The Scandal of Lady Eleanor

The Scandal of Lady Eleanor

A Regency Romance

Regina Jeffers

Published in the United States by
Ulysses Press
P.O. Box 3440
Berkeley, CA 94703
www.ulyssespress.com

ISBN: 978-1-56975-904-2
Library of Congress Catalog Number 2011921431

Acquisitions Editor: Kelly Reed
Managing Editor: Claire Chun
Editor: Sunah Cherwin
Proofreader: Sayre VanYoung
Production: Judith Metzener
Cover design: what!design @ whatweb.com
Cover photo: © Scala / Art Resource, NY—*The Honourable Mrs Graham* by Thomas Gainsborough

Printed in Canada by Webcom

10 9 8 7 6 5 4 3 2 1

Distributed by Publishers Group West

I dedicate this book to my readers, who believe,
as I do, that love is the most compelling of tasks.

Prologue

"WHAT DO YOU PLAN TO DO?" James Kerrington rasped as he leaned across Brantley Fowler, pretending to reach for the bowl of fruit. Kerrington watched Fowler's countenance tighten as the man stared toward where the Baloch warriors held the girl. Kerrington really did not need to ask. He and Fowler were the original members of a group the British government "lovingly" called the Realm. All seven of the unit ranged between the ages of nineteen and five and twenty. As he was the oldest among them, the others called Kerrington "Captain." In many ways, he had served as the leader of their unit, although the government never made any such distinction.

The others called Fowler "The Vicar" because he always wanted to *save* every lost soul he saw, especially the women and children. Surprisingly, through an authoritative persuasion, people confessed to Fowler nearly as quickly as they did an actual clergyman. He had joined Kerrington after a short stint with some shady seamen following the young man's alienation from his father and the title he would eventually inherit. His friend never said exactly what happened, but Kerrington's family knew Fowler's indirectly. James's mother, Lady Camelia Kerrington, had made her Come Out with Fowler's aunt, Agatha Braton, the Duchess of Norfield, and so James knew some of the family history. Fowler's father, the Duke of Thornhill, held a reputation for his lusty sexual appetite. Having seen his friend try to save more than one woman who suffered at the hands of a brute, Kerrington suspected some truth to the gossip.

Fowler gritted his teeth, offering a grim smile to the Baloch warriors sitting about the low table, while Kerrington immediately assessed the situation. Fowler hissed, "Each man who enters that tent gives the girl a rupee because Mir says that is all she is worth—one rupee—one shilling and fourpence in England." His friend's breathing became shallow, obviously biting back anger. "She is not yet sixteen."

"You cannot save the world, Fowler," Gabriel Crowden, another Realm member, cautioned.

Fowler insisted, "I can save her."

"Oh, Lord, here we go again," Crowden grumbled as he slid across the bench and into the shadows. "Give me time to get into place."

Kerrington stiffened in anticipation as the future Duke of Thornhill stood slowly and stretched, pretending to need to exercise his legs. "I think I will take a walk," Fowler announced, but before he could execute more than five steps in the direction of the girl's tent, a burly-looking soldier blocked his friend's path. Without saying a word, the man told Fowler to reconsider his choices.

Raising his hands in an act of submission, Fowler smiled largely and turned to Kerrington with a warning of what was to come. He shrugged as if to agree with the warrior, but in a split second, he struck the guard an uppercut, sending the man reeling with a broken nose.

A heartbeat later, Kerrington and Fowler stood back-to-back, taking on all comers, delivering lethal thrust after deathly jab. "I have it," Kerrington called as he parlayed a broken chair for a weapon. "Get the girl. Take her to the Bombay safe house." He shoved Fowler toward the girl's tent.

Kerrington's partner did not look back; Fowler knew he could count on James and the others in his group. Together, they would give him time to make a complete getaway.

Preparing for the next assault, he wondered about his own sanity. How many times over the past two years had Fowler gotten him in "a fight to the death" in order to save some female? Somehow, James had accepted his friend's "need" to rescue the disadvantaged. It seemed only fair, if he was to die, that James should do so in an effort to save some woman—an act of penance, so to speak. Kerrington could not save the woman he had loved—Elizabeth Morris—the woman he had married and had promised to love and to honor and to protect "as long as we both shall live." Unfortunately, Elizabeth Kerrington had lived but two years, two months, and ten days before she died in childbirth—his child—their child. Maybe by saving these women he might atone for what he could not do for Elizabeth, and what he did to Daniel—just walking away from the boy, unable to look at his own child without seeing Elizabeth and feeling the pain of her loss.

Turning his head, Kerrington saw Fowler pulling the scantily clad girl behind him, heading for the horses. James spun, twirling a sword he pulled from his walking stick, using the stick and the rapier in tandem with swinging figure eights to ward off three Baloch soldiers. "Now!" he called above the battle's clamor, and the Realm members synchronized their final strikes, leaving their opponents sprawled on the tent's floor. They dashed toward their tethered horses, swinging up into the saddles. They would distract their pursuers, heading in three different directions—all different from the way Fowler fled—to meet again in two days at their common house.

Racing toward the nearest hill, Kerrington pulled up the reins to take a quick look, making sure they all made it out safely. He felt responsible, although each man was quite capable and very menacing in his own right. "Let us depart, Captain," Aidan Kimbolt called from somewhere behind him. James had seen all he needed to see—they all were moving away from Shaheed Mir's tents. Turning the horse in a complete circle, he simply nodded to his riding partner before galloping away into the dying sunset.

Chapter 1

~ ~ ~

FIVE YEARS LATER.

"How are you, Sir?" James sat in the wing chair beside his father's bed. The Earl of Linworth suffered from a weak heart and had been abed for well over a year. James had returned home nearly two years earlier to assume the position as his father's heir.

"Your mother tells me you are off to Kent." James noted that the earl's voice seemed stronger than usual.

"Brantley Fowler finally returned to claim his title; Thornhill passed two months ago after a long illness. Fowler asked if I would come and take a look at the books for the estate. He says something does not seem right. I cannot imagine what it might be, but considering the late Duke was ill for some time, possibly someone took advantage of the situation."

"How long will you be away?" The earl shifted up in the bed, trying to use the many pillows as support.

James stuffed one of the smaller cushions into the stack to brace his father's lower back. "I can handle the books from anywhere, so unless you need me for something specific at Linton Park, I thought of taking in some of the Season. I will stay at Worthing Hall."

The earl gave a slight shake of his head in the positive. "You mean to look for a wife?"

"It is time, but I will not settle for the first girl out of the schoolroom. Daniel will inherit so I do not need an heir. I plan to just look. I heard from Crowden; he will be in London also. It will be more pleasant with old friends." James silently cringed every time he thought of Daniel and the wrongs he did to the boy. His poor Daniel still faltered and seemed out of place when James showed him any attention, and although he knew things were inherently better, he did not know exactly how to repair things with the boy, and so the awkwardness continued.

James knew his answer would not please his father, who wanted to see him married and starting up a nursery before the man passed. However, the earl tactfully said, "Did you see to the new seed?"

"Yes, Sir. Everything is ready for the growing season. I met with the cottagers and with Mackleroy; there will be no problems."

"You are a good son," his father looked directly at James. "I could not ask for better."

"Thank you, Sir."

The earl took on a serious mien. "I want you to look for a school for Daniel; the boy is old enough for Eton. We cannot coddle him forever."

James did not wish to send his son away; he had wasted too many years trying to kill the pain of losing Elizabeth. He realized his father was of the "old school," those who sent their children off to be educated by others, but, despite being an absent father for so many years, James had hoped to be an influence on his son's life—to show his child his love. "I will look into it, Sir." He would wait before parting with Elizabeth's child; once Daniel started school, James would see very little of him. He had recently decided that in his search for a wife he would consider Daniel's needs also. His son needed a mother, or, at least, a woman who would treat him with some kindness, maybe even affection. He would add those qualities to his list for his new bride.

"You will give Fowler our regards."

"Yes, Sir."

"And if you make the acquaintance of his aunt, the Dowager Duchess, hint that your mother might wish to renew their social relationship. Camelia spends all her time tending to me; she deserves a life of her own, especially when my time is over."

James looked uncomfortable, not wishing to speak of such a loss. "You have many years ahead of you, Father, and neither Mother nor I will hear of anything less. However, I will foster Her Grace's good favor for Mother's sake."

"That is superior." The earl paused, wanting to say something else but choosing not to. "You travel tomorrow?"

"Early—with the first light."

Eleanor Fowler rode across the estate, the late winter wind stinging her cheeks. Things at Thorn Hall changed the day her brother returned home. Now, Brantley was the Duke of Thornhill, and although Ella had not quite forgiven him for leaving her alone to bear the weight of running Thorn Hall and tending to William Fowler's regrets, she thoroughly enjoyed letting someone else deal with the disorder surrounding the title for a change.

Recently, she had told her brother she had a desire to travel—to see the world—to be independent—to never be subservient to a man again. Ella thought Brantley receptive to what she had said; at least, he had listened without censure. She had seen what a marriage based more on lust and less on love did to a person. She thought spending the rest of her life alone might bring her happiness, an eccentric daughter of an eccentric duke; she would not settle for a marriage of convenience. She would be out of her element in a romance, even an arranged one. "No," she thought, "it would be best if I simply chose not to marry at all."

Today, she rode her favorite grey, letting the horse kick up its heels and prance when it wanted. They both needed to simply run free with no destination in mind, and it was the perfect day to do so. "Come on, Sampson," she urged. "It is our time."

"You have no idea, Kerrington, how surprised I was to walk out of that gentleman's club to find my sister waiting on the steps." James sat in Brantley Fowler's study, having arrived less than an hour before. "And poor Ella…she has dealt with it all since the Duke took ill. For two years, Father lay in bed enduring the ravages his lascivious life had brought him."

James's brows drew together. "How in the world did Lady Fowler manage? An estate this size would cause most men to falter."

"Eleanor is quite resourceful. When the Duke, for example, had a lucid moment, Ella presented him with page after page of blank paper to sign so she could later write orders for supplies or work to be completed. Her farce perpetuated the rumors that Father suffered from a reoccurring bout of pneumonia."

James thought Fowler's sister quite ingenious. Few women would manage under such conditions. "I cannot imagine," James said with a hint of amusement in his voice, "that you willingly agreed to return to Thornhill. You were always set on ignoring the entailment, even if it came your way."

Fowler took another swallow of brandy, pointedly pausing before responding. "I refused, despite Eleanor's best arguments. My cousin Horton Leighton would inherit, and Ella promised she would not disclose finding me in Cornwall." His friend hesitated. "I should not have denied Eleanor's request. I was aware of Leighton's own depravity, but I could not relinquish my pride to save my sister from a life as Leighton's mother's companion."

James noted Fowler's culpability. His friend had spent years protecting the weak—searching for the noble cause. Now, Fowler admitted that he failed to "save" his own sister because of his personal ghosts. "What changed your mind?"

Fowler chuckled lightly. "Ella again. I underestimated her resolve. Women can be quite devious, Worthing," he observed. "Eleanor returned to Kent, but she sent me a package—two miniatures. One was of my mother—a reminder of what she suffered in order that I might ascend to the title."

"And the second?" James admired Lady Fowler's way of thinking. She had reached her brother's inner motivations.

"The second was of Velvet. I had wanted to ask Ella about her when my sister dwelled with me, but I did not believe I had the right."

James insisted, "Your commitment to Ashmita was for Sonali's sake. You do not have to deny yourself the woman you have loved all your life because you saved an innocent girl from a crazy Baloch." Every member of his Realm unit had dreamed of coming home and making things right—correcting the wrongs each left behind. Not a day went by without his spending time in anguish over losing Elizabeth. She rested in his heart and in his soul, and he could not let her go—could not forget what she had meant to him. Dutifully, he had accepted his fate: he had known the quintessence—the ideal love; and although he was likely to remarry, he would never know such happiness again. Despite that fact, he would remarry; he owed that much to his parents and to his title.

"Sonali's presence and the knowledge of my marriage has put a strain on my reunion with my cousin," Fowler disclosed.

"Do not give up." James offered a slow, triumphant smile. "My money is on you, Fowler."

His friend nodded his agreement. "Speaking of Velvet, she and I were involved in an unusual attack three days ago. Someone took a shot at us as we visited the cottagers. I assume my cousin has accumulated no enemies."

"Whereas you have, Fowler?"

"Whereas we all have, Worthing."

James tilted his head in an acknowledgment of the truth. "Are you sure there is no way it could have been an accident?"

"I considered that—hunters or poachers—but Velvet and I were out in the open—standing along the riverbank. No one could have mistaken us for animals. The thing is—whoever did this hit Velvet…just a graze, but it is now personal. I will not stop until I know *who* and *why*."

"Anything else?"

James watched as Fowler leaned back in his chair, fingers interlocked so he might mindlessly tap his chin. "Entries in my father's ledgers, several of them. Each simply say '3L.' Each for two to three thousand pounds."

"And what do you want from me?" James suspected he knew the answer, but he would ask just the same.

Bran looked at his friend—leveling a direct gaze, solidifying their understanding. "It is important to me to rid Thornhill of its negative reputation. That means I must tie up all the loose ends. So, besides enjoying your company, I need another pair of eyes and a different perspective." James knew this was his Thorn Hall mission even before he had arrived; Fowler held an undeniable desire to wipe away his father's reputation. Brantley Fowler wanted to be someone's "knight in shining armor."

"So, all we must do is to solve the mystery of missing estate funds, to absolve your family name, and to find a way to convince Miss Aldridge that you are the man she must marry." James's mouth curled in a sly smile. "Seems simple enough. All in a day's work for the Realm. Did you have any ideas on where we should start?"

Fowler frowned thoughtfully. "Well, I do have a plan to convince Velvet that my marrying Ashmita was my past. Velvet is my future."

The conversation reminded James of his and Fowler's first mission together. From the beginning, they had worked well as a team—their thoughts similarly detailed and predictable.

"I did not simply inherit the title; I also assumed my father's position as Velvet's guardian. Therefore, I plan to provide her and my sister a Season. When Velvet has had a chance to find another and, hopefully, has failed, I will claim her at the end of the Season; then we will be equal—she will see that things are not always as they are told in a fairy tale or novel—dreams change."

"It is a bold move, Your Grace. You are gambling with the prospect that your lady love will not choose another."

"It is the only thing I can think of doing. Do you believe it is a mistake?"

Fowler looked worried. James recognized the feeling of disorientation Miss Aldridge brought to his friend's life. He had known such anguish, too, in those early days of winning Elizabeth Morris's affections. "In the game of love, I suppose it is as good as any other move. What do I know? I keep Mary as my mistress because love avoids me like the plague."

Before they could continue, a light tap on the door announced Sonali's presence. "Papa," she giggled as she ran to where Fowler sat. "Look what I have." James enjoyed the girl's innocence. The child cupped her small hands lightly together. He sorely wished he had been at Linton Park to experience such moments with Daniel. She opened them enough for her father to see what she held. "It is a baby frog. May I keep it?"

Fowler glanced quickly at James before answering, "Does Mrs. Carruthers know of this, Sonali?" The duke manipulated her hold on the pet frog to keep her from accidentally crushing it in her palm.

The child shook her head rapidly. "Myles helped me catch it."

Bran conspiratorially winked at James. "I see." His friend took on a serious demeanor. "First, Child, as a frog is not really a house pet, I suspect it might be best to leave your catch in the pond where it might grow up naturally. However, before we speak to Mrs. Carruthers, say your good mornings to your Uncle James."

James noted the look of innocent mischief playing on the child's face. "Uncle James!" Sonali squealed and reached for him when she finally looked his way.

"Aah…!" Fowler warned. "Frog!"

The child froze in place before looking at her father sheepishly. "Sorry, Papa."

"March!" he ordered good-naturedly, pointing toward the hallway. Watching her go, Fowler turned to James. "I will be back in a moment. Make yourself comfortable."

James stood and walked casually about the room, taking a closer look at what William Fowler thought important to hang on his walls—he doubted that the room held anything much of Brantley Fowler's. His friend had assumed the title only recently—not long enough ago to claim the study as his own, although a jade elephant, a Persian folding screen, and an ornate ebony and ivory chess set reflected their time in the East.

He had circumambulated the whole room when the door suddenly flew open, and James came face-to-face with a golden-haired beauty, who, literally, stumbled and fell into his arms. Instinctively, he steadied her stance by encircling her slim waist, clasping his hands behind her back. Her awkward movements to right herself skimmed her soft curves against the muscular hardness of his chest and abdomen, awakening something in his soul, as well as his body. She was breathtakingly beautiful at this close range and just looking at her aroused him. Although nearly as tall as he, the lady refused to look him in the eye as he used his hand to edge her closer to him.

"I…I apologize, Sir," she stammered and blushed. Color waves flooded her face. James felt the heat of her body radiate into his, and something unknown stirred. He rarely acted so impulsively with any woman.

Tightening his hold on her, he whispered close to her ear, "I cannot say when I have enjoyed an accident more. You have my permission, my Dear, to fall into my waiting arms anytime you so choose." He had no idea why he acted so boldly. The woman was obviously a lady of good breeding and a member of Fowler's household, and he should apologize, but James found he enjoyed this moment of indiscretion more than he should.

Eleanor Fowler forced herself to look into his countenance. The man's steel-grey eyes sparked with silver and gold, flashing in unexplained recognition. Broad-shouldered and athletically built, he was solid—time spent in the saddle or in the fencing halls was quite obvious. Dark brows, closely set, framed those mesmerizing eyes into which she now stared. A strong jaw held a firm mouth, biting back a self-assured smile, and Ella realized too late that her hesitation had given him permission to continue to hold her; his hand pressed against her lower back, moving her inches closer to his flat abdomen. "I…I am…I am capable of standing on my own," she choked out.

"You may be, my lovely, but I find your presence leaves me quite incapable of even breathing without your aid. This close, you breathe out…and I will inhale the essence of you."

James Kerrington often found a beguiling female in his embrace, but when this one actually tumbled into his arms, he did not expect his world to shift on its axis. When he spoke of finding it difficult to breathe, he only half joked through the flirtation. The scent of lavender tempted his nostrils, and he willingly inhaled her essence. Taller than most women he knew, her angular, bony frame molded nicely to his, and James felt a rush of blood to his manhood. Besides the lavender, sun-warmed skin and a hint of cinnamon tea lingered, sending a new jolt of manly needs straight to his senses. Her red-gold hair shimmered like silk, and James fought the desire to loosen the pins and let it slide like satin through his fingers.

"Unhand my sister, Worthing," Fowler demanded from somewhere behind them.

Although warned, instead of jumping back as propriety might expect, Kerrington leaned in close once more and whispered, "It seems I must endeavor to breathe on my own, my Lady." Then he stepped back slowly and put distance between them.

Fowler came forward and placed his sister's hand on his arm. James noted how Eleanor Fowler's ears pinked with being caught in so compromising a situation. "I would introduce you, Eleanor," Fowler began, "except I am not sure I wish you to meet the Honorable Viscount Worthing as *honor* is lacking at the moment."

"I awkwardly stumbled," she hissed under her breath, pure embarrassment obviously racing through her. "Lord Worthing caught me before my misstep sent me tumbling to the floor. It was nothing more, Bran." The lady had no reason to defend him, but she did.

She surely realized James could have released her at once instead of pressing her to him. She impressed him immediately: He preferred a woman who did not faint away at embarrassing situations.

James faced them fully, having consumed several deep breaths to fight the bulging evidence between his legs. "*Shoma kheyli mehrban hastid*. You are very kind, Lady Fowler," he bowed deeply, meeting only the lady's eyes. "I am *honored* to be in your presence at last. Your roguish brother has spoken often of you; however, his Cambridge education shows its weaknesses. If he had attended Oxford, His Grace might know just the right words to truly describe a woman of such incomparable beauty."

"I agree with your estimation of Eleanor's worth." His friend gritted his teeth with annoyance. "But perhaps I do not look on my sister as other men might. I assume, Worthing, you will refrain from your usual perfunctory teasing and leave my sister to her status as a duke's daughter." An admonition played through the words, although neither Fowler's face nor tone betrayed his command.

Sophisticated superiority now rested on James's countenance. "I shall treat Lady Fowler with the respect she deserves. Forgive me if I in any way offered an offense; it was never my intention."

"No forgiveness is necessary, Lord Worthing, and please call me Lady Eleanor. I realize it is not standard usage, but my mother was Lady Fowler, and I could not assume her name." She gave James a quick smile, and his heart lurched in his chest.

"Thank you, Lady Eleanor, for accepting my apology. It will be my honor to address you as you have indicated—to be accepted as part of your brother's circle of friends." Her name made James immediately think of Eleanor of Aquitaine, mother of both Richard the Lionheart and King John—a woman who participated in the Second Crusade as Queen of the Franks—a woman who acted as regent while Richard was away in the Third Crusade—the wife of two different kings and the mother of two others. She was unique and unwavering in her own way. James wondered if Fowler's sister held such a powerful personality. His friend's earlier tales of Lady

Eleanor's manipulations to bring Fowler home spoke of her tenaciousness and her intelligence. Her name, literally, meant "sun's ray" or "shining light," and, predictably, her golden red hair gave off a sunny glow, radiating an inner light. He could not remember being so quickly enamored of a woman.

She gave him a quick curtsy before turning to her brother. "I came to ask you to join Velvet and me in the front parlor for some tea. It is Velvet's first day downstairs since her accident. She wished to thank you again."

"Certainly, my Dear. You go ahead and pour; Lord Worthing and I will join you in a moment." He patted the hand he still held in his. Without another word, she made a quick curtsy, but as she exited the room, she glanced over her shoulder to meet James's trailing stare. For a few elongated seconds, she paused, a shy smile gracing her lips. Primal male instincts shot through him again, and James made himself look away.

Ella stepped into the hallway, but she did not close the door completely. Instead, she listened to her brother reprimand his closest friend for Lord Worthing's actions. She knew her brother was correct, but for the life of her, she did not regret that brief encounter with the viscount. Although she thoroughly believed that living as an independent woman was her life path, she still wondered how it would feel to be held intimately in a man's embrace—a man who found her attractive for herself and not as an imitation of her mother. She did not approve of the way her body reacted to Lord Worthing—Ella recognized lust and would not succumb to such thoughts, but that did not mean she could not enjoy the effects of the viscount's flirtation. At age twenty, she had had no real experience with the opposite sex, except as her father's regent during the duke's illness. However, even an independent woman could store memories for her old age, and she would claim this one as her own.

"Lord Worthing," Ella pointedly began as she passed a generous-sized slice of seed cake to him, "what brings you to Kent?"

James shot a quick glance at Fowler; they had not discussed what story they would tell the others. "When I heard that your brother had returned to his ancestral home, I had to see it for myself." He offered up one of his best smiles to seal the lie.

"Yet, my cousin took up residence less than three weeks ago," Velvet Aldridge, the object of Fowler's attention, protested. James could see the similarity between Velvet Aldridge and Ashmita, although he preferred Fowler's sister, a woman of whose face his eyes could not seem to get enough. "How could anyone know so soon?"

"His Grace placed an order for new equipment and made inquiries into the Mayfair house's soundness. It does not take the gossipmongers long to latch onto the least clues, especially in light of the recent news of the former Duke's passing."

Ella appreciated the way the viscount twisted the words; she did not fully understand why Bran had brought his friend to Thorn Hall, but she knew her brother held a specific purpose. If nothing else, she knew her brother to be thorough in his dealings and to be a protector. If Lord Worthing had served with Brantley, he would be the perfect choice to help her brother tie up loose ends with the estate and with the recent accident. "May I translate for you, my Lord?" Worthing inclined his head in affirmation. "I believe His Lordship means Cousin Horton bemoans his loss of the title publicly." Ella's eyes sparkled in mischief.

"A lady of beauty and intelligence," Worthing declared; though he knew little of their Cousin Horton, he enjoyed the way Lady Eleanor's eyes lit up.

James watched with some amusement as Miss Aldridge screwed up her face in disbelief. She waited but a handful of heartbeats before she inquired, "Will you travel to London, Bran? Lord Worthing mentioned the town house."

Kerrington quickly realized he was also to be a part of his friend's plot to win Velvet Aldridge. Fowler took a sip of his tea, stalling before answering. "I wrote to Aunt Agatha and asked her to sponsor your and Ella's Come Outs."

James saw Fowler's sister react. Her brother's words shook her composure. Lady Eleanor's hand began to tremble, and, before she dropped it, Worthing reached for her cup. He enjoyed the brief touch of her fingers, but Eleanor Fowler's obvious distress bothered him. He would have liked to take her into his embrace and to tell her he would right her wrongs.

"Oh, Bran, we cannot; it is too soon." Her voice quaked with apparent anxiety. "The gossip will fly about our not maintaining a proper mourning period, and besides, I thought I made myself clear about what I would choose for my future." Worthing watched her closely; her unusual reaction piqued his curiosity, as well as his masculine need to protect her. Most young women would jump at a Season, but this woman evidently wanted nothing to do with one.

Fowler tried to assuage his sister's fears. "I beg to differ, Eleanor. As far as father's mourning period is concerned, blame me. I will simply say with father's extended illness, I deemed it improper to deny you and Velvet a Season; if not for this house's madness, you should have had one already. I can make such proclamations because I am a man and a duke. However, I have not forgotten our previous conversation. Instead, it is my conviction that before you are accepted in the manner we discussed earlier, you need Society's approval. After father's shunning of prescribed propriety, your refusing to accept normal conventions for a woman will never be tolerated. Before you choose your own manner of living, you must demonstrate you did not find theirs pointless by conforming to the *ton's* precepts. It is simply time you took your place in Society."

"I cannot bear a purposeful cut," she protested. "Father's reputation will follow us to London." James observed how she bit her bottom lip, choking back the emotions, and he found her anxiety stirred something inside of him. He wanted desperately to ease her growing agitation.

Realizing belatedly that he intruded on a family matter, James made to depart, but Fowler motioned him to remain. They had served together for four years; they knew each other's deepest secrets, especially regarding the former duke. "Father will always have his critics, but the *ton* chases one scandal after another. No one from this family has been to London for more than two years; the Fowlers will be old news. Besides, by the time we arrive in London, I will have introduced a different Thornhill to Society. I returned to Thorn Hall to obliterate William Fowler's memory from the books. No one would dare to offer either of you a direct cut. Eleanor, you are a duke's daughter and now the sister of one; in Society that means everything."

James observed how Miss Aldridge also took offense. "You want us—Ella and me—to join the 'marriage mart'?"

His friend tried not to betray his own anxiety at their entering the time of courtship known as the Season; yet, James ignored the tension between Fowler and Miss Aldridge. Instead, he turned his attention to Fowler's sister. In his short acquaintance with her, James had decided that Eleanor Fowler needed the confidence to claim her place in Society, and he firmly believed Fowler would need to lead her through the process. Despite her ladylike presence, a personal relationship might be her most difficult battle. If even half of what Fowler said about the late duke held true, Lady Eleanor possessed no models of what a marriage might actually entail. Unlike James, whose parents displayed a loving relationship, Lady Eleanor saw only devastation in marriage. Somehow that thought gnawed away at him.

Eleanor had feared this moment—the moment when her brother would force her to be William Fowler's daughter. She had hoped that when she told him she would prefer to travel the world, Bran would agree, and she could forget all Thorn Hall's ugliness. Being a man, her brother saw things differently from her; he thought he helped her by allowing her to become part of Society. However, all Eleanor wanted was to be left alone—alone with her thoughts, but not her memories. The memories were too raw. She wanted new memories—such as the one from today—to replace the abyss in which she had lived under her father's reign. She could be a bluestocking and simply live the life of an eccentric—a woman who had no desire to know marriage. She thought the only thing worse than her brother's proclamation that he would give her a Season would be if Bran arranged a marriage for her. If he did, she would refuse her household's alignment to another's.

Aware of Fowler's wavering position, James jumped into the conversation. "Well, I, for one, am looking forward to the new Season. Two such lovely ladies will make it most interesting. I am thankful to have an *in* and intend to claim my share of your dance cards." He wiggled his eyebrows in a jest.

James watched as Eleanor Fowler swallowed hard, trying to release her disquiet. "It will be reassuring to recognize a friend's name on my card."

"It would be my pleasure to be of service to both you and Miss Aldridge," he rushed to say, trying to bring her peace. "Especially in the Season's early weeks. When your brother is unavailable, please call on me, Lady Eleanor, when you are in need of an escort." Kerrington meant the words; he wanted to know more of this woman, although he suspected Fowler would not welcome that interest.

~ ~ ~

James sat in the library late in the evening. Accustomed to town, he whiled away the hours, reading an account of some of Wellington's greatest battlefield accomplishments. Under his breath, he cursed the book's many inaccuracies. It tempted him to find pen and ink and make corrections in the margin. Despite his somewhat "dangerous" reputation, even in London, one might easily find him at home at this hour. His reputation said one thing, but the reality of his life remained the reverse. He missed Elizabeth more than he would ever admit, even to friends such as Brantley Fowler. He had fallen in love with her from across a crowded ballroom—he a few months short of his majority and Elizabeth barely seventeen. He had elbowed his way through the crowd of young bucks lined up to claim her hand and surreptitiously maneuvered the last position on her dance card. From the moment he first touched her hand, James had never left Elizabeth's side. They married the day after he turned one and twenty, and for two years, he knew paradise.

Then the child came, and James lost her. The boy—his heir—did not turn, and the only way to save his child was to sacrifice the woman he had loved to the surgeon's knife. Elizabeth's eyes told him she knew her duty and would leave him, declaring her love the world's purest. Closing his eyes, he could see the angel looking back at him. Within three months, he was with what the public thought to be a group of mercenary soldiers, but, in reality, they ran covert operations against select targets. In actuality, the half-dozen carefully selected Realm members with whom he had served worked for a secret British government agency. James relished those years of self-imposed banishment, despite the sometimes harsh conditions under which they often lived. Those years dulled the pain of losing his wife.

A muffled footstep on the main staircase roused his attention, and he moved cautiously to discover its source. Fowler had told him of his suspicions regarding Miss Aldridge's recent injury, and for a moment, James wondered if he had stumbled upon an interloper sneaking about the sleeping household. Extinguishing the single candle, he worked his way warily toward the door. Listening carefully, he noted the intruder hesitated on the stairs.

"Now or never," his lips mouthed before he jerked open the door and leveled the pocket pistol he kept hidden in his boot at the uninvited guest. Heart pounding out of his chest, he drew aim on an intimately clad Eleanor Fowler. Gulping in air to steady his pulse, James slowly lowered the gun and stared dumbly at the vision standing rigidly on the third step. "Lady Eleanor," he stammered, assuming she had seen the gun and froze. "I apologize; I held no idea you too were a light sleeper. I suspected someone trying to pilfer the estate's riches."

Eleanor simply continued to stare *at* him, actually *through* him, and James self-consciously shot a glance over his shoulder to see if anyone else lurked in the shadows. Feeling totally discomfited by her hard gaze, he reached his hand toward her, unsure what to do. Wearing a white muslin gown, she was the picture of British female innocence, but his body reacted anyway. Her bare feet and ankles peeked from the hemline, and the thin material revealed her breasts' rosy nipples and the *V* of her triangle. James knew he should look away; propriety required he do so, but he could not. "May I help you find a book, Lady Eleanor?" He kept his voice low, not wishing to wake the others and let them witness this unexpected meeting.

Pausing briefly, Eleanor took the last three steps and crossed the hallway to the open door, but instead of taking his hand or even speaking to him, she glided through the portal, stopping only when she reached the room's middle.

James circled where she stood, moving slowly so as not to frighten her. "Lady Eleanor, are you well?" His voice was barely above a whisper. "May I be of assistance?" Although he now stood before her, Kerrington instinctively knew she did not see him. Eyes opened wide, Eleanor Fowler spoke to a ghost.

"Yes, Papa." Her words shot through him. He thought to reach for her, but James feared his touch might *truly* scare her to death. "I will be a good girl, Papa; I promise. No, do not take Velvet!" She looked desperately at him as she dropped to her knees and pleaded for her father to believe her. "I will not move, Papa; I swear I will not." She pulled at James's hand and leg, and tears streamed down her soft cheeks.

"It is all right, Darling." James encouraged as he tried to lift Eleanor to him.

"I am your daughter, Papa. Love me, not Velvet," she begged.

Kerrington's heart ached for the hurt he knew she had experienced at her despicable father's hands; she beseeched the man to love her. "Come, Darling." James took her arms and helped the sleeping beauty to her feet.

Eyes still not registering, Ella bit her bottom lip. "Will you love me, Papa?"

James could not resist touching her cheek to wipe away her tears' remnants. "Of course, Sweetheart."

"May I sit on your lap, Papa?" She clasped James's hand and pulled him to a nearby chair. Reluctantly, he followed and allowed her to push him down and then quite unceremoniously she climbed onto his lap and rested her head against his chest. "Is this right, Papa?"

"Oh, yes, Eleanor; it is very right." As she snuggled closer, James began to instinctively stroke her back and down her arm. "Rest, Sweetheart," he murmured into her hair. "I will protect you, Sweet Ella." He now twisted several of her curls around his fingers. The firelight captured the reddish tints, and her tresses glowed as he laced his fingers through to the tips. He thought it might be Heaven to brush it for her in the evenings, letting the softness of it fall down her back to tantalize his bare chest.

Innocently, she moaned and allowed her fingers to trace his beard's stubble. Her eyes were no longer open, and the angelic aura returned to her face. "You are beautiful." James's lips brushed against her temple, and despite the realization he should return Eleanor to her room, he tarried, enjoying holding a woman such as Eleanor Fowler in his embrace. It made him feel human again, and he was sore to lose her closeness.

She stretched, unexpectedly tilting her chin as if to receive him, and, of his own volition, James lowered his lips to hers and tasted sweetness. Immediately, he hardened; this was too much like an unspoken fantasy. Vulnerability shouted at him as he traced her mouth with his tongue and heard his own moan in response.

A shuddered breath forced his lips from hers. "Lord!" he gasped and made himself loosen his hold on her. "Let me return you to your chambers, Sweetheart," he spoke as he lifted her to him. James expected to feel her weight when he raised her to him—her long legs dangling down to his waist, but instead, he hefted less than eight stone, and it thrilled him to hold her so intimately. Her arms wrapped around his neck, and James envisioned what it would be like to take her to his bed and sate himself in her warm body.

The visions climbed the stairs beside him as he stole brief kisses at her temple and along the side of Eleanor's cheek, enjoying the taste of her skin. Finding her bedroom door ajar, he shoved it open with his shoulder as he maneuvered Eleanor's svelte body through the frame. "You are a temptation, Sweetheart," he mumbled as he lowered her to the bed and brushed strands of hair from her face. "Sleep well, Darling."

A noise behind him told him they were not alone. He spun around to find a maid sleepily emerging from Eleanor's dressing room. "M'Lord?" Accusation rested in her tone.

Aware of how this looked, James caught the woman's arm and hustled her to the hallway, not wanting anyone else to see him in Eleanor Fowler's room. "Shush," he warned as he edged the door closed.

"M'Lord, I must protest on Lady Eleanor's behalf." The maid, obviously loyal to her mistress, spoke defensively.

"I assure you nothing happened to your mistress. I found her downstairs, and I simply brought Lady Eleanor to her bed."

"Oh, Lordy, not again." The woman looked apprehensively at the door.

James followed her gaze. "What do you mean, *not again*?" he demanded in hushed tones.

The woman wrung her hands. "Maybe I should tell Master Brantley," she started.

"Tell me what you meant," he insisted. "I will discuss it with His Grace."

"My poor Lady Eleanor," she wailed in whispered tones. "M'Lady's been plagued with sleepwalking for years, but I be thinkin' she be finally rid of her demons. Not once since the old Master passed did my mistress leave her bed. I sleep close by, but

I did not hear Lady Eleanor tonight. Thank you, M'Lord, for protecting her."

"Will Lady Eleanor be well the rest of the night?" James wanted time to consider what Eleanor's maid shared.

"Oh, yes, M'Lord, but I be staying in the room meself."

"Then I will bid you good night." He needed to be away from Eleanor Fowler's room. Something was not right, but with fresh thoughts of the delectable lady on the other side of the door, James could not pinpoint it.

"M'Lord," the woman stopped his retreat. "No one else be knowing of Lady Eleanor's problem 'cepting me and Mr. Jordan."

James shot another glance at Eleanor's door. "I understand. Lady Eleanor's secret is my secret; I pledge you my word as a gentleman."

"Thank you again, M'Lord." She dropped a curtsy, preparing to return to her pallet.

Now it was James's turn to pause. "I believe it might be imprudent to advise your mistress of my interference tonight. I would not wish her such mortifications at knowing of my having carried her to her chambers."

"Yes, M'Lord. Lady Eleanor she be very sensible. That be very kind of you, Sir."

"Then it will be our secret." With that, he turned on his heels and strode to his chambers, his friend's sister having had an unexpected impact on him in more ways than one.

~ ~ ~

The next day James made a point to observe Eleanor from the moment she entered the breakfast room. When he had retired to his own quarters the previous evening, he had spent more than a few minutes staring at the four poster's ornate drapery in his guest chamber and reliving the experience of holding Ella, as her family called her, and as he now thought of her, in his arms twice in one day. Like most men of his age and station in life, James kept a mistress in town whom he visited when he needed a woman's touch. He had established Mary Cavendish, a war widow, as his when he returned to England. Mary was pretty enough, although a bit older than James, and she never made unreasonable demands on him. He bought her a house in a more posh neighborhood and had arranged for Mary's income early in their relationship to assure exclusivity, assuming he would continue their relationship long into his impending search for a wife. Now, he wondered, if he was to choose someone like Eleanor Fowler, or any well-bred woman, for that matter, whether he should subject her to this form of degradation. Although many aristocratic women accepted such dalliances as part of their existence, he knew he would never have looked twice at Mary if Elizabeth had lived. Maybe if he found the kind of companionship he sought, the idea of dismissing Mary might not seem so foreign.

Then his thoughts fell once more on his hostess's troubled mind. What experiences had driven Eleanor Fowler from her bed? James had seen the phenomenon before; one who spent any time in battle or intense conflict knew how the mind sometimes compensated by acting out in sleep, but what trauma burdened Ella? Obviously, it involved her infamous father. Then it struck him, her need for love—her father's deviance—and the need to protect Eleanor arose deep in James's soul. If William Fowler were not already dead, James would find his sorry arse and kill the man with his bare hands. "Damn him!" he mumbled as he punched the pillow. He had to know—somehow he had to know the truth.

As she slid into a chair at the breakfast table, James greeted Eleanor with a cheery "Good morning" before joining her. "Might I find something for you, Lady Eleanor?" He gestured toward the side table.

"No, thank you, Lord Worthing. Cook is preparing my usual. I fear I have a more than odd need for coddled eggs to start my day."

He chuckled, enjoying this new level of intimacy with Fowler's sister. Before he cut the sliced ham he piled high on his plate, he remarked, "It is pleasant to see a lady with an appetite."

"Do you prefer your women to resemble those depicted by Robert Lefevre, as in 'Madame Récamier,' or even those displayed by Baron François-Pascal-Simon Gérard?" Ella charged without considering her words.

James liked the way she flushed with color when she opened herself to his possible censure. He purposely waited to prolong her discomfort. "I once thought I preferred my women petite and dark, such as your cousin Miss Aldridge,...but of late, I am no longer sure."

Before she could respond, her brother appeared in the doorway. "Ah, Worthing, you are up early." Bran poured himself a cup of coffee.

"I am, Your Grace. I thought I might prevail upon you to ride out with me and show off your new home." James knew perfectly well that Bran had appointments with his steward and his father's solicitor today. He had overheard his friend make the arrangements yesterday.

"I regret I cannot; I have obligations to the estate this morning." Bran took the chair held by the footman. "Maybe we could induce my sister to be your guide. I dare say Eleanor knows the land as well as I, and she is recognized as an excellent horsewoman."

James swung his eyes quickly to Eleanor Fowler to capture her true reaction to his manipulations. "Might you honor me with your company, Lady Eleanor?"

He watched as Eleanor shifted her weight, obviously discomfited by both men's stares resting on her face. "That would be enjoyable, my Lord." Her agreement seemed stilted to James, and he observed throughout the rest of the breakfast that Eleanor picked at the eggs she had ordered. He never let his senses leave the presence of the woman as he and Bran reminisced about some of their closest friends, but James did not speak directly to her throughout the rest of the breakfast. He offered her a reprieve for the moment.

What could she say? She had internally decided to savor her memory of him, and although Eleanor found James Kerrington attractive, the idea of spending time with him alone sent her heart pounding. He was a magnificent sight, but she wanted nothing to do with any man beyond simple conversation. His intimate embrace yesterday still radiated through her body, and she could not help but feel breathless just thinking of it. Her brother and the viscount continued their exchange, but Ella spent her time trying to justify the way her breasts hardened and the way she felt an unexplained yearning between her legs every time she shot a glance at the all-too-handsome viscount. She could not explain the sensation. It was a hunger, but not one the coddled eggs would fill.

"And Crowden is in Staffordshire?" Fowler inquired.

"Gabriel is the new Marquis of Godown. I received a letter only last week. It gave me great pleasure to tell him of your restoration at Thorn Hall; I expect you will hear from him within days."

"Do you suppose we might persuade the new marquis to join us for the London Season?" The duke continued to eat his kippers.

James, out of the corner of his eye, noted Eleanor flinch with her brother's words. "Godown intends to establish himself as part of London's society, as will you, Your Grace—claiming your seats in Parliament and all."

"Who would think," Bran mused, "the seven of us who fought so closely might all end up in Britain's Parliament together?"

"Of course, Lowery and Wellston are minor sons, although word has it that the Earl of Berwick is near death, and Marcus will soon claim the title as his older brother is not right in the wits. The Earl has seen to it in the estate's papers. Marcus will provide Trevor a home, but he will be the new earl," James reminded his friend. "Lowery accepted a ranking position in Shepherd's inner circle." They spoke in a silent code of their former alliances.

"If you will excuse me," Eleanor stood as she spoke. "I will retire to change into my riding habit. Might we say twenty minutes, my Lord?" Her eyes never looked directly at James, which actually disappointed him, although it offered no surprise.

"I will have the stable saddle your favorite mount, Lady Eleanor." He stood to acknowledge her departure.

Eleanor curtsied and prepared to leave when Bran caught her hand. "Take one of the grooms, Ella." James hated the fact that Fowler made an issue of a possible indiscretion. Evidently, Thornhill knew nothing of Eleanor's troubled sleep, and James wanted no more guilt to plague her.

She nodded in agreement. "Everything will be as propriety demands, Bran. I assure you, I want no more scandal associated with the Fowler name."

Chapter 2

"ARE YOU SURE YOU CAN HANDLE LOGAN without our help?"

The groom pulled at his forelock. "Oh, yes, Lady Eleanor. If'n I walk him slow, old Logan will be fine."

Eleanor had shown Lord Worthing most of the property's points of interest, including the waterfall at the end of the nature walk and the large lake behind the north lawn. Now, she broke her promise to her brother by excusing the groom to return to the stables. "I will check on the horse when His Lordship and I return to Thorn Hall."

"Yes, Ma'am." The groom took the horse's reins. "A stone be all the problem. Logan be new as a bairn in no time."

Ella nodded her understanding. "Shall we continue, Lord Worthing?"

"Absolutely, Lady Eleanor."

As they rode leisurely along a tree-shaded path, James continued to observe Eleanor first-hand. From Fowler he knew of her manipulations to keep the estate afloat—a fact which sparked his admiration. But his interest in her lay along more primordial lines: Simply put, the lady stirred his desires. James wanted to be near her—wanted to touch Lady Eleanor—wanted to kiss her senseless—wanted to feel her body's heat pressed to his. She certainly did not resemble his Elizabeth, a mark by which he had gauged all other relationships. As he told her earlier, he normally preferred his women dark in coloring and petite, so he could not understand why in bloody hell he could not withdraw his eyes from this golden-haired Amazon, a woman who evidently had no desire to participate in Society's dictates for finding a husband? Did she not realize the gauntlet she tossed down with such words? They made him want to prove her wrong, and James knew other men would see it the same way. What would he do if…? *Bloody hell!* There he went again, thinking of Lady Eleanor as if she belonged to him. He had known the woman for less than a day, and if what he suspected had happened to her proved to be true, then he questioned whether any relationship might prove possible.

Riding out with the viscount had proven less stressful than Ella had imagined. When the groom had to return to the stables, she considered curtailing the tour, but a quick glance at her brother's friend changed her mind. He treated her with respect, and he listened to her. When she told him about the estate and what she had accomplished while she searched for Bran to resume the title, the viscount appeared duly impressed. Now, if he would not look at her with such intensity, she might be able to breathe again. "Have I offered an offence, my Lord?" Much to his embarrassment, James discovered Ella watched him closely.

"No,…certainly not, Lady Eleanor. You simply caught me woolgathering, I fear."

Ella impulsively smiled at him. "Dare I ask the source of your search, my Lord?"

"Would I embarrass you, Lady Eleanor, if I declared you to be the focus of my thoughts?"

Eleanor tried to play off what he said as being absurd, but secretly his words thrilled her. The thought that this man might truly find her attractive ricocheted through her. "Lord Worthing, my brother warned me of your silver tongue. I own a mirror, Sir. I am too tall, too thin, too opinionated, and too lacking in feminine wiles to be a source of anyone's musings."

James had a sudden desire to slide his "silver" tongue, first, between her full lips and then down Ella's body. "Ah, now, Lady Eleanor, you do me an injustice, thinking I purposely mislead any woman." He wiggled his eyebrows at her and watched as she broke into laughter. "And I know what I shall give you on your next birthday." He paused to reel her in. "A mirror that speaks the truth—one that reflects your splendor."

A flush of color spread quickly across her bust line and up her neck, a reaction that James appreciated. "Lord Worthing, I must admit I usually disdain such frivolous conversations, but I find your idle chatter to be just what I need today, although I place no merit on your spirited speech."

"Another wound?" he teased. "How will I survive?"

"I believe you will do well without my attention, Lord Worthing." Ella actually laughed at his prattle. "Now, I will show you how to please me." With that, she kicked the side of her gelding and took off across the open meadow at a full gallop—her laughter drifting back to him.

For a few heartbeats, James simply watched her go—her joy making him satisfied in his own mind; and then, he gave pursuit, rushing across the land—the heat of the horse's flanks radiating through his thighs. He chased the tinkling sound of her merriment. As his stallion closed the distance between them, James suddenly realized that he could not remember the last time he found so much enjoyment doing nothing more than riding hard.

Then the shot rang out, and he watched in horror as Ella's horse stumbled to its front knees, and she flew over its head, rolling on the ground—horse and rider entangled in pain's wild dance. Seconds behind her, James was on his feet and running before he reined in his mount.

"Ella…Ella," he called as he vaulted over the pawing legs of the gelding, pulling her away from the animal before it crushed her. "Ella, please," he turned her limp body in his arms, checking for a pulse and finding one. "Speak to me, Ella." He pushed the hair from her face, as he searched for other injuries, running his hands up and down her legs.

Holding her to him, James's eyes scanned the perimeter. From where did the shot come? No trees—just open fields backed up to a rocky overhang—*has to be*. His instincts knew where to look—knew the only place a shooter could hide, and a shadowy movement proved his assumptions correct. He could smell the fear of his opponent even though he was still too far away for an accurate shot with the pistol he pulled from the holster strapped inside his jacket. Resting Ella on the ground, he was at a run again, moving toward the rise—eyes locked on the crevice in the rock face—gun loaded and cocked—ready for the next flash before firing his own weapon. Heart pounding—just like in the old days—he moved steadily toward the opening. Locked on, James waited—breathed evenly—watched for the gun's glint in the sunlight—then he knew, knew when to drop and roll—saw the bullet leave the barrel before the sound found him. In one sleek movement, he lowered his shoulder to the ground and allowed his momentum to take him over—a complete rotation, and he was on his knee sighting down the gun, steadying it with his other hand. The gunpowder clouded about his face, but James never lost sight of the bullet. He saw its flight—straight and accurate—saw it hit its target—saw it go in the man's shoulder—saw him fall.

Traversing the rocky outcroppings, within seconds James reached the opening and pulled the man to his feet without checking for other wounds. He had him by the lapels, pure force lifting the scant fool inches from the ground. "If you hurt her, I will rip you apart limb from limb." Unable to control his anger, James's fist met their assailant's chin, sending the man flying backwards against the rock wall.

Not waiting to assess his attack's effect on the man, James pulled off his own cravat and bound the interloper's hands behind his back, and then half dragged and half shoved his prisoner to where Ella lay. "Open your mouth, bastard, and I will shoot you right where you stand!" Taking a strap from Ella's saddle, he tethered the man's ankles after removing his boots.

Leaving the man lying face down like a shorn sheep in the field's middle, James returned to where Ella finally stirred. Her horse continued to whinny in pain, so before she could witness the act, he reloaded the gun and put the animal out of its misery.

"Sweetheart." He cradled her head in his lap. "Ella, Darling," he drawled.

"Quit calling me *Darling*," she murmured as she tried to push up from the ground.

"Yes, Love." He smiled in triumph as he supported her back and head to a seated position.

Ella shook her head slightly, clearing the cobwebs. "I am not your *love* either, Lord Worthing," she insisted, still unsure what happened.

Smiling foolishly, James put a hand on her shoulder, keeping her from standing too soon. "Easy. You had a rough fall, Lady Eleanor."

Finally, the realization of what had occurred set in, and Ella looked quickly to where the grey gelding lay on its side, legs twisted. "Sampson?" she whispered, throat dry with grief.

James shook his head, unable to tell her what he had done. "He will suffer no longer," he assured her.

"My mother bought him for me right before she died." The words sounded very far away, and James suspected she remembered the happiness associated with that moment.

"I am sorry, Darling." James slid his arm around her shoulder, easing Ella into his embrace, allowing her to hide her sobs. After a few minutes, he edged her back. "I need to see you home, Lady Eleanor. Do you think you can stand?"

Ella nodded her understanding and allowed him to support her to her feet. When her eyes fell on the fettered man, they grew in size. "You were busy, Lord Worthing."

"Anything for you, Ella." Despite the impropriety, he helped her straighten her clothing and hat. "You need that mirror now," he teased. "You look quite delicious when you are rumpled."

"Wretch!" She pretended his familiarity offended her, but she squeezed his hand before letting go.

"Do you suppose you could hold the gun on our friend while I retrieve his mount?" If it were any other woman, James would expect a case of the vapors, but not Ella. Instinctively, he knew her strength. Somehow, this woman had survived William Fowler; she could handle herself.

She reached for the pistol. "I have never used a gun before. What should I do?"

"Just hold it steady." He adjusted her hand on the weapon. "It is not likely he can move, but this is a precaution. I will be back in a moment." Without a second look, knowing she would not panic, James scaled the rocky incline again. It took no time whatsoever for him to find the man's horse tied to a bush along the access road.

Returning with the animal, he loaded their attacker across the saddle, cinching the cravat and leather strap to the seat. Next, taking the gun from her grasp, he brought his own horse alongside; he mounted and then motioned to Ella. "You will ride with me, Lady Eleanor." He saw her start to object, but then the sensible Eleanor Fowler took control, and she accepted his extended hand. Placing her foot on the top of his in the stirrup, Ella climbed into his arms, settling on James's lap. Enjoying having another excuse to hold her, James teasingly whispered close to her ear, "Do not get too used to all this attention, Lady Eleanor. I intend to take a full look at this year's social offerings."

Not anticipating his denial of their closeness, Ella flustered, "I assure you, Lord Worthing, I have no such expectations!"

"As long as we have an understanding."

Ella muddled with indignation. "James Kerrington, you are the most frustrating…!"

Before she could finish her tirade, his mouth found hers. For a split second, she resisted, but then Ella relaxed into the moment. Although he fought to keep his senses clear, he was a possessed man. Her body's warm glow intensified his need—feeding it.

When Ella shivered, he allowed his tongue to trace the line of her lips—to touch her mouth's soft surfaces. She awakened a latent need in him—a need he could no longer deny. Every nerve in his body existed to know this woman. He pressed Ella closer to him, breathing in the scent of her hair—her skin—her innocence. James wanted to smother her with his passion, but, instinctively, he knew it was not the way to go with Ella. If he had guessed correctly, Eleanor Fowler had experienced some sort of maltreatment at her father's hand. She would need small doses of affection before she could learn to trust again. Last night, James had considered discussing his premise with her brother, but Brantley Fowler was known to use a hammer when a feather would better serve. Fowler's sister needed a different kind of touch. Hating to end it, James slowly withdrew his mouth from hers. "Nice." His grin reached his eyes. "I would wrestle another dozen men for such a reward." The thrill of her intimacy rocked his reason, and he wondered whether she might feel the same.

Ella blushed and hid her face in the opening of his shirt. "I should never have acted so impetuously," she rasped.

"It will be our secret, Darling." James tightened his embrace before offering her an excuse, something she would need to justify her own actions. "I do not want to face one of my best friends on the dueling field. It was just the shock of what happened." Ella's head moved in affirmation of what he said, but James felt her arms go around his waist, and he relaxed, knowing he had judged correctly how to handle the very complex Eleanor Fowler. After several such private minutes, he asked, "Did you recognize the man?"

Ella leaned back where she might see his face. "No,...but it has been some time since I was off the estate. Unless he was a cottager or a village merchant, I would likely not have seen him."

"We will let your brother question him." James turned the horse they shared toward the main stables. He laced the reins of the other animal to a lead strap. "Bran was quite the expert in obtaining information when the rest of us could not. We used to call him the *Vicar*, what with people making confessions and your brother's need to rescue every woman and child he saw."

"Bran?" she gasped.

"Your brother was one of my best men." James assured her. "Whatever is happening at Thornhill, Fowler will figure it out."

Ella looked at him with surprise. "Do you think, my Lord, someone wishes to hurt us?"

"Lady Eleanor, you are intelligent enough to realize that two shooting incidents in less than a week is not usual." James shifted her weight into a more appropriate position as they came into view of the house. "I do not wish to scare you, but please be careful."

Ella nodded in understanding.

"I want nothing to happen to you, Ella." James lifted her chin with his finger. "You have no idea how frightened I was today when I found you under Sampson's flaying hooves." They stared deeply into each other's eyes.

At the stables now, he knew he should release her, but James and Eleanor were lost to their closeness—lost in each other's eyes, the rest of the world did not exist. "My Lord," a groomsman's voice invaded the moment; he stood by a mounting block and reached up to help Lady Eleanor to the step. Reluctantly, James released her. Almost immediately, the Thorn Hall staff surrounded them, and Fowler came running, followed closely by Miss Aldridge. For those few exquisite seconds, lost in Ella's eyes, he saw his future—saw her by his side, and the thought did not shake him as he had once considered it might: It actually seemed to bring closure to his loneliness.

"Worthing, what the hell?" Fowler's voice held irritation as he encircled Ella in his arms, trying to determine who might be the culprit. Ella's appearance told everyone something bad happened.

"I brought you a present, Your Grace." James gestured to the trailing horse. "When I go after a shooter, I get my man."

It pleased James that Fowler lovingly adjusted Ella in his arms, protecting his sister. The woman needed such tenderness. Fowler bent his head to speak in her ear. "He shot at you?" He gestured toward the trailing horse.

Ella readily nodded. "Sampson went down; His Lordship took care of my horse after capturing that man." The strength of her voice surprised James. Clearly, she held that inner resolve, the one he had imagined for her, all along.

"Are you hurt?" Fowler demanded.

"Very sore and a bad headache…I was unconscious for a few minutes." Ella glanced around at the gathering crowd, and then her eyes followed the line of her brother's shoulder to find Lord Worthing. Someone had just shot at her; however, nothing else mattered but that intense moment she had shared with the viscount. This man just kissed her—she relived it in her mind, and without thought Ella's fingers brushed her lips in recollection. She could not keep her eyes from him. He still sat on his horse, an example of pure male, and she found that thought very pleasing, although a bit disturbing. The smell of him—musky sandalwood—clung to her. She had never acted so impulsively with anyone, especially not with a man of James Kerrington's apparent charms. In fact, Ella had only been kissed once in her life, and that was one of the stable boys when she was but ten years of age, and even then it was on the cheek. Now, she knew the power of a kiss, and she thought she might like to try it again.

As the others untied the captive, Fowler released his sister to their cousin's care. "Let Velvet take you into the house, Ella." As Eleanor leaned heavily on Miss Aldridge for support, James's eyes followed, still mesmerized by the moment they had shared. He had known many women in his lifetime, but for some unexplainable reason, Eleanor Fowler caught him by the shoulders and spun him around in circles. He desperately wanted to catch her up before him again and possessively ride off with her in his arms—to kiss the sprinkling of freckles along the slender line of her neck, which he had seen earlier today—to remove the pins and let her golden hair stream down over his waiting hands.

Fowler's words brought him to the moment at hand. "You men put Lord Worthing's captive in the root cellar. Place guards outside the door. I will send for the physician and the magistrate." Thorn Hall's footmen responded immediately.

Obviously not amused by James's preoccupation, Fowler demanded, "Would you care to join me in my study, Worthing?"

James chuckled when the duke did not wait for an answer. He slid from the saddle and followed Ella's brother to the house. "Hey, I thought I was the commanding officer," he called as he caught up to Fowler.

His friend's anger boiled over. "Not this time! This is personal."

For the next half hour, Fowler and James thoroughly dissected what had happened with the shooter. The duke sent for the physician for both Ella and the prisoner, but he withheld sending for the magistrate until he had some answers of his own.

"It just does not seem logical. A man does not just lay in wait, hoping a rider comes by; someone must know of your movements. Yet, even with that, no one could determine exactly where Lady Eleanor and I would ride today. We had no destination in mind."

"Ella was to show you the estate," Fowler reasoned. "Obviously, there are certain points of interest."

"But that does not guarantee we would be crossing that particular meadow." James thought aloud. "And who is the target? Lady Eleanor and Miss Aldridge were the recipients, but were they the objectives? Somehow, I cannot imagine either of them engendering such rancor. That leaves your father's enemies, your enemies as a Realm member, or your enemies in Cornwall. Do you have any ideas?"

"I made a mental list the other evening—after Velvet's encounter."

James just nodded; he knew this was how his friend's mind

worked—taking bits and pieces of information and making sense of them. "Then I suspect it is time for the *Vicar* to make a call on the prisoner."

Fowler stood slowly; James noted his uncomfortable frown. "Is there anything I should know regarding my sister?"

"Other than the fact that I find Lady Eleanor quite remarkable?"

"Ella seems perfectly in control and efficiently independent, but she is very vulnerable," Fowler cautioned.

James smiled, recognizing how he would feel in the same situation. "I promise you, Your Grace, I would never purposely hurt Lady Eleanor."

Begrudgingly, the duke said, "I am glad you stay with us, Worthing. I am in need of your reason, and, I suspect, Ella would prefer it that way."

Fowler secured very little from their prisoner. Even with the threat of hanging for attacking a peer, the man swore he did not know who had hired him. The prisoner, Harry Sparks, gave Fowler the name of the "friend" who had paid him to send a "message" to the new duke, but, for all intents and purposes, Sparks's partner likely knew as little as he did. Whoever made Fowler his target hid his trail well.

With James's encouragement, they decided to send what information Fowler coerced to their friend, the Marquis of Godown, asking him to meet them in London. James also called in some favors for information, in the form of Bow Street Runners, who sought connections to Sparks and his partner Lionel Stimpson, and, reluctantly, Fowler sent word to Shepherd. If this "message" came from one of the Realm's former interests, Shepherd, the Realm's government contact, needed to know. Eventually, Fowler and James turned Sparks over to the local magistrate, who insisted on transporting the prisoner immediately to London, declaring that such a nefarious attempt needed the attention of the best prosecutors the law could provide. They would house Sparks at Old Bailey. Within three days' time, word came that a Bow Street Runner had apprehended Lionel Stimpson in an abandoned building in Spitalfields. Shepherd took possession of both men and said he would inform them of any new leads as soon as they became available.

~ ~ ~

"Will you not join us, Bran?" Ella called from the library, noting her brother passing the open door.

Fowler stepped reluctantly into the room. Looking distracted, he simply offered them the required greeting. "I have work, Ella; I will beg your pardon. Please enjoy your game."

She and James Kerrington sat at a chessboard, preparing to start the match. "We might find other amusements."

James recognized the look on Bran's face—he had seen it often enough over the years. Any time Fowler held a puzzle where all the pieces did not fit, his countenance took on such gloom and doom. Releasing his friend to tend to the points of the investigation, he said, "Do you fear my besting you, Lady Eleanor?"

Predictably, Ella flushed with color, reacting to his attentions. "You should know, my Lord, I take no prisoners when I play chess."

"She does not, Worthing," Fowler warned before bowing from the room.

Alone again, James leaned forward to flirtatiously tease her. "No prisoners when you play chess, Lady Eleanor?"

"Absolutely not, Your Lordship," she smirked.

"When do you take prisoners, Lady Eleanor? I willingly sacrifice myself to such punishments."

Eleanor smiled despite her embarrassment. Her acceptance of his flirtation pleased James. She had over the past few days become more comfortable with him. Part of his plan. "You are a wretched man, Lord Worthing; you say the most bizarre things. I should chastise you for your forwardness, but you would just apologize and feign real remorse. Then I would have to forgive you despite the impropriety. We will skip all those steps and simply return to the game."

James's smile reached the corners of his eyes. "Yes, my Love."

"Lord Worthing, I must insist you not call me by such endearments," she protested.

"I will think of other endearments more appropriate. Do you prefer *Darling,* or *Sweetling*?"

Picking up the chess piece and making her first move, Ella rolled her eyes in disbelief. "There is no arguing with you, Lord Worthing. You are beyond reform."

"And you, Lady Eleanor, prefer me that way."

Ella said nothing, turning her attention to the board instead, but she thought him correct; she did enjoy Worthing's gallantry more than she expected. In fact, she thought about him all the time, which often vexed her more practical side, but, generally, Ella found spending time with Lord Worthing the most important event of her day.

~ ~ ~

Later in the afternoon, James sought Fowler in the duke's study. He knew Fowler's nature; the long solitary hours indicated his friend suffered from some sort of self-recrimination. "Your Grace, may I be of service?"

Fowler nursed a drink; half-heartedly, he gestured for James to join him. Kerrington poured himself a drink and took the suggested seat. They sat in companionable silence for several minutes before Fowler finally said, "It is so ironic. Ella and Velvet survived the self-imposed loneliness associated with living under my father's roof. They survived rumors of his lustful nature, and they survived running an estate in a world disinclined to value a woman's worth."

James did not respond for several elongated moments. "You wonder how it is you who brings danger to the women you love. I understand. If not for my weakness, Elizabeth would be alive. I rue the day I brought my lust to her doorstep." James would have reminisced, indulging himself in his personal anguish, but tonight his losing Elizabeth became secondary to protecting Ella.

Fowler continued, "I knocked Velvet to the ground when someone attacked us, and you saved Ella and captured her assailant. However, the peril is of my making. I must find a way to protect them in London. You will help me, will you not, Worthing?"

"Of course, Your Grace. The Realm serves together."

~ ~ ~

"You idiot! You were to wait until I told you to act!"

The man pulled out of his attacker's grasp. "I have my own agenda. I need Fowler's money, and the best way to secure it is to let him know that despite his title and his consequence, he is not in charge."

"There are bigger issues than your gambling debts! I told your business partner what I expected. I am after something that will make us all richer than Croesus. Now, you have put Fowler and Worthing on guard. I will have no way of making sure they do not have the prize, thanks to your meddling buffoonery. No wonder the British are tucking tail and running from Bonaparte. You are a bunch of pompous asses!" The dark-skinned assailant pushed the weaker nobleman out of his way as he strode from the darkened hallway and into the night.

~ ~ ~

Over the next week, Eleanor tried to forget those few sensational moments in His Lordship's embrace, but every time he walked into a room she melted. She clearly remembered the heat of his body—the way her breasts swelled in anticipation—and the shallowness of her own breathing. She thought that after the first one, he might try to steal a kiss in the garden or in an empty room, but he remained the perfect gentleman, at least, in action—sometimes he verbally flirted with her. No one could guess that they had shared such an intimate moment. Part of her prayed he did not pursue her, but the other half secretly wanted to know this man. Ella wanted to be free of her past and to leave William Fowler's memory behind. She had thought she might find satisfaction in travel and in her studies, but now she envisioned the handsome man who called her "Love" and "Darling." However, with his continued reluctance to approach her again, she began to wonder if she had imagined it. Maybe he was right; they experienced a traumatic moment, and the kiss grew from the joy of escaping death. Such a thought brought a scowl to her face.

Twice during the week, James found Eleanor in her nightgown, roaming the halls. Both times, he gathered her in his arms and carried her safely to her room. As he was leaving soon, he suggested Eleanor's maid make her pallet closer to the door, but secretly he took pleasure in holding Ella close to him. He dreamed of making her nightmares disappear, kissing her awake and sating his needs in her body. Never—even with Elizabeth—had he desired a woman so desperately. He did not know how he could watch her be the object of other men's attentions. If he thought Fowler might approve, and the woman might accept, a proposal hung ready on his lips. He would leave them on the morrow to return to his own town house, a posh dwelling on Pall Mall. His father rarely left the country estate, so James spent most of his time in town.

"Will we have the pleasure of your company in London, Lord Worthing?" Ella asked over supper, her question interrupting James's musings.

He teased, "As Briar House is less than a mile from Worthing Hall, you may need guards to keep me from making a pest of myself, Lady Eleanor."

A calmness she had not felt earlier with the knowledge of his leaving slowly crept across her face. She would see Lord Worthing again. Ella possessed no reasonable conjecture as to why that was important, but it was. "No guards, Your Lordship," she assured him.

James smiled—a contented sigh escaping before he could stop it. "I promised to claim dances from both you and your cousin, Lady Eleanor, and I am a man of my word."

"Where is Eleanor?" Aunt Agatha demanded.

"Here, Aunt," Ella swept into the room followed closely by Velvet. They had arrived at Briar House an hour before. Ella felt the situation's weight, and her dread smothered her. Her brother simply did not understand how hard this was for her. The only benefit, in her estimation, would be seeing James Kerrington again.

Aunt Agatha, the Dowager Duchess of Northfield, was their mother's older sister. Both Braton daughters married dukes, but Agatha certainly received the better bargain. Her only problem was that she had had but ten years of happiness. The previous Duke of Norfield lost his battle with a weak heart, leaving his wife a widow at the age of nine and twenty. Now, as she approached her fiftieth birthday, she spent most of her time matchmaking among the *ton's* members. Notoriously manipulative, Agatha Braton Norris had the connections and the money to be loved by everyone, including her niece and nephew. "Oh, Eleanor," she beamed, "I cannot look upon you, my Child, without seeing my dear sister. You look more like her every day."

"Thank you, Aunt." Ella bestowed a brief kiss on the Dowager's cheek. With the comfort of family, Ella allowed herself to breathe easier.

Velvet followed suit. "How are you, Child?" Agatha captured Velvet's hand and gave it a brief squeeze.

"I am well, Your Grace." Velvet made a quick curtsy. "It is most kind of you to offer your sponsorship for my presentation, Ma'am."

"Child, you know I live for such revelry." Agatha laughed lightly. "Do I not, Brantley?"

"That you do, my Dear." Fowler took a chair close to hers, before expelling a ragged breath as he surveyed the room. Ella recognized his uneasiness. She had noted that at Thorn Hall he had limited his residence to the east wing's rooms and the common rooms below. He had yet to enter those quarters once occupied by their parents. However, at Briar House, he would need to face his demons firsthand. Privately, she relished the idea that their coming to London also affected her brother's peace of mind; he certainly had caused her numerous moments of anxiety. "I am obliged to you for taking on Ella's and Velvet's presentations," he told their aunt. "What do you plan for my sister and cousin?"

Out of habit, Eleanor ordered tea, and they joined together before the hearth, but she took no pleasure in hearing of Aunt Agatha's preparations. "I am pleased, Brantley, that you came to town in time to order Presentation gowns for these two. In another week, the press of people demanding the best modistes will be many. I have fittings set for tomorrow; we will be about most of the day."

"Are the Presentation gowns as awful as everyone says?" Velvet could not keep the worry out of her voice. Eleanor listened intently; Velvet gave voice to her own fears about meeting the Queen.

"They are a bit cumbersome, but young ladies have survived them for years. Do not worry, my Child; I will teach you everything. In fact, we will begin this afternoon. We will borrow a tablecloth from the new housekeeper your brother hired and use it to practice the dress's train."

Ella glanced at Bran. "New housekeeper?" She wondered about her brother's maneuverings.

"I brought in Mrs. Smithson and Mr. Horace, as well as a few other key staff members from Cornwall. They may not know London, but they do know what I expect in my household."

Ella quickly realized he meant they would protect him; he knew these people. Obviously, someone at Thorn Hall had helped with the attacks. She understood his fear; Ella saw it in Lord Worthing's face that day. Bran wanted to take control. "Excellent idea," she observed.

"Brantley, I hope your pockets are deep," his aunt uncharacteristically blurted out, and Ella found herself smiling at the serious tone.

"Why might that be, Your Grace?" They adored their aunt;

when they were children, she had never spoken down to them. It was she who explained their mother's death. They always knew she would speak her mind, and right now, the truth—even if it hurt—was important to hear.

"Well, I do not wish to be indelicate, but if the gowns Ella and Velvet currently wear are indicative of their wardrobes, they simply will not do. The style is from at least three years ago. As the Duke of Thornhill, you must see to this deficiency." Agatha was not condescending, just matter-of-fact in her analysis.

Ella blushed immediately. "I do not remember my last new gown. Neither Velvet nor I have been off the estate for some time."

"Nearly five years," Velvet whispered into the suddenly silent room.

"Five years?" Agatha gasped. "Whyever so long?"

"Papa did not wish it." Despite her best efforts, Ella's voice came out small and vulnerable.

Several long seconds passed before Agatha finally let out a deep sigh. "Then we are agreed, Brantley; the ladies need new wardrobes."

Ella and Bran exchanged glances, their discomfort obvious. "Whatever you think best, Aunt Agatha."

Ella felt the mortification of her aunt's remark. Who was she fooling? She knew nothing about Society or even how to hold a polite conversation. She had had no friends since the age of thirteen when her father had fondled one of the girls visiting her at Thorn Hall. Her friends had left the house that day, never to return. After that, Eleanor shunned everyone's company, everyone of her own age. She had had no childhood.

"New gowns sound heavenly, do they not, Ella?"

Eleanor heard the words, but she could muster no enthusiasm for the idea. She swallowed hard, trying to recover her composure. "They do, indeed, Velvet. We must trust Aunt Agatha to make our Come Outs first rate."

"You will accompany us, Brantley, to the *ton's* many outings?" Agatha's question came out as a command. Ella could do without constant reminders of her upcoming social disaster.

"As many as my business and my establishing my name in Parliament will allow," he assured their aunt.

Agatha bristled just a bit with his exception. "And what shall your wards do if your obligations take you elsewhere?"

Ella looked on as Bran smiled at Agatha—she was always one to tell her own son his duty—she would not hesitate to take the duke to task. "Lord Worthing offered his arm as needed." The mention of James Kerrington made Ella's heart skip a beat.

"Worthing? Martin Kerrington's son?" Agatha's reaction was priceless; she eyed Bran with amusement. "I assume His Lordship is a friend of yours, Brantley?"

Her brother smirked, "Worthing recently spent a fortnight at Thorn Hall. I believe my sister and my cousin would find Kerrington a suitable escort. I also asked the Marquis of Godown to be a regular member of our party."

"Gabriel Crowden?" Their aunt nearly choked on her tea.

Bran's smile spread like butter. "Yes, Aunt. Is there a problem?"

"A problem? No, Brantley—no problem. My niece and our cousin will regularly be escorted by three of the *ton's* newest and most eligible bachelors. Definitely, there is no problem. It will only increase Eleanor's and Velvet's value as this year's debutantes."

Ella listened to this exchange. How could she attract Lord Worthing, or any other suitor for that matter? She had no social skills, and she wore outdated gowns. Now that her brother's friend was in fashionable London, he would not look twice at her. She heard herself saying the words, "I am sure His Lordship has other things to do with his time."

Her brother teased, "Do not go on so, Ella. I will set a bet at White's that Worthing calls today at Briar House."

She wanted to believe her brother, but a part of Ella always expected the worst. She only half listened as Aunt Agatha planned to have Lord Worthing and the Marquis of Godown show them about town. The Dowager Duchess thought it a social coup to have them seen on the men's arms. Eleanor thought little of the possibilities. She simply wanted the Season over. The disbelief in her aunt's voice brought Ella's attention to the ongoing conversation: one dealing with Bran's marriage and with Sonali.

Before their aunt could comment further on her nephew's choice of a wife, Ella interrupted. "Aunt Agatha, you will love Sonali. She is the most precocious child—so intelligent—and so beautiful." For some reason, Ella felt a need to protect her brother. He was family, and she always did what was right for family.

"Of course, I will love her. She is my dear Amelia's first grandchild."

"As you can tell, Aunt, Sonali has stolen Ella's heart."

Undaunted by the new information, Agatha waved a dismissive hand. "Well, it just proves I need to find you an appropriate match as well, Brantley."

Bran opened his mouth to protest, but Mr. Horace appeared to announce Worthing's call, and their friend bowed his entrance into the Briar House drawing room.

Eleanor was on her feet immediately; she missed him despite the foolishness of the concept and the foolishness of her previous personal chastisement. Bran and Velvet rose too, along with the Dowager Duchess. Ella heard Bran whisper, "I told you so."

James bowed to the room, but his eyes remained on Eleanor. *His Amazon* was in the same room as he, and his body reacted accordingly. "I came to assure myself you experienced no problems with your journey, Your Grace."

Fowler's voice betrayed a twinge of amusement. "As you can see, Worthing, we are well. Please come in and meet my aunt. I have just assured her you would serve as an escort for my family in my absence, and here you are."

"At your service, Your Grace." He aristocratically inclined his head.

Fowler motioned James forward. "James Kerrington, Lord Worthing, may I present my mother's sister, the Dowager Duchess of Norfield."

"Your Grace." James bowed graciously over the woman's hand. "Thank you for receiving me. My father asked that if I was fortunate enough to make your acquaintance, Your Ladyship, that I forward his regards."

Agatha chuckled. "You are certainly Martin Kerrington's son. Not only do you resemble the man as he was in his prime, you possess his charm. I will keep my eye on you, Your Lordship." The regally coiffed woman reminded James of his mother.

He often heard similar acknowledgments of his father's vitality as a young man. "I understand you have a long-standing acquaintance with my mother."

"Your mother and I spent our first Season together, with your father pursuing her from the beginning."

James gave her his best smile. "That does sound like the tales they each share of their courtship, Duchess."

"Come join us, my Lord." Ella gestured to the other half of the settee on which she was sitting and then rang for fresh tea.

"Thank you, Lady Eleanor." James's heart leapt with being close to her again. The past week was hell. He should have waited for his call, but he could not stay away while Eleanor was in residence at Briar House. When he returned to London, he had paid Mary a visit, thinking he simply wanted to satiate his rising need for a woman, but he ended up spending an evening on Mary's chaise and going home to an empty bed. The moment he saw Eleanor the blood rushed straight from his brain to his groin. *Damn! He had lost his bloody mind!* He was more in tune to this woman in this drawing room surrounded by her family than he had been to any woman in his life, even Elizabeth, although he did not like to admit that fact. His infatuation with Ella grew so quickly, he was sore to keep it under control.

James accepted the tea Ella offered and tried to relax into the cushions. It was the first time in a week he felt comfortable. "It will give me great pleasure, Your Grace, to inform my mother of making your acquaintance." James took up the conversation where they left off.

"May I ask after your father, Lord Worthing?"

"I am afraid, Lady Norfield, my father's remaining days are short. It has been nearly a year since he left his bed. My mother is a saint; she tends him herself."

Fowler's aunt looked uncomfortable with the news. "It is a shame, Lord Worthing…a crying shame we lose good men such as your father and my Harold too soon. I shall write your mother to see if there is anything I might do for her."

"I believe just knowing her former friends are thinking of her will make a difference, Your Grace."

Ella listened closely to James's description of his parents. All along she had assumed that, like Bran, Lord Worthing had left home to avoid interactions with his family; now, her suppositions proved to be in error. *Why did he leave? What would drive a man from the family he loved? Would Bran tell her?* Men thought differently about sharing confidences. It was not that women were more likely to gossip. On the contrary, men also obsessed over the comings and goings of their friends, as well as their enemies. Women simply needed to verbalize their thoughts to give them credence.

Noting her moodiness, James impulsively turned to Ella. He had not planned what he would ask, but somehow he needed to extend his time with her. "Lady Eleanor," he began, "I realize you only this day arrived in London, but would you allow me to escort you and your cousin on a brief tour of the city? The *ton* has not yet descended upon London in full force, and I recall your commenting on how long it has been since you were in the capital. It would give you the opportunity to become familiar with the city before the Season begins."

"I would enjoy a leisurely tour," Velvet added before Eleanor could respond.

"What might you have in mind, my Lord?" Ella asked softly, unsure she wanted to go, but positive she wanted him to stay.

"We might see the Royal Academy, or we could take a drive through Hyde Park, or whatever you may wish. I have no agenda—a purely extemporaneous idea."

"It has been a decade since we were here." Ella reasoned aloud.

Agatha looked on in surprise. "Surely, you jest, Eleanor." The news stunned James also. The late duke's total control of Ella bothered Kerrington.

"No, Aunt." He watched Ella's countenance glaze over in remembrance. "I was ten and Velvet nine. Our governess took us for a picnic in Hyde Park."

"Mrs. Holden *dash* Smythe." Velvet giggled. "Remember, Ella? That is how she would say it: Holden dash Smythe."

Ella nodded her head with the memory. "The lady was an odd bird, but we had fun on that holiday. Mother came to see doctors who might help her, while Mrs. Holden-Smythe escorted Velvet and me to see the Tower of London. If I had known the seriousness of her illness, I would have stayed with Mother instead." The conversation reminded James of Fowler's drunken confession that his mother suffered from the great pox—a "gift" from the late duke.

"Amelia would never have allowed it, Child. She wanted to protect you and Brantley as long as she could." Agatha set forward to emphasize what she imparted. James appreciated the woman's sensitivity for Ella's sake.

"Where was I when the two of you were playing about the London streets?" Bran teased.

"I imagine you were at school. Young boys have more freedom than young ladies," Velvet reminded him.

Ella's making her decision to join him thrilled James. "Would it be rude of us to accept His Lordship's offer, Aunt? After all, you had planned to begin our training for our Presentations."

"No, Child," her aunt thankfully agreed. "You and Velvet deserve some time to enjoy the city. God only knows we will be busy enough once the invitations pour in. Besides, we have all day to practice. A few hours with Lord Worthing will not jeopardize your Presentation."

"If you are sure, Aunt?" The corners of Ella's mouth quivered, but her response spoke of eagerness. A tender need to protect her spread through James. "Miss Aldridge and I would be pleased to join you, Your Lordship."

"Excellent." James beamed with how well things turned out. He could actually breathe again. Eleanor Fowler would be beside him, a place he instinctively knew was hers for the taking.

Velvet turned to Bran. "May we convince you to join us, Your Grace?" Ella had become more aware of the standoff between them over the past few weeks.

Ella thought her brother foolish when he refused. "It truly sounds like a delightful afternoon, but, as I wait for Sonali and Mrs. Carruthers, I must decline." Ella thought Bran and Velvet quite childish to fight their natural attraction to each other.

"Of course." Ella heard the disappointment in her cousin's voice and noted her brother's obvious chagrin.

Recognizing her chance, Ella stood before Velvet could change her mind. "If you will excuse us, Lord Worthing, my cousin and I will freshen our clothing and join you in a few minutes."

"I will enjoy your aunt's company until your return, Lady Eleanor."

Velvet tapped on the door before entering. "May I help you, Ella?"

Eleanor smiled with her cousin's entrance. "Would you mind lacing me up?"

For the next couple of minutes, her cousin dutifully pulled the laces tighter on Ella's corset and dress. "Lord Worthing is quite handsome," Velvet spoke the words as if they were an afterthought, but Ella immediately wondered at her cousin's interest in the viscount.

"Do you really think so?" Ella faced the mirror and tried to use it to see Velvet's true expression. Of course, she thought Worthing the most handsome of men, but she worried now whether her cousin might have set her sights on him. If so, Ella knew she would not stand a chance; Velvet outshone her in looks.

"My Heavens, yes, and he does admire you, Ella." Velvet tied the strings.

Forgetting her desire to appear uninvolved, as well as the worry of only a few seconds ago, Ella spun toward her. "What makes you say so?" She had hoped for such a possibility.

"One just has to look at the man; he can barely keep his eyes from you." Velvet pulled Ella to the bed to sit together. "I wish your brother looked at me that way."

Ella fought to control her breathing. "Do you speak the truth, Velvet, or is this one of your fairy tales?"

Her cousin caught Ella's hand. "Tell me you affect him also."

Ella looked away shyly. "Is it not absurd? I have always planned a life of independence, but I do admit I think often of Lord Worthing."

Conspiratorially, Velvet mused, "It is a shame to waste our time and energy with a Season when the only men we might consider sit together downstairs in the drawing room."

"Bran believes we would lose something by not having a Season," Ella defended her brother, although she did not agree with his assessment.

Surprisingly, Velvet chuckled. "I know he means well. Men always mean well, but they are so oblivious when it comes to women. You will not believe what I told Bran the other day. I told him I was anxious for the Season to begin so I could meet other men. I said I was determined to find a mate so he might be rid of me."

Ella gasped, "You did not? What did Bran say?"

"Well, nothing. That is when you and His Lordship rode in on one horse." After a brief moment of silence, Velvet blurted out, "Worthing kissed you, did he not?"

Ella burst into laughter, trying to hide her initial embarrassment, but finally she told the truth. Velvet remained as close as a sister, and

Ella knew she could trust her cousin. "How did you know?"

Velvet shrugged her shoulders. "I am not sure exactly. You looked different after that ride—more satisfied." She again caught Ella's hand in hers. "Would you help me win Bran? I will do everything in my power to aid you with Lord Worthing."

"Dare we?" Ella asked, nearly as excited as her cousin.

"The way I see it, Bran wants us both to find suitable matches this Season. We are simply following his wishes."

Ella smiled fully, the first time in a long time. "You are evil, Cousin."

"So, is it a deal?"

"Absolutely."

CHAPTER 3

~ ~ ~

TEN MINUTES LATER, they descended the main staircase, arm in arm. Ella leaned close. "May I offer a word of advice regarding Brantley?"

Velvet said nothing—just nodded her agreement.

"Bran is not likely to seriously look at any woman who could not accept Sonali. You barely speak to the child. Can you not, if you truly love him, begin to let his daughter into your heart? Sonali is part of Bran. Learn to love that part."

Velvet made no response, but she squeezed Ella's hand in understanding. "Let us do the Royal Academy," she whispered. "I will get lost, and you may spend time alone with His Lordship."

~ ~ ~

"Sir Joshua Reynolds." James pointed to the man's portrait. "He was the first President of the Academy. Benjamin West serves in that position at this time."

They walked along together, Ella's hand resting lightly on James's arm. "Did you address your estate business when you came to London, Lord Worthing?"

"I did, Lady Eleanor."

Silence. "I was sorry to hear you speak of your father's illness, and a bit ashamed I had not asked of your family before. It sounded as if you and the Earl are close."

"We are." Longer silence. "I...I avoided speaking of my father's illness knowing you just lost your own parent. I felt it might be too raw a memory, and I would do nothing to hurt you."

A still longer silence. "Lord Worthing, I am sure my brother shared some of our family's misery with you. You must understand my feelings for my father are not those one normally finds associated with grief."

James thought of Ella's tormented soul and of her "sleeplessly" begging her father to love her. "I would understand when you are ready to speak of it, Lady Eleanor."

"I am sure you would try, Your Lordship, but I am not sure I understand, and I lived through it."

The long silence returned. "A Gainsborough." He pointed to a large portrait surrounded by many smaller ones.

Ella did not respond; she simply walked by his side. "James," she said unexpectedly, "would you tell me why, if you love your family so much, you left home to spend years fighting for causes most would deem useless? You are your father's heir; I am surprised he allowed it."

He reveled in the knowledge that she used his given name, but he did not welcome the idea of telling Ella about Elizabeth. "Might we sit?" He gestured to a nearby bench.

When they were seated together, James impulsively caught her hand and brought the back of it to his mouth, letting his lips linger on her skin. "My dear, sweet Ella," he murmured. He paused to look into her eyes. "I do not know where to start. I am going to ask you not to interrupt. I fear that once I begin—if I stop—I may not be able to finish."

James turned his head slightly to the left, looking off at something not there. "Shortly before I reached my majority, I met a young woman, Elizabeth Morris, one of the most beautiful women I have ever seen, and I fell madly in love; but Elizabeth was not just beautiful on the outside; she had an adventurous heart as well. Anyway, I married her within six months of our meeting." James felt Ella try to slip her hand from his, and, instinctively, he tightened his hold. He refused to allow her withdrawal. "Elizabeth and I were ecstatically happy, and, for me, for two years, life was never so perfect. Then Elizabeth became with child, and I lost her. The boy did not turn, and the surgeon could not save my wife." He went utterly still, except that his Adam's apple moved painfully up and down as he fought back the tears. "I could not understand how I could go on living. Each day I visited the grave, and I prayed for God to take me too, and as painful as it is to say this now, I could not hold my child without blaming him for his mother's death. I had no other choice: Within three months, I walked away from everything I knew, and I took on every nasty cause I could find—trying to punish myself for continuing to live when Elizabeth did not, thinking if I tempted Fate often enough, I would lose." James turned back to Ella suddenly. "Then I found others who needed my help to survive, and I began to fight for them. Ironically, I saved myself as well."

"Is that what Bran did also?" Ella's voice was so quiet James was not sure he heard her correctly.

"All the men in my unit found what they needed, although none of us shared the depths of our reasons for losing ourselves."

Ella traced a circle on the inside of his palm with her fingertip. "And the boy?"

James smiled with the memory. "Daniel is nine, going on forty," he chuckled. "He is a phenomenal child; I would like for you to meet him some time."

"I would be pleased to do so." Ella released her hand from his. She was not sure what she felt. Ella needed to know of James's grief, but to know he had loved another woman—a beautiful woman, at that, made her doubt whether she might win his heart. "We should find Velvet; she must wonder what became of us."

James followed her to his feet. Impulsively, he cupped her cheek when he sensed the hint of panic in her stance. "Thank you, Ella." He knew she considered what he said—observed her questioning her own worth. James would teach her to love.

Eleanor said nothing more. She simply placed her hand on Worthing's arm and let him lead her off to find her cousin. She would need to think on this. Of late, she considered the possibility of winning James Kerrington's affections, but when he spoke of the woman who had stolen his heart long ago, she realized she would never be able to replace Elizabeth Morris in his life. For some women, the affection he showed her might be enough—they might allow him to keep the woman he had loved in his heart while he showered them with the "here and now." But, Ella was not so sure she could accept only a "liking" from Lord Worthing. All her life she had desired someone to love her—to place her above all others. Ella did not think Worthing could do that, and she was unsure whether she could settle for anything less.

After enjoying a cream ice from Gunter's, they arrived at Briar House to find an excited child dancing about the foyer.

"Aunt Ella." Sonali was in her arms as soon as Ella entered the hall. "Papa says we can all see the animals at the Tower of London. And you must come too, Uncle James," the child said in breathless excitement. James reached out to smooth Sonali's hair in a gesture of love.

"That sounds delightful." Ella placed the girl on her feet before allowing James to help her off with her cloak. "Where is your father?" Ella asked as she took the girl's hand. "Excuse me for the moment, Lord Worthing." Ella allowed Sonali to drag her toward Bran's study.

Before he could respond, Velvet quickly took James's arm and directed him toward the same drawing room as earlier. "Lord Worthing, I wish to speak to you," the woman announced quite unexpectedly.

"Of course, Miss Aldridge." He allowed her to lead him to the privacy of the empty room. To date, the woman had said very little to him beyond polite conversation. Evidently, she had an agenda, and he was to be privy to it.

"You will think me quite forward, Sir, but desperation makes me so." Velvet crossed to the window and motioned for him to follow her. "I have been in love with Brantley Fowler since I was eight years old," she proclaimed before he even came to a standstill. "You will think that foolish, but I have no time to debate. You see, it is my belief, Sir, you know how Bran feels about me."

James just smiled at the urgency in her voice. "Go on, Miss Aldridge."

"Bran has it in his mind he must let me choose another in order to protect me or because he thinks that will make us even. I suspect you know the truth of his marriage, but I will not ask you to divulge Bran's secrets. I do not care about five years ago; I care about now." The woman rushed through the words. "I want Brantley Fowler, and I will do anything to win him."

"And you are telling me this for what purpose, Miss Aldridge?" James could not help but continue to smile at her forwardness. Fowler always thought "his Velvet" to be innocent and naïve; James was discovering otherwise.

"Because you, Lord Worthing, are going to help me figure out how to get through Bran's thick head and make him see I am the one woman for him."

James glanced toward the open door, hearing a footman in the hallway. "Without betraying my friend, I suspect His Grace already knows you are the right woman, Miss Aldridge."

"However, I must destroy his mantle of honor."

"And how do you propose to do that?"

"Make him jealous."

James laughed lightly. "Poor Bran—he has no idea what awaits him."

"You will not tell him!" A moment of anxiousness escaped.

"I will keep your secret, Miss Aldridge."

"Good," she declared confidently. "Now, Lord Worthing, I need someone with whom to flirt."

James held up his hands to stop her. "I will not be a part of your plan in that manner, Miss Aldridge."

"Of course not, Your Lordship. Actually, I thought of you originally, but then I observed how you look at Ella."

"How… how I look at Lady Eleanor?" he stammered. "How do you think I look at your cousin?"

Velvet's eyes lit up with amusement. "Like you want to hold her and never let go."

James paused before responding. "Am I that obvious?"

"Only to those who are looking for love."

"What do you require of me, Miss Aldridge?" James resigned himself to aiding her.

"Help me find someone to make Bran insanely jealous—enough that he will declare himself rather than let me go."

James hesitated before answering. "Fowler may have supplied his own undoing. I know just the man. Gabriel Crowden, the new Marquis of Godown. He and Fowler are so competitive—whether it be cards or swords or clothing…"

"Or women?"

"I have never known them to compete over a woman, but I imagine it would be so. Surprisingly, they were at university together before joining me in our adventures. Godown is more dangerously introspective than Fowler—do not forget my warning on that point, Miss Aldridge."

The woman appeared satisfied with her thoughts. "Would the Marquis help me?"

"If it meant bedeviling His Grace, I suspect Godown would be willing," James said guardedly.

"Would you speak to Godown on my behalf? Seek out his help?" she implored.

"What do I get from all this?"

"More time alone with my cousin." Velvet walked away from him. "You really did not think I became lost this afternoon, did you, my Lord?"

James self-consciously slid his hand in his pocket, fingering the pebble his son had given him. It was silly, but he carried it everywhere he went. Touching it now made him think of Daniel and of Ella and how they might all be together some day. "No, Miss Aldridge, I suppose I did not."

"Then I have your assent, Sir?"

"Most definitely, Miss Aldridge. Operation Velvet Touch is underway," he teased.

Velvet's smile grew with the thought. "Oooh! I like that, Lord Worthing. Operation Velvet Touch! Perfect!"

Shortly, Ella appeared at the drawing room door. "My brother sent me, Lord Worthing, to request your joining him in his study."

James turned suddenly upon hearing her voice. "I thought to take my leave, but I will see what His Grace needs." He crossed to where Ella still stood in the open doorway. Impulsively, he paused; mere inches separated them, and their eyes locked on one another.

Realizing the impropriety of standing so close, where everyone could see, James pushed off to step past her, but then the lightest touch held him in his place. A glance down showed him the source. Ella's hands remained at her side, but, intuitively, her index finger reached out to him—extended, it seductively stroked the back of his hand. No one could see the gesture, but James felt his breath catch in his chest.

"Would you be able to join us for supper, Lord Worthing?" When she licked her lips to add moisture, James swallowed his moan. "It will be a simple fare…only the family…even Sonali."

James's vision rested on her mouth and the way her tongue glided across the seam of her lips and imagined being able to taste her whenever he wanted. "It would be my pleasure, Lady Eleanor. Thank you for including me." Despite not wishing to do so, he stepped away, moving through the hall toward where her brother waited.

Ella glanced over her shoulder to watch him go before turning to her cousin. "Aunt Agatha wishes us to meet her in her sitting room."

Velvet moved at last, catching up with Ella as they climbed the stairs. "That was some display of flirting," Velvet sniggered. "How did you learn to do that?"

"Do what?" Ella asked, confused.

Velvet whispered, protecting their words from servants' ears. "Hold a man's interest so intently."

Ella responded with surprise, "Did I do that?"

"As well as any woman would ever do." Her cousin squeezed Ella's hand. "I need to start taking notes."

"It was great fun. I did not plan it." Ella smiled all at once. "Lord Worthing makes me feel different—as if I could be pretty."

"You are pretty," Velvet insisted.

Ella shook her head. "I am a duke's daughter; that is my appeal…what I have to give a suitor, but with, His Lordship, I feel he sees me, not my father, or Bran, or the dukedom. Is that bizarre?" She reveled in the intimacy she just shared with Lord Worthing, although the desire—the sensations it caused frightened her.

"That, dear Cousin, is love."

"So, Shepherd believes Shaheed Mir seeks revenge for our foray all those years ago?" Worthing sipped on a brandy.

"Until of late, we kept our identities to a minimum recognition level. Now, each of us claims our place in British Society."

Worthing had to ask. "What does your family know of Ashmita?"

"Not the truth, if that is what you ask." Fowler shifted uncomfortably.

James paused for a long time. "And Shepherd's contacts found out what exactly?"

"Mir claims one of us walked out of that confrontation with an emerald the size of a man's fist. The Baloch wants it back."

"An emerald?" James mused. "Who had time to look for an emerald?"

Fowler steepled his fingers before him, tapping them to his lips. "I cannot see any one of our men taking something of that value without the rest of us knowing."

"I assume, as you confide in me, you do not suspect I am culpable?"

"As we fought back to back through much of the hostilities, I cannot imagine your having the opportunity to rummage through Mir's tents; but even if that were not true, I would never suspect you of such thievery."

"Then what do we do next? I cringe with the knowledge that our families are in danger."

His friend became businesslike. "Obviously, we need to inform the others, although Shepherd feels we should not mention the emerald. If one of us has it, that person would know the Realm would not look on it in a positive manner. We need to find out if anyone else suffered attacks such as what I experienced." James simply nodded, digesting what Fowler had just said. Engrossed in those thoughts, James did not anticipate the shift in the duke's line of thinking. "Now, Worthing, do you want to tell me what you know of my sister's sleepwalking episodes?"

James looked about uncomfortably. "I suppose the proper thing would be to respond in the negative, denying any knowledge of what you speak."

"But you will not offer me such prevarications."

"I will not." James experienced anxiety's twinge under Fowler's close inspection. "I…I came upon Lady Eleanor my first night at Thorn Hall. I…I said nothing because I chose not to embarrass the lady. On two other occasions, when I found her wandering alone, I returned Lady Eleanor to her room." Fowler waited in silence to see what else James might divulge, but James knew the technique—used it himself on more than one occasion. "When did you discover your sister's meanderings?"

"Actually, I have not encountered them firsthand. Eleanor's maid sought me out before we left Thorn Hall. As my sister's sleepwalking incidents increased and as no one here was aware of them, Hannah thought I should know. She let slip your involvement. I am not sure, Worthing, that I appreciate your intimacy with Ella."

"I assure you, Your Grace, that any interest I have in Lady Eleanor is purely honorable."

"Really?" Fowler sat forward in his chair, resting his arms on the desktop. "You affect Eleanor?"

James swallowed hard. Fowler was five years his junior, and he did not enjoy being on this side of the "desk"—questioned by Ella's brother. "If I thought Lady Eleanor would accept my plight, I would make my feelings known immediately. As it is, I plan to be somewhat of a nuisance during the Season and pray Lady Eleanor chooses me by the end. So, Fowler, you should prepare your objections if you have any; otherwise, I will expect your permission when the time comes."

His friend simply smiled at him. "I wish you success, Worthing."

"Thank you, Your Grace." James started to stand and then thought better of it. "Bran..." he paused again, "find out what happened to Lady Eleanor while you were away. Something is driving your sister from her bed."

Fowler's head snapped up in attention. "Do you know something else about Ella you are not sharing?"

"I cannot say for sure, but it seems odd to me that your sister's somnambulant sessions stopped with your father's passing and began again when you announced this upcoming Season. Remember her words when you told Lady Eleanor your plans. Your sister expects censure because of your father. There must be a connection." James finally stood, not wishing to add his personal assumptions to the conversation.

Fowler let out a long sigh before following James to his feet. "You give me much to consider, Worthing."

"I want Lady Eleanor free of her demons, and I will do what is necessary to protect her from her past, and, if required, from you."

"Is that a threat, Worthing?"

James's pretense at nonchalance dissolved immediately. "It is a guarantee, Thornhill."

Because Fowler had an appointment with Shepherd, he left "his" ladies on Bond Street, ordering ball gowns, morning and day dresses, intimates, hats, gloves, pelisses, ball slippers, half boots, and everything else needed for a successful Season. By silent assent the women had decided to begin the Season in colors of half-mourning, not wishing to seem callous over William Fowler's passing. In reality, they should wear black, but no debutante would appear in black for the Season. Again, under Bran's orders, they would tell everyone the late duke's long illness served as the mourning period.

Fittings for Presentation gowns took up much of the morning. Queen Charlotte expected young ladies to take a step back in time—unfortunately, they stepped back while wearing hooped skirts. "I think this might be the place to show respect for your late father by having the Presentation gown made in black," Agatha conjectured.

"Black?" Eleanor and Velvet exclaimed in unison.

"Queen Charlotte is a stickler for decorum. Your father passed but three months ago, Eleanor. If he was a simple nobleman, we might consider ignoring the Queen's edicts without engendering censure; but as a duke is directly below a prince in peerage, I would not wish to upset Her Highness. Black should be the color."

Ella looked at Velvet, trying to judge her cousin's thoughts. "We bow to your opinion, Aunt Agatha."

However, she heard Velvet murmur, "So much for using my Presentation dress for my wedding."

James waited patiently beside his carriage for the ladies' appearances. After sending his own carriage home, carting boxes and boxes of new items, Fowler called on Shepherd for the latest on the investigation, but Fowler's footmen still stored many more purchases in James's coach. He had brought his mount, intending on riding beside the coach where he might observe those whom they passed along the way. Yesterday, at the Royal Academy, he had noted a swarthy-looking man closely following them. He did not tell Fowler what he marked as unusual, but today James searched the crowd milling along the busy street.

Beside him, Gabriel Crowden lounged leisurely against a support beam of the nearest shop. The marquis had arrived in London late the previous evening, but had called on Worthing early enough for a morning ride along Rotten Row and through Hyde Park. Amused with his captain's constantly shifting eyes, Crowden smirked when those same eyes met his.

"What?" James seemed irritated.

Crowden pushed off from the building. "I just wondered what it was about Fowler's family that has you on alert."

"I will let His Grace explain it to you when he sees you later." Finally, James's gaze found her—*his Amazon*, moving gracefully along the street. Ella and Miss Aldridge closely followed the indomitable Dowager Duchess. When they were near, he advanced and took the elder woman's arm on his.

"You are a sight for these old eyes, Lord Worthing," the duchess exclaimed. "I forgot how tiring spending money can be."

James chuckled with her frankness. "I am happy to be of service, Your Grace." He led her to the waiting carriage.

Crowden stepped forward to do his duty and bowed nicely to the women. "Your Grace, may I present my acquaintance, the Marquis of Godown. Crowden, this beautiful lady is the Dowager Duchess of Norfield." The marquis bowed again; then James turned to the woman who consumed his every thought. "I wish you also to make the acquaintance of Lady Eleanor Fowler and Miss Velvet Aldridge."

"Fowler spoke so fondly of you both; you will excuse me if I claim a prior acquaintance."

"It is always pleasant to greet one of my brother's dear friends." Ella smiled at Crowden, but the flicker of excitement belonged to him, and James drew in a sharp breath of desire.

His duty carried him forward, as he reached to steady the Duchess's entrance to his carriage. "Let us see you ladies home," he said as he braced Velvet on the step. In reality, Eleanor should precede her cousin by rank, but he knew Ella would not object, and he might hold her hand those few extra seconds if she went last. "You look beautiful today, Lady Eleanor," he murmured close to her hair as he handed her into his carriage, a place he would wish her to readily accept.

With the ladies settled, he and Crowden mounted and followed behind his town carriage. James continued to survey the streets, but he saw nothing out of place. Crowden moved close enough to speak. "So, that is Fowler's Miss Aldridge. She is everything he described."

"I suppose she is." James's thoughts lay on another in the carriage.

"Does Fowler still hold her in high regard?"

James glanced at his friend. "Fowler is funding his cousin's Come Out, but I believe he secretly hopes she will not find another. It is all tied up somehow in Fowler's perverted sense of honor…all that situation with Ashmita and her child."

"Then I should look elsewhere?"

"If I tell you something, will you keep Miss Aldridge's secret?"

Crowden edged closer again. "Is it something I will enjoy knowing?"

James tugged the reins to keep his horse in line. "Miss Aldridge looks for someone to make His Grace jealous enough to declare himself."

"She does, does she?" A smile crept across Crowden's face. "Tormenting Fowler was always one of my favorite pastimes."

"So I explained to the lady." James said nothing more. If Crowden wished to become involved in the craziness of Fowler's life, then he was free to do so.

"How is Mary?" Crowden asked suddenly.

James flinched. His thoughts rarely fell on his mistress these days. "I have seen her but once in nearly a month, and even then…" He did not finish his thoughts.

"Ah, like Fowler, you have the sweet love fever, I see." Crowden never let his smile fade.

"Why do you say that?"

Crowden's horse sidestepped a sweeper before he could answer. "When a man employs a mistress but never *employs* that said mistress, a woman of the upper class is at fault. As you spent the last few weeks with Fowler's family, I conjecture it to be the lovely Lady Eleanor."

Irritated that his attentions were so obvious, James ignored Crowden's last remark and edged his horse forward where he might see Eleanor as she sat in his carriage. The previous evening, they had spent time together on the pianoforte bench—shoulders touching—arms brushing against one another. Now, he needed to look upon her again.

"You and Lord Godown will join us for tea, will you not, Lord Worthing?" Ella asked through the open window when James came close.

"I believe I have told you, Lady Eleanor, that unless you employ hired guards to protect Briar House, then I shall be a nuisance."

Ella traced his form. She could not but feel a rush of desire, seeing Lord Worthing as he sat a horse. He was very masculine, and she knew it—her body recognized his. "Still no guards, Lord Worthing," she teased. When he smiled at her; Ella found anticipation skimming her nerves. The blatant provocation scattered her thoughts and weakened her knees. He dared her to live again. "Never to you."

Returning to Briar House, James was sore to leave Eleanor so he encouraged Godown to entertain the three ladies, and even Sonali, with tales of their unusual adventures. Laughter emanated throughout the room. "I swear," Godown gestured with fingers barely apart, "they are no larger than this."

"But they are snails!" Eleanor wiped at her eyes, laughing joyously, making her more beautiful in James's estimation.

"Oh, yes, escargot are truly snails," he assured her.

Godown, standing before the mantel at center stage, pulled himself up to his full height. "Be exact, Worthing," he warned good-humoredly. "Not every snail is used. Only the *petit-gris* or the *Helix pomatia* make good escargot. Did you know, Miss Aldridge, they actually have snail farms in France?"

"You tease me, Lord Godown? Maybe we should speak to Brantley, Ella, about converting some of the cottagers to snail farming. After all, if a Frenchman can do it, an Englishman must be able to do it better."

From the doorway behind them, Fowler joined the conversation. "The British farmer prefers his crops above ground," he observed as he strode forward to join the group. He extended his hand to the marquis but did not interrupt the flow. Instead, he lifted Sonali and took the seat she occupied, placing the child on his lap.

"Between the escargot and the roe, we were quite surprised, even those of us who had made a Grand Tour and thought we knew everything," James added.

The Dowager Duchess turned to him. "Roe? You mean venison?"

"*Roe* in French cuisine are fish eggs, usually in a salty sauce," Fowler informed them.

"What else?" Velvet demanded, focusing all her attention on the marquis, a fact of which Fowler quickly took notice. James watched a scowl cross the duke's face.

Godown did not hesitate in his response. "The Persian food surprised me; I expected something spicy, along the lines of what I found in India, but it was different...more herbs than spices: saffron, cinnamon, and diced limes. His Grace was quite fond of *sesanjan*, were you not?"

"*Sesanjan*?" Ella tried the word. "What is that?"

"Nothing out of the ordinary. *Sesanjan* is chicken in a pomegranate sauce with walnuts."

"That sounds delicious," Ella observed.

James rejoined the discourse. "I preferred the *ghormeh sabzi*. It is lamb with herbs and lemon—quite a subtle concoction."

"I would like to try it sometime." Ella shot a quick glance his way, and he winked at her. The way he spoke to her, as if she was important, gave Eleanor the contentment she had never known. It was not in what they discussed; it was that Worthing found her a valued companion. It was a heady experience, and she did not want it to end, although she secretly feared it might. And it brought more confusion to how she felt about James Kerrington. At moments such as these, she thought they might make a loving couple, and then she would remember that he had once loved another. It was all very puzzling, and, like her brother, Ella did not enjoy unsolved puzzles.

"Do you remember how much wine Behrouz could drink?" Godown began another tease.

Fowler explained, "Behrouz was our guide."

Godown continued his thoughts. "Behrouz loved to quote the Quran about wine. Some of his fellow tribesmen thought it a decadent activity, but Behrouz claimed the Quran encouraged wine drinking when it speaks of giving the fruit of the palm and wine. I cannot remember the exact words, but Behrouz quoted the passage often."

"Who was the prince from Gurgan he quoted?" Fowler looked from one friend to another.

James took up the answer. "Kaikakavos."

"Behrouz extolled Prince Kaikakavos. As before, I cannot remember his exact words, but they dealt with the ancient belief that drinking wine was a transgression. The prince supposedly had said that if one was to commit a transgression, it should not be a flavorless one."

James expanded on his friend's story. "And if you drink wine, make it the best. If you are to end up in purgatory in the next world for your sins, at least in this one you should not be branded a fool." Everyone laughed at the ease with which the stories flowed. Good friends made both Ella and Velvet feel more comfortable about the upcoming Season.

"Lady Eleanor, would you and Miss Aldridge care to join me for a ride in Hyde Park tomorrow morning?" he asked as he prepared to leave.

"We would be pleased to join you, Lord Worthing."

"I will call for you at eight, if I may? Hyde Park is relatively clear at that hour."

"May we prevail on you to join us also, Your Lordship?" Miss Aldridge boldly turned to the marquis. James supposed she would put her plan into place.

Godown evidently agreed in principle to help her because he gave Ella's cousin his best smile. "I can think of nothing more delightful, Miss Aldridge."

James wondered how Brantley Fowler would take to Crowden's attention to Miss Aldridge. Over the years, he had broken up several fights between Fowler and Crowden, as their "friendly competition" sometimes turned to blows. Fowler had told them all, thousands of times, how he would return to England some day to claim his cousin. Now, they both played at games: Fowler granted Miss Aldridge a Season from which he hoped she would choose no one, and the lady flirted with one of Thornhill's friends, trying to force the duke into declaring himself. He thought they might both pay the price for their deceptions. James did not like such games, and he respected Ella for not being so blatantly circuitous. He wanted to court Eleanor Fowler in a deferential and timely manner; he wanted to make her his wife.

He called for the ladies promptly at eight. "Lord Worthing?" Ella questioned when she saw him holding the reins for the chocolate-colored mare. The Briar House groom presented horses for her and Velvet.

James bowed to her. "I know it is presumptuous of me to do so, but I had Athena sent to London from my home in Derby. I thought her the perfect complement to your riding. If you like her, I will speak to your brother about transferring Athena to the Briar House stable." In reality, he planned to present the animal to Eleanor as a wedding gift if she accepted him.

Tears misted her eyes. "To replace Sampson?" she murmured.

He stepped closer so only Ella could hear. "I could not bear to see you so forlorn, Lady Eleanor. I wished only to ease your pain."

She bit her bottom lip in hesitation. "No one else has even considered my attachment to Sampson."

James thought, *No one else knows you as I do*, but he said, "Then let us give Athena an audition, shall we?" He lifted Ella to the saddle and handed up the reins. She squeezed his fingertips in reward, and James's heart lurched in satisfaction. After mounting his own horse, he carefully led them through the London streets, avoiding hawkers displaying their day wares. "Those who want to have full freedom during their ride come even earlier. I have several friends who miss the openness of the country. They are here at dawn's crack to ride breakneck across Rotten Row and around the Serpentine, trying to capture the excitement of a full gallop."

"I imagine you among their number, Lord Worthing," Ella's cousin teased.

"I am, Miss Aldridge, upon occasion."

They entered Hyde Park off Grosvenor, where they met the marquis. "Ah, Ladies, it is rare to see two such beautiful gems so early in the day." He touched his hat with his riding crop in an acknowledgment.

"Lord Godown, you appear in good spirits today," Eleanor remarked as she brought her horse alongside of Worthing's.

"What man would not be as such in your company, Lady Eleanor?"

Although Fowler trailed them along the park's complementary streets, James noted the man's appearance, and he was sure from the raised eyebrow that Crowden did also. James assumed somehow that the marquis and Miss Aldridge had come to some sort of understanding—a joint venture to drive Brantley Fowler crazy with jealousy. *It must be working,* James thought, *because Fowler is making a fool of himself.* Ignoring their childish games, James forced his horse to turn Ella's toward a far-off tree line. "Shall we race, Lady Eleanor?"

"Absolutely, Lord Worthing." And she kicked the horse's side and flicked the reins.

As before, he waited to a count of three before giving chase. Then he gave pursuit in earnest. He knew enough of Ella's nature to know she would find it offensive if he purposely let her win. He admired how well Eleanor handled the horse. She had ridden Sampson for years, and this was her first time upon Athena. She held the reins a bit too tightly, but Ella could manage well; she was an excellent horsewoman. His mount closed the distance between them, but he saw Ella lean forward along the horse's neck and take off into the tree line leading to the Serpentine. "Come on, boy," he encouraged his mount. "The ladies are getting away."

James followed her lead. He had purposely given his hat to the groom before he took off after her. Now, he was glad he did. Just staying on the horse as they cut and zigzagged among the trees took all his equestrian skills. Bursting through the forested line, he spotted her—*his Amazon*—dismounting as Athena edged toward the water.

Eleanor whipped off her hat, and James slowed his mount to take in her countenance fully. The early morning sun glinted off the Serpentine and danced in the fine golden hair framing Ella's face. The race's flush colored her cheeks, and James knew he was truly in trouble. As he suspected, Eleanor Fowler consumed him completely. When she tilted her neck back to let the sun kiss her face, his groin flicked to life. Remaining in a constant state of erection seemed his destiny, at least as far as Eleanor was concerned. Dismounting, he came to stand beside her. "You and Athena are a worthy challenge, Lady Eleanor." He caught her hand and brought it to his lips. Needing to touch her seemed all-important.

"She is a glorious ride." Eleanor patted Athena's long neck; she held the reins loosely in one hand. "Thank you for bringing her for me today."

"She is yours to use any time you choose to ride. Athena cannot replace your mother's gift, but you needed to ride again." James stood behind her, spooning her body with his. His hands rested on Ella's shoulders as they both stared out over the water.

Eleanor turned her head to look up at him. "How can I thank you, Your Lordship? You are too kind—too good to me."

James considered kissing her. She tempted him greatly, but he feared frightening her if he moved too quickly. Instead, he said, "I would like to be the one who shows you kindness, Eleanor—the one who is good to you in every way possible." He whispered close to her ear, afraid to venture the words aloud.

He watched as tears misted her eyes. "No one," she began but choked up when she tried to finish.

"I understand, Darling." James found himself swallowing hard, trying to control his need for her. "No one has ever loved you and you alone. I plan to change that, Eleanor, if you will let me. Your brother wishes you to have a choice—to know the pleasures of Society and of a Season. Fowler feels a need to make things right for you, to give you all the things you were denied as William Fowler's daughter, and I have assured him I will wait. If you find another, I will step aside, for I want you to be happy above all things. You deserve to be happy, Eleanor."

Tears now streamed down her cheeks. She used the sleeve of her riding habit to blot her face. "We should ride again, Lord Worthing," she rasped out.

"Of course, Lady Eleanor." James led her to where Athena nibbled on some grass, and without ceremony, he lifted Ella to the horse's back.

When he remounted, they rode side by side. At first, there was silence, and James wondered if he had said too much. But then she said, "I always welcome your company, Lord Worthing. You make me feel special."

"You are special, Eleanor."

Obviously a bit uncomfortable with all his honesty, she simply smiled before changing the subject. "I wonder what has happened to the Marquis and Velvet."

James cocked an amused eyebrow. "I imagine they are dealing with His Grace. Your brother trailed us to the park."

"Bran?" she gasped. Then she too laughed at the situation's absurdity. "Well, would you not like to be a fly on the wall and hear that conversation?"

Chapter 4

ELEANOR AND WORTHING RODE casually toward where they last saw the Marquis and Velvet, allowing their horses to cool naturally. After such an exhilarating ride, Eleanor's complexion glowed with life, and James continued to think her the most beautiful woman of his acquaintance. Wisps of golden hair framed her face, having worked lose from her chignon, and he wanted so badly to push them behind her ear and touch her again. For a few brief seconds, he focused on her mouth, on its fullness and what it would be like to kiss Eleanor as he did at Thorn Hall. So absorbed with her, too late he saw him—the one from the art gallery—saw him raise the gun and aim, and instinctively, James reacted. He bounded from the saddle, throwing his body in the air to protect her.

The bullet burned his flesh, but he ignored the need to address it because, as he scrambled from the ground, he discovered Ella's safety still in jeopardy. Athena bucked and turned, trying to throw Ella from her back, and James frantically sprang to his feet to reach her. However, the mare skittered away and cantered off at full speed.

Ignoring his wound, in seconds he was on his own horse, turning it to give chase, but as he spun around, he saw along the periphery of his vision the shooter running toward the far side of the park, as well as Brantley Fowler and others closing in on Ella's flight. Realizing the others would reach Ella before he could, he gave pursuit of the gunman.

Riding flat along the horse's neck, he once again dodged low-hanging branches and raised tree roots, weaving in and out, tagging after the man. Two carriages loomed ahead, and Kerrington knew he must reach the man before the assailant made a successful getaway. The shooter cleared the trees, and in the open his progress improved, but James followed suit. Catching the retreating form at last, he left the saddle once again, landing squarely on the man's back, taking them both to the ground. Rolling in the dusty pathway, he struggled to right himself while fending off a barrage of fists and kicks. In return, he pummeled his enemy with carefully designed blows to incapacitate the man.

A strike across the man's Adam's apple sent his opponent staggering backwards, clutching his neck in contorted pain. As James prepared to strike again, a gun pointed at his face pulled him up short. *"Monsieur."* The masked accomplice gestured with the gun for him to step away from his partner. *"Pardonnez-moi, en ami."* Before James could react, the disguised adversary struck him with the gun's butt along the side of his head, knocking James to the ground and allowing the two men to escape to the waiting coaches. His eyes rested on their retreat, but something unusual happened. The men separated and headed toward their respective carriages. James chose to follow the dark-skinned man, trying to memorize his carriage's markings as it rolled away. Staggering to his feet, he found his horse and pulled himself painfully into the saddle. *Ella,* he thought. *Have to find Ella.*

When Kerrington anticipated the attack and leapt from the saddle to protect her, Eleanor did not at first understand his madness until she witnessed the bullet strike his shoulder when he flew through midair. Then chaos exploded.

Ripping away part of Worthing's sleeve, the slug landed within an inch of Athena's front hoof, sending a spray of dirt and rock fragments covering the animal's forelegs. Had she been riding Sampson, Ella could probably have brought the horse under control, but the courser reacted to the sudden particle shower by bolting forward and trying to dislodge Ella from her back before Eleanor could take control of the reins. The melee began, and all she could do was hold on.

The reins slipped from her fingers, and Ella grasped the horse's mane, trying to convey her need for the animal to stop its undulations. Then, miraculously, he appeared—a stranger reaching for the reins and turning the horse in a large circle, slowing its progress; and finally, the animal moved no more. It stood perfectly still, snorting and stamping its displeasure.

As she leaned back, adjusting her bonnet, the first person Eleanor saw was her brother skidding his mount to a stop. Instantly, he was on the ground and pulling her from the saddle and into the safety of his arms. "Ella, oh, Ella," he cooed as he kissed the side of her head, shoving her hat away where he might see her face. "Oh, God, Ella!" he clutched her to him again.

"Bran," she choked out his name as she buried her face in his chest, clutching desperately at his lapels.

"Are you hurt?" Seeking to assure himself of her safety, he gently brushed Ella's hair from her face.

Ella shook her head in the negative, but she kept her head tilted to the side so the growing crowd could not see her clearly. The onlookers hung back, taking close note of the unusual happenings to share with others over their afternoon tea.

Heart racing, Bran looked over her shoulder at her rescuer, who was dismounting from his own horse.

Reaching the scene at last, Velvet unceremoniously slid from her horse and raced to her cousins. Fowler simply opened his arms and took her into his care.

Ella clung to her cousin and to Bran. The three of them had always seen each other through the worst, and as much as she still needed them, a part of her cried out for Lord Worthing's closeness.

Fowler kissed her cheek and their cousin's forehead, and then he released Ella to Velvet's care by saying, "Let me deal with your rescuer, and then we will see you home."

Ella kept her back to their unwelcome audience and accepted Velvet's help in righting her disheveled appearance. Her cousin used Bran's handkerchief to wipe away the dusty trail of tears across her cheek, and Ella closed her eyes to Velvet's ministrations. The horror of the last few minutes still played in her head. She saw it all, a shadowy drama behind the one image she was unable to shake: Lord Worthing had risked his life to save her. She knew subconsciously that he had ridden off after their attacker, but she had a desperate need to know his fate, to show him that she cared for him. Earlier, he had professed his affections, but she had given him no return besides an acknowledgment of enjoying his company. Now, she saw the folly of such milk-and-water replies. Ella could have lost him today without His Lordship knowing the depth of her regard. She would not let the opportunity to tell him so pass again.

So resolved, Ella opened her eyes to a new future, but a past nightmare loomed over her shoulder.

"Are you well, Miss?" the stranger stood with hat in hand before them.

Ella heard Bran's shaky voice respond, "My sister and I owe you our eternal gratitude, Sir."

"My reward is your sister's safety." The gentleman offered a bow.

"I am Thornhill," Fowler returned the greeting.

"Thornhill?" The stranger's voice rose in surprise. "The Duke of Thornhill?"

Now her brother sounded suspicious. "I fear you have me at a disadvantage, Sir."

"Forgive me, Your Grace. I am Levering. I did not realize you had assumed your father's position. My parents were great friends of the former duke."

Ella heard her brother's conversation as if in a dream. *It could not be—not now.* Gulping for air, she swallowed her fear, trying not to betray her agitation to the others.

"Sir Louis?" Her cousin politely renewed the acquaintance. "Lady Eleanor and I did not know you were in London. Look,

Ella, your rescuer is Louis Levering. How many years has it been since we last saw you?" Velvet gave the man the obligatory curtsy.

"Before my Grand Tour, Miss Aldridge, nearly six years ago."

Ella, arranging her appearance as best she could without a mirror, purposely turned to offer her own thanks. "Sir Louis, how do I express my appreciation? You came at just the right moment, and to consider the coincidence of our former acquaintance." The name Levering ricocheted through Ella, but she fought to push away her doubts, praying the baronet's reappearance would not destroy the happiness she had known of late.

"I am sure His Grace would have done as well. Your brother was only seconds behind." The man's face showed nothing but concern for Eleanor's safety.

"You must allow us, Levering, to offer you our hospitality at Briar House. As you are already familiar with my family, it will be a *homecoming* of a sort." Ella's shoulders stiffened with her brother's invitation.

Yet, before Levering could accept, Worthing rode up. Dusty and bleeding from behind his ear, he slipped from the saddle and caught Ella up in his arms, and she allowed herself to breathe. The viscount was safe, and now he offered his protection. "Thank God, His Grace reached you in time." His genuine concern for her spoke of hope. He smelled of leather and of sweat and of maleness and of safety, and for a brief moment Ella allowed herself to cling to him—the dream renewed. Not wanting to leave his protective embrace, she reluctantly backed away. Seeing the trickle of blood she stifled a gasp before pressing her own handkerchief to his head. "Actually," she told him, a flush of color covering her face, "Sir Louis reached me before His Grace."

Worthing turned his head to see the other nobleman standing beside Fowler and presented the man a painful bow. "As I am sure Thornhill has done, I offer my thanks for Lady Eleanor's protection."

"Sir Louis is the son of one of our Kent neighbors," Velvet chattily explained. "The Leverings assumed possession of the Huntingborne Abbey several years ago. I believe it was a little over three years since you inherited with your dear father's passing. Is that not correct, Sir Louis?"

"I could not have said it better, Miss Aldridge. You are a purveyor of the latest news in our little section of the world." Ella heard the same derisively sarcastic tone she remembered as characteristic of Sir Louis's attitude. She noticed how her brother's and the viscount's bearings shifted as if they too heard Levering's impertinence.

"Viscount Worthing," her brother bristled as he made the introductions, "may I present Sir Louis Levering. Levering, the Honorable Lord Worthing." Bran, apparently, judged Levering—his first impression less than stellar, and he placed Sir Louis, a mere baronet, on the social ladder. Her brother reminded the baronet that the man spoke to a duke and a future earl. From what Ella knew of the Leverings, Sir Louis would take offense.

She noted how Levering bit back a retort. "Well, Your Grace, now that we know everyone is safe, if you will excuse me, I have appointments to which to attend."

Thornhill simply nodded. "Of course, Sir Louis. Thank you again for your efforts." Ella wondered what Bran really wanted to say to the popinjay.

Levering stepped forward, took Velvet's hand, and brought it to his lips for the traditional air kiss, and then he turned his full attention on Ella. Instead of a kiss several inches above her knuckles, Sir Louis brought Ella's hand to his mouth and held it there for several seconds before letting it go. "Lady Eleanor, may I call some time in the next few days to assure myself you did not suffer from this episode?" Ella cringed with the possibility. Sir Louis's acquaintance was not one she wished to renew.

"Of course, Sir Louis." Ella discreetly withdrew her hand. She prayed she had not betrayed her anxiety to either her brother or the viscount.

Looking about him and bidding the group a collective farewell,

Levering strode to his horse, mounted, and rode away. It was a weight lifted from her shoulders.

"Let us see you home." Ella touched Worthing's arm in an act of concern.

"I will find my own way," James began, but a collective "No" from the Fowler party told him not to do the gallant thing.

Her brother helped Ella and Velvet to their horses. They could not discuss what had actually happened in the park's middle. "I insist," she told James, "that I see to your injuries myself."

"It is not necessary," he told her.

"Lord Worthing." A reprimand rested in her tone. "You suffered your injuries for my sake. You will not deny me the satisfaction of repaying your kindness."

James lost himself in the glittering hope of her admonition. "I would deny you nothing, Lady Eleanor."

When James and his guests entered Worthing Hall some fifteen minutes later, his staff snapped into a quick response. Ella, used to commanding her own home, demanded bandages and oil of chamomile be brought at once, while James tried to order tea and refreshments. Ultimately, Ella won out, and he sat resigned to her ministrations. Cutting away his shirtsleeve, she tended to the torn flesh of his upper arm before addressing a bruise along his temple.

A little later, once the servants withdrew, having finally brought the service for which Kerrington asked, Fowler turned to speak. "What did you see today?"

James grimaced as Ella dressed the wound behind his ear. "A man shot at your sister and me from the tree line. I saw him at the last second; I had no way of warning Lady Eleanor."

"So you jumped in front of me?" Ella's voice was barely above a whisper.

James waited until she lifted her gaze to him. "You must understand, Lady Eleanor, I could do nothing else." Their eyes rested on each other for several raxed seconds before he continued. "When

I remounted, I observed you closing on your sister, so I gave chase to the gunman."

"From the looks of your clothes, I assume you found him," the duke observed.

"I managed to wrestle him to the ground, but an accomplice pulled a gun on me. The second man left in one coach, while the gunman escaped in a small black carriage with a red stripe across the back where the luggage might be strapped to the chaise."

Fowler's eyes indicated he filed the information away for later use. "Did you recognize either of them?"

"The accomplice wore a makeshift mask made from his cravat, but he had an unusual shade of eyes—nearly a black brown—his hair a chocolate color—and he spoke only French."

"And the gunman?" Fowler prompted.

"I saw him when I escorted your family to the Royal Academy. I had hoped I was wrong, and he was just interested in the same exhibits; but that is why I noticed him today. When I saw him at the gallery, I thought *swarthy*—dark complected, sable hair and eyes."

"A Baloch?" Fowler made the necessary connections.

James considered his response. "Quite likely—at least, in appearance."

His friend stated the obvious. "Then one of us is the target, and through us, our families."

"If one of us is the target, Fowler, then why did the gunman simply strike me down? Why not, at least, take me prisoner? And the Frenchman, his accent was more British, and he used only basic French."

"None of it makes any sense."

Ella ventured, "Maybe we should return to Thorn Hall until everything is safe."

"Attacks came at Thorn Hall also," her brother reasoned.

"What if someone is hurt next time?" Miss Aldridge ventured, although she just now began to see what the others obviously knew.

Fowler assured them, "We have contacts working on this, and we have some ideas."

"Who are *we* exactly?" Ella inquired, realizing belatedly how her brother and the viscount would feel about exposing their loved ones to danger.

Fowler caught James's eye for approval before continuing. "The men with whom I served during my private service: Lord Worthing, of course; the Marquis; Carter Lowery, second son of Baron Blakehell; Baron Swenton; Marcus Wellston, third son of the Earl of Berwick; and Viscount Lexford. All have been alerted to the possibility that someone seeks revenge for our previous life."

"But why now?" Unsurprisingly, Ella's quick mind already accepted her brother's assumptions and moved on to the matter's crux. "It has been five years since your service."

James answered, "We are coming into our estates or our governmental positions, as with Lowery. Our names and wealth are more well known."

"So no matter what—all seven could be targets?" Both her eyes and her voice indicated her mood had taken a downward turn.

"Exactly, my Lady," Worthing summarized, but he watched carefully as Ella's expression became a mask of cautious reserve.

Fowler knew that any other information would have to wait until he and Worthing could speak privately. "I shall escort my family home, Worthing. We have experienced enough excitement for one day."

"Thank you, Lord Worthing." Ella dutifully joined her brother.

James followed her to his feet. "I should be thanking you, Lady Eleanor, for tending to my wounds." He brought her hand to his lips and kissed it tenderly; he found he most thoroughly enjoyed the flush of her skin as his lips skimmed her fingers. "Hopefully, next time, our ride will be less eventful." James reluctantly let her leave him alone in a house that should be hers to command.

Ella wanted to ask if there would be a next time, but instead she followed Bran and Velvet outside to where the groomsman held their horses. They had said their good-days in the drawing room, but she knew she could not leave him without a private word. She still needed to tell him she would welcome his plight. Suddenly, she grasped Bran's hand to secure his attention. "I have left my gloves in Lord Worthing's drawing room; I shall be right back. Help Velvet up. I shall only be a moment."

Before he could object or send a footman instead, Ella quickly scurried up the steps and tapped on the door. The butler opened it immediately. "I apologize; I left my gloves," she mumbled her excuse and entered the drawing room without his permission. His Lordship was where she hoped he would be.

His voice rose with surprise as he stood to behold her. "Lady Eleanor?"

"I left my gloves." She lost her courage before she could say more.

He retrieved them from a nearby table and carried them to her. "These gloves?" he said smoothly—a chuckle, which she thought sounded of seduction following.

"Yes." Her body melted when he came near—his intensity holding her with his gaze.

"Anything else, Lady Eleanor?" He pushed back her curls, and Ella turned her cheek into his touch.

Ella swallowed her fears and breathed her answer. "Yes." Her eyes did not shift from his even for a second.

The viscount's eyebrow rose in question. "Might I say you look well in my home, Eleanor?" he whispered close to her ear. She could feel his heat along her front.

"I need…I must go. Bran and Velvet wait for me." She loved the desire she saw in his eyes—that heavy-lidded look; yet, she hesitated.

"Certainly." He knew he affected her, but he stepped away. From where the freedom came, Ella could not say, but, miraculously, she grabbed his open shirt and kissed him—a full-mouthed kiss that spoke of anticipation and hope. His arms pulled her closer; she quickly realized how much she had missed his touch—being in his arms. When their lips separated, he murmured, "I would take a bullet every day if you would continue to kiss me so." Seductively, he licked the seam of her lips teasingly with his tongue. "I want to taste you, Ella; I want you under me in my bed." His lips brushed against her cheek in a soft caress. His words brought an unfamiliar ache between her thighs.

Her bravery waned, and Eleanor shot a glance at the door, expecting to see her brother bursting through the portal. "I must go," she mumbled, and then she was out the door before he could stop her and before she could observe disappointment in His Lordship's eyes.

Through the window, James watched the groomsman help her to the saddle. *Did Ella purposely leave her gloves? She had kissed him—of her own free will; Eleanor Fowler had kissed him.* God, he hardened with the memory. A smile opened across his face. Had he gone too far by telling her he wanted to make love to her? Truthfully, he did not think so. Ella would not readily come to him, but he would have her, nonetheless.

Riding the mile to Briar House, Ella's mind drifted to Viscount Worthing. The heat of his mouth remained on her lips. *I want to taste you, Ella. I want you under me in my bed.* His words shocked her—thrilled her—scared her beyond belief. *Could she let any man touch her in an intimate way again? Would Worthing even want to touch her if he knew the truth?* Ella nearly moaned out loud with desire and with frustration.

"You will not, at least, thank me for saving your life?"

"Thank you?" the dark-skinned man exclaimed. "I should throttle you! I followed Worthing and the women the day the Fowlers arrived in London. It was all planned. I would take one of the women and use her in exchange for the emerald. But before I could act, you fools shot at them again, placing the gentlemen more on guard. You are not even a good shot; you missed by a mile.

If Worthing had not jumped to save Fowler's sister, you would not have hit anything."

The Englishman disliked the foreigner, but he hid it well. He wanted his share of the prize the tawny-complected man offered. "We did not know you planned your own attack. We simply wanted to create a situation where Thornhill might need a new ally. I had thought you were to keep us informed."

"I report to no one," the intruder protested. "My orders give me the freedom to make my own plans."

The Englishman looked away in annoyance. "Then do not blame us if your plans cross with my friend's."

~ ~ ~

"Sir Louis," Ella nervously greeted the man with a curtsy as she entered the blue sitting room. "It is so kind of you to call." Eleanor spoke the required words, but she wished to be anywhere else but in the room with this man.

"Lady Fowler, I came to appease my conscience and assure myself of your continued well-being." He offered her a correct bow and a warm smile.

Eleanor gestured for him to retake his seat. "As you may behold, Sir, I am quite well, and I have no reason to suspect your conscience needs appeasing."

To her dismay, Levering feigned a polite laugh. "So little you know of my conscience, Lady Fowler."

"I would prefer to keep it that way, Sir Louis." As she so vividly recalled, the man's polite boldness made her uncomfortable.

"We all have our secrets, do we not, Lady Fowler?" he observed, stressing the word *our.*

Ella clenched her hands together in her lap. "Some people are more open, obviously, Sir Louis, but I believe we all have a right to *our* privacy." Ella prayed she did not sound as ill at ease as she felt.

"Of course, Lady Fowler. I meant no disrespect. God only

knows, my own family has its deepest secrets." Again, he gave her a smile of familiarity, which sent fear shivering through her.

Ella shifted uncomfortably in her place. Needing to be away from him, she lied, "Sir Louis, I do so appreciate your solicitude, but I fear I have other obligations today that I may not postpone. I pray you will forgive me if I shorten our meeting."

"Of course, Lady Fowler. It was crude of me to call without notice." Thankfully, he stood to take his leave.

"It is perfectly acceptable, Sir," Eleanor added, trying not to be inhospitable. "My cousin and I prepare for our Presentations, and we have duties to that effect."

"I look forward to your first forays into Society, Lady Fowler. I shall be honored if you accept my company upon occasion." He lifted Eleanor's hand to his lips.

Ella fought the urge to slap his hands away. "My cousin and I would welcome your presence."

~ ~ ~

For the next week, preparations for their court Presentations would consume all of Ella's free time; so tonight, James joined the party at the Haverton musicale. The Season was not yet upon them, although less than a fortnight away, but the Dowager Duchess deemed it acceptable as long as the cousins remained in Fowler's company. As their guardian and their chaperone, respectively, Bran and Aunt Agatha gave them the respectability they needed.

"Lady Eleanor," James whispered into her hair, "you are exquisite this evening."

"Only in your eyes, Lord Worthing. No one else says such outrageous things to me." Ella used her fan to hide her blush. He had become very fond of these intimate moments.

He smiled knowingly at her. "I doubt that, Lady Eleanor, but if it were so, I would not complain. Exclusivity would be divine."

"You will come to tea tomorrow, Lord Worthing?" she blurted, apparently shaken by his declaration. James had purposely accelerated his wooing of Eleanor Fowler. Since the second attack, he had felt an urgency to have her under his protection.

He teased, "Still no guards at Briar House, Lady Eleanor?"

"Never to you, James," she whispered.

The sound of his name on her lips drove him nearly over the edge. "Oh, Ella," he murmured, "my dear sweet Ella." He placed her hand on his arm and led Eleanor to a seat behind her aunt. Leaning in close as he seated her on his right, he sighed, "Exquisite."

Eleanor glowed under James Kerrington's attentions. With him, she no longer felt dirty or unworthy. Every time she was near him, her heart exploded with desire, and her dreams of traveling the world expanded to include having him by her side. Yet, she still worried whether she might earn his love. Knowledge of his former wife haunted her insecurities. Ella thought she might be falling in love with the viscount, but she needed him to return that love. She realized he desired her, at least, on some level. She also realized that they might be happy together without the love, but that would mean settling for something less than what she desperately required, and Ella did not think she could do that.

~ ~ ~

The Presentation day found Eleanor and Velvet bedecked in the black gowns. The Dowager Duchess had commandeered Lord Worthing's carriage also, as the dresses were so elaborate that fitting both in one carriage was impossible. Queen Charlotte expected the gowns to have old-fashioned hoop skirts and to be worn with a stomacher, lying over the triangular front panel of the stays and held in place by the gown's lacing. Most of the young unmarried women waiting in the halls for their moment with the Queen wore white, which made Ella even more uneasy, although Velvet took it all in stride. Low-cut and with short sleeves, the black silk complemented Velvet's natural coloring and her coal-black hair, but Ella saw herself as a scorched tea kettle with golden curls. The single towering ostrich feather, pulled downward by the black veil attached with black pearl hairpins, threatened to topple from her thin blond hair.

They waited in their carriages for two hours outside St. James's Palace before being admitted into the too-warm hallway of St. James's Gallery, where they waited another hour. As the daughter and sister of a duke, Eleanor would be among the first to be presented. Velvet would wait with the others in order of precedence, as her parents, the Viscount and Lady Averette, were of middle importance in the line of nobility.

The time arrived and Aunt Agatha escorted Ella to the Queen's receiving room. As the door opened, Eleanor heard her aunt caution, "Breathe, Child," forcing her to suck in a deep breath and let it out slowly. Then Ella stepped forward and handed her card to the Lord Chamberlain while a gentleman-in-waiting spread out the ten-foot train, which was attached to her dress, behind her.

"Lady Eleanor Fowler, daughter of William and Amelia Fowler, the Duke and Duchess of Thornhill," the man's voice boomed throughout the hall.

Eleanor began her progress across the great room, praying with every step she would not trip on her train or finally lose the ornate headdress before she could complete the required curtsy. Before the throne, at last, Ella made the deep obeisance necessary for the Queen, murmuring "Your Highness," as she did so. Then she gave a briefer bow to the rest of the court before dipping low once more to her monarch. This one she held, waiting for the Queen's release.

"Your niece, Your Grace?" the Queen asked, although she knew Agatha's relationship to Eleanor.

"Yes, Your Highness. Lady Fowler's mother passed some seven years ago."

Queen Charlotte motioned to both ladies to stand. "And your father, Lady Fowler?" Hearing herself addressed by her proper title eased Eleanor's nervousness. It was as if she were another person, playacting a role. From the beginning, she had never wanted to be called *Lady Fowler*, as that was her mother's title. But even before her mother's death, Ella shunned the proper reference to her position as the duke's only daughter. She never wanted her name associated with his, so she always insisted on being *Lady Eleanor*, never *Lady Fowler*.

"Passed three months ago, Your Highness." Ella prayed that Aunt Agatha had made the correct move by having her wear black.

"Ah, we had forgotten. We are pleased that you chose to show the proper respect for your family, Lady Fowler. Not many of the young cling to the old ways."

"Thank you, Your Highness." A sigh of relief nearly slipped out, but Ella swallowed it.

Queen Charlotte motioned to one of her courtiers, who made notations in a gigantic book he held, before returning her attention to Eleanor. "Your brother has assumed the title?"

"Yes, Your Highness. His Grace returned from the Continent and entered upon his duties as Thornhill." Ella began to become nervous all over again. Any conversation with the Queen was unusual. This one of some substance was infinitely unlikely.

"Your brother claimed his place with the King?" Queen Charlotte demanded.

"His Grace has seen to his duties, Your Highness."

"Excellent...excellent, indeed." Queen Charlotte paused before adding, "And you cared for the late Duke during his illness?"

"My father was abed for nearly two years, Your Highness. I did what I could to ease his suffering."

"You perform your duties well for one so young, Lady Fowler. You may tell His Grace we do not believe mourning clothes appropriate for a daughter of England during the Season."

"Thank you, Your Highness." Again, Ella curtsied, aware her time was complete. Later, Velvet would be asked to kiss Queen Charlotte's hand, but as the daughter of a duke, Eleanor received a different acknowledgment: Queen Charlotte kissed Ella's forehead. Then, very carefully, Ella rose; another gentleman-in-waiting helped her drape the train over her arm, and she backed from the room, constantly aware of the liveried footmen who tactfully guided her steps.

~~~

"You were a success with the Queen," Worthing declared as he entered the blue sitting room at Briar House. He came forward and kissed Eleanor's hand, bowing over it a few extra seconds—a warm, unexpected desire shooting straight to her secret spot. "I heard of nothing else all morning," he assured her. "The *haut ton* will fall at your feet, Lady Eleanor."

Ella was so glad to see him after her stressful day that she nearly threw herself into his arms; she had thought of him more than a dozen times during the day—a dozen daydreams of the viscount's voice—his eyes—his countenance—his muscular body. "I was petrified I would do something to disgrace the family," she confessed.

"You could never be a disgrace," he asserted; however, Ella involuntarily winced with his words. "Have I spoken out of turn, Lady Eleanor?"

She plastered on her best smile. "No, Lord Worthing. You never offer me an offense."

He led her to a nearby settee and joined her on it. They were alone in the room with the exception of Ella's personal maid sequestered in a far corner. "Was Miss Aldridge as successful?"

"Queen Charlotte showed my cousin a like kindness."

"I am happy to hear it. It will go a long way to support your cousin's reputation in Society."

Ella raised her eyes to his. "And what of my reputation, Lord Worthing?"

"You, my Dear, will rule Society this Season." Ella rolled her eyes in disapproval of his words. "Do not go on so, Lady Eleanor. Your father has passed, and the *ton* has a short memory. Despite what you believe, you will not be judged by his actions, but rather by your
~~~

own." Ella prayed that he spoke the truth. Before she could respond, Mr. Horace tapped on the door and announced Levering's presence.

"Show Sir Louis in, Mr. Horace." Despite her efforts to control her reservations, the unexpected visit turned the animated, happy Ella into Eleanor of the subservient bearing with just those six words. "Sir Louis, so kind of you to call." She dropped the obligatory curtsy.

"Lady Eleanor." She noted how he had purposely switched to her more familiar name, making a silent claim on her acquaintance and causing every nerve in her body to balk in revolt. "I came to offer my congratulations on your success at court today." He came forward to kiss her hand, a habit Ella wished he would break. "Yet, I see Lord Worthing has beaten me to it." Levering gave James a look of pure contempt.

Ella gestured to a nearby chair before indicating to Hannah that she should have tea brought in. Resettling herself on the settee beside the viscount, she explained, "As Lord Worthing is my brother's closest associate, and as he loaned us the use of his carriage so both my cousin and I could attend Queen Charlotte today, it is natural that His Lordship is often in our company."

"Of course," James put in to let Levering know where things stood, "I consider Lady Eleanor as close an associate as I do His Grace." Ella thought she could kiss him for putting a claim on her before the baronet.

"Naturally," Sir Louis sneered. "Actually, I am surprised His Grace continues his association with you and Godown, Worthing; I mean, now that he is Thornhill."

Ella started to react, but Worthing interrupted before she could say something offensive. Instinctively, she knew he protected her reputation. She had just completed a social coup, something that would go a long way in paving her path into Society. He would not allow her to experience censure at the hands of a pompous ass such as Louis Levering. "And what, pray tell, do you see as my and the Marquis's 'association'?"

She recognized an implied warning in His Lordship's words, but Levering ignored it. "Everyone knows you chose private wars to the honor of fighting for your country—money over integrity," he charged. "His Grace followed suit, but he should separate himself from that memory now that he is Thornhill."

"What do you insinuate, Levering? That my men and I did something illegal?" The viscount's hands balled into fists, ready to pummel the man senseless, and Ella tensed in anticipation.

However, Sir Louis pretended shock at Worthing's challenge, keeping his tone noncommittal. "Of course not, Worthing. It was an observation; I spoke out of turn. I am sure in whatever you and His Grace participated, you had your reasons."

"Please, Gentlemen," Ella cut them short before a duel became necessary.

Levering's toothy smile spread across his face. "I apologize, Lady Eleanor. I meant my remarks only as a caution to your family. As your closest neighbor in Kent, I felt it my duty to protect your family name from further disparagement."

"My brother will choose his own friends, Sir Louis, as will I."

"Well, obviously, I have overstayed my welcome." Belatedly, Levering stood and pulled on his gloves. "I hope this will not affect our relationship, Lady Eleanor."

Eleanor rose to see him out. "Our relationship remains the same as it has always been, Sir Louis." She thought: *nonexistent*, but Ella fought the urge to speak the word aloud. "Thank you for your kindness today."

"Lady Eleanor." Levering bowed to her before saying, "Worthing." He offered James no such symbol of courtesy before making his leave.

"Pompous prat!" The viscount hissed under his breath.

Ella did not respond; she feared she had not seen the last of the combative Sir Louis, and if that were so, she was in more trouble than anyone could imagine.

CHAPTER 5

ADDITIONAL DAY OUTINGS occupied the ladies' time, but no more attacks occurred. James's and Fowler's frustrations rose as they hit a dead end in the investigation. James worried extensively over the two attacks coming at Eleanor's expense. He wanted her in his life; yet, as the danger mounted, he worried that even he might not be able to protect her. At night, he dreamed of stripping Ella naked and bringing a lovely blush to her pearly white skin, burying himself deep inside her and never coming out. He had enjoyed Mary's ministrations for several years, but he had never lusted after her—had never seen her face when he closed his eyes. Not since Elizabeth had he wanted a woman as he did Eleanor; however, he desired her safety foremost.

The Capertons' ball would be James's and Eleanor's first opportunity to be seen as a "couple" in Society. The Capertons officially opened the Season with one of the most attended events of the yearly social calendar. James looked forward to claiming his dances with Ella. He had reserved two dance sets with her several days earlier, and, miracle of miracles, Eleanor had penciled him in for both waltzes. He would hold her close—close enough to smell the lavender on her skin and the apple blossom of her hair. The thought made his groin react. He had been hard since he met her. In addition to the pleasure of her in his arms, he would not have to suffer the pain of seeing her being led into such an intimate dance with any other man. James did not believe he could tolerate her being in another man's arms. Straightening uncomfortably, he stood to stare out his study window. "Soon," he murmured. "Soon, I will claim Eleanor as my own."

Aunt Agatha paved the way for clearing the last hurdle to their acceptance. The week the *beau monde* returned to the city, the Dowager Duchess hosted her first bi-weekly at home. With Briar House long in nonuse, those in town easily accepted, wishing to see for themselves that Thornhill had survived the scandalous ways of the previous duke. Among Agatha's most honored guests were Lady Jersey and Princess Esterhazy, two of Almack's infamous patronesses, making the Dowager Duchess's first social event of the Season remarkably successful.

As a result of Aunt Agatha's manipulations, both Eleanor and Velvet received the required acknowledgment—a voucher for Almack's first gathering. Having passed "inspection," so to speak, both ladies could now accept invitations to waltz in public. Without the patronesses' acceptance, neither could have partaken in what would have been considered a scandalous display by many of the older set.

Velvet saved one of her waltzes for Godown, but the after-supper one she purposely reserved for Bran. Not wishing to be with anyone else, Ella marked both of hers for Worthing. Aunt Agatha chastised her judgment in showing the viscount so much favoritism, but Ella easily accepted her aunt's reprimand. It was a fair exchange for being held close by James Kerrington.

The Capertons' ball was a major squeeze for so early in the Season. Fowler escorted his three ladies, following other members of the nobility up the steep staircase and through the receiving line. He walked with Aunt Agatha, but was very aware of the gentlemen watching Eleanor and Velvet as they trailed closely behind him. Taking Queen Charlotte at her word, both wore the traditional white gowns associated with those making their Come Out. Velvet's coloring contrasted well with the purest white, but Eleanor chose a beige-white so as not to let the lack of color wash out her fair complexion.

Entering the ballroom at last, Ella's eyes scanned the room for the one man she wanted most to see. Each day she grew more attached to the future earl. Then he appeared, and she heard her own quick intake of air, a mixture of fear and anticipation. Tall and broad-chested, with a tapered waist and no extra fat found anywhere, he was all male, and she could not control her body's reaction to him.

Lord Worthing watched the door for her entrance and smiled seductively when her eyes met his. The green pools danced with excitement, and James felt the heat hit his groin. Ella's cream-colored gown clung to her deceptively feminine curves, accentuating her elegance. About her neck she wore a single drop ruby on a gold chain, with ruby-tipped pins holding her golden curls close to her head. Delicate miniature embroidered roses decorated her neckline, and a deep red velvet ribbon emphasized her bustline. *His Amazon! Damn, she was perfection!*

"Your Grace." James exchanged bows with Fowler before turning his attention to the duke's party. "Lady Norfield, will you partake of the dance tonight? If so, I must claim your dance card immediately." Worthing bowed over the Duchess's hand.

"You wretched man!" Agatha struck James's arm lightly with her fan. "I must continue to warn my niece of your falsehoods, my Lord. I should accept your challenge and steal you away for myself."

"Then I would be the most blessed of men," he taunted.

"I will take your arm, Lord Worthing. I see Lady Kramer over there, and I shall keep her company." She laced her arm through his.

"Certainly, Your Grace." He helped her to a chair and brought her a lemonade from a nearby refreshment table. "Now, if you will excuse me, Lady Norfield, I must claim my cousin Alma's hand for the opening set, or my uncle will be most vexed with me."

"Your cousin?" She raised her quizzing glass, an accessory she always wore, but rarely used.

"Yes, Your Grace."

Agatha actually smiled this time. "I should be pleased to make your cousin's acquaintance, Lord Worthing."

"And so you shall, Lady Norfield." James bowed out of her company.

Fowler placed Eleanor on his arm for the first set, a country dance, to lead her to the floor. "You look lovely, my Dear," he whispered close to her ear. "I hope you no longer regret making this trip to London."

"It has been more pleasant than I anticipated. Of course, having your friends as part of our group gives Velvet and me a familiarity others may not have. I know if you are not available, one of them will step up and offer us his protection. It is quite extraordinary."

"Aunt Agatha was not amused to see you saved two dance sets for Lord Worthing, and both were waltzes," he cautioned. "Is that wise, Ella? I do not wish familiarity to soil your good name, nor do I wish it to be too comfortable, where you will let no others into your life."

Ella edged closer as they took the few steps to the floor's center. "I cannot imagine the dance's intimacy although I know the steps. How could I trust such closeness to a complete stranger? And dancing as such with my brother would seem sordid."

"Do not forget that Worthing is still a man, Ella. He is not immune to your charms."

Ella stopped suddenly and looked beseechingly in her brother's eyes. "Do you think it possible, Bran?"

"I think it more than possible, Eleanor." He set her in the line across from him.

Sir Louis claimed the second set, a prospect to which Eleanor did not look forward, but as he called regularly at Briar House, she felt she had no choice. Now, as she took his hand to pass him in the form, Ella thanked the Heavens for her gloves. She imagined his skin as scaly as a snake and probably as slimy.

"You look lovely, Lady Eleanor," he murmured as he passed her.

Ella stifled the urge to pull away from him. "Thank you, Sir Louis."

When they came together again, he met her eyes. "Might I call on you tomorrow, Lady Eleanor, and take you driving during the fashionable hour?"

Just the sound of his voice made her want to run away and hide, but Eleanor steadied her pitch in response. "I have promised that honor to another, I fear, Sir Louis."

"Worthing, I suppose," he hissed.

Ella bristled with his accusatory informality. "That is my business."

They parted, and for several seconds, Ella breathed again. Unfortunately, too quickly, they came face-to-face again. "I beg your pardon, Lady Eleanor, for the offense. You know I think only of your family when I voice my objections."

She made several turns before she faced Levering again. "Your concern speaks well of you, Sir Louis, but as we have had this conversation previously, I will not repeat my disdain for what begins to feel like interference in my life. I do not let others choose my friends, nor do I choose theirs."

James watched her go. He pretended interest in the conversation regarding a "fine set of greys" Lord Sherlwood sought at Tattersalls, but, in reality, he watched Ella. He observed her interaction with Sir Louis. Instinctively, he knew the moment the man returned to his favorite subject of late: the inappropriateness of James Kerrington as a possible suitor. James saw her bristle with Levering's assertion. He might have only known Eleanor Fowler for a little over a month, but he fancied he knew her better than anyone, even her brother. He recognized her mannerisms indicating her nervousness, her gestures showing her excitement, and her facial expressions when she hid her true feelings. James looked at the false smile she wore as Levering returned her to the Dowager Duchess's care. *His Amazon* steamed with contempt for her dance partner.

Ella paused only long enough for Sir Louis's retreat before she excused herself to the ladies' withdrawing room. Moments later, James was on the move, following her, making sure Levering had no dishonorable intentions. It appeared Sir Louis had considered trailing her, but Lord Chatterton latched onto the baronet's arm and led him to where a group of wallflowers gathered. Evidently, Chatterton recruited Levering as a possible dance partner. When the baronet looked away to his new admirers, James slipped into the darkened hallway.

Finding one of the doors lining the wall unlocked, he stepped into the empty room where no one would see him and waited for Ella.

Surprisingly, she spent very little time in the women's retiring room, indicating she needed to recover her composure, not her appearance. Although he could not see her, James sensed the moment she exited the comfort room. The hair along the back of his neck stood on end, and his breathing quickened. He timed it perfectly; as Ella reached the portal, James let the door swing open, caught her wrist, and pulled Ella into the blackness.

She started to fight him, but, for some inexplicable reason, she allowed him to drag her into his embrace as he closed the door behind them with his foot. Neither of them spoke, just held tightly, as if peace lay in the other's arms.

"Oh, God, Ella," he whispered to the air. "I have missed you."

"You see me every day, James." She snuggled closer to him and ran her hands under his jacket and along his back muscles.

He was making similar forays down her back and over the rise of her hips. "It is not enough, Ella. It is never enough unless it is all day, every day, and every night." His breathing became shallow. "I mean to kiss you, Lady Eleanor. If you do not want this, turn and walk out the door now."

Ella did not hesitate; she leaned against the door, pulling him with her, plastering herself to the wood with his frame. His mouth found hers, and bliss shot through his body. Eleanor opened her lips, allowing his tongue to search her gum's soft tissue and the concave shape of the roof of her mouth. He heard her groan, and James doubled his intensity. Coming up for air, at last, his lips hovered over hers.

"How did you know it was I when I caught your wrist?" With his lips, he covered her face with feathery caresses.

Ella looked away but then turned back to his closeness. "It is foolish, but I know your touch." She kissed the side of his face. "The smell of your cologne."

He tipped her chin up as if he could see her eyes, and, surprisingly, he could see the depths of them—the moonlight giving her an angelic glow. James growled under his breath, "You are mine, Eleanor Fowler. You may enjoy your Season; every woman has a right to one, but when it ends, you are mine. I mean to claim you—to bind you to me."

"Yes." The intensity so encompassing she could barely breathe.

James wondered about the sanity of making such a declaration, but he knew in his heart what he said was true. He wanted her with him, as he had never wanted anything else.

"Will you let me touch you, Ella?" he whispered in her ear. "I know you are frightened, but I want you to know how much I worship you—how precious every inch of you is to me."

James cautioned himself to go slowly—not to alarm her. In his gut, he knew her father had committed some sort of maltreatment against her. He did not know what, but something had happened to Eleanor in William Fowler's household.

She did not answer him directly, but Ella leaned into him, letting her body respond to his urging. James returned to her mouth, a slow, tantalizing trip to ecstasy. As Ella angled her mouth to meet his invasion of hers, James eased his way along her waist until he touched her breast. He felt Ella stiffen, so he used his tongue to trace along the line of her lips. "I will not hurt you," he coaxed as he weighed her breasts in the palms of his hands, caressing them gently, squeezing the full weight of them in his large hands. They swelled with his ministrations, and as his thumbs lightly crisscrossed her nipples, the buds hardened to his touch.

His groin swelled painfully, but it was worth it to finally feel her respond to him. God, he wanted her, but James made himself stop. As he eased away from Ella's curves, she moaned in frustration. Her audible disappointment went a long way in proving he was correct in how to handle her. "You are so beautiful," he murmured as he ran a finger from her temple to her chin line.

She turned her head to kiss his palm. "I wish I was truly beautiful." She thought of what he said about his wife. "I would like to be beautiful for you."

"Lord, Eleanor," his voice raised a bit in volume, "if you only knew what you did to me, you would never question when I say you are exquisite. I can think of nothing else but you."

"Truly, James?" she questioned.

James smiled with the tone of hope he heard in her voice. "Truly, my Love." He brushed her mouth with his. "I need to return you before people realize neither of us is in the ballroom." His fingertips traced her lips. "I wish there was enough light in here to see your mouth right now. I am sure it looks delicious—your lips swollen from the pressure of my kiss."

Teasingly, Eleanor let her tongue lick the pads of his fingers. "How will I be able to dance the waltz with you after what we just did?"

"Simply think of it as a prelude to supper. The waltz is the supper set. You do wish to sit with me, do you not?"

"Of course, I do."

"Then come." He caught her by the arm and reached for the door. "Return to the withdrawing room and freshen your appearance. I will claim Miss Aldridge's hand for this set. I believe the Marquis waits for you. Then we shall dance for the first time." He kissed her temple and eased the door open, stealthily disappearing into the passageway.

James returned to the ballroom's merriment and retrieved Miss Aldridge from the Duchess's side.

"Is my cousin well?" the lady murmured as he escorted her to a place in the form.

James chuckled but did not deny her assertion. "Do you suppose others noticed?"

"I doubt it." She acknowledged recent acquaintances. "Sir Louis upset Ella." It was more of a question than a statement.

"The baronet seems intent on separating Lady Eleanor from my company."

"As if anyone could," she whispered.

James found that he really enjoyed his new intimacy with Velvet Aldridge. He needed to occasionally say aloud what he felt for Eleanor—to give his blossoming desire credence. "From your lips to God's will."

"Why do you not simply declare your intentions, Your Lordship? I cannot imagine my cousin would refuse."

James moved closer, securing the privacy of his words. "Continue to smile at the crowd, and do not react to my question," he cautioned. "How much do you know of Eleanor's relationship with her father?"

"The former duke ignored Ella, generally. I always thought she reminded him too much of her mother." They spoke in hushed tones, barely looking at each other.

"Are you aware of Ella's sleepwalking episodes?"

"Still?" she hid her surprise. "My cousin knew such fits when she was younger. Have they returned?"

"They have."

Velvet bit her lower lip, a habit that she shared with her cousin. "What might I do?"

"Allowing Lady Eleanor to speak of her feelings is the best

medicine. Encourage her to confide in you. Ella is experiencing many changes. That is why I will not complicate her life with one more. The *newness* of having Bran home, having her first Season, and having to find her place in Society are stressful enough without my complicating it with my plight, although Lady Eleanor is well aware of my interest."

"You really love my cousin?"

James hesitated—*did he love Ella?* He had accepted the fact that he could not imagine spending his life without her. She was the air he breathed, but was that love? Then he raised his eyes to the door, and Eleanor reentered the room, scanning it for Gabriel Crowden, her next dance partner. He watched as her eyes finally met his, and nothing else mattered but that moment of shared understanding. "Yes, Miss Aldridge, I do."

"Then I will do what I can, Lord Worthing, to help you. Eleanor deserves someone to love her unconditionally."

~ ~ ~

And so it began. The next morning young bucks of varying titles and positions in Society filled the Briar House sitting room. While many sought Velvet's attentions, as a duke's daughter, only those of a certain rank considered approaching Eleanor. The room filled quickly with bouquets of all sizes and colors, and during the appropriate hours, the men fawned and fidgeted, many declaring their devotion to both women. Ella, more uncomfortable in such situations, often turned to Aunt Agatha for guidance, not knowing how to respond to such pretense. The Dowager Duchess, in her element, orchestrated the proceedings with a gypsy ringmaster's grace. She let no man monopolize either of the women's time, purposely redirecting conversations to allow each caller to play to his strengths. She knew the men's families—knew each title—knew each man's financial needs. Ella's dowry of thirty thousand pounds made some men desire her for that purpose alone, but the Dowager wished to find a loving match—if not a love match—for her niece. Velvet's thirteen thousand pounds was more than respectable, and many saw her as a more desirable match—beauty, vitality, and wealth, mixed together in the perfect package.

When her brother made a brief appearance in the sitting room, Ella's nerves nearly came unglued. He asked her to join him in the library when her callers departed. The gentlemen's false attentions had discomposed her. All Ella wanted was James Kerrington and a small drawing room and maybe another of those bone-melting kisses from last evening.

Less than an hour later, Eleanor entered the library, taking a chair across from him. As no formality was necessary between brother and sister, she removed her slippers and curled her toes into the thick carpeting.

"How did you perceive your first day of receiving callers?" Her brother asked nonchalantly.

Ella rolled her shoulders, trying to release the tension of the past two hours. "I never thought such poppycock could exist without exploding. The conversation, at best, lacked merit. Most of the gentlemen in that room would feign listening to my opinion on the best place to purchase ribbons or the most fashionable bonnet, but Heaven forbid, I might wish to discuss politics or agriculture."

"I have little experience with the majority of the gentlemen I observed today, except for Lawrence and Whitmore, who were mates at university, but, in general, men of Society do not expect their wives to be as well versed in current information as are you, my Dear."

Ella frowned deeply. "Then I am to pretend disinterest in everything but frimp and frills if I seek a matrimonial match?"

"You have no need of pretense, Ella. A man who wishes more than your dowry will accept the sharpness of your mind." Fowler set his teacup on the small table beside his chair. "I did not see Worthing among your callers," he ventured.

With the mention of James's name, Ella relaxed into the cushions. He had that effect on her. "I am to ride out with His Lordship this afternoon. Lord Worthing comes to Briar House daily; he has no need of morning calls."

"Perhaps Kerrington made his presence known at another fashionable address," Bran teased.

Ella sat forward, such a thought having never occurred to her. "Do you believe His Lordship might be engaged elsewhere? If you knew of such an attachment, you would tell me, would you not, Bran?"

Her brother's lips twitched in amusement. "It was a jest, Ella. James Kerrington is an honorable man; he will not play with your affections."

Ella relaxed into her thoughts of the man. "Would you tell me what you know of His Lordship's former wife?" She wanted to know whether she might actually compete with Lady Worthing's memory.

"I did not meet Kerrington until a year after the lady's passing, but, he spoke of her often in those early days, and afterwards, I became acquainted with others who knew Lady Worthing well—his cousin Alma, whom you met last evening, for example. Most who speak of Elizabeth Kerrington speak of her beauty, and from the renderings I have seen of her, she was attractive." Ella's frown returned. "Elizabeth Kerrington was pretty, Ella, but no more so than you. She was dark—more along the lines of Velvet's coloring. A person could not compare the two of you."

"His Lordship says his wife was all kindness." Worry lines appeared around her eyes.

Her brother smiled solicitously. "I am sure Worthing would say so. He speaks as a man who remembers the early bliss of love, but, Ella, please understand that part of grief is selective memory. Those who speak of Lady Worthing remember a girl, not a woman; she was not even your age when she passed, Kerrington having married her when she was but seventeen. He remembers the exuberance of the young girl, but that does not mean as Kerrington matured that his wife might follow suit. I have heard Worthing's mother say she never thought Elizabeth Morris her son's equal in intelligence or depth of character, and Alma speaks of the lady's spoiled nature, always needing to be the center of attention. Lady Alma once commented on her doubts of Lady Worthing being able to love the boy—not being willing to share His Lordship's attention with her own son. Alma seemed to feel that once Worthing grew older he would tire of having to attend to his wife's every wish, especially after he became Earl. He would have less time to cater to her demands. Of course, none of us will know that for sure, but it is my belief, Eleanor, that you could be more to Kerrington than his late wife. A man of twenty sees the world differently from a man of thirty, and he needs a different type of woman to fill those changing needs. I seriously doubt Kerrington would even feign interest in ribbons just to please you."

Ella laughed lightly. "Did you hear our near battle over the advantages of railways over the canal system two evenings ago?"

"I doubt if Worthing could find someone at White's to give him such a setdown."

"Am I too fiery in my opinions, Bran? Should I try to soften my approach?"

The duke leaned forward as if to share a secret. "Do you wish to attract Worthing? If he made a declaration, would you accept?"

Ella licked her suddenly dry lips. *Should she admit the depth of her interest in James Kerrington?* "I value Lord Worthing's opinion more than I should on such short acquaintance. I fear I prefer his company to that of all others, and as far as a declaration, I would seriously entertain such avowals."

"Then let us give Worthing some hope," Fowler declared. "He expressed an interest in making his overtures at the Season's end. If I interpret what you say correctly, it would be acceptable to you if he did so before that time?"

Ella swallowed hard, understanding what her brother asked of her. "I would not wish to wait to come to an understanding with Lord Worthing, but neither would I wish to force him into acting before he is ready."

"I have observed how the man looks at you, Ella. I doubt Kerrington would think himself forced into an offer of marriage, but I will assure him he may speak earlier if he wishes." Bran reasoned, "As your official Come Out ball is less than a fortnight away, we should not upset Aunt Agatha by announcing a betrothal before then. I intend to suggest Worthing wait at least a fortnight following your ball before securing your hand as his own. That gives you a month, Ella, to change your mind if you so wish."

"And if I change my mind, would I disappoint you, Bran? His Lordship is a dear friend, after all."

Her brother took her hand and brought it to rest over his heart. "I would only be disappointed, Eleanor, if you chose someone who could not make you happy. I would agree to a cottager or a vicar or an earl, as long as you could find comfort and joy in your life by sharing it with him. You are what is important to me, not Society."

Immediately, she was in his arms, her fake veneer—the one she showed the world, of the reserved duke's daughter—slipping. "I love you, Eleanor," he whispered close to her ear. "No one will ever replace you in my life. I would move mountains for you; I promise to never fail you again."

When Kerrington called to take Ella driving, the duke motioned him into his study as Mr. Horace sent a maid to find Eleanor. "Have a seat, Worthing." Fowler gestured to the chair before his desk. "I thought I might bring you up to snuff on the Baloch emerald. Lexford reports someone broke into one of his smaller properties and ransacked the rooms, leaving things in disarray. It could be vandals in the neighborhood, but it might have something to do with the emerald. Maybe not surprisingly, John thwarted a similar incident at a manor house on his Yorkshire property. There are some parallels in the manner in which the culprits entered the dwellings. Shepherd sent out warnings to the others. I told him I would speak to you and Crowden."

"I need to contact Mr. MacKelroy, my father's steward—have him check the outlying holdings." He motioned to the foolscap lying on the desk, and Bran nodded his agreement. James took up the pen. "Have there been other attacks?"

"None of which Shepherd is aware."

James finished his short directive to his estate's steward before looking up at Fowler. "Any leads on the coach or the shooter in the park?"

"Shepherd believes he has a lead on the coach." Fowler handed over the hot wax after James wrote the directions on the outside. "Other witnesses saw a coach. It bore a crest, but the street hawker who first took note of it could not identify it. The coach nearly ran him down in its flight to escape you. With what you shared, I suspect the coach the hawker observed belonged to the fake Frenchie, rather than the Baloch." James used his signet ring to seal the missive. Fowler rang for a footman to send the message on its way. "I had another reason to speak to you, Worthing."

Leaning back into the chair, James eyed Fowler suspiciously. "I am all ears, Your Grace."

"I spoke to my sister after her morning callers departed."

James shifted uncomfortably. "Were there many?"

"It was a packed house between those who wished to see Eleanor, those to see Velvet, and those who would take either. It made me wish to clean my gun before them," he mused. Fowler swirled the brandy he sipped. "I find I drink more often than I once did. It dulls my response to my cousin's presence. Tell me, Worthing, how do I let her go if Velvet chooses another?"

"I assume that is a rhetorical question, and you seek no response from me."

Fowler handed the footman the letter before returning to their conversation. "I noticed you not among Eleanor's admirers," he half mocked.

"As you must subjugate your desire to make Miss Aldridge your own, I find I am not so magnanimous regarding those who would place a claim on your sister. I am not of the persuasion to share Lady Eleanor's attentions with a room full of would-be lovers." James sighed deeply, accepting his fate.

"You will be happy to know, Worthing, that my sister prefers you to all the others."

James sat forward, hands on the edge of the desk. This mad obsession with Ella consumed him. "Do not tease me, Fowler; I am not a schoolgirl seeking news of my latest infatuation. If you wish to speak to me of Lady Eleanor, then do so directly and truthfully."

"I have told Ella," Fowler smiled, the corners of his mouth turned up mockingly, "I would entertain a petition for her hand before the Season's end if she found someone to her liking. I suggested some time—perhaps a fortnight, shall we say—after her official Come Out ball. It would be unseemly to do so before that event. Aunt Agatha would be most livid."

"Do you speak the truth, Fowler?"

"Make her happy, Kerrington. Teach Ella to love. I wish never to see her begging for my father's attentions again. My sister received ill treatment of the worst form, and I cannot bear to think she might spend the rest of her days without knowing love." Fowler leveled a stare on Kerrington. "Tell me you really love Eleanor, and I will fight the heavens and the earth to bring you together."

James did not flinch. "I love Lady Eleanor with every inch of my heart. You will not believe this, but when I am with Ella, I do not think of Elizabeth—never has that happened."

"Then you have a month to convince Ella to be your wife. After that, any exclusivity I have allowed you as my friend will no longer exist," Fowler warned.

"I understand, Your Grace." James stood to make his leave.

Fowler gestured to stay him. "One thing more, Worthing; get rid of Mary. If Eleanor finds you have a mistress, it will kill her. I will not see her hurt ever again. If you choose to make Ella your wife, you must do so with the understanding you find pleasure only in her arms. If I hear of your doing something contrary to that, you and I will meet on a dueling field, and I would dislike losing you as a brother."

"I have seen Mary but once since the day your sister stumbled into my arms at Thorn Hall, and even then I left to spend my evening alone. I think of no one but Eleanor. I give you my word on it. If Eleanor is mine, I will release Mary to another protector." James finished his speech and strode from the room. Although he knew he could not keep Mary if he engaged Lady Eleanor, he certainly did not relish the idea of his friend issuing such orders.

From behind him, Eleanor's voice stopped him flat. "My Lord," she began. Without thinking, she touched his shoulder lightly. "James." Her hand caressed his arm. "May I help?"

Chapter 6

WHEN HE LEFT THE ROOM, James nearly went straight to his curricle and freedom, but then her voice came to rescue the depths of his soul. Her hand stroked the line along his shoulder and down his arm, and James's anger dissipated instantly. *May I help?* she said. *Did she not realize that she just did?*

"I am well, Lady Eleanor." He turned to give her the perfect smile. "I was simply anxious to find you; I had finished my business with your brother. Would you be ready for our outing?"

"I would, my Lord."

"Then let us be about it." He took Ella on his arm and led her to his vehicle. "I have waited for this moment all day, Lady Eleanor—the moment when you returned to my side."

For the next week, their lives became the Season's routine. Each evening comprised a number of invitations, and they chose among the ones the Duchess deemed most worthy: dinners, soirees, musicales, balls, and the theatre. For the ladies, the days filled with entertaining callers, shopping, and attending at-homes. The men attended to Parliamentary duties, fencing or boxing, and afternoons at White's.

James arranged an outing with Ella every day. Recognizing Eleanor's need for intellectual activities, they spent a great deal of time at lectures and museums. He combed the papers daily for entertainment he thought she might enjoy.

Much to Ella's chagrin, Sir Louis became a regular among her callers, often bullying others into withdrawing or monopolizing her attentions with his constant references to her father and to his parents. He made no pretense of also desiring Velvet; the baronet spent his time in the Briar House drawing room and then withdrew to his personal business interests. Every time he called, Ella died a new death. Only James Kerrington gave her any hope for the future.

On one particular afternoon, James and Eleanor enjoyed exploring the antiquities at the Historical Society—relics from ancient civilizations—gold and silver and gems glistening in the lights. "Can you imagine of what their lives must have consisted?" They dwelt over a display of artifacts from Egypt.

"Your brother and I spent nearly a year in Persia. The civilizations are similar." James stood as close to her as possible, where he might enjoy the heat of Ella's body along his.

Ella leaned over the glass case for a better look at a golden torque. "I would love to travel and see the world some day."

"Let me take you, Ella. Let me show you the world," he murmured close to her ear.

She turned her face to him. The pure intensity of her gaze mesmerized him—in it he saw the hurt and the loneliness he recognized from his own soul, but James also saw the passion and the zest for life resting under the surface. He had served with her brother in what one could only call the most harrowing situations, and he had survived. He had survived for this moment with Ella. He and Eleanor both needed saving. They would fill the gaping holes in each other's souls. "Can we have this, James? Can there be happiness out there? I am afraid—afraid to hope such a connection can exist—afraid if it does, someone will snatch it away."

He laced their fingers as they rested them on the glass, unable to do more in such a public setting. "I have told you, Ella, I want to see you in my house, by my side, and in my bed. I want to be the one who gives you comfort—who brings you joy, but it will never be perfect, Eleanor. Outside forces will interfere always. We can only find that peace we both seek in each other." He brought the back of her hand to his lips. "I will protect you with my body and with my title."

Something in his tone induced her feminine embarrassment. "I am sure that if you knew everything about me, you would not think so highly of me." Eleanor turned her head, purposely refusing to look at him. All of her self-doubts rushed to the forefront. Her countenance said, "I am undeserving of anyone's devotion."

James draped her hand over his arm and walked slowly to the next display. He needed a moment to consider what he should say. Eleanor held no idea of his suspicions about her life. *Should he tell her?* "Eleanor," he began cautiously, "I will tell you what I know about you. You possess a quick wit and a strong intelligence, a delightful sense of humor, a loving heart, and a compassionate personality. You would make an excellent mistress for my estate; I have seen how you run a household. I have also observed your interactions with Sonali, and although I do not expect you to love Daniel as your own, I cannot imagine your ever being purposely cruel to Elizabeth's child. My son could learn much from you about empathy, respect, and responsibility."

James paused to maneuver her to a nearby bench. Eleanor continued her pretended examination of the display, and he knew he was on a precipice with their relationship. What he said in the next few minutes would make pathways or close recently opened doors. He distractedly ran his fingers through his hair. "Ella, I want to tell you about my first night at Thorn Hall, where I came across a scantily clad beautiful wood sprite on the main staircase." Her head snapped around to look at him, pure horror implanted upon her face. She started to speak, but James silenced her with a touch of his finger to her mouth. "Let me finish, please." He saw her swallow her dread, and he prayed he was correct in his evaluation of her.

"I held this riddle in my arms and tried to offer comfort while my beauty cried softly against my shoulder, and then I carried this wood sprite to her bed. This apparition came to me on three other occasions during my stay at Thorn Hall, and each time I held her close, my heart opened to the pain she had suffered, and I wanted to protect her from such anguish. True—I do not know exactly what my wood sprite suffered at the hands of a despicable, foul overlord, but it did not destroy her, and like the phoenix, she rose to be my life's light. Without her, only darkness looms on the horizon, and now that I have seen the light, I can no longer live in the darkness; for the light is love and truth. Some day I may be worthy of holding the light in my arms."

Tears coursed down Ella's cheeks, and she forced the sobs down deep within her chest. "You know some of my secrets and still want me in your life?" she whispered hoarsely. His words stunned her senses. "You knew about my nighttime ramblings, but you still kissed me?" Disbelief played across her face.

"Actually, I have kissed you several times since then, and I would gladly do it again if you need reassurance," he teased.

"James, I cannot fathom how you entered my life."

Ella seemed pleased with his earlier responses, and he allowed himself a sigh of relief. "Actually, Lady Eleanor, you stumbled into my arms. Fate has a wicked sense of humor, does she not?"

"She does, Lord Worthing; yet, I am blessed she has showed me such favor."

It was the closest to a declaration of affection he had ever received from Eleanor Fowler, and James beamed with happiness. "I have a strong desire for a cream ice. May I interest you in a side trip to Berkeley Square, Lady Eleanor?"

"Decadence, my Lord?" she taunted.

"The way to a man's heart, my Lady." He meant it as a tease, but Ella contracted when he touched her arm. Instantly, James regretted his words. "Eleanor, it was a jest," he whispered to her hair. "Nothing more than a jest. You must believe me."

"It is fine, my Lord Worthing. Just a taste of reality—it is sometimes a bitter pill to swallow."

"But you do trust me?"

"With my life, my Lord."

~~~

Two days before her Come Out ball, Ella joined James Kerrington, along with the rest of the Fowlers, at the theatre, her brother making use of his private box. Although they spent time together every day, the *ton* only suspected the viscount's preference for Thornhill's sister, having seen them in each other's company only upon occasion, for they were generally in the company of her brother and her aunt, the Dowager Duchess of Norfield. Occasionally, someone made a comment regarding their public embrace after Ella's horse tried to throw her, but they all explained it away as being true concern for dear friends. As they became better known to the gossips, they both took more care to assure their privacy. However, on this night things changed. Ella entered the theatre on James's arm. In a fortnight, he would declare his intentions publicly, and then they could make plans for a marriage. Having Eleanor by his side gave him contentment—his life finally coming together after so many years of loneliness.

"It is a beautiful building; just look at the architecture," she spoke softly to James alone.

"Only you, Ella, would come to the theatre for one of Shakespeare's finest and comment on the building itself."

"Do not tease me, Lord Worthing. You know my nature."

"Indeed, I do, Lady Eleanor." They shared a moment of intimacy before turning to the crowd.

Climbing the stairs behind Fowler and the Dowager Duchess, James had never experienced such pride as he did at that moment. Then, his world tilted, for at the top of the steps, a figure appeared, and he felt himself stiffen: Mary Cavendish stood on the upper level, clinging to a gentleman of some fifty years or so. She blushed and took a step back from the railing when their eyes met. James suffered a twinge of guilt, seeing the fear in her eyes—she thought
~~~

him upset—after all, he still paid her bills—technically, Mary was his mistress, although he had called upon her but once in two months.

Having Fowler and Godown as part of the group complicated the situation. None of them could acknowledge Mary in public, especially with fine ladies on their arms, but James could tell she wished to offer an explanation as to whom her escort might be. Yet, Mary would not risk his wrath; she knew her place in his life.

Ella felt the change in the tension in James's arm, in his bearing as they climbed the stairs. He hid it well, but something he had seen affected his mood. Her eyes began to search the crowd gathered on the upper landing. She half expected to see Sir Louis; such was the way Lord Worthing reacted to the baronet's frequent intrusions, but Levering was not in the throng making its way to the seating.

Nearly at the top, Ella caught the slightest tilt of her brother's head as he passed a rather buxom lady and an elderly gentleman on their right. They exchanged no words, but recognition was obvious. *Who was the woman?* It was not the man to whom Brantley inclined his head; the gentleman looked off to the side. *It was the woman.* Her eyebrow raised in amusement as Bran walked past, and then it was her turn. She and James came abreast of the couple, and Lord Worthing purposely turned his gaze away and increased their pace. Ella had never seen him give anyone a direct cut, and she could not help but to glance over her shoulder at the woman who dropped a quick curtsy to Gabriel's simple nod of acknowledgement.

All at once, she felt sick—her stomach began to turn. Her brother and Lord Godown at least recognized the woman's presence, but James did not. That meant that all three of them held an acquaintance with her, but Ella feared that only Lord Worthing knew the woman intimately. She thought she might swoon. Instinctively, James steadied her steps with his weight, but he did not look at her. His mouth remained set in a tight line; his thoughts were not on her, and Ella knew it.

They entered her brother's box, and Worthing intentionally allowed the Marquis and Velvet to join Bran and Aunt Agatha on the front row. Normally, Ella would have enjoyed the privacy of the second row, thinking it romantic to be separated from their party, but not tonight. Tonight she wanted answers. Her eyes searched the crowd. The gentleman from before seemed well to do, but not fashionable, so although she realized it seemed snobbish, she did not search the plusher boxes for the couple. Instead, her eyes scanned the boxes and alcoves at the stage level until she found them in one of the two-chair box seats on the side incline of the pit area.

The gentleman seated the lady and then moved in close where he might hold her hand. Ella watched the woman smile at the man, but, predictably, her eyes came to where James sat. Ella noted how Lord Worthing stared intently at the empty stage as if expecting it to perform some sort of conjuring trick.

Needing to know and needing to know now, Ella caught his hand resting in his lap, oblivious to the fact the lights had not yet dimmed for the performance. He turned his head to look at her and tried to smile, but it came strained at best. Leaning toward him, she whispered in his ear, "Would you care to tell me who the woman at whom you are trying not to look might be, Lord Worthing?"

He looked deep in her eyes, obviously searching for an answer. "What woman?"

Tears sprang instantly to Ella's eyes. He had lied to her. "Excuse me," she said loud enough for the others. "I will step to the ladies' retiring room before the play begins."

"Shall I go with you?" Velvet offered.

Ella shook her head in the negative before springing to her feet. As she reached the draped opening, she turned to the left, needing to be away from him. Lord Worthing had looked in her eyes and lied to her. *If he lied about the woman, where were the other lies?*

She was nearly ready to break into a run when he caught her arm, pulling Ella off balance and back into his side. "Do not run," he hissed under his breath. "We will settle this. *Ba man bia.* Come with me." Opening the door to a closet containing brooms and mops and buckets, he pulled Ella in and blocked the door with his shoulder.

"Leave me alone!" Ella pushed against him trying to escape the semi-darkened space.

James set her away from him, as gently as possible. "Not until you listen to what I have to say."

"Why? So you can lie to me again? Are you going to try to pretend you did not just lie to me? How could you?" Tears flowed, but Ella never backed down.

"Eleanor, please." Panic constricted his breathing.

"Did you or did you not just purposely tell me an untruth?" She threw up her hands in disgust.

"Yes, I lied," he sneered, "but I did it to protect you."

Deflated by his words, Ella turned her back on him. "I do not need protecting, Lord Worthing. In fact, it is I who protects the others in my family. Remember, I am the phoenix—I survive." Her voice came out hard and unforgiving.

"Ella," he pleaded, "*Bebakhshid.* I am sorry. I never wanted to hurt you. You have been hurt before, and I promised I would never let it happen to you again."

"But you did hurt me, James, by not trusting me." She turned slowly to him. "You hurt me as no one else can because I allowed you to see me—to know my hopes and dreams." Alarm spread through her veins.

Something between anger and desperation colored his tone. "She means nothing to me, Ella. I swear it."

"The woman means something, James. You gave her a direct cut—she means enough that you wish to hide her from me."

"What do you want of me, Eleanor?"

Ella took a half step forward. "I expect you, Lord Worthing, to first tell me your relationship to the lady, and then I expect you to be the gentleman I know you are. You will acknowledge the woman and her escort by introducing me to them."

"Ella, it is just not done. His Grace would be furious." He tried to reason with her.

"My almighty brother at least inclined his head to the woman," she asserted.

Indicating defeat, Worthing just shook his head in disbelief. "You are like no woman I have ever known. May we, at least, wait until the intermission, Lady Eleanor, to meet the woman who was once my mistress?"

Ella swallowed hard, not wanting him to see how much his words affected her. "The lady's name?" she insisted.

"Mary Cavendish."

"And when did Mary Cavendish stop being your mistress?" Again, the thoughts of his being with anyone else ripped through her.

Kerrington rolled his eyes up in an act of supplication. "Do you realize how embarrassing this is?" He waited for a response, but when none came, he answered her question. "Mary is still my mistress although I have not been with her since before a *demanding... totally irritating...Amazon* stumbled into my arms one day in Kent. I should have released her; I know that; I do not intend on keeping Mary—I guess I did not know how to tell her. She is a kind woman. Mary is a friend; I have never treated her as anything less than a friend until tonight."

"Then why did you do so this evening?" Ella let hope back into her heart.

"I thought I was doing the proper thing by you. Most women of the *ton* would be appalled."

"I am *not* most women of the *ton*, Lord Worthing. I have empathy for a woman who must shackle herself to a man in order to survive. Society gives us so few options. The fact that you speak highly of Miss Cavendish addresses the lady's true character."

"Actually, she is Mrs. Cavendish, a war widow."

"Then I will meet Mrs. Cavendish, and you will release her from your service before we take the next step."

"Just like that."

"Just like that." Ella looked as determined as before, but the anger had disappeared.

The viscount took a cautious step toward her. "Eleanor, are we well—I mean, *us*?"

Ella snaked her arms around his neck. "*We*, Lord Worthing, are better than *well*, but if you ever lie to me again, there will be hell to pay." She went on her tiptoes to brush her lips across his.

Breathing a sigh of relief, James quickly deepened the kiss, pulling Ella into his embrace. "I should have known better than to take your brother's advice."

An eyebrow raised in amusement. "Bran gave you advice about your mistress?"

"More about how to handle you than Mary," he confessed.

"The man who cannot make up his mind about how to win his cousin's love? That man? That is whose advice you accepted about me? I swear, Lord Worthing, sometimes I wonder about your intelligence," she taunted.

He smiled in agreement. "When you put it as such, it seems you might be correct, Lady Eleanor."

"Then you are saying I am right?" Ella's answering smile met the corners of her eyes. "I love being the one who is right."

James grinned largely. "If you tell any of my friends I allowed you to win this argument, I will be the laughingstock of White's."

"It will be our secret, Lord Worthing." Unable to resist a little jab, she added, "Have you noticed, my Lord, that you speak Persian when you are frustrated?"

"Do I now, Lady Eleanor?" He teased, feeling a bit easier about their relationship.

"You must teach me some day. I have always wanted to see the world.

"And since I met you, Ella, I have wanted to give you the world."

Eleanor and James returned to their seats after the play began, which eased their party's questions, but not the close scrutiny of the *ton*, which now made them the newest point of interest. "Watch the play," James instructed as he adjusted his seating. "We are being observed."

"I have noticed," she whispered out of the corner of her mouth.

After the third act, when the house lights were relit, the audience began to stretch and mingle for the intermission. "Will you join us for some refreshments, Ella?" Her brother asked emphatically as he assisted Aunt Agatha to her feet.

"I think not." She reached for her fan and reticule. "I have asked Lord Worthing to introduce me to Mrs. Cavendish."

She noted that both her brother and Godown fought the urge to openly react. Bran caught her hand and leaned in close. "It is unacceptable, Eleanor. Viscount Worthing knows better." He shot a look of warning in James's direction.

"Lord Worthing and I will have no secrets between us," she insisted. Her eyes told her brother this issue was not one upon which she would look favorably for his interference.

Fowler pointedly released her hand, registering his objection. "If you must do this, do so with class," he whispered.

Ella simply nodded her understanding before turning to Worthing's proffered arm. James caught her hand to his side, and directed her through the curtained opening, and then led Ella on a slow, ambulatory circle of the lobby. Periodically, they paused to exchange pleasantries with acquaintances, but they had a destination, and they moved accordingly.

Finally, in a less brilliantly lit passageway, they found the people they sought. Mrs. Cavendish and her escort stood outside their seating area. Mary blushed when she saw him approach, but she did not look away, a small act of defiance. It was one of the qualities James had always admired in the widow.

"Lord Worthing," Mary intoned as she dropped a curtsy.

"Mrs. Cavendish." James bowed properly. "It is pleasant to see you, Ma'am. Would you do me the honor of introducing your friend?"

Mary looked uncomfortable. As she was his mistress, Worthing should not be seeking her company, especially with a lady of fashion on his arm. "Lord Worthing," she began unsteadily, "may I present my late husband's brother, Sir Neville Cavendish. Sir Neville, this is Viscount Worthing."

"It is of the greatest honor to have your acquaintance, Lord Worthing. I have met so few of Mary's acquaintances on this London trip."

James turned to Ella and smiled with a close familiarity, signaling their relationship. "Sir Neville, Mrs. Cavendish, may I present Lady Eleanor Fowler of Thorn Hall in Kent."

Mary gestured her understanding with the simple raise of an eyebrow. This introduction of Brantley Fowler's sister would serve as an acknowledgment of Ella as his own. With the simplest of acts, James told Mary that her status as his mistress had changed.

"Lord Worthing speaks of you with the highest praises." Ella offered Mary a compliment, an act unheard of among the *ton*.

Mary dropped a quick curtsy. "I thank you, Lady Fowler."

James addressed Sir Neville. "How long are you in London, Sir?"

"A brief fortnight, Viscount Worthing. I have made a special journey from Warwickshire to reacquaint myself with Mary. It is foolish of an old man, but I have hopes of convincing her to return with me. We were friends—she and I—before she married my younger brother, and I think we might do well together."

James saw Mary's eyes dart from him to Sir Neville. "I have explained to Sir Neville that I have obligations."

Ella tightened her hold on his arm, but James realized what he must do. "Far be it from me, Mrs. Cavendish, to offer you advice, but Sir Neville seems a reliable fellow, and his offer appears an honest one. If I were you, I would consider it before replying with a refusal." He owned her and settlements needed to be addressed, but he released her publicly from his protection: Mary could choose Sir Neville as her own, just as he obviously did with Eleanor Fowler.

She stammered, "I…I have many legal and monetary issues with which to deal before I might respond."

Ella told Mary and James what she expected. "I am sure, Mrs. Cavendish, that if you need legal advice, His Lordship would be happy to assist you. Perhaps one day next week he might call on you to set your affairs in order." James recognized the lack of resentment in Ella's tone. During the play's three acts, he had observed how Eleanor spent time considering this situation with Mrs. Cavendish. He did not fool himself: Ella knew Mary provided him sexual favors, but she also knew him to possess many layers to his character. In fact, she knew him better than anyone. He had never regretted his time with Mary: She had helped him to reconcile his loneliness. If he had not done so, he and Ella could not be falling in love now. Ella would not resent Mary's time in his life, but she would not share their marriage with anyone in that way. That was blatantly clear, and James had no qualms in declaring his absolute loyalty to her.

"That is right decent of you, old Chap," Sir Neville was saying. "I am sure Mary would be agreeable to your kind offer, Lord Worthing."

"I will send word, Mrs. Cavendish," James brought the encounter to a close, "when I will be able to address your business."

Mary looked relieved, but also a bit disconsolate. "I shall be expecting your card, Your Lordship. It was an honor to make your acquaintance, Lady Fowler."

Then it was over—both their exchange and his relationship with Mary Cavendish. She had served him well—helped him deal with Elizabeth's loss, but his future lived in Eleanor Fowler—a woman of strong opinions and undying trust—a woman to match his passion and challenge his intelligence—a woman devoted to family—a woman to love. Unlike many of his fellow aristocrats, James had found a true love match—there would be no marriage of convenience for him. "Thank you, Ella," he whispered close to her ear. They returned to the duke's box. "You are incomparable—beyond imitation."

Ella smiled openly. "It is I who should thank you, James. You have changed my perspective of the world."

Noting the empty hallway, he impulsively pulled Eleanor into a darkened box. "Ella," James murmured as he trailed a line of heat from her temple to her mouth's corner with his fingertips. "I have seen portions of this world, but I never saw the beauty of England until I saw you. You changed my perspective of home." He reverently lowered his mouth to caress her lips. "We must return to His Grace's box. Yet, I would be happy to spend the night in this empty one with you in my arms."

Ella sighed deeply. "Nothing could compare with such perfection."

The ballroom swelled with floral arrangements, the smell of an English garden comforting and enticing. Yellow roses and daisies and lavish greenery filled every vase and urn in the room. Two crystal chandeliers and wall sconces every three feet lighted the room with hundreds of candles. French doors and windows stood open to the late spring night, where outside colorful lanterns and ribbons adorned the garden walkways and balustrades. The orchestra, on the raised dais, tuned their instruments and arranged sheet music upon stands.

Fowler, all in black, except his white linen, stood aristocratically at the receiving line's head, followed by Aunt Agatha, who wore a dark green—nearly black—gown with matching hair plumes and who looked remarkably handsome for a woman of her age. Velvet chose a shimmering gown of the palest lavender, accessorized with silver about her neck and woven within her dark curls.

Ella wore a creamy satin gown, with short puffy sleeves and a low décolletage, draped with a golden mesh and making her look very royal. Gold picks sporting yellow petals were woven into piled-high hair—a double gold chain and locket draped about her neck. When he saw her, James's first thought was of the goddess Ishtar. He once saw a statue of the Babylonian goddess of love and war, supposedly shedding her garments before entering the nether world. Covered in the thinnest gold, he thought it a splendid representation of artistic excellence, but it paled in the brilliance of Lady Eleanor Fowler. She was elegant and ethereal. Of late, he found himself impatient to claim Eleanor as his own and to make his life perfect. Seeing her beauty increased his desire for her. James purposely matched her in choice of clothes this evening; after Velvet let it slip Ella would wear cream and gold, he ordered his fawn-colored breeches and black and gold waistcoat.

The opening dance belonged to Fowler, but James never removed his eyes from Eleanor. She flashed him a smile across the crowded floor, and his heart leapt in response. He championed one of the other debutantes from his home country for the set; and although she was very pretty, Miss Alice Westerly lacked the exuberance found in *his Amazon*.

As before, James appeared to claim Ella's hand for the supper waltz. "Lady Eleanor," he bowed politely, "I believe this is our dance."

Aunt Agatha snorted. "Lord Worthing, do you not think another should have the pleasure of my niece's company for the waltz?"

Without missing a beat, James bowed ridiculously low to Ella's aunt. "As I assume you plead for my attentions for yourself, Lady Norfield, I would beg off from Lady Eleanor in order to please you."

Agatha meant to chastise him for increasing the gossip regarding his relationship with Ella, but his feigned seriousness caught her off guard, and the Duchess barked out a laugh. "I should call you a Renaissance man and claim the dance for myself just to quell your impertinence, Your Lordship," she threatened.

"I beg to differ. I am never impertinent with you, Your Grace. I speak the truth."

Blowing out her breath in exasperation, the Duchess shooed him away with a flip of her wrist. "Go on with you, you wretched man, but you must guard my Eleanor's reputation."

"With my life, Your Grace," he murmured. Then James conspiratorially winked at Ella's aunt. The music began as he walked Ella onto the floor. Tonight he would dance with an Amazon goddess.

"You are spectacular," he breathed the words close to Ella's ear. "My eyes never tire of looking upon you."

Ella blushed, "Lord Worthing, it is too much. I cannot contend with your words."

James held her gaze, assuring Ella of his sincerity. "I am a man who has been taught by a frugal father to manage his estate and his title wisely. I live comfortably, but not necessarily extravagantly. I see to my tenants and my staff. I provide for my family, but I rarely see to my own needs beyond food and clothing. However, with you, I find I am a greedy man. Eleanor, you have quickly become essential to my existence. You must recognize that fact."

"Is it truly possible?" she asked again for the hundredth time.

It would take James a lifetime to convince her of his devotion. To emphasize his intent, he used his fingers to edge Ella a bit closer. "You must learn to trust me, Eleanor, and to trust yourself. You know my nature, and I fancy that I know yours. Can you imagine either of us allowing anyone or anything to take what we have away from us?"

He led Ella into supper after waltzing together before the *ton*'s inquiring eyes. The gossip swirled about their relationship, but they kept most of the tongues from wagging with their attention to propriety, at least in public. Tonight, they sat with their inner circle—Fowler, Aunt Agatha, Velvet, and Crowden. The only difference was that Fowler brought the widow of a childhood friend to the table, the first time he had showed attention to anyone, including Velvet. Mrs. Lucinda Warren recently left behind her widow's weeds. At three and twenty, her husband had fallen in a past campaign. A bit plain in her appearance, except for her mesmerizing eyes, the lady had followed the drum until her husband's passing and only recently returned to London. Fowler met her purely by accident at a soiree; tonight he singled her out with his attentions.

Mrs. Warren, used to being one of only a few women surrounded by men, spoke with an ease, which James could understand Fowler appreciating. She was honest and outspoken in her opinions, and the woman understood how men who faced war and battles thought—something Velvet Aldridge would never be able to offer Fowler. Plus, Mrs. Warren might actually accept Fowler's child as her own, even if she knew the truth of Sonali's birth. Even though he had developed an affection of sorts for Ella's cousin, James was not sure Miss Aldridge would be so indulgent. She was too immature to understand Fowler's obsession.

He and Ella watched with amusement as Miss Aldridge doubled her flirtations directed at Gabriel Crowden, trying to draw Fowler's eyes to her. "My cousin may be sitting in the Marquis's lap soon," Ella whispered close to James's ear.

"That sounds delicious." He smiled broadly with mischief. "Although I would prefer a different lady."

"Anyone I know, Lord Worthing?"

"A most intimate acquaintance, Lady Eleanor," he suggested seductively.

When they rose to return to the ballroom, Ella stayed him for a moment. "You will linger when the others leave, my Lord?"

"I would think you to need your rest, my Lady."

"I am too excited, Lord Worthing, to sleep. Might you keep me company?"

James simply smiled, happiness filling his every pore. *Would he willingly spend private time with Eleanor Fowler? Indubitably!* "You know I would like nothing more."

CHAPTER 7

~ ~ ~

THE LAST OF THE GUESTS DEPARTED, all declaring the Fowler ball a huge success. Ella and Velvet officially became the most popular offerings of the Season, a rarity in the fact they were not straight from the schoolroom but still experiencing their first tastes of Society. At nineteen and twenty years of age, they were perceived to be more marriageable than those of seventeen, the normal age for making one's debut. Crowden made his farewells, agreeing to escort Mrs. Warren to her lodging, although Fowler offered his carriage for her use. Now only Fowler, the Duchess, Velvet, Lord Worthing, and Eleanor remained in the blue sitting room.

"Aunt Agatha, you are a social genius, my Dear," Fowler reached over to pat her hand. They sat together on a settee, both lounging into the cushions, exhausted by the evening.

The Duchess's eyes twinkled with delight. "It was quite delicious, was it not? All the obstacles are behind us; my girls simply need to enjoy the rest of this Season's activities."

"They both deserve it," Fowler nodded at Velvet and Eleanor, "and they owe their success to you, Your Grace." He stood as he spoke. "As I have an early appointment with my solicitor, I am to bed." He bent to kiss Ella's cheek. "You were magnificent tonight, Eleanor. I have never seen you look more beautiful. Our mother must be beaming in Heaven this evening as she looks down upon her daughter." She reached up to cup his jaw line with a loving caress. Then Fowler took Velvet's hand and brought her fingers to his lips for an extended display of affection. "My Dear, you are a diamond among pearls. Our family is blessed to have you amongst us." He wanted to say more, but he judiciously withdrew instead.

Not ten minutes later, Agatha followed. "My old bones need their rest. I shall not be available before noon tomorrow. You are leaving soon, Worthing?" indicating he should not stay without a chaperone.

"I am, Your Grace," he assured her, but he would not leave until Ella sent him away.

For another twenty minutes, he, Ella, and Miss Aldridge made small talk. Ella's cousin gave both Fowler and the Duchess time to reach their beds before she made her own announcement of retiring. "I will tell your brother I saw His Lordship leave," she proclaimed out of nowhere, and then she stood to depart. "Please do not tarry too long, Eleanor. I do not wish to be in Bran's bad graces."

He looked on as Ella squeezed Velvet's hand and mouthed the words "thank you" before hugging her cousin good night. James considered his own gratitude. Miss Aldridge kept her word of providing them time together. "Release the staff," Ella told Velvet. "I will see Lord Worthing out." James's heart skipped a beat. Miss Aldridge nodded and left the room, pointedly closing the door behind her.

Nervously, Ella turned to where he now stood. She had asked for this privacy, but she, apparently, had never expected it to happen so easily. On impulse, she had requested that he stay simply because they needed each other's company. Now, *his Amazon* knew not what to say or do, and he found that very endearing.

James knew what to do, however, and he immediately crossed the room, locked the door, and then turned to take her into his embrace. He lifted her chin with his fingertips and lowered his mouth to Ella's, needing a long, slow kiss to quench his thirst. She tasted of wine and of Eleanor—a totally delicious combination, and he was drunk with desire. Ella opened her mouth, an invitation in which he gladly partook.

"Come," he said when he finally released her. James led her to a settee, before extinguishing all the lights but one located on the far wall, leaving them draped in shadows and in secret. Returning to where she sat, he gathered her into his arms and lifted Ella gently to his lap. "I have been picturing this since supper," he whispered into her hair, as Ella leaned her head on his shoulder and slid her arms around him.

"I should protest your forwardness, Lord Worthing."

"But you will not." He traced lines of heat up and down her arms with his fingertips.

Ella spread light kisses along his jaw line and cheek. "No... never where you are concerned."

James returned to her mouth, drinking deeply of her lips—exploring it with his tongue. "God, Ella, I want you," he moaned. "I mean to have you as my own." He growled as he invaded her mouth again, exploring her warmth. And then he cupped her breast. Unlike before, Ella did not stiffen with his touch, and James gloried in the knowledge she was learning to trust him. Continuing to kiss her with all the desire he held, he squeezed and stroked, feeling her breast swell under his ministrations. Finally, he slid his fingers along the dress's neckline, teasing the nipples, fondling them with his contact. The buds hardened, a delightful reward, and Ella groaned in response.

She tilted her head away from him, and James let his mouth slide to her neck and finally to the swell of her breasts. He trailed wet kisses all over her, sucking gently at her skin, and raking along her pulse with his teeth. Ella's chest rose and fell with desire, and he was so swollen he thought himself in pain, but he ignored it all. Ella needed him to teach her about love, to take it slow, and so he would.

"Let me taste you," he whispered close to her ear before sucking once on the lobe.

Her eyes opened wide, but James silenced her objections with his mouth. "I will not hurt you, Ella. I will wash away all the evil that once surrounded you. Let me love you, Ella. You deserve to be loved by someone who worships you," he coaxed.

Making a conscious decision, Ella relaxed across the settee's arm, allowing him access to his desires. As he kissed and licked and nipped at her neck, James loosened her ties from behind with his left hand, while continuing to caress her breasts with his right. Finally, he raised his head, and quite ceremoniously, he lowered the front of Ella's gown and exposed her breasts to his stare. They were round and full, and, oh, so tempting, and he knew she reddened in embarrassment, for he felt the heat of her against his fingers. "Beautiful," he murmured. "Breathtakingly beautiful."

Purposely, he moaned as he lowered his head to lick her nipples, tracing the bud with his tongue and blowing a stream of warm air over the wetness, aware of how Ella arched toward him, pressing her breasts to his mouth, requiring something she did not even know existed. When he placed his lips over her nipple and began to suck, Ella sighed with relief.

Her reaction fueled James's madness, and he sucked harder, taking her into his mouth—scraping his teeth over one bud while palming the other with his free hand. Soon Ella's breathing became shallow, and her body began to thrust as if needing an elusive intangible to push her over the edge.

James knew what she sought, and as he continued to suckle her, he reached down to catch the skirt's hem and began to edge it upward. Captivated by this new intimacy, he questioned whether he should elevate this experience to the next level after having, literally, lowered her "guard," but his hand moved on its own, enthralled by her hips' rotations, seeking release. Fully exposing her legs to his touch, he moved his fingers in small circles along her inner thighs, pushing closer to her most private part. Higher and higher he traced lines across her pelvis before loosening the ribbon holding her drawers and opening them fully, rendering her to him. He cupped her mons in his palm, feeling the heat of her explode against his hand. Ella's hips lifted to his warmth, thrusting again and again.

Laying his head across her chest to block Ella's view of what his hand was doing to her nether zone, James's mouth found her other breast. He wanted her to simply feel the pleasure, not to think about it. His fingertips parted the lips, and then he slid a finger into her opening. He heard Ella gasp and her breathing become faster. While sliding the finger in and out of her, sometimes slowly and sometimes with a rougher rhythm, James continued to lave her breast with the rough texture of his tongue.

When she quickened her force against his hand, James returned to her lips. As he did so, his thumb began to circle the nub at the opening to her wetness. He slid the one finger out all the way, and before she sighed in complaint, he guided two in, feeling her lift to him. Now, his tongue mimicked the glide of his fingers. He touched the inside of her and rubbed her core with a demanding desire to satisfy her completely. Ella gave herself up to him, arching to him again and again, riding the crest of pleasure he invoked in her. And then she became painfully still, and he knew when the dam broke, and she quivered into his palm. The muscles inside her contracted around his fingers while his thumb milked the last of the climax from her.

Tears trickled from the corners of her eyes when he raised his head to look at her. Ella's bottom lip, swollen from the pressure of his kiss, trembled with desire and relief and an unspoken devotion. "You are my bane, Eleanor Fowler." His own breathing fought to return to normal as he lowered her skirt across her legs.

"What was that?" she whispered. She lay across his lap, her breasts fully exposed to his sight. She did not open her eyes, languidly enjoying what had just happened to her.

James brushed his lips over hers. "That, my Love, is passion—pure, unaltered passion. When you are mine, I plan to drown you in it—to smother you in love." He kissed her closed lids and the tip of her nose. Restoring the front of her dress to its proper place, he lifted her to him. "It will be a Herculean act for me to leave you, but I cannot defile you even though every nerve in my body is screaming for more. You must now understand how very precious you are to me, Eleanor. As soon as your brother allows, I will declare myself openly to the world, and if you agree, we will marry before the Season ends."

She wrapped her arms around his neck, happy in the contentment he brought to her life. "You will call tomorrow?" she murmured close to his ear.

"Not until later in the day." He sat her forward and began to tighten her dress's strings. "I am to call on Mrs. Cavendish tomorrow so I might release her to Sir Neville's care."

"Shall you be sorry?" Ella now stood so as to adjust her clothing properly; James lingered behind her, tying off the ribbons. Never fully assured of her own power over him, Ella looked away.

Recognizing her body's tension, James kissed her neck's nape. "It is time. Maybe if I had found someone else, I might still require Mary's services upon occasion; although for some time, I have seen the arrangement's futility." He turned Ella into his embrace. "Eleanor, I loved Elizabeth with a young man's fascination, and I decided some time ago I could not remarry unless I found a love of equal merit. Then you walked into my life, and my world tilted, sending me off the end and plunging me into a desire to protect and love only you. I need no one else; you are the blood that courses through my veins. Without you, I do not exist."

Ella's mouth tilted upward for a kiss. "Then I will see you at the Donne's soiree?"

"You shall, Lady Eleanor." He caught her hand. "You must be to bed," he said as he pulled her toward the main hall. "Without me," he winked and then teasingly ran his hands up and down her arms before he reached for the door. Pausing, he added, "Yet, that shall not be for long. Once we marry, you and I will sleep in each other's arms for the rest of our lives. Good night, my Love." He kissed her cheek before letting himself out the main door.

Eleanor slid the bolt into place and then returned to the drawing room. She straightened the pillows and retrieved her discarded drawers, making sure nothing in the room would betray what had happened there. "How can I ever enter this room without thinking of James?" she whispered aloud. He had called her *his love* and said she was *the blood* that kept him alive. How marvelously salacious! Ella hugged herself joyously and twirled around the room before rushing up the stairs to her own chambers. The heat of James Kerrington's mouth on her lips and her breasts and the feel of his hands upon her body still lingered. Tonight she would dream of a marriage proposal and a wedding before the Season's end.

~~~

The room filled in the afternoon, a plethora of gentlemen vying for their attentions, but neither Velvet nor Eleanor cared. Velvet minded only the fact that Brantley Fowler called on Mrs. Warren at her lodgings. In fact, she was so vexed by his sudden interest in this particular military widow that she was very nearly rude to all her potential suitors. Eleanor cared only for her dreams of last night, and her disinterest in her callers showed. Both women feigned exhaustion from their Come Out ball and sent the men on their way earlier than usual.

"How could Bran?" Velvet whined once they were alone.

"I am sure my brother is simply looking for a suitable companion. He assumes you do the same," Ella reminded her.

Velvet slammed the pillow she clutched into the chair and then followed it down. "But we both know I am only trying to make him jealous."

"Evidently, you succeeded in convincing Bran you took Lord Godown seriously."

Frustrated, Velvet bit her lower lip. "I do not know what else I might do to make Bran notice me."

"Maybe you should just tell him the truth—stop playing games," Ella suggested. She thought how such silliness would never work with James Kerrington, and her brother and Lord
~~~

Worthing shared some of the more essential qualities.

"Oh, yes, I can hear me now: 'Bran, I want you to love me as I love you.' He would laugh me out of his study and marry me off to the first interested caller." Velvet punched the pillow again. "The thing is—how may I compete with Mrs. Warren? She knows how to talk to men about something besides hats and parties. She knows how to kiss a man—fuel his desire."

"You know about things other than fashion," Ella protested. "Did not Bran seek your help with the cottagers?"

"But I do not know how to kiss a man and make him want me."

Ella laughed lightly. "I should hope not, Cousin."

"How do you kiss Lord Worthing?"

Ella flushed with color. "I beg your pardon."

"Come, Ella; it is important. How did you know what to do? Lord Worthing is definitely besotted with you."

Ella looked about uncomfortably, wishing she had never partaken of this conversation. "I have no secrets to share, Cousin. I simply allowed His Lordship some freedoms, and he showed me what he wants from his partner."

Velvet considered this tidbit carefully. "Maybe I should petition Bran to teach me how to kiss," she thought aloud.

"I do not think I want to hear this. The less I know of your schemes to win my brother's heart, the better."

Suddenly, Velvet was on her feet. "I need to make plans. Some way, I need to convince Bran to teach me about love. It is sure to work; I am positive of it. How can your brother resist me once we kiss repeatedly?"

Ella stammered, "I…I still believe telling Bran the truth would be best."

"Forgive me if I seek my own counsel," Velvet declared. "You have just admitted you know nothing about making a man love you. It is obvious that His Lordship adores you, but you did naught to earn his regard. He pursued you; you did not have to even lift a little finger." Velvet was already moving toward the door. "With

Bran, I have to do it all, but one day he will thank me for showing him what he needs in life."

"Velvet," Ella called, trying to stop her, but her cousin was halfway up the stairs. Alone in the room, Ella rested across the settee upon which she had shared intimacies with Kerrington the previous night. *Was Velvet right? Had Lord Worthing pursued her?* She knew him to be more experienced, and for the most part, she let him lead the way, but she took chances, like the kiss in his library. Did she need to do more? *She had not even told James of her devotion to him.* He expressed his adoration all the time, but she only accepted his words—never saying them back to him. *Tonight. Tonight, I will tell James Kerrington how much I love him.*

Some time later, engrossed in her thoughts of Lord Worthing, Ella resented the tap on the door that interrupted her private time. A footman brought in a note on a silver salver addressed to her. She lifted it from the tray and examined it. She did not recognize the handwriting nor was there a marking in the wax. She hoped it was from James, but she knew inherently it was not, even before she opened it. Her hands nervously broke the seal, and she unfolded two pages, one nestled inside the other.

The inserted page resembled one from a diary or journal, and she curiously turned it over in her hand several times before opening it.

3 November

The young girl is lovely—looking no more than fourteen or fifteen at most. Evidently, Robert had visited her before, for she did not seem at all surprised to see him or her father.

Ella's breath came in short bursts; her hands shook so violently she could barely see the paper. The page spoke of her.

Her father, bare-chested, sat behind her, after stripping off the child's nightgown. He held her to him, her naked form pressed against the Duke's chest, his arms around the girl's thin waist. With his own hands, he cupped his daughter's developing breasts and lifted them so Robert's mouth might touch them. I watched with some fascination as my husband took pleasure in the young girl's body. Robert suckled her like a babe, and I found my own breasts swelling in response.

I never wanted this; I simply wanted my husband to touch me again as if he desired me. The wine and the black powder Robert shared made my head dull with reason, but I could not look away as Robert began to touch himself as he suckled the girl. It was too much. Like a wanton courtesan, I shoved Robert back on the girl's bed and mounted him.

Ella remembered that evening as if it were yesterday. Her father often came to her room late at night when everyone else was asleep. Her mother was but two months in the grave when he first came to her, telling her he needed to know she loved him. When she swore she did, he begged her to prove it. *No one has ever truly loved me, Ella.* And then he would plead with her to touch him because people who loved one another showed it by touching. He placed her hand on him and began to move until he screamed out in what sounded like pain, but which later she found out to be pleasurable for him. For a few weeks, he brought his friend with him, both of them smelling of alcohol and his friend of a sweet tobacco. Her father allowed the new baronet to touch her breasts—only her breasts—although the man bargained for more. That particular night, the Duke brought the man and a woman. When her father caught her to him, he told Ella not to move. If she did, he would make Velvet love him instead. She promised her obedience, and he held her for his friend's pleasure.

I do not know what happened to the girl the Duke called Eleanor. The last I saw of her she clutched her gown to her as she slipped from the room. It was a night of love such as I had never known before. When Robert finished with me, he gave me off to

William Fowler. They were a powerful duo, but I am proud to say I gave them back as good as they got.

The realization of what this meant shook Ella to her core, making her stomach lurch in disgust. Someone knew her secret, someone from the *ton*; her worst fears had just become a reality. James. James would never understand—she would lose him.

Frantically, she flipped to the second page. It was in a different handwriting.

My mother's diary is very explicit. I found it most enlightening. You will have an immediate change of heart, Lady Eleanor, and openly receive me, or else individual pages of the diary shall be mailed to each and every member of the ton. They will all know your shame, and Thornhill will be ruined forever. I shall await you at the Donne's soiree this evening.

L.

Sir Louis Levering. He had proof of her greatest shame: his mother's diary. Levering held all the cards, and he planned to ruin her. Tears sprang to her eyes. She—her stupidity—ruined everything. Because of her—Bran, Velvet, Sonali, James, Aunt Agatha—they would all suffer—because she allowed her father's sickness to invade her life. What could she do now? If she did not do as Levering asked, all of Society would know. The tears flowed easily now, but she dashed them away with her knuckles. She needed to think—needed to find a way out of this mess. Oh, Lord, James! She was to meet James tonight at the party. After what they had shared, how could she ever convince him she cared for another?

First things first—despite how she felt about the baronet, she was going to have to see Louis Levering once more; it was pointless to think otherwise. She would meet Levering tonight and find out what he wanted from her. Somehow she would protect them from herself, after all, she was the phoenix.

Ella wanted to be any place but the Donne's soiree, but her duty to family forced her to do the impossible: accept Louis Levering over James Kerrington. Entering the main room of the Donne's stately home, her eyes automatically searched the assembled throng for Worthing; however, the viscount seemed nowhere to be found. Customarily, he arrived before the Fowlers and greeted her after acknowledging Bran and Aunt Agatha. Part of her applauded his absence, keeping her from having to face him; part of her prayed he was in attendance, wanting desperately to be in his arms and to let him solve this dilemma for her. However, she was alone, as she always was, facing the worst of what William Fowler rained down on them; she could do it again. Somehow she would prevail.

Gabriel Crowden joined them after bowing nicely over the ladies' hands. "I fear I bring bad news," he told the group. "Lord Worthing sends his regrets. The Earl has taken a turn for the worst, and Her Ladyship summoned Kerrington home. He sent word he will return to London as soon as possible."

"Oh, poor Martin Kerrington!" Aunt Agatha exclaimed. "I do so hope this is not as serious as it sounds."

"I will write Worthing in the morning to see if we may be of assistance," Fowler declared.

By silent assent, they began a slow promenade about the room, needing to greet the others in attendance. In doing so, Crowden dropped back to walk with Ella, offering her his arm. "His Lordship was most distressed about missing your company this evening, Lady Eleanor. He asked that I might give you a personal note if you wish to accept it."

"I would, Lord Godown," she whispered.

Without releasing her arm, he took a carefully folded piece of paper from his glove. Bringing her hand to his lips in a show of respect, he helped her palm it for safekeeping, and moments later, Ella slipped it into her reticule to read in private. When they paused to speak to the next of Agatha's "friends," Godown returned to Velvet's side.

At least, I can confront Sir Louis without hurting His Lordship, she thought. However, before she could adjust to that idea, Sir Louis approached with all the confidence of one who had achieved an easy victory. Toadying to the group, he spent time in greeting Fowler and the Duchess with great pomp and circumstance before turning to Ella. "Lady Eleanor, may I prevail upon you to take a stroll with me about the room?"

Ella gritted her teeth, but she managed to say in a civilized tone, "That would be very pleasant, Sir Louis." Ella could feel the look of confusion storming across her family's faces. More than once, they had all expressed their contempt for their neighbor. They would have questions. Placing her hand lightly on the baronet's proffered arm, she forced herself to give him a smile of welcome.

They walked in silence over a quarter of the room. "I do not see Lord Worthing present this evening," he noted with some smugness.

"I believe His Lordship had other obligations." Ella would not discuss James's absence.

Levering clamped his arm to his side, bringing Ella closer to him. "I had hoped you sent the man packing as I asked," he hissed.

"I have had no opportunity to do so, Sir Louis."

He mimicked Crowden's kiss of her hand, keeping her knuckles close to his mouth for an few extra seconds. "Join me on the balcony, Lady Eleanor." The normalcy of his tone frightened her, and Ella considered refusing; but a shake of her head indicated her agreement, and Levering led her onto the darkened terrace. Finding a place where they might speak privately, he guided Ella to the balustrade overlooking the Donne's garden.

"What exactly do you want from me?" Ella demanded, unable to control her need to know the worst.

"Well, ..." Levering stammered. "I was prepared for niceties before our negotiations, but if you prefer to meet my demands right away, then let it be so. As others suspect, my father's passing left me with a pile of gambling debts and unsavory loan connections, but he also left me among his personal effects something more valuable: my mother's diary, written in her own hand. I assumed he originally kept it for sentimental value, and it proved beneficial to both of us. Imagine my surprise to find my parents' intimacies described in such detail. One never knows one's parents, does one?" he half smirked.

"When I first discovered my mother's *musings*, I spoke to the late Duke, and he and I came to an understanding. He paid me for my silence, and things went well initially. Your father's *contributions*, as I called them, kept away my creditors and allowed me some freedom to enjoy my own pleasures. Unfortunately, your father fell ill, and my source of additional income faltered."

Ella interrupted, "If it is just money you need, I have a small income. I will pay you to forget this."

"Ah, Lady Eleanor, you do have a kind heart, my Dear," he feigned compassion. "And there was a time I might have considered such a solution, but I no longer look so kindly on the prospects. First, my own indulgences caused me to rethink how I meet my obligations. I thought, before your brother's return, that I might have a kindred spirit at Thorn Hall; your Cousin Leighton shares some of my proclivity for the finer things in life, but His Grace's succession eliminated that point of union."

Levering paused to give her time to fathom the depth of what he would propose. "So, all this leaves me with few choices. I need money, and I need it quickly. As your brother has such strong connections with those in the government, I cannot conceive he would be willing to negotiate for the sale of my mother's diary. Your brother holds a reputation for his rashness; it is likely he would simply allow Thornhill to suffer. He has thumbed his nose at Society on more than one occasion. But I believe your dowry will go a long way toward making Huntingborne Abbey debt free."

"You expect me to marry you?" Ella stood agape. She had anticipated having to pay Levering for the diary; she had never thought he would demand her personally.

"I insist that you marry me, my Dear." He touched her cheek with his fingertip. "I found myself quite aroused upon reading my mother's account. I decided I wanted to taste you myself. A woman of such wanton ways can be very stimulating, and I mean to have you—to use you over and over again." His voice became menacing, as his finger dipped into the cleavage displayed by her gown's low décolletage. "Your brother and his friends have treated me with a certain amount of contempt. It will be extremely satisfying to see Worthing suffer, knowing you are my wife, and I have rights he will never hold."

"Eleanor," Velvet's voice came from some ten feet away, "Aunt Agatha requests that you join her."

Neither Levering nor Ella said any more, but a satisfied smile played across his face. Ella simply turned to follow her cousin into the crowded room, while Sir Louis remained in the darkness.

"Ella," Velvet hissed, "what were you thinking?"

Ella had plenty of which to think, but she hid her feelings. "The baronet and I were simply speaking of Kent and our parents. I lost track of time is all."

"Explain it to Bran."

Ella would love to explain it all to Bran and let him handle the baronet, but she suspected a certain amount of truth in what Levering said. Bran would try to stare down the *ton*, daring them to defy what he said, while they all would know of what she did to convince her father to love her. "I will not answer to my brother or anyone else. If I choose to keep company with the baronet or any man, it is my prerogative. Bran brought me to London against my wishes so I might meet a variety of suitors. Sir Louis saved my life, and now he wishes to call on me. I should, at least, give him the benefit of the doubt."

"What of Lord Worthing?" Velvet resisted what she saw as Eleanor's unreasonableness.

Ella stopped suddenly, needing to convince her closest confidante. Like a yawning, gaping hole, James Kerrington's absence produced a physical pain—a hurt that Ella was not sure she could survive, phoenix or not. "It is likely His Lordship will be in Derbyshire for some time—either nursing the Earl back to health or dealing with his father's passing. Am I to become a recluse just as the Season is becoming its most active, simply because Lord Worthing deals with family responsibility? That hardly seems fair. Besides, it will give me an opportunity to see if Lord Worthing is truly a proper choice or whether I look at him through rose-colored glasses."

Velvet looked doubtful. "But you love Lord Worthing!"

"I love the idea of Lord Worthing," Ella corrected. "His absence will allow me to decide if I might find other men equally agreeable. I believe I am acting quite responsibly."

"If you are sure, Cousin."

They reached the Duchess's side. Ella stood tall, daring any of her family to defy her before they had even expressed their concerns. She needed time to somehow figure a way out of this mess, and she did not have the patience to deal with their allegiance to Lord Worthing. My goodness, did she not also hold an allegiance to the man? But she needed to protect herself. She noted that Velvet gave Bran a warning shake of her head as they approached, and, fortunately, her brother swallowed his objections and made no comments.

As she hung back in a large palm's shadows, she replayed the entire conversation with Sir Louis. He needed her dowry to vanquish the debts of Robert Levering, as well as the baronet's own accounts. Sir Louis also knew in what she participated as a young girl, and he now demanded that she allow him liberties a gentleman would not request of his wife. If she married the baronet to save her family, such perversions would be the norm. The thought of it sent a shiver down her back. How could she tolerate the baronet's touch after the love she experienced in James Kerrington's arms? How could she live such a life? She would be dirty again. Her past would soil her future. Fleetingly, she considered running away—going to America or Australia to lose her identity in the wilderness—or even going to the extreme of ending it all, taking her own life—but Bran and Velvet and Aunt Agatha, and even James, would continue to suffer. The baronet would see to that if she tried to foil his plans by removing herself from the picture. No! She would face this and persevere.

Chapter 8

~ ~ ~

THE NEXT DAY, TO HER FAMILY'S DISMAY, Ella rode out with the baronet in the afternoon during the fashionable hour, but she offered no explanation as to what brought on her extreme change of heart. She refused to read Worthing's note; it remained tucked away in a pocket inside her evening reticule. Ella knew that if Kerrington spoke of his love, she would never be able to deal with Louis Levering's demands.

"Thank you for accepting my company, Lady Eleanor." The baronet maneuvered his curricle through the busy London streets.

Ella stared at the buildings, refusing to look at him. "Did I have another option?"

"Please do not sound so bitter, my Dear." He took her hand, placing it on his arm. "Despite what you might believe at this moment, we will do well together."

Ella left her hand on his forearm, but kept the muscle taut, in reality, barely touching him. "I am not what you think, Sir Louis. I was a young girl seeking the love of a difficult parent. My naiveté does not make me the type of woman of which you speak."

"However, such affections are not foreign to you. Any man would welcome a gentlewoman willing to accept her husband's desires."

"If I do all you ask, will you turn over the diary to me?" It was time for her own negotiations.

Levering paused as if debating over what she asked. "I would have you and your fortune; I would have no need of the diary any longer." Eleanor wondered if she dared to believe him. He turned his carriage into the main gate to Hyde Park. "We will make one pass through the park, Eleanor." She tried not to cringe with his use of her given name. "I expect you to give me the proper attention. Now, smile, my Dear."

Although she did not trust him explicitly, Ella took some comfort in his acknowledging he would meet her demands. They spent the next hour greeting acquaintances. Most of their acknowledgments were met with badly disguised shock or curiosity. A duke's daughter would rarely consider a baronet a good match. Taking five steps downward in peerage simply was not done unless theirs was a love match, and that was not likely. Plus, the *ton* wondered what had happened to Lord Worthing. He had been paying exclusive interest to Eleanor Fowler, and now, it was rumored, he had left town.

"Just yonder is where I reined in your horse." The baronet broke their silence, pointing off to the left.

Ella placidly nodded, thinking how it was all so ironic. She wished desperately that that day had never happened.

He leaned close to give her a mocking smile. "You were never in any danger."

Ella looked confused when she turned to where he sat.

"I only meant to frighten you," he confessed.

Quickly, the truth registered on her face. "You arranged my attack?"

"It was not an attack, my Dear—simply a way for me to renew our acquaintance. Of course, your friend Lord Worthing created a real hubbub with his misplaced pursuit, but it all worked out." He gestured to a passing acquaintance. "I wanted you to know that although your brother is a duke, he does not hold all the power, and even someone like me can wield revenge."

"Revenge?" she whispered, her movement suspended by the menace in his voice.

"You never asked, Lady Eleanor, how my mother died." He scowled in remembrance.

Eleanor swallowed hard, afraid of the answer he was likely to give. "What caused Lady Levering's demise?"

"I suspect my mother's death had the same source as did your mother's. Her relationship with your father and mine cost my mother her life. The great pox—although truthfully, I prefer to call it, as did William Blake, 'the youthful harlot's curse'—is the enemy of both our families, but the initial source of our losses is your father's baseness."

"As much as I despise that for which my father stood, I must protest the premise of your accusations. My father never forced your parents to participate in his entertainments. They made the choice as adults to enjoy those pleasures. My mother loved my father, and she wanted children; she knew her duty as a gentlewoman of the aristocracy, and despite her awareness of the risks he took in his personal life, my mother chose to accept him into her bed. Those were my mother's reasons. I cannot explain why Lady Levering chose to join your father in his pursuits. She, obviously, had her seducements. Can you honestly say, Sir Louis, you know your mother's thoughts? From the excerpt you so 'kindly' shared with me, Lady Levering experimented not only in your father's earthy pleasures, but also his opium habits. My father never found a need for clouding his senses. You may charge my family with the downfall of yours, but you will be in error, Sir." Ella braced herself for his retort.

However, Levering said nothing for several minutes, letting his cold silence invade her thinking. "I can see you are no milksop, Lady Eleanor—a fact I will savor as our relationship progresses—yet, I must warn you, I will not tolerate impudence in public. You will behave as I instruct you." He did not finish the threat—his tone filled with danger. "I will give your logic points, my Dear, but emotions do not bow to reason. My mother was the only one who ever truly loved me. For some unexplained reason, I was a disappointment to my father. I will retaliate in her memory in the only way available to me." They finished their turn through the park, and he edged his team out into the street traffic. "So, as you can see, I possess several legitimate arguments for seeing this through: my mother's death, my mounting debts, and Society's snubs."

"Then you will not reconsider—will not simply accept my buying your cooperation?" She seemed resigned to what he purported.

"By the week's end, I will present myself to Thornhill. The announcements will appear in the *Times*, and the banns will be called. I expect you to convince your brother of your heart's change." He reined in the team before Briar House. "Now, offer me a smile as I hand you down. Your cousin watches from the window, and I would have her see your growing affection for me." Levering hopped down and extended his hand for her support. As he instructed, Ella smiled at him before dropping her eyes. Levering kissed her knuckles and then escorted her to her door. Raising the knocker, he murmured close to her ear, "We will attend the theatre tomorrow evening—alone." The door opened, and Ella slipped in, thankful for not having to respond verbally to his demands.

~ ~ ~

James Kerrington sat at his desk at Linton Park. His father still teetered on the brink; his health could go one way or the other. Yet, as much as he worried about his parents, his thoughts dwelled on one person: Eleanor Fowler. What was she doing? Did she miss him as much as he missed her? Every time he closed his eyes he saw her face—her neck's sleek line, the glow in her eyes when she looked at him, the smell of lavender she left on his clothes, and the feel of her lips under his mouth's press. It had been three days since he had seen her, and James ached with a need he could not explain. "I love you, Eleanor." He heard the words ringing in his head.

He had written her again today. It was an act of impropriety; they were not engaged, but he could not resist. Eleanor instantly had become his life's light, the all-sustaining air he breathed. He hoped she would break the rules and answer his messages. He needed for Ella to understand his absolute devotion to her and his dreams of their future. Sealing the letter with blue wax, he sent it on its way. Soon, he would return to London and claim her as his own—*his Amazon*.

~ ~ ~

Every day, his letters came as regularly as clockwork. Her Aunt Agatha buried her objections, obviously hoping Lord Worthing's words might save her niece, but Ella maintained her feigned "devotion" to the pretentious Louis Levering. She did not like deceiving her family. She too had counted the days to His Lordship's declaration, but not for the same reasons. The Dowager Duchess saw the advantages of temperament and status. Worthing would soon be an earl, an appropriate connection for a duke's daughter. However, Ella desired James Kerrington because he taught her love—accepted her past mistakes as childhood gullibility. And what could Levering offer her? An unacceptable diminished status. A questionable title drenched in debt. Rumors of impropriety nearly as corrupt as that of the late William Fowler.

"Another letter from Lord Worthing?" Her aunt watched as Ella slipped the missive into her pocket. They sat in the morning room, enjoying a late breakfast. "Does His Lordship speak of his father's health?"

"I would not know. I have read none of them." Ella busied herself by spreading jam on her toast—anything to keep the focus off her words.

Aunt Agatha put down the newssheet she surveyed for the latest gossip. "I am not an advocate of His Lordship's bending the rules of etiquette by writing to you directly, but it seems that if you choose not to read them, you should return the letters to Kerrington. Accepting them indicates that you also accept his attentions, my Dear."

"I suppose you are correct, Aunt." It was all Ella would say on the matter. She should send the letters back if she was to accept Sir Louis's proposal, but Ella kept them for selfish reasons. She would spend a lifetime with Levering, and James's letters would be her salvation. She would cherish them and keep them safe and remember when someone actually loved her. Otherwise, she would spend her whole life unloved. Therefore, each day she locked them in a box of mementos—things cherished from her childhood and from happier times.

"You wished to speak to me, Bran?" Eleanor knew why he had summoned her to his study; she had seen Levering make his call earlier. She stared at her hands and frowned.

Bran rose to meet her. "Come in, Ella." He led her to the chairs before the hearth—more personal than the desk chairs. "I wish to consult with you on a matter of importance."

Stalling, she straightened her dress's seams. "I suppose I know of what you speak." She did not look at him directly; Ella always had trouble lying to her brother and purposely avoided the eye contact.

"Sir Louis called earlier. He tells me he has made you an offer of marriage, and you have accepted. Is that correct, Ella? You accepted Louis Levering?"

"I have, Bran. It is acceptable to me in every way." Since the baronet made his demands, she had spent the past week generating *excuses* for her acquiescence. "Louis is agreeable, and he expresses a growing affection. I believe he and I will get along well together. However, the main reason I seriously considered the baronet's plight is that Huntingborne Abbey is our nearest neighbor to Thorn Hall. I might see you regularly—daily if I like. Our children will grow up together. We were separated for so long, Bran; I cannot bear it again, and if you and Velvet resolve your differences, we might all go on as before."

Bran's suspicious look did not go unnoticed. "What of Lord Worthing?"

"His Lordship is nearly ten years my senior. We have so little in common; I was unaware of the discrepancy until I became more acquainted with Sir Louis. The baronet and I have had many similar experiences." Ella thought it best to speak the truth—although not the whole truth.

"You have explained this to Lord Worthing? He has expectations."

"I never promised anything to the Viscount. Even now, I refuse to answer his letters. I do not wish to give him false hope." Ella fought her emotional allegiance to Lord Worthing. For weeks, she had thought only of him. Now, she thought only of herself—of her survival.

Other than the span between their social ranks, Ella knew that Bran had no legitimate reason to deny the baronet's request, but she realized he would not honestly give her his blessing. However, to convince him she would remind her brother of his promise to allow her to marry whom she chose. Ella saw him bite back his objection. "It was my wish, Ella, for you to enjoy a Season. Your devotion to Thorn Hall denied you that experience. It was not my desire for you to give yourself to another. Like you, I do not want us to part so soon after our reunion. May I suggest a compromise? Your relationship with the baronet seems a bit impetuous. I would prefer you wait until the end of the Season to announce your engagement. It will give us all time to become familiar with Levering and to welcome him into our family."

Fear coursed through her. How would she silence the rumors for so long? "I am sure Sir Louis will insist on a speedier course of events. He would like the announcement next week and the banns called immediately afterwards." Ella wondered how Levering would react to Bran's stipulations. She knew he would not be happy; Sir Louis would see it as another snub.

Bran smiled his assurance. "Eleanor, you are the daughter of a duke and the sister of a duke; your wedding will not take place in some out-of-the-way chapel. You will be married, at a minimum, at St. George; your family will want to plan a magnificent wedding. One cannot do that in a matter of weeks. You know what Aunt Agatha will do if we try to spurn our responsibilities. Having you gloried in the best light is the Dowager Duchess's motivation for coming to town this Season."

Ella looked away nervously. "I have never desired such opulence."

Her brother ignored her objection. "It is your birthright, Ella. I will not have you denied your place in Society."

"Sir Louis will insist on, at least, an *understanding*, a pre-nuptial agreement, being apparent between us."

Bran stood to end the conversation. "I will speak to Levering personally and explain what it means to marry into the dukedom. The connections will benefit him; therefore, the baronet will accept what I say as the final conditions to your union. He is a sensible man and will agree once I explain things to him."

Ella prayed that Bran was correct; she could not imagine Levering to be so benevolent. With his plans ruined, she would likely pay the price.

If Ella had considered her brother's nature, she would have realized that Bran plotted against her hasty decision; but Ella was too consumed with the misery of her own life to understand that the man who would rescue complete strangers in trouble would call upon all his resources to save his only sister from making the worst mistake of her young life.

"You have convinced the baronet to wait?" Crowden asked as he sipped a brandy, casually extending his leg across a hammock.

Fowler snarled his dislike of the subject. "Levering is most anxious to finalize his marriage. Considering he asked three times the conditions of Eleanor's dowry, I suspect he is spending her settlement before the nuptials are read."

"Has Lady Eleanor told Kerrington of her change of heart?" Crowden looked worried. Everyone associated with the Fowlers had recognized Worthing's obvious love for Eleanor. They all hated to see his heart crushed again.

"She has not." Bran absentmindedly ran his finger around the glass's rim. "I take it upon myself to inform him. I will not have Worthing return to London expecting Eleanor to receive him nor will I have him hear it secondhand."

"What do you want me to do?"

"Find out everything you can about Levering. Leave no stone unturned. I want to know when he gets up in the morning and when he goes to bed at night and everything in between. What attracts my sister to the man? Everything I know of Ella says she should feel revulsion, not affection. Something in my gut says Levering is not what he appears. I demanded a delay to make this right for Ella."

The Marquis finished off his drink. "I will see to it immediately. Possibly, we need to bring in someone the baronet does not know."

"John Swenton or Aidan Kimbolt?"

"I was thinking both. Kimbolt can weasel his way into anyone's company, and Swenton knows every gaming hell in London. If Levering has debts, John will discover who holds the baronet's blunt."

Bran made himself some notes. "You will take care to bring them up to date?"

"Absolutely, Your Grace." Crowden eased from the chair. "Will you escort Mrs. Warren this evening?"

"I must marry eventually and set up my nursery. I am just looking at the possibilities."

His friend nodded his understanding, but Crowden made his own suggestion. "Look at *all* the possibilities, Your Grace. It is an important decision for any man."

~ ~ ~

James hesitantly opened the letter from Brantley Fowler. He had heard from Ella's family only once—right after his return home—now it was a fortnight later. He had continued to write to Eleanor each day, but he had yet to receive even one word in response. At first, he had told himself it was because Eleanor would not want anyone to know of her growing ardor; however, each day had brought him such disappointment. His heart ached for her. Feeling the ax preparing to fall, James reluctantly read the letter: Bran's message spelled things out quite plainly.

Worthing,

I pray this letter finds you well. We at Briar House remember the Earl and all your family in our daily devotion. If you require anything, a simple word will send me rushing to your side. You are one of my closest friends.

As such, it falls on my shoulders to inform you of my sister Eleanor's acceptance of Sir Louis Levering's proposal of marriage. As you are aware, I wished Ella to enjoy a Season, so I have insisted that the couple wait until the end of this year's social calendar to exchange their vows. Ella has expressed a desire to remain close to Thorn Hall after all our years of separation, and Sir Louis's estate is our nearest neighbor. We may see each other daily if we choose. Our children will know one another as more than distant cousins.

As your friend, I would not have you return to London without prior knowledge of these events.

Thornhill

Pure cold rushed through his veins. He had lost her, but there was no way James could purge Eleanor Fowler from his heart or from his mind. He reread the short note three times trying to comprehend how it could be so. The night before he had left London, he held Eleanor in his arms and gave her pleasure. He knew her—inside and out. James knew her eccentricities and her delights. *How could she willingly give herself to another man?* Did she not understand she was the other half of his heart? These sobering thoughts plagued him.

"Sir Louis!" He screamed as he threw the nearest thing upon which he could get his hands. A Grecian-styled urn smashed and crumbled against the far wall, and he did not stop there. One after another he destroyed decorative pieces he had cherished for years.

For elongated minutes, no one entered the room, until Lady Linworth jerked open the door. "James Martin Kerrington, put down that vase this moment!" she ordered. "Have you lost your mind?"

It was a moot point; James turned slowly to his mother, utter agony evident on his face. "Yes, Mother, I have lost my mind and my soul and much more than I can ever explain." With that, he strode from the room, barking orders to everyone in sight.

He had ridden hard most of the day, hoping the pounding and the abuse his body took would ease his heart's pain, but it made little difference. Now, as he finished off his first decanter of brandy, alone in his own chambers, James found that no amount of alcohol lessened the hurt. *How could Eleanor Fowler pretend that nothing had happened?* Had he misjudged her so completely? *Maybe she was as wanton as her father's reputation!* Yet, even as he thought it, he knew it was impossible. Ella's innocence was never in doubt. As he further analyzed each of their interactions over the last few months, he saw how his obsession had grown. He could not get enough of her, but, in reality, as he considered it, only once did Ella kiss him without his initiating it; and that was after the attack in Hyde Park. Could she have just been tolerating his advances? The kisses—possibly, but not what happened after her Come Out ball. She had maneuvered his presence in the family room. Ella wanted him; he was sure of it.

Sitting in his chambers in the dark, he forced himself to face the truth. Eleanor simply did not care for him even a fraction of what he felt for her. He was her *security*—someone to whom she turned when she felt uncomfortable around strangers. He was, after all, her brother's friend. Well, she would not see him again; he would be no one's second best. Whether his father improved or not, James would not return to London this Season—maybe ever. He could choose a lady from the country when he was ready to take a wife—someone like Miss Alice Westerly. She was pretty enough, after all. With Daniel, he had his heir; it was not necessary for him to produce another. He might never marry again. Trying to replace Elizabeth was foolish in the first place; a perfect love could not be found twice in a lifetime. A second decanter awaited him as his declaration sprang to his lips. "To hell with you, Eleanor Fowler!"

~~~

"James," his mother tapped on his study's door. "May I come in?"

Still half inebriated—a hangover from the brandy dulled his senses—he forced himself to his feet to welcome his mother to his private domain. "Certainly," he said as he went to lead her to a nearby chair.

Lady Linworth no more took her seat before she began her prodding. "James, I am concerned about what happened yesterday. It was so uncharacteristic of you; I have not seen you so distraught since Elizabeth's passing. I would like to be of support; your father's illness takes much of my time, but you are still my son, and I worry about you. I was never one to simply visit you in the nursery; I doted on both you and your sister."

"I apologize for giving you any moments of concern, Mother. It will not happen again." James assumed the responsibility for his family with his father's afflictions. He felt guilty for demonstrating his weakness.

Lady Linworth's eyes teared with his words. "I do not criticize your emotional outburst, James. In fact, I am proud that you are not ashamed to show your feelings; it speaks to the depth of the man you have become. My only moments of disquiet come from the fact you suffer alone. I cannot resolve your problems, but I may serve you by listening."

James looked away, uneasy with anyone knowing his grief. "I assure you, it is nothing of consequence."

"Who is she?" Camelia Kerrington probed.

"Really, Mother!"

Her Ladyship ignored his brushing aside her scrutiny. "Considering you spent much of the last month and a half with Brantley Fowler's family, I assume it is someone of His Grace's acquaintance."

James rolled his eyes in disbelief. Last evening over his first decanter of brandy, he had sworn never to say Ella's name again. He wanted to avoid speaking of Eleanor Fowler, but his mother was relentless once she latched onto an idea. Resigned to telling her, he
~~~

began, "I developed a fondness for Fowler's sister Eleanor. That lady, however, has accepted Sir Louis Levering."

"Is Lady Fowler beautiful?"

He smiled at her insistence even though it was a bit frustrating. "Mother, did you not hear me say Lady Eleanor will marry another?"

His mother shook her head in the negative. "The chit is not married, and until she is, do not give up hope. If you really want Lady Eleanor, then you should stake your claim to her. Now, tell me about your lady."

"I wish I had your faith, Mother, but I fear the worst when it comes to Fowler's sister." Could he survive such heartbreak a second time? "Yet, even as I tell myself to forget her charms, I cannot wish her to throw her life away on a man of such low repute as the baronet. According to His Grace, Lady Eleanor speaks of accepting Levering in order to remain close to Thorn Hall and her brother, but the Eleanor I know wanted to see the world and claim her independence." He now fell into an easy narrative regarding Ella.

"You would love her, Mother. Lady Eleanor defies what you think I might choose." He smiled in remembrance. "I often thought of her as *my Amazon*, not that the lady is so warrior-like, but Ella is tall and majestic with golden hair and the greenest eyes one ever saw. The odd thing is, when I found Ella, I quit grieving for Elizabeth. I actually spent whole days when I did not think about what my life was. Instead, I considered what it might be. I suppose that sounds foolish."

Lady Linworth sighed deeply. "It sounds like a man in love."

"But Ella chose another." Kerrington paused for a moment of acceptance. "I must walk away—allow her what happiness she may find elsewhere. However, I shall not return to London for the Season. I must accept Lady Eleanor's choice, but that does not mean I need a front-row seat to watch it happen. Even worse, I also will probably lose my best friend. How might Fowler and I continue as before knowing my feelings for Lady Eleanor?"

"It is a quandary. I will make your heart part of my nightly prayers. It should know peace at last. However, I want to make one point: You must ask yourself whether the woman you just described would willingly turn from you to Levering."

James stood and helped her to her feet. He accepted her interference because he knew she acted out of love. He leaned in for a kiss on his mother's cheek. "I knew perfection once with Elizabeth; I should be satisfied with my lot. Many men never hold happiness in their hands. Why should I think I deserve to feel such purity twice in a lifetime? Fate chose otherwise."

Camelia Kerrington caressed his cheek. "I will agree to stay out of your personal life as you are a man and know your own heart, but I will not tolerate your saying you do not deserve what you desire. You are the best of men."

James chuckled, "You may be prejudiced on my behalf."

"Never," she protested good-naturedly. "I always tell the truth. It is not just a coincidence, however, that the best of men is my son. Your father and I would tolerate nothing less from our boy."

"Then I am fortunate to have such righteous parents. Come; let us have tea. Good English tea solves all our ills. It was one of the things I missed most when I traveled the Continent."

~ ~ ~

And so Ella's life became one long internment, burying her feelings and her ideas and her hopes and her dreams to protect her family. She endured Louis Levering's dictates because she had no choice. She tolerated his bullying, placing a half-turned smile on her lips. What was most difficult was his forwardness in touching her. He often stroked the side of her leg or ran his finger across the rise of her breast. Each time Levering touched her, Ella suppressed the shiver of revulsion running through her veins.

"I look forward to burying myself in your radiance, my Dear," Levering whispered close to her ear as the back of his hand brushed against her breast when no one was looking. They sat in a rented box at the theatre, surrounded by the *ton*, the same people who would celebrate the idea of her opprobrious situation. "I promise you will enjoy every moment of our coupling."

"Please, Sir Louis, do not speak so intimately. We are not yet wed," Ella offered a protest, hoping to ward off what she knew he would next say. His verbal familiarity became more and more explicit by the day. "We are in a very public setting, after all."

"First, I cherish the blush my words bring to your cheeks, but why can I not tell my betrothed how I long to bury my cock in her wetness?" He placed her hand over his manhood and squeezed it against him. "See how hard you make me," he murmured. "The lights are down, and no one can see. I want you to rub your hand over me. The idea of your touching me in public is quite ribald."

"Please," Ella pleaded softly. "Do not make me do this."

Levering squeezed her hand tightly, purposely bending two fingers backward to the point of pain. "All I ask is for you to show me affection, Ella," he hissed. "Of course, I understand your objection. I am, after all, *purchasing* your fondness with my mother's diary. However, I had hoped you might soon care for me more than you do your precious Fowler heritage."

Swallowing hard, Ella could not look at him, but she nodded her agreement, and Levering released his grip. Slowly, she moved her hand across his groin, feeling him pump his hips against her. She heard his breathing go shallow, but she never turned her head. Instead, she stared at the stage, tears streaming down her face.

"Excuse me," he gasped close to her. He quickly stepped behind the curtained area at the back of the box. She could hear him as he frantically toyed with the buttons on his breeches to free himself. The sound of sporadic gulps of air told her exactly what he did steps away, shielded from view by the darkness and the velvet drapery. Ella had seen her father do the same thing, knew how Louis's hand moved up and down his own tumescence until she heard his stifled shudder. A few moments later, he returned to sit beside her as if nothing happened. "Thank you, my Dear," he murmured. "That was quite stimulating."

Ella thought she might lose her stomach. "Might we leave, Sir Louis? I could use some fresh air."

"No, my Dear. We will sit here and pretend we have not just delved in the forbidden."

Ella choked back a sob, hiding her face behind her fan. With a convulsive swallow, she stiffened and sat tall, the perfect example of a daughter of the aristocracy. This would be her life—moments of debauchery hidden behind a façade of refinement. How could she live like this? Her only hope was that Sir Louis would leave her at Huntingborne Abbey while he took his perversions elsewhere. If she could live her life in solitude, then maybe she could survive. Solitude. It was her unanswered prayer.

"We will make a trip to Nottingham next week for a house party," Levering announced on their way to Briar House from the theatre.

Ella's head snapped around in surprise. She was purposely watching the busy streets through the carriage window, trying to avoid Levering's close examination. "I do not believe His Grace will approve of our traveling together."

"Then you will come up with a way to convince him. Tell him you travel with a female friend. Your brother does not need to know what we do with our time." Ella recognized the menacing threat behind the flippant tone of his command.

"And if I am not successful?" she ventured.

Levering looked away, pretending to take interest in a drunken ruckus on a lighted street corner. "I noticed Miss Aldridge prefers to walk in Hyde Park each day. Would it not be a shame if she lost her balance and slipped into the murky waters of the Serpentine some day."

He made no effort to mask the warning behind the words. Either Ella complied or Levering would find a way to hurt Velvet. "I will think of something."

"Of course, you will. You are quite resourceful, one of the qualities which endears you to everyone who knows you."

~ ~ ~

Less than a week later, she and Hannah journeyed to Nottingham in Sir Louis's carriage. She had taken an unmarked hack to meet Levering at a posting inn on the London Road. Bran had surprised Ella by allowing her to travel with her "new friend" Miss Nelson to a house party in Leicestershire. Her maid's presence was her brother's only stipulation. Reluctantly, Levering had agreed to tolerate Hannah's traveling with them in the carriage. He would have preferred that Ella's maid ride on the top with his coachman, but Ella had convinced him Hannah would alert Bran of any such impropriety. Persuading Hannah to not disclose they did not journey to Leicestershire would be difficult enough without adding to their duplicity. Ella knew Levering had planned to take advantage of her in his coach's privacy as he had in the theatre box's privacy, more than likely worse than what happened that night.

His plans thwarted, the baronet was not in the best of moods, so both she and Hannah took their cues and sank quietly into the barouche's squabs. Ella pretended to nap while Hannah did so in earnest. Ella listened and watched the man to whom she had committed herself. Besides the blackmail and the inherent threats, Levering of late had taken pleasure in physically hurting her, as he had hurt her hand at the theatre. He always chose a place not readily visible to others. Just the day before yesterday, he had pinched her side so violently he had left a bruise and had brought tears to her eyes. Her offense for his retaliation was tarrying in speaking to Gabriel Crowden in the park. She had felt safe with Godown's closeness and had purposely talked to him longer than the baronet thought appropriate. He had expressed his discontent with the secret abuse.

Now, Ella recognized the man sitting across from her to be a real monster. She had never feared stories of ghosts or goblins as a child, but she recognized evil when she saw it. Louis Levering was pure evil. He did as he chose and blamed everyone else for his failings. That made him a dangerous man. He would hold her responsible for his lot in life, and she would pay the price. In the past few days, she had quit accepting her fate at his hands, and Bran's insistence on her waiting to marry became a blessing of a sort. It gave her a chance to formulate a way out of this mess. She needed to discover where Levering kept the diary and take possession of it before she could withdraw, but, at least, now she hoped to be free of him.

Ella realized that once she became the baronet's wife, nothing could save her. By law, Levering would have the right to do what he wished with her. A husband could legally punish his wife without fear of retribution. Even Bran could not save her, although she was sure her brother would gladly kill Levering for what she already had suffered; but, she would not let her brother give up Thornhill by calling out Levering in a duel. Ella knew Brantley could kill Louis, no matter how much her future husband bragged of his prowess. However, dueling was illegal, and Bran would be forced to leave England again. She refused to let that happen.

It was funny of sorts; as a child and a young girl, she had thought her father the most base of men. Yet, she never once knew of his forcing his attentions on anyone. Even her own mother welcomed William Fowler to her bed. Every maid and bar mistress he had enjoyed over the years accepted his natural persuasion to become involved with him. Many of the household staff served him for years without his demanding their participation in his lust for carnal release. He asked quite often, but William Fowler accepted a refusal even from a lowly maid, and there was no retribution. Hannah, for example, was but a teen when she came to serve seven-year-old Eleanor. Hannah had never suffered because of the late duke—she avoided any dalliance her employer offered.

Ella could not imagine Louis Levering, however, accepting a denial from any servant in his household. If she became the baronet's wife, Ella would leave Hannah behind. She would force no one else to suffer her private hell. When she sought her father's attentions, wanting him to lessen the loneliness after losing both her mother and Bran in one fell swoop, he did love her in the only way he knew how. Her father's fixation lay in desires of the flesh. It was as if he could not help himself. She remembered his crying and begging her forgiveness after touching her, but he returned to her time and time again. However, he never did more than fondle her. In fact, what James Kerrington gave her the night of her Come Out ball was much more intimate than any way her father had used her. It was not as if Ella had forgiven the former duke for how he had manipulated her; she had not—she would not, but she understood the difference between the love Kerrington offered and the obvious sickness from which her father had suffered.

She remembered also how Levering's parents had cleverly attached themselves to the duke, and, needing his own form of acceptance, her father had opened himself to them. Her memories, those she had suppressed for so long, had returned over the last few weeks. She recalled once hiding behind a screen in one of the guests' rooms while witnessing Robert Levering tying his wife to the four-poster and using a whip to take his true pleasure on the woman. She could imagine Louis Levering trying something similar with her. Ella was made to undress in front of them that evening, but they did not touch her—just watched with bestial delight before turning to their own form of profanity. Finally, she had escaped with her father's help. He had strode openly into the room and had wrapped her in his arms. "I will not tolerate anyone hurting Ella," he had declared to the Leverings. "It will not happen." That was the last time she remembered the Leverings being guests at Thorn Hall.

She had never seen her father so incensed. It was the only time she really felt his love. That time, and when, with his last lucid moments, he had told her she was a "good girl." At the time, she had thought he meant to compliment her diligence in caring for him during his sickness and for the estate in his absence. As she reflected on the moment, Ella now wondered if he had hoped to arrest her belief that she was not worthy. It was James Kerrington who had taught her to truly trust herself. He saw a woman he admired—a woman he wanted to love just as she was. She liked the person she saw reflected in His Lordship's eyes.

Quite different from the image she observed when looking at Levering: His countenance hid the ice that flowed through his veins, the flash of a mocking smile, the stony cold roughness barely below the surface. In the inn's private dining room the previous evening, he had twisted her arm behind her back when she resisted his advances, before forcibly pulling her dress down to expose her breasts wrapped tightly in her corset. She had feared he might take her there, but he had amused himself with fondling her breasts and invading her mouth with his tongue.

Setting her away from him, Levering had quickly unbuttoned the front placket of his breeches, freeing his swollen member. Ella had closed her eyes as he encased his rigid manhood in his hand. "Look at me," he hissed. "Watch how I pleasure myself. Of course, I will let you touch me instead if you insist." When she shook her head to refuse, Levering chuckled. "I thought not, but someday you will come to enjoy this as much as I."

Then, in a shameless display, he ignited his own passion, focusing his gaze on her displayed bosom until his jaw locked in fervent pain, and Levering released his seed into the palm of his own hand. Taking the linen napkin from his place setting he wiped himself clean before tossing the cloth into the corner of the room. "Fix your dress," he ordered as he restored his own clothing. "Go to bed and dream of our joining. It will be glorious," he had instructed. "I will have a few drinks with the locals at the bar."

Ella did not argue: She simply escaped as quickly as possible, finding comfort behind a locked chamber door and Hannah's presence on a pallet before the cold hearth.

Chapter 9

~ ~ ~

"IT IS NOTHING BUT A HUNTING BOX," Ella gasped as Levering's carriage rolled into the circular drive before the small house. "I thought we were to meet some of your acquaintances for a country party."

"We are," he taunted, reaching for the coach's handle. "It will be a more intimate party than what you anticipated, my Dear, but it will be a party like no other you have experienced." He stepped from the coach and turned to help her down. "Come, Lady Eleanor, and meet my friends."

Reluctantly, Ella placed her hand in his. *What did the secretive baronet have in mind?* Ella had expected interludes similar to what she had experienced in the inn the previous evening, but she had thought that with the number of people at a house party, she could limit her private time with him to a few incidents. Despite his obvious wish to possess her, until now the baronet had respected her virginity. However, as four gentlemen appeared with their "ladies" to greet Levering, she quickly determined her situation was dire. The men were too casual and the women too free in their attire.

"Ella," he did not even use her title, not a good sign, "these are my old friends, Heath Montford, Gavin Bradley, and Danver Clayton. We have known each other since our school days, and this is a relatively new acquaintance, Allister Collins."

None of the men even offered her a bow of acknowledgment, an indication of the lack of Society she was likely to find inside the house. "And the ladies are Susan, Louisa, Fanny, and Millie." Louis gestured to each woman, accepting a rather passionate kiss from Fanny as he did so. "Hannah, you may join the other staff in the kitchen. I am sure Mrs. Blossom could use your help. Ella will send for you when she needs you."

Realizing Levering wanted no witnesses to what he planned, Ella sent Hannah to the house, assuring her maid she would be fine for a few minutes.

"Let us go inside," Bradley called as he wrapped his arm around Louisa's waist. The others followed suit: Each man claimed one of the ladies as his own, but none of them treated the women with formal respect; they draped their arms about the women, caressing and fondling as they returned to the house.

"How could you bring me here?" Ella demanded as they trailed the others into the house. Levering pulled her close, although he showed no more respect than did the other men.

"My friends wished to meet you, my Dear. I have told them all about you," he tilted his head closer so she might hear him.

Ella jerked her head around to look at him. "You told them what?" she hissed.

"Oh, you mean the diary. No, that is our secret alone, but I told them I believed you to be willing to share your affections with them also."

"You told your friends I would act as a complete wanton?" Ella came to an abrupt halt, forcing Levering to join her before they entered the still-open doorway.

Levering gave her a toothy smile of reassurance. "A complete wanton? No. I said no such thing. I simply indicated you might be willing to participate once you observed the others."

"You simply indicated?" she accused. "I realize you feel a odium for my father's part in your mother's death, but do you despise him so much that you are willing to use me most ill? Have you no respect for me as a person that you offer me up to complete strangers?"

"They will not be strangers long, my Dear. Montford, Bradley, and Clayton are business partners, as well as friends. I owe a great deal of blunt to Collins. He is willing to accept your charms in payment for some of it. It is nothing personal; it is all purely business."

"I am a possession—no better than your dog or your horse." Ella's eyes flashed in anger.

He gave her a soft laugh. In her innocence, she had opened herself up to the perfect retort. "Nonsense. I shall enjoy mounting you more than any horse; whether it be as a dog or not, I am sure I will not care." Levering's lethal smile returned as he caught her chin in his grip, forcing her mouth to his in a demanding kiss. "Go to your room and freshen your clothing," he ordered through clenched teeth. "I will call to bring you down later." To emphasize his point, he brought her arm up sharply behind her back, wrenching it hard for extra measure. "Do as I say when I say it," he warned brazenly as he shoved Ella toward the open entranceway.

Wiggling free of his grasp at last, Ella stumbled toward the stairs—his violence and her own naiveté weakening her ability to move. She was in the middle of nowhere, at least ten miles from the nearest village or farm with no transportation of her own, and no one to help her but an equally naïve maid.

It was suppertime before Louis Levering appeared at her chamber door. Ella would have been happy if he had never called for her, but she did not think that likely. As it was, Levering reeked of alcohol and a sickly sweet tobacco smell, which she had remembered from his father. On the stairs, he pulled her passionately into his arms for a kiss. "I apologize if I hurt you earlier, Eleanor. I forget sometimes you are a duke's daughter and have not experienced life outside Thorn Hall. Collins says I need to treat you with more tenderness." Ella did not answer—she only dropped her eyes in submission. In his current state, she suspected Levering's newfound tenderness to be short-lived.

Downstairs, supper was a plain cream soup, cold meats, and cheese, but Ella could barely swallow any of it. She saw no end to this insanity.

Apparently, all the men were minor noblemen, too low on the family tree to ever inherit and too lazy to accept commissions in the military or some other such honorable occupation. Levering's father had inherited Huntingborne Abbey, evidently, by a total fluke. Three cousins, all ahead of Robert Levering in the succession line, were killed in a carriage accident, sending them to their deaths in a Yorkshire lake. The women, all except Fanny, were his friends' mistresses. The hunting box was to host a week of decadent pleasure.

Throughout the meal, she could feel Allister Collins's eyes on her. Although he was as inebriated as the others, the man seemed different; she found her eyes drifting to him more often than they should have. He told the same crude jokes as the others, but his seemed less offensive somehow. "I am happy to see you welcome Collins with your eyes, my Dear. I may leave here debt-free if he likes you." Ella started to protest Levering's assertions, but as she thought about it, if she were to have to participate in a dalliance, she much preferred the depth of character she found in the stranger's eyes to Levering's revolting depravity.

When they retired to the drawing room, the women curled up in the men's laps to enjoy themselves. She sat beside Levering on a settee, tolerating his kisses along her neckline–eyes closed against her body's violation.

"I think we all need another drink," Collins's voice interrupted the heated moments evident in the darkened room. He held a small tray with two brandy glasses out to Levering and Ella.

Breathing deeply, she reached for the nearest one, leaving Louis Levering the final offering. "Thank you, Mr. Collins," she spoke softly, taking a sip from the glass. Levering swallowed deeply from his, not happy to have Collins intrude.

"Possibly, Ella, you would consider joining me on the chaise lounge." Collins reached for her hand.

Ella instinctively looked to Levering, thinking he would stop her abandonment, but he nudged her forward, and she reached for the stranger's hand. It tightened around hers, and he led her across the darkened room. She had no more than left Levering's side when Fanny slid into the baronet's welcoming arms. "Your betrothed loaned me his mistress for the week," Collins whispered close to her ear, "but I find you far more fascinating."

"The baronet's mistress," she said with a sneer. "I should have known."

Before she could say more, Collins pulled her into him, kissing her tenderly. Feathering light kisses across Ella's cheek, he lingered by her ear. "Lady Eleanor," he whispered as he continued a line of softness down her neck and then back to her ear. "I am not really Allister Collins." He caressed her cheek when he felt her reaction. Pulling her into his embrace was purposeful; he had blocked her body from view with his own. "My name is Aidan Kimbolt, Godown's friend."

He paused, his lips hovering above hers. "Viscount Lexford," she mouthed in recognition.

A slight nod of his head told her it was true. "I am afraid, Lady Eleanor," he nibbled on her ear again, "you and I are going to be more intimate than I would like, but understand it is for show." He lifted her into his arms and laid her along the chaise, following her down with his own body.

"Wrap your arms around me and kiss me," he murmured. The others in the room were fully engaged in their own pleasures, in various stages of undress.

Lexford draped himself across her, but Ella did not object. "I must get you out of here," he murmured so softly she needed to listen with her whole being. "I have been watching you for a fortnight. How is Levering controlling you?"

Ella considered a lie, but if Godown knew, then so did Bran. "He has something that will ruin Thornhill." She kissed his jaw line, maintaining the ruse.

Lexford nodded his understanding. "I have drugged the brandy; our 'friends' will sleep soon. You and I will simply lie here until the drug takes effect. I cannot send you away in a coach without my new acquaintances knowing I helped you. I am onto something important here besides Levering's blackmail." He took time for a long, tender kiss. "I arranged for a man in a wagon to take you and your maid to safety; Levering will never know. He cannot ask Bran because you are not supposed to be here."

"Sir Louis will follow me to London," she protested between kisses and his hand rubbing up and down her arm.

"You will not go to London. I am sending you to Kerrington."

Ella stiffened, unable to breathe. "Lord Worthing must hate me."

"From what I know of Kerrington, he will forgive you." He purposely nuzzled into her neck, sliding kisses along her shoulder line. "Just do me a favor; do not tell Worthing about this. He is a better shot than I, and I am sure he would call me out if he knew." Lexford looked down at her, a mischievous grin spreading across his face, and Ella let out a slow steadying breath. "Worthing will forgive you because he loves you, and you love him." Things from the other side of the room became quieter. "We will lie in each other's arms for now in case any of my new associates are still conscious on some level. They will see us passed out together." The viscount gathered her into his arms. "Worthing is one lucky bastard." He kissed her forehead before lowering his face into her curls.

For a half hour, Ella laid against Lexford, the first time she had felt safe in a month. It was odd; she had known the man for less than six hours, but she trusted him with her life. When he stirred and helped her to her feet, she almost cried from deprivation. He placed a finger to her lips and led Ella through the darkened halls to the servant quarters.

When they entered the room, Hannah breathed with relief at seeing Eleanor. "My Lady, I was so worried."

"Come." Lexford pulled a cloak about Eleanor's shoulders. "We need to hurry."

"What about Lady Eleanor's bags?" Hannah protested.

Lexford looked vexed by Hannah's insistence. "There is no time. I will bring them to Linton Park myself in a few days." He caught Eleanor's hand, dragging her behind as he worked his way to the back entrance. "The servants are loyal to Bradley," he whispered. "They cannot know I helped you. Listen carefully. A quarter mile down the main road, a man named Lucifer waits for you. He has a supply wagon. It will not be comfortable, but you will be safe. Kerrington's estate is some fifty miles. You should be there by mid-morning. Tell him the truth—the whole truth—and he will protect you." She started through the door he held open, but Lexford's hand caught her wrist. "The whole truth, Lady Eleanor. Tell the captain you are sorry and tell him how much you love him. The man has known enough sadness."

Ella impulsively kissed his cheek. "Thank you." She caught Hannah's hand, and away they ran into the night. With each step they took into the unknown, she prayed Viscount Lexford was correct, and that it was not too late to make James Kerrington love her again.

With the late morning light, Lucifer turned the wagon team into Linton Park's circular drive. Lexford had given him very specific orders. He had hidden the two women in a vented box under several bales of hay. No one had pursued them, something Lexford had feared. Lucifer pulled up the teams. Footmen scrambled to have him remove the dilapidated-looking wagon from the entranceway, but Lucifer ignored their protestations. A gigantic hulk of a man, he easily moved the hay away from the hiding place and lifted the lid. Both women gasped, taking in large gulps of fresh air.

"We are here, my Lady." He helped Ella to her feet and braced her until she could get her legs under her. Then he did the same for Hannah.

Ella pushed the hair from her face; she had no bonnet to protect her head so she released the braid and ran her fingers through her locks to straighten them. Brushing the dust from her cloak, she let her eyes fall on the stately mansion before her. "It is beautiful," she murmured.

"Aye, Ma'am, it be one of England's finest," Lucifer told her. "Let us find Lord Worthing."

"Maybe he is not in residence." She stumbled forward trying to keep up with Lucifer's long strides.

He stopped suddenly, realizing how weak she was. He caught Ella's arm to steady her. "His Lordship tends his father; he will be here."

Ella took a deep breath. She had not seen Worthing since the night she laid in his arms. *How would he receive her?*

James Kerrington had tarried at the breakfast table. Normally, by this time of day, he would be at his desk reviewing the books, but his sister Georgina had arrived late the previous evening, and he enjoyed just listening to her many tales of Devon and her life as Lady Amsteadt. It seemed a lifetime ago since she was here. Despite the fact that her confinement was well upon her, Thomas Whittington, Lord Amsteadt, had allowed her to return to her childhood home, all of them fearing it might be the last time she would see her father alive. He was thankful on multiple levels, but mainly because Georgina might provide moments when he could forget that Eleanor Fowler had chosen another. Because of Georgina's condition, she would spend her confinement at Linton Park. Life would come to his home—a home where death lingered—and James was glad for Georgina's company.

"Will Amsteadt join us soon?" James asked as he buttered another of the hot rolls he mounded on his plate.

Georgina opened her mouth to answer, but a tap at the door delayed her response. Mr. Lucas opened the sliding door to announce, "Lady Eleanor Fowler, Your Lordship."

James did not hear the butler's words, but his heart knew she was there. It could not be she—but he, instinctively, knew she had come at last. Eleanor Fowler stood in the doorway of his dining room, a place he had imagined her for months; yet, he never pictured her as such: dirty cloak, rumpled dress, smudged face, and golden hair streaming over her shoulders. The woman he loved with all his heart had miraculously reappeared, and he cared not whether anyone else remained in the room.

With the second beat of his heart he was on his feet and moving toward her. "James," her lips moved, but no sound came out as she swayed, trying to remain standing, but finally crumpling into his arms just as he reached her.

"Ella," he pleaded as he scooped her up and lifted her to his chest. Unable to stop himself, James lightly kissed her cheek.

"I need your help."

"I have you," he assured her as he headed for the stairs, ignoring the thousand questions bombarding his senses. "Lucifer, bring Hannah and come with me," he ordered upon seeing the viscount's bodyguard and Eleanor's maid waiting in the hallway. "Mr. Lucas, send for a bath and something to eat," he barked as he hit the landing and turned toward the guest rooms. James waited for no one's response. He knew they would see to his wishes. Ella was in his arms, and the emptiness of not ten minutes earlier now swelled to overflowing with love and need and protectiveness.

Ella laced her arms around him and held tightly. "I am sorry," she repeated over and over again. "I never meant to hurt you."

"Shush! You are here now. That is all that matters." He pushed open a door with his shoulder and carried her to a bed. Laying her against the pillows, James pushed the hair from her eyes. "*Delam barat kheyli tang shodeh*. I missed you," he whispered so the others could not hear.

"And I you." Her fingers caressed his face as if trying to memorize his features.

He kissed the palm of her hand. "Let me deal with this, and then we will talk." James turned to face Lucifer, whom he had left waiting at the door. "Where is Lexford?" he demanded.

"Some fifty miles from here, Your Lordship, *on business*." The man would give James specifics later. "The Viscount seemed to think you would wish to protect Lady Fowler yourself. He bid me bring the lady and her maid to you. Unfortunately, I had to hide them in the wagon under some hay."

"Thank you, Lucifer. Why do you not show Hannah the kitchens? Procure food for the two of you, and we will see to your lodgings. Hannah, Lady Eleanor will send for you later. Get some rest. I am sure you are exhausted also."

Hannah offered James a curtsy. "Thank you, Lord Worthing." Then she followed the tender giant who had saved her and her mistress. "Lucifer be an unusual name," James heard the maid say as they left the hallway.

"James," a soft voice came from behind him. Turning quickly to the woman who held his heart in her hand, he found her sitting up, ready to deal with her condition. "We must speak."

A shiver of anticipation ran up his spine. "Will it not wait, Ella, until you have had a bath and some food?" For some reason he did not want to know what had brought her here. He wanted all the hurt of the last month to go away and let them start anew.

"It must be said, James. You must know it all, and if I do not tell you soon, I may lose my courage."

The maids rushed in with hot water, followed by a footman carrying a hip bath, setting it up behind the screen. "I will join you for breakfast in a few minutes, and then we will talk."

"I have nothing else with me," she whispered.

"I will find something for you." He kissed the top of her head and then left the room.

Once the water and bath soap was added to the tub, Ella slid in and began to scrub away the road dust but also the dirt Levering had left on her soul. It would take more than water and soap to remove the filth in her life; it would take James Kerrington's forgiveness.

Leaving Eleanor to her bath, James returned to the morning room. He had left Georgina and his mother in mid-sentence; nothing else had mattered but Ella. Now, he owed his family some sort of explanation. He put on a carefree face, but his mother's words wiped that away.

"So, that is Eleanor Fowler," she said in wonderment. "An *Amazon* is the perfect description, Darling."

"Mother tells me you are in love with her," Georgina squealed. "James, I am so happy; you have been alone too long."

He collapsed into the nearest chair. "I do not know why she is here." He wiped his face with his hands, trying to clear his thinking. "Lady Eleanor is in some kind of trouble. Viscount Lexford rescued her and sent her here for my protection. What if all she needs is my safekeeping, and then she moves on? I lost Elizabeth, and I lost Ella once; I do not believe I can stand to lose her again."

"You will not lose her, Darling. No woman worth a grain of salt can resist you." His mother patted his hand. "I told your father about Lady Eleanor; I think it will do him good to meet her while she is with us. He wants to see you settled before the inevitable."

James took a couple of deep breaths, forcing his heart back to normal. "First, I must discover what is wrong and plan how I might be of service to Lady Eleanor. Then maybe I can renew my plight, actually ask Ella to accept me. Georgina, may Lady Eleanor borrow some of the gowns you left in your former room? It appears that whatever the Viscount did to extricate her, Eleanor's things were left behind."

"Certainly, let me send for Mari. She will know exactly what to choose for the lady. It is not as if I will need them anytime soon." She patted her increasing girth in a humorous gesture of love and disbelief.

"Eleanor is a bit taller than you, but, otherwise, she should be able to manage. Thank you, Georgina."

"Of course, James. The lady shall be my sister some day."

"From your mouth to God's ears." He paused for a moment in an act of supplication. "I believe I will find Lucifer and see what he knows before I talk to Eleanor again. I suspect I will be several hours, trying to decipher what is best to do about all this."

Georgina rose to summon her maid. "You will entertain Lady Eleanor in one of the guest chambers, James?" It was half tease and half warning.

He felt a surge of panic in his chest. "Believe me, if I thought being found in bed with Eleanor would have made her agree to marry, I would have planned a seduction two months ago. She is a stubborn woman, but inherently, I know that room spells safety for Ella right now. I am more likely to learn the whole of it if Eleanor feels safe."

"Then do what you must, Darling. Your sister and I will call on Lady Eleanor later today; I am most anxious to meet the woman."

"Collins, where is Ella?" Aidan Kimbolt lay face down on the chaise, pretending to be in as bad a shape as the others.

Kimbolt staggered to his feet. "How in the bloody hell am I supposed to know?" He wiped at his mouth as if what he drank left a bad taste.

"She is not in her room and her maid is gone also," Levering continued.

"Did she go for a walk or something?" Aidan staggered convincingly, making his way to the breakfast room and ignoring Levering's bravado. "I am not the lady's keeper, Levering. Should that not be your job? After all, you are the one who is supposed to marry the woman."

Levering's voice took on a menacing tone. "The last I saw of her, Ella was on the chaise with you."

Kimbolt turned on Levering, matching him tone for tone. "Maybe your unspoken threats scare women, Levering, but they do nothing for me. I do not fear you." Aidan purposely turned his back on the baronet and helped himself to some toast and eggs. "I remember kissing the lovely Eleanor, but I do not remember much else."

"None of us remember much of anything," Bradley wandered into the room, straightening his clothes. "Obviously, no one made it to bed last night."

"I think the drink or the food was tainted." Levering still ranted on as if he actually cared for Eleanor Fowler.

"Maybe it was that crap you brought back from the Continent." Aidan sat at the table shoveling in the food. He knew that those who used opium often had large appetites the next morning, more from thirst than from real hunger.

"There was nothing wrong with the powder," Bradley took offense. "Plus, Levering, if the food and drinks were contaminated, would it not also affect your betrothed?"

"The lady barely ate, and I only saw her take a sip of the brandy," Montford joined the conversation. "She was upstairs until supper so I doubt if Levering's lady friend was the culprit who doctored the food and drinks. She would not have had the opportunity. But then her maid may have. Did you not send the woman's servant to help Mrs. Blossom?"

Fanny entered the room and reported directly to Levering. "Your lady's clothes are still in her room."

"That brings us back to you, Collins," Levering accused. "You were the last one to see Eleanor."

"Well, I am not the woman's nursery maid," he said flippantly. "It seems to me you have more reason than any of us to keep track of her. First of all, you bring your mistress to your play week and expect your betrothed not to notice. Lady Eleanor is not a stupid woman. Then you hand her off to me as if she was some sort of whore. How did you expect her to act? She was willing last night, but I would bet it was the stimulant in the food and drinks. She took in less than the rest of us, and when she saw her chance to get away, she took it. I am betting she just walked away from your indifference. However, it seems to me you had best be making your regrets. I thought you needed her dowry. She may think twice about the way you have been treating her."

Levering declared in a less than convincing voice, "She will marry me."

Kimbolt just smiled at the baronet's posturing. "It sounds as if you have an 'in' with the lady's family."

"I have better than an 'in'; I have a personal warranty."

"Then I expect you had best find her." Viscount Lexford sat back in his chair, carefully observing the changes in the group's attitudes and behaviors.

Levering started for the main hall. "Bloody hell! I will teach the chit a lesson or two when I get my hands on her. No one runs away from me!"

"How are you going to find her?" Aidan called casually over his shoulder, trying to learn as much as he could without making an issue. "I thought the lady's family believed she was in Leicestershire for the week. She is not supposed to be with you."

"I do not know. I will figure out something before I return to London."

Fanny nearly whined, "You are returning to London? What about our holiday?"

"It will have to wait. If you wish, you may return with me." Kimbolt thought it amusing how the baronet tried to find a way to rid Fanny of her disappointment. It would cost Levering an expensive bauble—money Sir Louis did not have at the moment. Under Fowler's instructions, the Realm knew minute details of Sir Louis's life.

The man's mistress's lip stuck out in a pout. "I guess I have no other choice. I will pack my things." She slipped from the room to tend to her luggage.

Aidan rose to his feet, pulling at his rumpled clothes. "I believe I will clean up and then make my own exit. Obviously, if Levering is taking Fanny, and Lady Eleanor is no longer here, there is not much sense in my remaining." He started for the door but paused long enough to add, "What do you say, Levering, to my taking some of your lady's things with me? Fanny is too well endowed to find any use for them, and I know a sweet young thing near Brighton who would fill them out well. If Roslyn likes them the way I think she will, I will take the cost off your debt."

"Hell, take the whole damn wardrobe for all I care. I certainly cannot transport them to London and deliver them to Briar House. If Roslyn rewards you for the gifts, I will be thankful for the reduction in my obligation."

Chapter 10

AN HOUR LATER, JAMES TAPPED on Eleanor's door. She was in the accompanying sitting room enjoying a light repast. "I am happy to see you eating something." He slid into the chair across from her without an invitation. If they were to get through this, it would be as friends first. He had spoken to Lucifer and knew the nature of the party from which Lexford had rescued her, although he certainly did not know why Aidan Kimbolt had been in Levering's company. He guessed that Bran had manipulated the situation somehow. He promised Lucifer he would let Ella tell him her side, however. With the news, James had again taken his frustration out on the wall of his study. The irony of the havoc he had created in that room in the past month was not lost on him

"I have eaten very little for several days." She set her teacup on the table. "I need to thank whomever you persuaded to loan me these clothes. The fit is a bit snug, but I am most appreciative of her generosity."

"My sister Georgina," he nodded to the dress, "one of her dresses from her Come Out Season, I believe. As her confinement is upon her, I am sure she has no use for it any longer. She and my mother will stop in later to check on you and to introduce themselves."

"You are being so kind. I certainly do not deserve it." Ella looked away for a moment, gathering her courage. "I promised Viscount Lexford I would tell you the whole truth, and as much as it will hurt me, and I suspect you, as well, I beg you not to interrupt. Locked in Lucifer's wagon last night, I tried to imagine how I might explain this madness to you so you would not hate me for what I did, but I do not expect it to be possible."

James started to tell her he could never hate her, that he would make her his wife tomorrow if she would agree to go to Scotland with him today, but a flip of her hand silenced him for the moment.

"You know of my sleepwalking, and you suspect it has something to do with my father. You said as much before, and you were correct. When Brantley argued with our father over our mother's death, I lost the two people who meant the most to me in the world. I was thirteen and tall and quite homely looking, and like most young girls I wanted my father's love. I tried to be everything to him—as with me, he had lost two people he had loved. The thing with Father was he knew only one way to show love." By now, the tears streamed down her cheeks.

"You do not have to say it if you do not wish." Immediately, James was on his knees before her. "I understand what you went through."

"I must say it, James. I must repent with sackcloth and ashes. I have felt so dirty for so long, and it is the only way I can be through with it."

He nodded his understanding, but instead of returning to his chair, he sat on the floor at her feet and rested his head on her lap. She stroked his hair and lovingly ran her fingertips along the line of his cravat. "When my father would come to my room, he was usually drunk." The emotions vibrated through her words. "He would sneak into my bed and wake me by touching me. He never entered me as a man; I am very much a maiden, but he did touch me and touch himself." Ella gulped for air, but she continued. "The next day he would feel remorse and beg my forgiveness, but he would always return. He could not help himself, but he knew that if he did to me what he had done to my mother and several of the maids, I could die the same kind of death. He visited me for nearly two years, and I know no one with whom he took his pleasures during that time. I believe my mother's death scared him from his habits."

James thought it did not scare him enough to keep him from invading his daughter's childhood with his perversions. If he could bring William Fowler back to life and kill the man all over again, he would, and he would enjoy every minute of it. James thanked God for the justice by which the late duke suffered for his crimes against women.

"Then Robert and Lillian Levering became the Baronet and Lady Levering by a freak accident in Yorkshire. Being socially motivated to climb the ranks, the Leverings saw a way of connecting themselves to a dukedom—their son could court either Velvet or me, but neither of us were old enough to truly consider marriage so instead the parents attached themselves to my father, becoming his closest—actually his only—friends. Like their son, they were vile people, more depraved in many ways than my father." Ella paused as if searching for how to explain the unexplainable.

"I assume that somewhere in the nearly nightly gatherings and drinking, the subject of passion arose. I am not sure how it happened, but after leaving me alone for nearly a year, one night my father woke me from a sound sleep. Only this night was different—this night Robert Levering joined him in the room. This continued until they added a third person: Lady Levering. One particular night, my father and the baronet were naked except for their breeches, and Lady Levering wore only her chemise." She heard James curse, but he did not raise his head from her lap, and Ella made herself continue the tale. If Lord Worthing was to choose her, no secrets could lie between them.

"My father removed my gown and held me from behind, my back pressed against his chest. I was sixteen by then, and my body was changing daily. Father wrapped his arms around me and lifted my breasts, offering them to Robert Levering's mouth. He told me to sit still, and it would soon be over. Levering reached into his breeches, releasing his manhood, and as he licked my breasts he rubbed the length of himself, growing more and more involved. Finally, Lady Levering climbed in the bed and mounted him. My father released me as he reached for Lillian Levering's breasts. When I slipped out of the room, they were a tangled mess of arms and legs."

"Oh, my sweet Ella." James's hand stroked the inside of her calf. He wanted to take her in his arms and give her comfort, but he knew she was not ready.

She sighed deeply. "The Leverings came often to Thorn Hall, and more often than I care to remember to my room. I suspected Lillian Levering wanted to rid herself of her husband and become the new duchess, but Father would have none of it. When he refused to allow them to involve me any further in their lust, they fought with him, and he banned them from the house. I prayed it had been a bad memory until I met the new baronet again in London. It seems Lillian Levering kept a diary account of her evenings at Thorn Hall. The entries describe in detail the experiences she enjoyed, but the worst for Thornhill and me, it tells of my father's and my participation. Robert and Louis Levering blackmailed my father with it until his illness prevented Levering from getting any more money out of the estate. Lady Levering caught the pox and died quickly from it. I am unsure what caused Robert Levering's death, but Sir Louis now has the diary. When he thought Cousin Horton would inherit, everything seemed in place, but Bran's return altered those plans. He needs money for gambling debts, and my dowry is most tempting. Plus, he wishes to take a certain amount of revenge on Thornhill for his mother's death. In fact, he staged the Hyde Park attack. Your pursuit of the shooter nearly ruined all of Sir Louis's plans."

"Levering is blackmailing you into marrying him?" James was back to his knees. "Why did you not tell Bran?"

"The baronet threatened to mail the diary's individual pages to *ton* members if I told Bran. His mother rarely uses either of their names, but my name and Father's are used quite liberally. Plus, you know how Bran is. He would make it an issue, and everyone would know.

"I agreed to accept the baronet's proposal so as to save Thornhill, but I cannot do it. I cannot allow him to publicly treat me as he has. He forced me to lie to Bran regarding a house party; it was his close friends and their mistresses. He owes money to Viscount Lexford, whom he knows as Allister Collins, and Sir Louis gave me to Collins in payment for some of his debts. I cannot tell you of the other degradations I have suffered in the past month, for they are too vile, and I know your nature."

"Ella, you do not have to face this alone; I will take care of it." If he could find Sir Louis Levering at this moment, he would introduce the man to some very unique ways of torture he learned in Persia. "Bran will follow my orders, and we will recover the diary. Lord Godown can move through a house like a ghost. Wherever the diary is, we will bring it home to you to destroy page by page in your favorite fireplace. I promise you: No one will ever hurt you again." He leaned in and kissed her tenderly. "I love you, Eleanor, with all my heart."

"And I love you, James."

"Then you will marry me?" He put a finger to her chin, turning her head to face him. "I want to spend the rest of my life earning your trust, your respect, and your love."

Eleanor squeezed her eyes shut to hold back the tears. "I will not bring my family's perfidy to your household. I love you too much to bring shame to your parents or your sister."

"Then I will find the Levering diary, and you will have no excuse to deny me."

She whispered, "No excuse."

James pulled gently, bringing Ella to her feet. He held her gaze, solemnly, his hands sliding up and down her arms. "God, I have missed the feel of your skin under my fingers." James's breath caressed her ear, his possessiveness suffusing Ella's body with the heat she now recognized as desire. He kissed her thoroughly, like a starving man; his tongue explored her mouth's soft tissue as she opened to him.

She melted into him as a moan escaped her throat; enflaming his desire further, she pressed herself to him, her body trembling with longing. Her heartbeat hammered in her ears as every nerve thrummed to the power of his persuasion.

"I will have you as my wife, Ella."

She relaxed, sliding her arms around his waist. "What a wonderful fantasy." Ella leaned forward for a slow, lingering kiss.

"I will make that fantasy a reality, my Love."

A light knock at the door forced them apart, but not before he stole another kiss. He answered the door to find his mother and sister waiting in the hallway. "We brought fresh tea," his mother announced as she swept into the room, followed by a wobbly Georgina.

"Lady Eleanor," she grasped Ella's hands in hers before Ella could even offer a curtsy, "I am so pleased to make your acquaintance at last. Please, you must be exhausted; have a seat."

Ella shot James a quick glance, unsure how much he actually had spoken of her. "I am mortified, Lady Linworth, for my unexpected entrance to your home this morning. I am most appreciative of the hospitality you have extended to me."

"Nonsense. You are a special friend of my son's, and that gives you leave to come to Linton Park any time. This is my daughter Georgina, Lady Amsteadt. As I said, I have brought fresh tea so we might all get to know each other. Let us sit. As you can easily see, Georgina cannot be on her feet long."

Ella sighed contentedly as James's mother enveloped her in her arms. She had needed a mother for so long. Ella prayed to know Linton Park as her own. "Ladies, if you will excuse me, I have some business to address in my study." James announced to the room. He gave Ella a secretive wink, indicating that he would contact her brother immediately.

Ella genuinely smiled for the first time in weeks when James's mother waved him away before circling Ella's waist with her arm and leading Ella to a nearby chair. "My, how little you are, Lady Eleanor!"

"*Little* is never a word associated with me, Lady Linworth." Ella laughed nervously.

"Oh, but you are, is she not, Georgina?"

"I would say so. I wore that dress when I was barely seventeen. How old are you, Lady Eleanor?" Georgina was not as tactful as her mother, but between them they would learn everything they could of her. At first, Ella balked with their apparent intrusion into her private life, but she realized that she knew nothing of family. Thinking such, she forced herself to relax into something foreign to her experience. Lady Linworth and Lady Amsteadt loved James as did she. If she had a chance of becoming part of this family, she owed them the truth.

"I shall be one and twenty next month."

"And dear Agatha Braton is your aunt?" Lady Linton added, "She and I shared our first Season, Georgina."

Ella breathed easier, thankful of the hearts opening to her. Tears overflowed her eyes. "Aunt Agatha told us recently of that Season. She claims Lord Linworth pursued you quite relentlessly."

"Martin was most persuasive as I believe Harold Norris was with your aunt."

"His Grace, may he rest in peace, left Aunt Agatha too soon. I am afraid that, other than his portraits, I remember very little of him." Ella stirred the tea they had offered her.

"You will have to ask my dear Martin about him. I am sure he will have tales with which you may torment your aunt when you return to London."

Ella glanced to James's mother and smiled, a brief happy smile of family and how it would feel to be James's wife. If this happened, she would have a mother again, a glorious thought. "I would enjoy that, Lady Linworth."

"As I am sure Martin would. He is most anxious to meet you."

"Lady Linworth, I do not wish to mislead you. I have not accepted James's proposal; I have a problem, which could bring me personal shame, and I will not let that hurt His Lordship nor any of you. It would not be the honorable thing to do."

"Oh, pooh, Lady Eleanor. You love my brother, do you not?" Georgina ignored Ella's protestations.

A hundred possible responses ran through Ella's head, but she opted for honesty. "Yes, Lady Amsteadt, I do."

"Then that is all of which we care, is it not, Mother?"

Lady Linworth's eyes misted over. "We want James to know happiness again, and you make him happy, Lady Eleanor. I am afraid you may be stuck with us, my Dear. I cannot imagine James would willingly let you go now that you are at Linton Park."

"If I know my brother, he most certainly will not."

Another knock came, tentatively, and Lady Linworth moved to answer it. "Well, Daniel, what are you doing here?"

"Grandpapa wants you. Mr. Lucas told me you were here. Do we have another visitor?"

Lady Linworth stepped to the side. "Come in for a moment. I have someone I would like you to meet." The boy eased into the room. He did not look like James, except for his eyes; Ella imagined how much the boy must remind James of his late wife. She felt her heart squeeze tightly, remembering what Lord Worthing had said of his child. "Lady Eleanor, may I present my grandson, Daniel Kerrington. Daniel, this is Lady Eleanor Fowler. She is Brantley's sister. You remember your father's friend Brantley Fowler?"

The boy bowed properly. "Of course, I remember His Grace. It is pleasant to meet you, Lady Eleanor. Will you be staying with us long?"

Lady Linworth answered for her. "We hope Lady Eleanor will enjoy Linton Park so much she would hate to leave us."

"That would be capital. I would enjoy someone else with whom to talk." The boy shifted nervously from one foot to another.

"Why do you not show Lady Eleanor the library?" Lady Linworth suggested. "Georgina and I will go see Grandpapa."

"Yes, Ma'am." The boy cleared his throat. "Would you care to see the house, Lady Eleanor?"

Everything decided for her, Ella joined James's son, who stood very erect, trying to be a man. "I would love to see some of the house. It is gracious of you to serve as my guide, Daniel."

"Right this way, Lady Eleanor." They walked in silence to the main staircase.

"Do you like to ride, Daniel?" The words sprang from her mouth when she tried to think of a conversation starter.

The boy spun around quickly on the stairs. "I love to ride, but Father does not let me go very often."

"I am surprised; His Lordship is an excellent horseman. Maybe Lord Worthing will let us ride together. I must wait a day or two for my trunks to arrive, but I would love to ride out across the estate. Of course, I must warn you that whatever I do, I take no prisoners. When we play cards or partake of chess or ride horses, if you can beat me, you must never *let* me win just because I am a woman. I will never purposely let you win because you are a child. Otherwise, how will you ever become a man?"

"Would you play me a game of chess now?" Daniel's eyes lit in anticipation.

Ella smiled; her instincts were good. She would treat James's son as she used to treat Bran. "No prisoners."

"No prisoners, Ma'am. I promise."

"There you are," James came looking for his son. "Mr. Weston is a bit vexed, Daniel."

Daniel jumped to his feet, eyes lowered in repentance. "I am sorry, Father. I shall apologize to him."

Eleanor and Daniel had played chess for over an hour, but more importantly, they had talked about everything. James's son not only had his natural charm, he possessed his father's intelligence, and Ella thoroughly enjoyed the quiet quickness of the boy's mind. "Mr. Weston?" Ella's eyebrow rose in concern, after observing Daniel's sudden subservience to his father.

"The boy's tutor, Lady Eleanor. Daniel has missed a lesson." James surveyed the scene. She and Daniel building a relationship was part of his dream of Eleanor Fowler.

Eleanor recognized the problem immediately; she had done the same thing as a child. Daniel wanted to be perfect for James; the boy wanted his father's love. In her mind's eye, Eleanor saw herself in the same repentant stance praying she had not displeased her father. If not for her insecurities, she would not have made such poor choices as a young girl. She would not let Daniel Kerrington starve for James's love. "Far be it of me to tell Mr. Weston what is proper for a young man's education," Ella began, "but it seems Daniel did all that was necessary for a budding gentleman. He spent time keeping his grandfather company, and then he and I read several of Shakespeare's sonnets, debating over the true interpretation of them. For the past hour, we have had a hotly contested game of chess, something, which surely must increase his intelligence as much as working on sums. During the game, we discussed my brother's new plan for crop rotation and the possibility of cross-breeding a line of horses, both important for a future master of Linton Park. Yet, more importantly, your son kept me company and politely listened to my ramblings, a true sign of a gentleman."

James observed how his son raised his head to look at Eleanor. She accepted him, and an instant respect passed between them. Just the picture of Eleanor defending Elizabeth's son made James love her more. "Well, it seems Lady Eleanor recognizes something neither Mr. Weston nor I considered. A boy learns in many ways. Not all have to be formal lessons in the schoolroom. I suspect it is time I begin grooming you as the future Earl. Would you care to join me in my study on a regular basis to learn about the estate?"

Daniel's eyes lit with excitement. "May I, Father? That would be capital; I have so many questions."

James smiled at the boy. "Hopefully, not too many questions," he teased.

However, Daniel, not used to his father's attention, immediately began to withdraw. "No…no, Sir," he stammered.

Ella saw and came to Daniel's rescue. "I believe Lord Worthing offered you a tease, Daniel. From what I know of your father, he is unique in that he is able to keep a straight face when he presents a taunt. I will try to teach you what I know of his proclivity in that area," she said as an aside. "I assure you Lord Worthing welcomes your questions."

James reiterated what she said. "Of course, I invite your curiosity. How else will you learn?"

"Thank you, Father." Daniel beamed.

"Would you join us, Lord Worthing?" Ella motioned to the game.

James nodded, coming forward to look at the board. "Who is winning?"

"I am, of course." Ella smiled at him. James sensed his son's change, and he gave up being master of the house for a few minutes to be a father.

"Oh, Son, you did not fall in Lady Eleanor's trap?" James teased again. "You must learn, my boy, to not let a lady's beauty distract you in the game." He took Daniel's chair to analyze the next move. James ruffled Daniel's hair when the boy moved a hammock to sit beside him. "Of course, Lady Eleanor does not need to cheat at chess; she is one of the best. The London Chess Club should admit her as a member, but, alas, she is too beautiful for membership." He winked at Eleanor.

"You mean because she is a woman, Father?" Daniel watched closely as James took up the game. "That does not seem fair. If Lady Eleanor is better than other members, being a woman should not matter."

James chuckled softly. "I suspect, my son, that you have just won Lady Eleanor's heart with those words. The lady does not approve of men who want a woman to be quiet and docile."

"No prisoners," Daniel asserted, looking at Ella.

"Absolutely. No prisoners, ever," she declared.

"I beg your pardon. Did I miss something?" James seemed amused by the interplay between Ella and his son.

"It is nothing, Father…just Lady Eleanor does not like men who purposely let her win at games or horseback riding or…"

"I am well aware of Lady Eleanor's ability on a horse," James assured his child.

"May we all go riding while Lady Eleanor is with us, Father?"

James smiled at her, thankful that she had opened up lines of communication with his child. "Would you enjoy that, Ella?"

"To steal a line from Master Daniel, that would be capital." She moved the piece across the board. "Checkmate," she announced with a flourish.

James leaned close as if sharing a secret. "I warned you, Son."

Daniel whispered, "Have you heard Lady Eleanor speak of medicine or of the railroad system? She knows so much of both." The boy was as enthralled with Eleanor as his father was. Daniel, obviously, needed someone besides a tutor and a distant father in his life. James reluctantly realized that he would have to fix this too.

"I was taken to task by Lady Eleanor regarding the merits of the rail system previously, but I was unaware of her knowledge of healing." James peeked at Eleanor as he spoke.

"Lady Eleanor once wanted to be a doctor," Daniel informed him. "While her cousin read fairy tales and stories of knights and dragons, Lady Eleanor read books about science and what causes people to take ill."

"I wanted to cure my mother," Ella admitted sheepishly.

James accepted her explanation. "I suspect you should find Mr. Weston now, Son. Later, I will explain to the man that I wish you to have different types of lessons, and that you are to spend more time with me and with your grandparents and with Lady Eleanor, for as long as she is here."

"Thank you, Father." The boy scrambled to his feet. He presented James with a proper bow and gave Ella a separate one. "Lady Eleanor, I enjoyed our game and our talk."

"So did I, Master Daniel."

Then he was gone, out the library door and taking the steps two at a time.

"You were quite a success with my son. Thank you, Ella."

"Daniel needs to see your love, James, not just hear you say it."

"So I recognized; I saw my son quite differently today. A fresh set of eyes showed me how special he truly is—apparently, I looked for perfection, did I not?" His eyes searched hers for the truth.

Ella glanced away, his stare too intense for her own insecurities. For a moment, she considered keeping her opinions to herself, but she continued, "You knew perfection with Elizabeth, but I cannot offer you that. I am quite flawed. The question is the same for both your son and me. Can you love us even when we fall short of your expectations? And if you can, how will we know? Will you freely show it, or will we forever be trying to please you?" Sickening memories made her throat tighten. "Daniel did not kill Elizabeth. You know it; you even openly stated such, but when was the last time you let your son know you do not blame him for your wife's death? He was raised in a household of servants whispering of how you could not bear to look at him because he reminded you of your loss and how you left him with your parents as you went off to discover peace in someone else's misery. And although you never said those words to him, you did nothing to persuade him otherwise. Daniel cowers in your presence because he seeks the love he never knew from you. As much as you proclaim to want to know him better, you keep Daniel at arm's length, never allowing him the closeness he desperately needs. I suspect it is because you cherish Elizabeth's memory and do not want to lose your last connection to her, so you protect yourself with a moat of formality, keeping Daniel in close proximity but never in your embrace. When was the last time you hugged your son for no reason except that he is your son? And do not give me that foolishness about men not needing to be hugged."

Worthing pursed his lips and thought for a moment. "You learned all this in just a few short hours with Daniel?"

She narrowed her eyes on him. "Not exactly. I learned it at the hands of William Fowler, a man who never saw me when he looked at me. He saw Amelia Braton, the one woman he truly loved, and there was no room for Eleanor in his heart. As my father could never forget his wife when he looked at me, you cannot forget Elizabeth when you see Daniel. Your son and I are very much alike—fighting the good fight to earn the love of a father who cannot see us for his own loneliness."

All teasing sympathies evaporated from his lips; his eyes crinkled with hope as he gazed at her. "Ella, I promise to see only you when I let my eyes rest on your face. I will see a woman who has known pain, but who has learned from it—a woman who has such empathy in her heart that she embraces the insecurities of another woman's child and makes them her own cause—a woman who would gladly suffer the worst a man can present to protect those she loves. I see a woman I can easily love with all my heart." He pulled her into his arms and lowered his mouth to her lips. "Ella," he whispered as he lost himself in her determination to survive. "I love you." His lips brushed hers.

Her fingers laced through his dark curls, holding onto the one solid in the liquid mire of her life. "I want to be yours; I want to belong to you completely. I want you to make me clean again with your love; I am so weary of being dirty. Please come to me tonight."

His eyes darkened to a deep onyx. "Ella, are you sure?" In his mind, she had already been his wife long ago; making love to her, at last, would be as natural as breathing; but she must give herself freely.

Ella's knuckles stroked along his chin line. "You will make me beg, James Kerrington? Here I thought you were obsessed with me." She nibbled on his bottom lip.

"Obsessed—possessed—preoccupied—haunted—tortured—maddened—pick your participle, Ella, and it describes your mastery over me. When I thought I had lost you to Levering, I nearly destroyed everything in my study. I wanted to kill Sir Louis for taking you and kill myself for losing you. For the past month, I have been an empty shell—a desert, and then by a miracle, you walked back into my life. If you want me in your bed, it would take an army to keep me otherwise."

She slid her hands up his chest, linking them behind his neck and leaving trails of heat wherever they touched. She kissed him gently, very ladylike. "Your official invitation," she teased.

In response, he ravaged her mouth with his tongue—the hunger remaining. "My official acceptance."

A light knock came at the door. She started to move away, but James refused to loosen his grasp. "This is where you belong, Ella."

"James," his mother did not react to their closeness. "Your father is feeling better today. He would like to meet Lady Eleanor if you would take her up to his room."

"Yes, Mother."

"And then maybe Lady Eleanor could join me for tea in the blue sitting room."

James smiled, recognizing his mother's ruse. "I will show Lady Eleanor the way myself." He caught Ella's hand. "Let us meet the incomparable Earl of Linworth, Ella." They climbed the stairs, hand-in-hand. "I hope you like Linton Park," he murmured. "Obviously, my parents do not wish you to leave."

"I have no desire to leave, but we must deal with Levering. I will marry Sir Louis before I allow the *ton* to know what happened years ago at Thorn Hall."

"I understand; I am already working on it. I will meet your brother on Wednesday in Northamptonshire. I asked him to bring Crowden and any of the others we need to stop Levering."

"Is it possible?"

James kissed the back of the hand he held. "*Mitoonam ke komaketoon konam?* Can I help you? I will make it possible, Ella. I will not rest until everything is right for you."

They turned to the right and made their way down the long hall to the master chambers. James paused long enough to make sure his father was awake and ready for them before leading Ella into the bedroom. "Look at you," he called cheerily as they approached the bed. "Sitting up and everything."

"I do not often entertain young women in my bedroom," the

Earl's eyes sparkled. "I could not do so if I looked unkempt. What would your lady think of me?"

James brought Ella beside the bed, holding her hand wrapped about his arm. They stared down at the earl. "She might think she chose the wrong Kerrington," James mocked.

"Introduce me, James," the Earl demanded. "I am most anxious to meet the lady. My grandson came flying in here on his way to the schoolroom to announce that Lady Eleanor knew everything about chess and horse breeding and railroads and Shakespeare and medicine. I must meet such a woman immediately."

"Well, that is two of the Kerrington men. You are the last hope we have, Father, of not succumbing to Lady Eleanor's wiles," James taunted. "However, I doubt if even you are that strong." James chuckled with the irony of how quickly Daniel had told his grandfather of his time with Ella. "Lady Eleanor Fowler, may I present my father, Martin Kerrington, the Thirteenth Earl of Linworth?"

Ella curtsied before adding, "Your Lordship, I am honored to make your acquaintance. My Aunt Agatha, the Dowager Duchess of Norfield, speaks so fondly of you and Her Ladyship."

"Yes, James shared some of the Duchess's stories when he returned recently. I was pleased to hear that Agatha thrives. She lost Harold Norris too soon."

"She did, Your Lordship."

"Here, sit down, Lady Eleanor." Martin Kerrington patted the place along the bed. "Tell me about your family."

Ella stiffened a bit, but James moved to sit on the other side of his father, giving her the confidence to speak honestly. "My mother Amelia Braton was Aunt Agatha's youngest sister; she married William Fowler, the Duke of Thornhill. Neither my mother nor father are living so my brother Brantley assumed the dukedom some three months ago."

"You remember Bran, Sir?" James redirected the conversation. "I spent time with him in Kent recently."

"Of course, young Fowler. When you traveled to Kent, James, to help Thornhill with the estate, none of us expected that you would return with such a prize." The earl directed his attention to Ella again. "You and your brother have different coloring, Lady Eleanor."

"I favor my mother, Sir."

"Then the former duchess must have been an extraordinarily beautiful woman." The earl gave Eleanor an approving look.

James's smile spread across his face. "Queen Charlotte spoke at length to Lady Eleanor at her Presentation. Ella was the talk of London, Sir."

"Her Highness's favor—quite a feather in your cap, young lady. Of what else can you brag about the woman, James?" The earl's affection for his son showed through easily. Ella felt the twinge of regret at not knowing such family harmony.

"Well, let me see," James caught Ella's hand across his father's body. "The former duke was abed for two years while Fowler was away in Brittany. Ella ran the estate in the absence of both father and son. Without her, Thornhill might not have survived."

"That is too much praise," Ella protested.

"My son was taught to speak the truth, Lady Eleanor. If James says as much, it must be so. It sounds as if you are a survivor, Lady Eleanor. That is who a man of my son's mettle needs by his side, a woman like my Camelia, a woman who will thwart propriety for the sake of her family. We Kerringtons celebrate such women. I understand you have not officially accepted my son's offer, but I want you to know I would be proud to call you *Daughter*."

Ella's eyes misted with tears. "I do not wish to contradict you, Sir, but you barely know me."

"That is where you are wrong, my Dear. I knew the first time I laid eyes on Her Ladyship the kind of woman she was, and I see the same lift of your chin and tilt of your head and bristle of your shoulders as I saw in her. I have known you, Lady Eleanor, for many years. You are what this earldom needs to survive into the next decade and beyond."

"How may I thank you for such words of praise?"

Martin Kerrington's eyes sparked with mischief. "Marry my son soon and start a family. I cannot hold out forever, and I want James settled at last."

"Such threats make me wish to deny His Lordship in order to keep you with us, Lord Linworth." Ella straightened the blanket across the earl's chest.

"I will not wait, Ella," James snapped.

The elder Kerrington raised his hand to still his son. "I like your logic, Lady Eleanor, but God will not relent. He may give me a reprieve, but I will not foil His plans for me. Keep my advice in mind, my Dear. You and James will make a handsome couple."

"You need your rest now, Sir. It is time for your medication." James rose to fill his father's water glass and count out the pills.

"I hate that abominable brown pill. It upsets my stomach," his father grumbled.

James handed his father the glass and the medication and waited for the earl to swallow the pills, obviously suspecting the elder Kerrington might not do so on his own. "I will send up some dry toast." James checked off the procedure in his father's care. "Ella and Mother are to have tea, and I believe I will check on Daniel."

"Is something wrong with the boy?" the earl looked concerned.

James adjusted his father's pillows. "No, Sir. Lady Eleanor pointed out earlier that Daniel needs other types of lessons. I thought I might take him to the stables to see the new stud I bought at Tattersalls. I thought he might be interested in the horses I hope to raise and sell."

"Excellent idea." The Earl settled back to take a nap. "I told you Lady Eleanor is a prize."

"Of course, you did, Father. We will both see you later." James caught Ella's hand to lead her from the room.

"You will come back, Lady Eleanor?" the Earl called from the bed.

Ella impulsively pulled away from James and returned to the bed. She leaned down over the ailing earl. "I will come often, Your

Lordship," she whispered. "It has been a long time since I had a father, Sir, so I expect you to stay around for me." She pushed the hair from his face.

"I will do my damnedest, my Dear." He winked at her before closing his eyes to rest.

Chapter 11

~ ~ ~

SHORTLY AFTER THE SUPPER HOUR, Viscount Lexford's carriage rolled into the Linton Park entranceway, and within moments James ushered him into the drawing room to pay his respects to the ladies. Lexford made his bows to James's family before turning to Eleanor. "Lady Eleanor, I am pleased to see you again." He did not say the words, but she knew what he meant.

"And I you, Lord Lexford." Ella breathed deeply trying to control her embarrassment, considering their parting less than a day ago. Neither of them wanted Worthing to know the extent of the ruse they had created to fool Levering.

Anxious to confer with his friend, James interrupted their reunion. "His Lordship and I have some urgent business if you ladies will excuse us." Before much else was said, James left the room, and Lexford bowed out to follow.

"That was a bit rude," Lexford laughed lightly as he strode into Kerrington's study. He took a quick glance at the room's condition, and his laughter became louder. "I see you are redecorating," he mocked.

James simply shrugged his answer before pouring them each a glass of brandy. "You know my mother. She would keep you talking about nothing for hours, and I need to know what you learned of Levering. I meet Fowler late tomorrow to decide what to do about Lady Eleanor." James ignored the comment regarding the room; he knew it appeared a shambles as he repaired the holes his anger had created earlier.

Lexford collapsed into the nearest chair. "How in the world did the lady become involved with such a seedy character?"

"The baronet is blackmailing Ella over something she did as a teen under the late duke's guidance. Lady Eleanor is trying to protect her family's reputation for Fowler's sake. What do you know of Sir Louis?"

Lexford took a sip of the brandy. "If I tell you, you are not going to blow up, are you?" He eyeballed the holes gouged in the wall, a bemused smirk on his face.

"That bad?" James swallowed hard, trying to steady his breathing.

"The baronet has some bawdy personal tastes, and he has involved your lady in them." James's anger rose immediately. He clenched and unclenched his fists, but he kept his temper in check as the viscount continued. "Fowler forestalled the proposal, giving Levering only an *understanding* with Lady Eleanor, trying to find time to thwart the bastard's plans. Godown contacted Swenton and me, and we moved forward. I became 'friends' with Levering by making him my debtor. The man is spending Lady Eleanor's dowry before he even receives it."

James became extremely quiet, imagining the many ways he would like to make Levering pay. "Go on," he said, his voice deadly cold.

"You will not like what comes next," Kimbolt warned.

"Nevertheless, I need to know it all."

"The baronet placed Lady Eleanor in several embarrassing situations. Recently, I followed them to the theatre where I observed them closely. Although she protested and openly wept during the stage performance, he placed her hand over his manhood and moved against it, stimulating himself in public. Then he stepped behind the box's curtain to relieve himself."

"Damn!" James muttered. "Poor Ella. However did she bear it?"

Lexford sat forward as if to share a secret. "There was a similar incident at an inn this week, where the baronet took his own pleasure before her. He bragged about it when he brought your lady to Heath Montford's hunting box. Levering manipulated Lady Eleanor into thinking he was escorting her to a house party. There were only five of us there, and each man brought his mistress for a week of lustful fun; Levering brought Fanny Houghton."

"The bastard brought both Ella and his mistress?" James's fists balled in anger.

"Levering brought Fanny for himself; he gave me Lady Eleanor in order to pay part of his debts. When I found out his plans, I negotiated the exchange. Levering claimed he did not care whether his future bride was an innocent or not. Luckily, Lady Eleanor seemed to understand I would not hurt her and came willingly to me. I drugged the others so I could send the lady to you with Lucifer's help."

"Thank you, Aidan, for saving Ella from Levering's debauchery."

Lexford smiled mischievously. "Please tell me you have a plan to make Levering pay."

"I plan to turn him into a eunuch and ruin him completely, but I have one problem to solve first. I need to find a diary belonging to Levering's mother. Lady Eleanor will not be safe until that time."

Lexford leaned back into the chair. "How may I be of service?"

"I hate to ask, but could you get the baronet to take you into his confidence? I need to know where he has secured the diary."

"I think that is possible; I will just insist Levering pay up immediately, or I will send him to debtor's prison. Although Levering knows me by the name Allister Collins, I am still a viscount, after all. My word should be worth something. I know his type; Levering will swear he has a way to make the Fowlers pay, and I will demand to see this 'miracle balm' for his money woes before I extend him time to pay his debts."

"Do you think you could buy up more of his blunt? I would help finance, making Levering greatly in debt to you. I am sure Fowler would buy into it also. That way we could control him completely."

Viscount Lexford considered the idea. "Swenton can tell us to whom Levering owes money. We could go from there; it would increase the pressure I could put on the man to show me the diary."

"Once you know where it is, I will send Godown in to retrieve it."

Lexford chuckled softly. "The Ghost stalks again."

"It will be good for Crowden to exercise his talents," Worthing asserted. "If we retrieve the diary, I will then orchestrate Louis Levering's permanent downfall."

"Then I suppose I should be to London tomorrow. I convinced Levering that Lady Eleanor took the chance for her escape; the baronet took Fanny and returned to town."

James looked a bit wary. "He would not follow you here, would he?"

"I doubt it; Derby is west of Nottingham. Why travel west to return south? Plus, he has Fanny with him, and she was not happy about cutting their holiday short. Levering is too narrow-minded. He imagines using Lady Eleanor's flight against her—keeping her a pawn in his scheme. He has been physically hurting her for several weeks—a twisted arm, a blow to the ribs—things such as that. He plans to make her pay physically and sexually for her withdrawal. Sir Louis is not the type to believe he has lost complete control of his pigeon."

James clutched at the edge of the desk, trying to restrain his anger. He would enjoy inflicting pain on Levering. "When Lady Eleanor returns to London, she will do so as my wife. Levering will have to go through me to get to her."

Lexford barked out a laugh of pure delight. "In some ways, I pity the man. The Realm's full power is about to lay him out cold."

"I cannot see it happening to a more deserving ass." James topped off his friend's drink. "You will ride with me to Northamptonshire. I plan to meet Fowler and Crowden there. You can share what you know."

"Oh, Lord," Kimbolt swore, "I forgot about Fowler's revenge. What an idiot Levering is! He dared to cross both Brantley Fowler and you. I am going to enjoy this more than anything since I returned to civilian life."

James pushed open her bedroom door, and his breath hitched at the sight of Ella's silhouetted figure in the dimly lit room. His first instinct was to take her in his arms immediately, but he paused to fully survey the goddess before him. She stood by the window reading a letter.

"What do you read, my Dear?" He closed the door behind him.

"Your letters…they were in my luggage. I never allowed myself to read them while I dealt with Levering. I knew I could not face him if you spoke of our relationship. I kept them to help me control what seemed to be an endless imprisonment."

James took a tentative step forward. "I meant every word, Ella. You are everything I never knew I wanted." He paused, unsure of Ella's thoughts. "Is this what you sought, Ella? Do you still want our joining?"

"I wondered how much longer I would have to wait, Lord Worthing." She laid the letter on a nearby table.

"Did you?" With each slow step, his heart raced faster.

Ella studied his face for a moment before smiling. "What means this teasing of yours?"

His grin widened. "Anticipation, my Love. It deepens the fascination."

"Ah-h. You realize, of course, I am likely to see this as *terrifying* rather than fascinating."

"Terrified of me, Lady Eleanor?" He stepped up beside her where he might caress Ella's face. "I am your chivalrous warrior," he mocked.

"And I am your Amazon," she countered.

James's smile spread to the corners of his eyes. "I will gladly be your captive, Ella." Her exquisite beauty held him in place. Blonde gold curls draped over her shoulders in twisted strands, cupping her breasts.

For several elongated moments, they said nothing, but their eyes spoke of desire and of need and of something like love. He opened his arms, and Ella walked willingly into his embrace. This moment was different from the other times he had held her to him. Ella would give herself to him tonight.

Her voice a bit breathless, she murmured, "So much for anticipation…will action follow soon?"

"Oh, yes, Ella." His lips brushed hers lightly. "Anticipation is over." The softness of her lips drove James over the edge, and he was lost only to her.

She gave herself up freely to his ministrations; he was the perfect answer to a difficult question. He tasted of brandy and of male and of power and of James. The taste was intoxicating, and she swayed under its supremacy.

James caught her close to him, trailing light kisses down the curve of her neck. "Ella," he sighed against her skin, before lifting her into his arms and carrying her to the bed.

Pressing her against the pillows, they both gasped for air. James's mouth was everywhere, while Ella's hands tugged at his shirt so she could touch his skin. He sat back to look down at her, his clothing askew; then he tugged off his jacket and his waistcoat, but never once did his eyes leave hers. "You are so beautiful; I ache for you."

"Come to me," she whispered and reached for him. James shed his shirt, throwing it into a corner, wanting only to share her skin on his skin.

When he crawled across the bed to lie beside her, Ella's fingers traced the line of his shoulders. "Mmmm," she moaned.

His lips returned to hers, tender at first, but then crushing hers, demanding her submission. "May I look upon you?" he implored.

Ella gave a quick nod of her head and then squeezed her eyes shut. She worried for the possible disappointment in his face, but Ella had nothing to fear. He could see only the exquisiteness of her form. James raised the gown slowly, exposing her ankles, her slender legs, her stomach…up the white muslin slid, revealing Heaven. He flipped the gown somewhere behind him before cupping a breast in his hand. "Open your eyes, Darling, and see how I adore you."

Instinctively, he lowered his head to her breast, first lifting it to his mouth with his hand. His tongue traced circles around her nipple, finally taking the tip between his lips to suckle her. She was the most beautiful—most heart-stopping woman he had ever seen.

Ella gasped, his body's heat radiating through her. Gripping his shoulders, she arched into his mouth. Waves of pleasure making her breath shallow and her hands tingle, she melted into him. James shifted to lavish attention on her other breast while sliding his hand down across the flat of her stomach to palm her mons. His hand nudged her legs apart as his mouth returned to hers. Teasingly, his fingers twisted the curls found along the fatty swelling of her most secret desire. Ella impulsively arced her hips and moaned seductively. His fingertips traced along her opening's dampness, parting the lips and stroking lightly across as his tongue mimicked the movement within her mouth.

Slick and wet, she clutched the bed covering, fisting the material in her hands. Completely absorbed in what he did to her, Ella willingly spread her legs to welcome the finger James buried in her. Methodically, he moved to where he could see his finger slide in and out of her wetness, totally mesmerized by pure passion rushing through him.

"Will you come for me?" he asked softly at her ear. "I want to see you lost to my love." He caught the lobe with his teeth and bit gently. His hand's rhythm increased as his mouth returned to her breast. Now, James sucked harder, using his teeth to rake against the nipple. The tension inside Ella increased, and her body moved of its own accord, rising to his touch before she cascaded into pleasure's pool pulsing through her, whimpering sounds escaping her lips.

James waited to allow the climax to subside before standing to remove his boots, breeches, and underthings. Ella's eyes grew in size at seeing his length, the proud erection pointing at her when he knelt between her legs.

"Do you wish to touch me?" his voice broke with emotion.

Ella could not remove her eyes from his manhood. "Do you wish me to do so?"

"I want you to feel familiar with me, but I will not force you, Ella. You must want to know my body."

Ella took in his countenance: He was a man who would never try to dominate or subjugate her, a man who would accept her as his equal. "Is it wanton to have such desires?"

James smiled slightly; he recognized her war between propriety and need. "There is not a man alive who would refuse your curiosity, my Love. It is natural between a man and his wife, and even without the vows being read, that is how I see you. You are my wife, Ella—the life that breathes and lives within me. Touch me if you desire it."

Tentatively, Ella's fingers touched the velvety softness, spreading milky drops of wetness across the surface. He jerked with her touch, and then closed his eyes with the experimental strokes of her palm as it slid the skin up and back over the head, driving the thoughts from his mind. She gently massaged his sacks, and he could not suppress the groan escaping his lips. James clenched his jaw in passion as Ella increased the pace—the only sound in the room being the rapid inhalation and exhalation of their attempts to breathe.

"Do you wish to drive me absolutely crazy?" He caught her hand, stopping her before he could no longer control his hunger.

"I want you to want me," she protested.

"Oh, Lord, Ella. If I wanted you any more, I would explode." He smiled seductively. James eased her back, spreading her legs with his own. "I will be gentle, but this may hurt; however, the pain will pass quickly."

He placed his member to her opening and edged into her. It was all he could do not to plunge deeply, taking her fast and furiously, but James made himself go slowly, a few inches at a time, allowing her body to welcome his breadth inside her. "I love you," he whispered against her mouth as he pushed past her maidenhead to open her to him completely, catching her protest with a deep kiss. He felt her flinch, but he pulled out almost all the way and plunged in again.

"Feel how much I love you," he growled as he set up a rhythm of withdrawal and thrust. Soon, her body responded, meeting his plunge with her own push. He briefly returned his attention to her breasts.

James felt her tighten around him as he began to pound his body into hers. A high keening and a thrumming of impulses along his length sped up his drive—faster and faster until he threw his head back and exploded, releasing his seed into her, love's waves making him shiver before collapsing on top of Ella.

"That was unbelievable," he whispered into her neck.

"You were quite magnificent, Lord Worthing." Ella ran her fingers through his hair and pulled his mouth to hers.

"Ella," he tilted her chin to where he could watch her face, "when Elizabeth died, I thought my life had ended. I was content to live alone, thankful for having known a wonderful girl. Yet, I am no longer the young man who loved a sweet, innocent girl. When I joined my unit, I left Elizabeth's memory, but I also left the memories of a young man behind. I saw things, which changed me, and I can say in all honesty that sweet, innocent Elizabeth Morris would never interest me now. I need a woman who does not faint dead away whenever life opens the wrong door. I need you, Eleanor Fowler, every day—every hour. I do not wish to live another minute without you."

Tears crept toward her hairline, and emotions danced across her countenance. "I…I know I can never replace Elizabeth in your heart," she stammered.

James touched her mouth with his finger. "Listen to my words, Ella. The James Kerrington who loved Elizabeth Morris died with her, and it was not an unpleasant death. They loved completely, but young blood has its own time. As Ovid said, 'How different from the present man was the youth of earlier days.' You lie with a different James Kerrington, a man who loves only you. We will grow old together, surrounded by our children and grandchildren. You are the missing part, the one who makes me whole."

For a long moment, she simply clung to him. He knew her; he knew what Ella needed. She needed family and love, both of which he would give her. "I love you," she whispered, and then said it again to make it so, to give credence to her declaration. "I want to be your wife."

"Before you return to London," he avowed.

"What of Sir Louis?" She clutched at him for safety.

James distracted her with several well-placed kisses across her stomach. "You trust me to cherish your body and to nourish your heart; trust me, Ella, to see to your safety. I will not fail you. Within a fortnight, Louis Levering will know my vengeance. No one hurts the people I love."

"You do not know the extent of the mistakes I have made of late." Ella looked away, apparently fearing his questions.

"I know everything, Ella. I know about how Bran forestalled the engagement to find time to locate Levering's weakness, and I know how the baronet publicly shamed you at the theatre and at the inn in Buckinghamshire." Ella's lip trembled in humiliation. "The man will pay for his audacity."

Ella's voice begged him for forgiveness. "I acted foolishly. Please understand I meant you no harm; I wanted only to protect Thornhill. If you indulge me in this, I will be the best wife any man has ever known. I will bring no more disgrace to you."

"There is nothing for which to offer absolution, Ella. God, you have no idea of some of the choices I made as part of the Realm. We go forward from here. All that you demonstrated was the depth of the love you possess. Heaven help anyone who would harm our children or the name Kerrington. Now, no more of this foolishness. Tomorrow, I ride to Northamptonshire to confer with your brother. I will secure a special license, and we will marry privately in the Linton Park chapel by the middle of next week."

"Will Brantley agree?"

"If necessary, I will admit to deflowering his sister and then gallantly agree to a speedy marriage. I have no qualms about doing anything and everything to make you permanently mine, but I doubt it would come to that. Fowler wishes you to be happy, and I am arrogant enough to believe I can make you so."

Ella smiled mischievously. "Arrogant, are you, my Lord?"

"Arrogant. Lustful. Madly in love." He began to rotate his hips against hers.

"You wish to make love again?" He enjoyed her innocent surprise.

James began to trace a line of kisses from her ear to the throbbing pulse of her neck. "Again…and again…and again. I can never get enough of you."

"Are you sure you will not tire of me?" Ella kissed the side of his face.

With her, light, not darkness, ruled his world. He would make her whole again—make her forget her past degradation—make her forget everything except the desire coursing through her. "Tire of you? Not bloody likely. There are too many ways for me to please you."

Ella's voice became seductively husky. "Other ways?"

"Oh, yes, my Love." His lips brushed her breasts on their way to the shallow dip of her hipbone—the flat of her stomach. "You will beg me to stop and beg me to stay both at the same time." His lips kissed the rise of her mons. "Open for me, Ella. Let me pleasure you again." His mouth sucked the bud of her sex, arousing her instantly and pushing her closer to a new kind of love.

"James," she gasped, "you are wretchedly evil." She pushed one shoulder and pulled him closer with the other.

Her words made him double his efforts, feeling her grasping for that sublime moment. When his tongue touched her, Ella cascaded to that place where stars explode before one's eyes. He pressed harder, milking the last of the shudders of desire from her body.

Wiping his mouth against the blanket, James rose up to enter her again. "Are you ready for me, Ella?" He pressed into her, feeling her body clench against his erection. "You are so tight; I will not last long." Plunging deeply into her, he immediately set up a frantic pace, pounding, maddeningly losing himself in her body's heat. "Ella," his voice very sharp and raspy. "Ella," he repeated before going very still and then collapsing onto her—sweat mingling.

When their breathing returned to normal, James rolled to his back, bringing Ella to him, resting her head in the crook of his shoulder. "Sleep, my Love. I mean to have you again before I leave for Northamptonshire. You will need your strength."

"Other way, please," she murmured.

James chuckled before kissing the top of her head. He would like to teasingly call her a "true wanton," but he knew Ella was too sensitive for that. She matched his passion with her own, and he considered himself blessed among men. "How may I please you; let me count the ways," he bantered as he pulled the bed linens over them; yet, she did not answer; Ella breathed sleep's breath. "*Dustet daram*. I love you," he murmured, closing his eyes to the happiness he held tightly in his embrace. "Ella." He knew contentment at last.

~ ~ ~

Ella entered the breakfast room in midmorning, glowing from her night in Worthing's arms. He had left her with the first streaks of light—taking her to a moment of ecstasy before leaving her tucked in her bed. He told her to write three letters with specific dates and give them to Mr. Lucas. The butler would see that they were mailed, part of the complicated gambit he planned to free her from Levering's manipulations. Worthing shared part of his artifice with her before he left, and Ella marveled at the way he managed so many stratagems, bringing them all together in perfect harmony. Now, she slipped into one of the ornately carved chairs after filling a plate with coddled eggs. Evidently James had told the cook of her preferences. Ella felt hope—hope that he could rectify everything she most feared.

"Good morning, Lady Eleanor." James's mother looked exhausted. She filled a teacup and joined Ella at the table.

"Lady Linworth, did you have a rough night? Is there something I may do to serve you?" Ella was on her feet immediately to help Camelia Kerrington.

"His Lordship did not sleep well," Camelia shared. "I worry for his continued health."

Ella brought the toast and jam to the table. "I will sit with Lord Worthing. I had promised Daniel a ride, but I am sure we can postpone."

"Nonsense. His Lordship would want you to tend to Daniel. The boy has very few opportunities to be a child."

"Then I will sit with your husband after my ride; you need your rest also." Ella brought a plate of fresh fruit to the table.

Lady Linworth caught Ella's arm. "My James is correct; you possess a generous spirit, my Dear." She squeezed Ella's hand. "What is this?" Her voice rose as she turned Ella's hand over to examine the ring now prominently displayed. "Please tell me this is what I think it is."

Ella blushed, but she smiled brightly. "Viscount Worthing renewed his proposal, and I accepted. He will meet with my brother later today and earn Bran's approval."

"Oh, my Dear, I am so happy." Camelia stood to take Eleanor in her embrace. "You are so beautiful." His mother touched Ella's face with her fingertips. "When? When might I call you *Daughter*?"

Ella helped Lady Linworth to sit again. "James and I would prefer to marry as soon as possible. He hoped it might please his father to know of our union. He will purchase a special license, and we plan to marry by next week's end. I agreed we would marry in the Linton Park chapel, making the transition of his reign as the Fourteenth Earl of Linworth easier when the time comes."

"Next week?" Camelia stuttered, "but do you not wish a large wedding, Eleanor?"

"I am not one who seeks the *ton*'s approval. A wedding with close friends and family would be most perfect for my taste. My only concern is I need a dress. Aunt Agatha will be sorry that I wore black for my Presentation gown."

"We will not bother Agatha," Lady Linworth declared. "I have the ideal dress for you. It was James's grandmother's dress. We can get a seamstress in here tomorrow to make alterations. It will be magnificent, I promise. Please say you will allow this kindness."

Ella smiled widely, brilliantly happy that Worthing's family accepted her. "If it is no trouble."

"Women live for such moments, Eleanor." She brightened, starting to eat with more gusto. "Martin shall be beside himself with happiness. I cannot wait to tell him. Oh, but you may want to break the news to him yourself."

Ella laughed lightly, truly excited, caught in Lady Linworth's enthusiasm. "You have my permission, Lady Linworth, to tell His Lordship if you believe it will make him happy to hear it."

"I guarantee it will be a turning point in his recovery."

"Whose recovery, Mother? Is Papa feeling poorly again?" Airily, Georgina bestowed a kiss on her mother's cheek as she entered the morning room, Lady Amsteadt's girth preventing her from bending too far.

Lady Linworth caught Ella's hand again, shoving it toward her daughter. "Look what that brother of yours did last evening after we retired!"

Georgina caught Ella's eyes, recognizing how James must have gone to Ella's room, although she said nothing to that effect before her mother. *Believe me, if I thought being found in bed with Ella would have made her agree to marry, I would have planned a seduction two months ago.* Her brother's words rang in Georgina's head. "Well, that scoundrel!" Georgina teased. "He proposes and then leaves before we can wish him happy. You must reprimand him, Mother, for his thoughtlessness."

"It gets worse," Camelia's voice sparkled with joy. "James and Eleanor will marry next week."

"Then I am pleased to be home for the event, and Lord Amsteadt shall arrive in two days." Georgina lowered herself into a chair across from Ella.

Eleanor lowered her voice. "I request the opportunity to tell Daniel myself."

"Of course, my Dear." Camelia nodded her approval. "The boy should hear it from you."

"I believe it important not to speak down to James's son; adults often assume children are unaware of important events simply because of their ages. Children are closer to the truth because they have not known the depth of evil."

Georgina paused to evaluate what Ella had said. "That is very wise, Lady Eleanor. You will do well with Daniel; he just needs attention. I believe you might be surprised by the boy's reaction."

"I hope so." The words spoke of a false bravado. What did she know about being a mother? "If Daniel accepts me as a friend—someone he trusts—that will be a satisfying beginning."

~~~

They had meticulously planned how they would bring about Levering's downfall, from Kimbolt's strong-arming the baronet to Crowden's invasion of Levering's home to retrieve the diary. The reason they had known success in the East was that they had planned for all contingencies. Each of their strengths complemented the strengths of others in the group, and no egos existed when they took on a challenge. "We will teach Sir Louis Levering not to cross the Realm," James summarized. Four of the six men he supervised as part of the Realm sat across a table in a rural country inn in Northamptonshire. "We all know what we are doing?"
~~~

Fowler grumbled, "As long as I do not kill the bastard first."

"You may have to get in line," James commiserated with his friend. "The moment Levering commits social suicide, you are welcome to him, my friend, but I must eliminate any chance Eleanor's reputation could be soiled by that dodgy prat. If he even looks at Eleanor again, I will cut his eyes right from his head."

"And I plan to rip his tongue from his mouth." Thornhill gulped his drink to quell his anger.

Kimbolt smiled deviously. "Are you two not the bloodthirsty ones?"

"Some day you will know how we feel," Fowler warned.

"I suppose I will, but it shall not be anytime soon." The viscount poured them all another round of drinks.

"Kimbolt, you have contacted the baronet?" James checked off all possibilities.

"I did. I told Levering I expected payment of his debts as soon as I arrived in London. I also warned the 'gentleman' I would tolerate no defection on his part."

Crowden leaned back in his chair. "Do we have any idea where I should begin my search?"

"Soon." Kimbolt acknowledged with a salute of his glass.

"Bran," James began again, "everything depends on your convincing Levering you know nothing of his machinations."

Fowler rolled his eyes in disbelief. "I am not that *good* of an actor."

"You will do what is necessary," James ordered, suspecting Fowler's euphemism.

"Yes, Captain," Fowler mocked, grudgingly.

James stood to end the meeting. "I will expect all of you at Linton Park next Friday," he announced quite unceremoniously.

John Swenton laughed. "And for what purpose would that be, Captain?"

Fowler stood also, lazily draping his arm over James's shoulder. "The Captain has decided to take orders from my little sister."

The others at the table congratulated the man they had followed into some of their lives' most hair-raising escapades. "It is time, Worthing," Kimbolt declared privately. "Lady Eleanor will be the perfect complement to your brashness."

James thought of the woman to whom he had made love only a few hours ago. "Of course, having Fowler as a brother is a detriment." He shrugged off Bran's arm. "However, Lady Eleanor makes up for her brother's shortcomings."

"A toast to the Captain," Swenton came proudly to his feet, and the others followed.

"To the Captain," they called in unison as they raised their glasses.

~ ~ ~

Daniel took the news of her marriage to his father rather well; at least, Ella thought as much. She sat in a large wing chair in the earl's bedchamber, having relieved Lady Linworth of tending to the ailing earl. Martin Kerrington excitedly made plans for James's succession until he had worn himself out, but the color had returned to the man's cheeks, and Ella thought him more animated than she had expected.

Now, James's father rested, his medication making him sleep. Ella tried to read the historical essays she held in her hand, but nothing on the page made sense—her mind was elsewhere. Worthing's family embraced her as their own, and she wanted so much to believe her life had changed last night. Even the household staff had offered their solicitations, obviously wanting Viscount Worthing to find happiness with his future wife. Such ruminations brought a mental picture of the man—naked and in all his glory—to her mind. In another week, she could lie with him legally every night, wrapped in his arms. Just the thought of him sent the blood pooling to her most private parts. Impulsively, Ella squirmed in the chair, feeling guilty about such salacious thoughts.

A rapid tapping at the door caught her attention, and Ella scrambled to answer it before the noise woke the earl. Cracking the door only a few inches, she peeked out. "Daniel," she hissed, "what are you doing?"

Obviously distraught, the boy blushed before fixing his gaze on Ella's face. "Lady Eleanor, you must come quickly. Aunt Georgina..." Daniel paused, totally out of breath. "Aunt Georgina is lying on the floor, and there is blood everywhere! I could not get her to wake up!"

"Where is she?" Ella demanded, shoving the door wide.

The boy went pale, swaying a bit with fear. "Outside her room."

"Daniel, you must listen to me. I need you to be the man of the house in your father's absence. Can you do that for me?" Ella tried to do what she always had done—take charge.

His voice shook, but the boy rolled his shoulders back with resolve. "Yes, Ma'am."

"First, go to your grandmother's room and tell her I need help. Then do the same with the housekeeper. Tell her I require clean bandages and hot water immediately. Tell Mr. Lucas to send for the midwife. Do you have all that?"

"Yes, Ma'am."

"I am counting on you, Daniel." She was off at a run, never looking back, knowing the boy would do her bidding.

Seconds later, she turned the corner leading to the hallway of the family quarters. "Oh, my God, Georgina." She motioned for a footman who was coming up the stairs to follow her.

James's sister lay in a wet heap on the floor. Ella knelt by Georgina's side, not knowing where to begin. The footman rushed forward. "Get her into the bed," Ella ordered as the bulky servant lifted her almost-sister from the floor. Rushing forward, Ella led the way into the room as the man gently put Lady Amsteadt on the bed and then left.

Lady Linworth half-staggered into the room, sleep and shock making her look years older and frailer than Ella imagined her to be. This family had lost James's wife to childbirth; now they all feared losing his only sister too. Ella could not let that happen. "Will she?" Camelia Kerrington whispered.

"I do not know," Ella looked about, trying to figure out what to do first. "You and I," she told Lady Linworth, gripping the woman's hand tightly, "must do something now, or it might be too late by the time a midwife or a surgeon gets here."

Camelia wavered for a split second, but then moved to her daughter's bedside. "Tell me what to do." She placed all her trust in Eleanor Fowler.

"Let us help Georgina out of her corset and stays." Ella said a quick prayer so she might make good choices. James's sister was unconscious, but she breathed normally, and that seemed positive.

"Her water has broken," Mrs. Mooreton, the housekeeper, attested as she came to help. "Here are the smelling salts."

Once they settled Georgina against the pillows, Ella waved the pungent spirits under Lady Amsteadt's nose, and the woman came around, although she was still a bit groggy. "What happened?" she seemed confused.

"The baby is coming." Lady Linworth wiped Georgina's face with a damp cloth.

Fear crossed her daughter's eyes. "It is too early!" Georgina protested.

"It will be fine. Eleanor and I will take care of you."

Georgina turned her gaze fully on Eleanor. "Save my child," she stated flatly. "Do you hear me, Lady Eleanor? Save my baby."

A minute nod of Ella's head gave Georgina the comfort she needed. Relief played across her face; the woman had accepted her fate. Ella swallowed hard, afraid she could not change what was happening. If Georgina lost her life, it would kill James. Ella would lose him to his grief. "Let us make you more comfortable," she began to arrange the pillows. "We will need to move you to the birthing chair soon. It seems to me that a walk would speed this up and help our chances. Are you willing to try, Georgina?"

"Anything you say, Lady Eleanor. My life is in your hands."

CHAPTER 12

~ ~ ~

"WHAT IN THE WORLD IS THIS?" Ella exclaimed as she helped Lady Linworth undress Georgina.

Lady Amsteadt looked at the linen sash fastened about her middle. "It is a Tansy Bag. The midwife at home insisted I wear it. She and Thomas feared the journey from Devon too strenuous on a woman so far advanced, but I needed to come. Father and all." Ella nodded her understanding. She would have done the same even for William Fowler.

Removing it, Ella laid the poultice on a nearby table. "Tell me what the midwife said of the bag." Besides being curious about the herbal medicine, Ella wished to keep Georgina Whittington's mind from the situation.

"Mrs. Woodson, the midwife, swore the bag would stop a miscarriage if a woman was frightened somehow or there was some other accidental cause." Georgina took several deep breaths. "You do not think the bag hurt my child, do you, Lady Eleanor? I would die if my foolishness has caused me to lose this child."

Ella braced Lady Amsteadt's back as her mother slipped a muslin gown over her daughter's head and shoulders. "I cannot believe you could do anything foolish, Lady Amsteadt," Ella assured, although she privately wondered about the folk remedy. She smoothed the woman's hair from her face as she removed the pins holding the chignon in place.

"It is just that Mrs. Woodson told me to wear the sack from time to time, sometimes in the morning and sometimes at night." Ella noted how fear returned to Georgina's face. "I thought, you see..." She caught Ella's hand tightly. "I thought if sometimes was good to prevent...to prevent a miscarriage, using the bag every day in the morning and at night would make my chances better."

"Nothing you did was wrong," Lady Linworth declared. "Do not go on so, Georgina."

Tears misted the girl's eyes. "But what if it was wrong, Mama?"

Ella took control. "Besides a good handful of leaves of tansy, was there anything else in the sack?"

"Nothing...I swear by all that is holy; there was nothing else in the sack, Lady Eleanor. We just sewed the leaves in the sack of gill and heated it upon a warming pan. Then I laid the bag across my navel," Georgina's voice rose with the recitation.

"Georgina, listen to me." Ella cupped the girl's face in her hands, forcing James's sister to look directly at her. "Lady Linworth and I will let nothing happen to this child. You must believe me."

For elongated seconds Lady Amsteadt stared deeply at Ella. "I believe you, Lady Eleanor." Ella prayed she had not made the mistake of promising something she could not deliver. However, it seemed important to win the girl's trust until help came.

As Ella picked up the discarded clothing about the room, Lady Linworth came up behind her and whispered, "Could the treatment have hurt Georgina?"

"Probably not the tansy leaves, but maybe the heat," Ella murmured. "Truthfully, I have no idea. Do you suppose the midwife will come soon?"

"I pray so," James's mother continued. "What do either of us know of delivering a child?"

Ella thought things could not get worse, but when word came that the local midwife tended to the birth of twins in the next village and the nearest physician had left for London yesterday, she bit back the desire to scream in frustration.

They correctly settled Georgina on the bed rather than on the birthing chair, although Lady Amsteadt swore the pain increased to the point of delivery. "What are we going to do?" Lady Linworth pleaded as she caught Ella's arm.

Ella forced herself to smile although she had not a clue as to what she was doing. True, she had once read a medical text, part of which was on giving birth, but that was several years ago. Also, while her father convalesced, she had seen her share of animals being born on the estate. Yet, she, like Lady Linworth, was a genteel lady. *What did she know of childbirth?* "We are going to deliver Georgina's baby." She stated the obvious, praying James's mother would take the lead, but Her Ladyship looked to her for guidance. "Help me position Georgina to give birth to her first child."

The countess nodded her understanding. They prepared the birthing chair for later, prepared additional bandages, and laid out medicine available from the estate's housekeeper.

Not surprisingly, the earlier walk and the movement triggered Georgina's urge to push, and the girl let out a blood-curdling scream, causing her mother to shudder with gut-wrenching sobs while Ella flinched with shock. "Georgina." Ella's tone demanded the girl's attention. "I need for you not to bear down and not to hold your breath when the pains come. You *must* breathe as normally as possible. If you push before the baby is ready, you will hurt it. You must let it come naturally. Can you do that, Georgina?"

"I will do what is necessary for this baby, no matter what it takes." It crushed Ella to hear Georgina hint at her own demise.

"Lady Linworth, you hold Georgina's hand and keep sponging her face with the water." Ella firmly pressed against Lady Amsteadt's abdomen, examining it for its fullness. "It will be a while." She did not know that to be true. Somewhere Ella remembered hearing stories of women spending several hours in childbirth; her own mother claimed nearly seventeen hours in delivering Brantley. It seemed important to ease everyone's distress by pretending everything was normal.

"Eleanor is correct, Georgina. I spent close to ten hours waiting for you," Camelia confirmed. Lady Linworth's agreement gladdened Ella. Maybe her instincts would prove her capable, after all.

Six hours later, Georgina still gritted her teeth and worked her way through the birth process. Ella took to timing how long the discomfort lasted and how long between the spasms. Again, she had no reason to do so; it just seemed natural. The pains were now between ten and twelve minutes apart, according to the mantel clock, down from twenty minutes when they had first carried Lady Amsteadt into the bedchamber.

"Is there not someone else to help us?" Lady Linworth whispered, close to where Ella stood. They changed out the water used to bathe Georgina's face.

"I have my maid in the kitchen taking care of the water and medicine if we need it. However, none of the household staff wishes to be held responsible, as your daughter is a month early in the delivery. They fear Elizabeth's fate." Ella wrung out the cloth they used, preparing to return it to Georgina's forehead.

Lady Linworth sighed deeply. "So do I."

"We will get through this; you and I are strong. Your husband says we are very much alike. I do not plan on giving up on Georgina, and neither will you. As with your daughter, we will do what is necessary, no matter what it takes."

"I am so thankful that God placed you in this house at this moment. I could not have done this alone."

Ella thought about what had happened to her in the last month, and she knew she would suffer it all again with a glad heart if it meant her presence at Linton Park would make a difference in saving Georgina Whittington's life. Ella smiled slightly, admiring the older woman. "I beg to differ, Lady Linworth. You do not have to be alone. I am here, and we will save your child and her child."

~ ~ ~

Bran reluctantly answered the room's door. He had drunk too much during the evening and had been abed less than two hours, but he staggered to where the sound came. When he released the bolt and cracked the door, a sliver of light assaulted his eyes, and he squeezed them closed.

"Fowler," James Kerrington's voice came from the near-darkness of the inn's passageway. "I am leaving."

Bran eased his eyes open, letting the light in a little at a time. "Leaving? What time is it?"

"About four." James lowered the candle to take away the light's sting.

Bran looked confused. "Four? Why so early? Cannot stay away from my sister?" Bran's alcohol-saturated mind could not think seriously.

"No, not exactly." James paused in his explanation. "There is just something—something is not right—a gut feeling. I cannot shake it. We have always listened to our instincts."

Bran shook his head to clear it. "Levering do you suppose?"

"I do not know; I just need to go. You will deal with things in London?"

"It is done, Worthing. You may be assured of it."

James shook his head, already moving to leave. "I will see you soon." Then Worthing disappeared into the darkness, taking the light from the candle with him.

Within minutes, Bran heard the carriage's rattle in retreat. He crawled back into the bed, pulling the blanket up over his head. He would rise in a few hours and return to London. The more he thought of the possibility of Levering being in Derby, the less likely he considered the notion. Worthing simply missed Eleanor and wanted to start his new life. It was a nice dream; Bran knew it too. In fact, he suspected that each Realm member held like desires—a chance to find love and happiness. Thoughts of Velvet Aldridge renewed these prayers in him, and Bran welcomed his favorite dream of the dark-haired beauty.

~ ~ ~

"Lady Eleanor!" Daniel pounded on his Aunt Georgina's door. "Help, Lady Eleanor!"

Ella, exhausted by her constant vigil over Georgina's bed, reeled in place before jerking the door open. "What is it?" she snapped, not disguising her high dudgeon with the newest interruption and then regretting snapping at the boy.

Daniel stepped back, momentarily stung by her tone, but he shot a glance toward the earl's room and plunged ahead. "Grandpapa is getting out of bed. He says he wants to see for himself what is happening; he will not listen to me."

"I will go." Lady Linworth's drained spirit came from behind Ella.

Ella looked closely at James's mother—the woman's appearance was fagged and haggard. "If the Earl sees you, it will worry him. Neither of us has much color, but your husband will notice it more on you. Besides, you have a calming effect on Georgina. I will tend to His Lordship." Motioning to Daniel to lead the way, Ella followed the boy to his grandfather's room. Her frustration and her fear increased with each step, and by the time Ella reached the earl's room, she exploded. "What do you think you are doing, old man?"

A man used to having people at his beck and call, Martin Kerrington stood less than three feet from his bed, a satin robe sashed tightly around his waist. Her words inflamed him. "I am to see my wife and daughter," he snapped aristocratically. "I will ask that you not try to stop me, Lady Fowler."

If the earl wanted highborn, Ella would match his high-toned pretentiousness with some of her own. "That is right, Your Lordship. Hobble your way to Lady Amsteadt's room, and allow your loved ones to worry for your demise. They have no other concerns than you at the moment. Make Lady Linworth feel guilty for choosing to stay with her daughter right now rather than to hold your hand. Please do come to your daughter's bedchamber. Obviously, if you are able to stand on your own and to maneuver your way to Georgina's room, you are feeling better. Your wife and I could use your help."

"Who do you think you are?" he flared.

"I am the woman who is trying to save your daughter's life and that of your second grandchild. If you will excuse me, Your Lordship, I have no time or energy to tend to your bruised ego. Do us all a favor: Return to your bed. Let your grandson tend you as I have asked him to do. Allow Lady Linton and me to concentrate all our energies on Georgina's well-being. When we know anything, you will be apprised." Ella's hands now fisted on her hips, and her chin rose in defiance.

Martin Kerrington leaned on a cane, but he made no other move as they spent the next few minutes daring one another to say anything else. "Bloody hell," he grumbled, turning toward the bed. "Did Camelia teach you that stance or does it come naturally to you also?" he called over his shoulder.

Having expected James's father to continue to argue with her, Ella needed a second shake of her head to clear her thoughts. She stuttered, "I...I suppose it is natural."

Jerking the blankets back, the earl motioned to Daniel to come support him. "I will need to warn James about your temper," Kerrington said flatly. "You might match his mother in intensity."

"I will take that as a compliment." Ella made an amused, half-hearted curtsy to leave.

"Lady Eleanor." His voice held her in place, returning to a more familiar address. "Please give Camelia and Georgina my love. Daniel and I will offer special prayers. Will we not, my Boy?"

"Yes, Sir."

Ella rotated slowly to his voice, happy to have won the battle. "It will be my pleasure to convey your affection to your loved ones, my Lord." She curtsied again and then slyly sidled up to the boy whom she would soon call her son. "Master Daniel," she draped an arm over his shoulder in an act of conspiracy and of apology for her earlier reaction, "if His Lordship chooses to ignore all our best advice, you have my permission to wrestle him into submission." With that, she swept from the room, the sound of Daniel's laughter and the earl's sputtering drifting through the open doorway.

"Thank God, you are back." Lady Linworth seemed relieved although Ella had been gone less than ten minutes. "I think she is ready."

Ella simply moved to where she could support Georgina's weight, helping the woman to the birthing chair, a weird-looking contraption designed to place a mother in a better position to deliver a baby naturally. Settling her soon-to-be sister in a very unladylike position, Ella half-laughed at how much she had changed in the past month. If she had not spent an intimate night with James Kerrington less than two evenings ago, the current scene might have shocked her. However, now she took it in stride, realizing that the human body was not a tool for evil.

The contractions now only minutes apart, Lady Amsteadt screamed and began to push, her hands clutching at the straps on the wood-armed chair. A flush of blood told Ella that Georgina's time drew near.

"Breathe," Ella ordered as she moved to where she could assist the baby. Camelia Kerrington tried to soothe her daughter's brow.

"Another one," Georgina gasped and gritted her teeth. Jaw locked tightly, she held her breath and concentrated her energy on the pressure between her legs.

Less than an hour of sweat and anxiety brought them to the delivery. Georgina was early but not so early that it was impossible for Lady Amsteadt to survive. The child was a different story. So, expecting the baby's head, Eleanor watched in morbid curiosity as a miniature hand, arm, and shoulder appeared. "Oh, Lord, no!" She felt the panic coursing through her veins. *What could she do now?* The baby could not survive such a delivery, and they had no way of surgically removing the child. They might lose both mother and child.

"Can you see it…the baby?" Georgina panted breathlessly.

"Not…not yet," Ella stammered, trying to determine what to do next. If Georgina pushed again, it might be too late to do anything. She glanced at James's ring on her finger and knew what she must do: She must save Georgina from Elizabeth's fate.

"Georgina, listen to me," Ella's voice held no chance for argument. "The baby did not turn. I can see the child's arm and shoulder, but it cannot come out this way without hurting the child, wrapping the cord around it. I need to slide the arm back in you somehow and turn the shoulder enough so the head comes first. You must not push until I finish." She slid the ring from her hand and slipped it into her pocket for safekeeping. James's love would be her guide through all this.

"I am frightened," Georgina gasped. "I do not think I am capable of what you ask."

Ella pressed her suit, "Georgina, will you leave Lord Amsteadt to suffer the way your brother did with Elizabeth, where he must live with the loss of his wife or his child? Will you put James through that again? He will not survive a repeat of such grief. Help me to save them both—I love James, and I know you love Lord Amsteadt."

Georgina's eyes widened in disbelief, but she shook her head in understanding. "Do it quickly, Eleanor, before I have time to think about it."

Ella did not want to consider how this would be. She would do the unthinkable for a lady of noble birth; yet, she caught the tiny arm and locked it close to the child's body before shoving it upward into Georgina's opening, saying a private prayer she did not hurt the baby. She instinctively bumped against Georgina's legs, opening them further.

"Easy," Ella continued to coach. "Almost." She did not know whether what she did made a difference, but she worked the baby's shoulder free from Lady Amsteadt's opening. Blood gushed from the womb, and Ella wondered why it did not repulse her. "Hold…hold…"The baby seemed to shift at the opening, and she could see bright red hair and an ear. "Nearly there." She had her fingers in Lady Amsteadt's opening, touching the matted locks of the woman's child. Ella had once seen a groomsman reach up into a mare to turn a colt. This was not the same, but she could not eliminate the image from her mind. Slimy mucus coated her fingers, but Ella continued to touch the top of the head, working it fraction by fraction toward the opening. "Lord Amsteadt has red hair," she laughed at the absurdity of what she said. "Another minute, Georgina," she ordered, but never looked up.

Georgina said nothing, but Ella could hear her labored breathing and sense the pain the woman suffered.

The ear was no longer evident, and all Eleanor saw was tangled red locks. "Push, Georgina," she rasped out.

Lady Amsteadt gulped for air and bore down, needing desperately to release the pressure she felt. Ella watched carefully as the baby's head crowned and stretched the opening. "Again," she barked before feeling the baby's face in her hands. Gently, Ella guided it forward. "It is there, Georgina. A couple more times," she encouraged.

This time the baby's full head and neck appeared. Ella released the breath, which she had held throughout the ordeal. Georgina rose up and pressed forward, Lady Linworth supporting her daughter's back. Ella did not release the head she held tenderly in her hands. Somehow it seemed important that the child know someone would protect it. Finally, the shoulders cleared, and the trunk followed.

Ella reached for the swaddling cloth and began to wipe the baby clean, clearing her mouth and nose. "Come on, Sweetheart." Ella rubbed the child's back and chest trying to convince it to breathe on its own.

"Tap it hard," Lady Linworth ordered, taking the child from Ella's hands. "Cut the cord," she hissed, holding the baby away from Georgina's body. "Hurry! The cord is wrapped around its neck."

"Mama!" Georgina pleaded, but Lady Linworth ignored her daughter.

Ella grabbed the razor she had taken from James's room and made two cuts after tying off the cord with strings.

As Ella tended to Georgina's safety, Lady Linworth worked the cord free of the baby's neck and pushed hard on its back. A moment's silence followed, and then a weak twitter of air, much like the chirp of a bird, echoed through the room.

Georgina's sobs, no longer stifled, filled the space, symbolic of what they all felt.

Lady Linworth continued to massage the baby's back, but her shoulders no longer held the tension of a moment ago, and Ella began to relax. A whimper and a cry reassured them all that they had done the impossible. "It is a girl." Camelia Kerrington wrapped the child in a soft blanket. "Eleanor is correct; Lord Amsteadt shall never be able to deny his daughter. Look at her hair." True joy radiated from her words.

"Let me see," Georgina begged as Lady Linworth placed the child in her daughter's arms.

Ella moved on wobbly legs toward the nearest chair. "I think I need to sit down." She gulped for air and bent over at the waist, fighting away the blackness creeping into her head.

Lady Linworth touched her back lightly, gently massaging her shoulders. "Now, you become frightened?" Amusement in the situation hit both of them.

"I did not have time before," Ella whispered loudly, slowly raising her head to look at her future mother. All about them, the room had changed with the baby's first breath.

"Look at my daughter, Eleanor." Georgina moved the blanket away from the child's face. "Is she not beautiful?"

Ella took a deep breath and stood, testing her legs before moving to where she could see the child. "I never thought myself capable of delivering a child." She touched the baby's cheek gently. "Welcome to the world, Little One."

"Give me my granddaughter," Lady Linworth demanded. "Eleanor, can you and Mrs. Mooreton see to Georgina's state? I will introduce this child to her grandfather; I am sure Martin is beside himself with worry."

Ella stepped to the door to summon Georgina's maid and the housekeeper to aid in the cleanup. Before she could stop her laughter, she turned gleefully to her future mother. "Please tell His Lordship I sincerely apologize for my earlier outburst."

"Was Martin his usual demanding self? He fancies he is in charge of this house; men are such weaklings, are they not, Ladies? Could you see any of them doing what we just did?" The relief of the past few minutes allowed them all freedom to speak openly. The three of them bonded in a way no one else could have understood.

"The Earl accused me of taking lessons from you, Your Ladyship."

"Good for you," Camelia declared before returning her attention to Georgina. "Do we have a name for this child? Martin will want to know."

"I planned to seek Lord Amsteadt's counsel, but *Eleanor* seems most appropriate to me. Thomas will agree. If not for Lady Eleanor, tragic circumstances might be our fate instead of the joy we all feel."

Tears misted Ella's eyes. "I am honored, Georgina."

"It is the least homage I can offer. I owe you—we all owe you so much more. God placed you here because this family needed you…James and Daniel and Papa and Mama and me. We all need you, Eleanor."

Ella swallowed hard, unable to control her emotions. "A family—I never thought it possible," she whispered.

~~~

At noon, Kerrington's carriage rolled into the Linton Park driveway. A feeling of dread had followed him across the Peak District, and he was glad to experience the normalcy of his footmen welcoming him home. Alighting from the carriage, he bounded up the stairs to the entrance, needing to see for himself that his family was safe. He handed his hat and cane to Mr. Lucas and had just turned to the stairs when Daniel flew down the steps at full blast.
~~~

"Papa!" the boy called as he jumped over the landing and kept coming. "I am so glad you are home." He rushed to his father with open arms.

James could not remember the last time his son had called him *Papa* instead of *Father* nor how long it was since Daniel had willingly given him a hug. James dropped to a knee and held the boy close to him, a chasm of loneliness narrowing with the embrace. Breathing deeply, James closed his eyes with contentment.

However, Daniel squirmed for release, and Kerrington reluctantly loosened his hold. "Papa, you will never believe what has happened."

James smiled at the boy as he stood and looked again to the stairs expecting the others, especially Eleanor, to greet him. "Will you tell me, or shall I guess?" he said distractedly.

"You will never guess," Daniel declared. "Not in a million years. Lady Eleanor called Grandpapa *Old Man* to his face!"

James sputtered, but he managed to catch Daniel by the arm to lead his child to some privacy. This was, obviously, not a conversation to have before the household staff. Leading Daniel to the nearest room, James closed the door for confidentiality and then demanded an explanation. "Start at the beginning, and tell me all."

"Lady Eleanor and I went riding yesterday, and she told me you planned to marry her." James wanted to interrupt to weigh his son's reaction, but he simply gestured for Daniel to continue with the story. "We returned early because Grandmama was feeling poorly. Lady Eleanor sat with His Lordship so Grandmama could rest. Later in the day, when I finished my lessons, I was going to see if someone would play chess, but when I went looking for Aunt Georgina, she was lying on the floor and bleeding."

"Bleeding?" James's fear became apparent. "How badly?"

"Badly, Papa. I was really afraid so I went to find Lady Eleanor."

Impatient to know, James pressed. "Tell me quickly, Daniel."

"It is a big story, Papa, but I will try. Lady Eleanor and Grandmama helped Aunt Georgina with the baby."

"They what? Where was Mrs. Matthews?"

"Mrs. Matthews tended a woman with twins in the village. Lady Eleanor did it all, Papa, but Grandmama helped too! Aunt Georgina named the baby Eleanor, and she has bright red hair just like Lord Amsteadt."

"What about your grandfather?"

"Grandpapa tried to get out of bed. He and Lady Eleanor yelled at each other. She called him an *Old Man* and said he was stubborn. He said she was just like Grandmama, and he would have to teach you how to handle your new wife."

James laughed lightly. He could imagine the confrontation if the Earl placed himself in Eleanor's way. "He did, did he?" Sarcasm snuck into his tone.

"I do not think Grandpapa really knows how to handle Grandmama. He does what she says, especially when she puts her hands on her waist like Lady Eleanor did."

James enjoyed his son's evaluation of his grandfather's claim of dominance over his wife. "I suspect you are correct, Son, but do not tell your grandfather your opinion. The Earl prefers to think he rules his own house."

"Will you listen to Lady Eleanor when you marry her?" Daniel seemed fascinated by the possibility.

"As Lady Eleanor is one of the most intelligent women I have ever known, it is likely I will seek her opinion regularly."

"Lady Eleanor is very knowledgeable," Daniel observed.

"Then you shall not object to my bringing Ella into our lives?"

Daniel looked up suddenly surprised that his father sought his approval. "I really like Lady Eleanor." Daniel fidgeted before adding, "She says we shall be friends."

James nodded in understanding. "Will that be acceptable to you?"

The boy paused, an elastic silence stretching between them. "I do not wish to forget my own mother, but do you think Lady Eleanor might let me call her *Mama* some time?"

James breathed easier, realizing his instincts regarding Ella correct. "Lady Eleanor has a large loving heart, and she will welcome you as her own. I imagine she would prefer to give you time to accept all the changes in your life that her presence as my wife will bring. It might be best to call her *Ella,* with her permission, of course, at first. But I believe you will both know when the time is right for you to switch to *Mama*."

This idea seemed to please Daniel. "Everyone is asleep right now," he announced. "It took a long time for the baby to be born."

"Is my new niece in the nursery?"

"Yes, Baby Eleanor is in a crib. Mr. Lucas sent for a wet nurse, but one of the maids tends to her at present. Could we go up and see her? I only peeked at her once."

James ruffled his son's hair. "I cannot wait any longer. Let us go together."

Following a few steps behind Daniel, they moved quickly through the passageways leading to the nursery. James nodded to the maid, who scrambled to her feet when they came in. "The babe sleeps," she told him before dropping a curtsy.

"We just want a quick look." He caught Daniel's arm, and they inched forward in unison to peer at the sleeping child. "Lord Amsteadt will love the hair, will he not?" James bent to whisper close to Daniel's ear.

"Aunt Georgina says Baby Eleanor is small but beautiful." Daniel's response was not as secretive.

James peeled away the blanket with the tip of his finger, getting a better look at his niece. "God has a way of making all his children beautiful. Of course, I thought you the most remarkable child I had ever seen." James rested his hand on his son's shoulder, and he felt Daniel swell with pride.

"Truly, Papa?" Daniel searched James's face for honesty. James saw in his child what Ella had described only two days prior. Daniel sought his approval and his unconditional love. Everything in James's life had changed with the introduction of Eleanor Fowler.

James tilted Daniel's chin higher, looking deeply into the boy's face. "You have a lot of your mother in your looks, and she was the most handsome of women." Baby Eleanor began to fuss, so James motioned his son from the room. "You should return to the schoolroom; Mr. Weston will be looking for you."

"Yes, Papa."

"You will dine with us this evening?" James wanted to keep the closeness flowing between them.

Daniel smiled broadly. "Thank you, Papa."

James laughed at Daniel's retreating form. The boy seemed happier, and Worthing attributed it all to Eleanor's influence.

Making sure the hall was clear, James slipped into Ella's room, locking the door behind him. Walking quietly, he came to stand beside the bed and eased the drapery aside to look at her. Eleanor's golden locks spread out across the pillow, and her innocence sent a shot of pure lust straight to his groin. James reached out to touch the strands with his fingertips.

Engrossed in looking at her face, he did not notice the slight shift of Ella's hand by her side, so when her hand shot out and caught his finger, James's reaction was one of pure surprise. "It is about time, Lord Worthing." Ella's seductive tease warmed him clear through.

He placed a knee on the bed's edge and leaned over her to kiss the side of Ella's face. Her eyes remained closed, but a smile turned up the corners of her mouth. "You missed me, Lady Eleanor?"

"I was too busy to miss even you, my Lord." She rolled to her back and opened her arms to him.

No other words were necessary. James jerked off his jacket and sent it sailing toward a nearby chair. He lay on top of her, enjoying the closeness and how freely Ella kissed him. "Was it awful?" he asked between intimacies.

Ella eased her eyes open. "I thought we might lose both Georgina and the child. I was so frightened, James." She clutched at him for comfort. "The baby had not turned all the way."

He held his breath, imagining her trials. "What did you do?" he asked softly.

"I had no choice; I pushed the baby's arm into Georgina and then maneuvered the child's head toward the opening." James knew he stiffened in her embrace, but he could not control his reaction. *His Amazon*—his Ella—had saved Georgina's life and the life of his niece. She had kept Georgina from meeting Elizabeth's fate.

"Thank you for Georgina's life." The words nearly stuck in his throat; his mouth was so dry he could not swallow. "You are an incomparable woman, Eleanor Fowler, and I am so blessed you love me." Caught in the moment, James began to smother her with kisses, and Ella responded by arching to his touch.

"God, Woman, you have no idea how much I want you." His mouth found hers in a moment of passion.

"It is the middle of the day," she protested.

James sucked Ella's ear lobe, causing her to moan. "If you believe, my Love, that once we marry that I will desire you only at night, you are sadly mistaken. I will want you every minute of every day. You will suffer my lust often." His teeth raked across her neck. "You are fully clothed, but I am as randy as a schoolboy for you. You consume me, Eleanor. I am nothing without you."

"I have found a family at Linton Park. I never knew that so much love could exist in one place." Ella's voice came out small and insecure.

"Sweetheart, I brought the special license with me. We can marry at any time." He brushed the hair from Ella's face. "I want to pledge my love to you before God, and then we will begin our own family. A half dozen blond-haired beauties would make me happy."

"I was thinking a grey-eyed, mahogany-haired master might be more to my liking."

"In a few more days, you will be mine forever, and we can begin our family in earnest." They both knew that, in reality, Ella already could be carrying his child, but it was important to say the words aloud. He rolled to his side to lie beside her. "You rest now; I need to check on Father and Georgina. I will see you at supper if not before."

Ella recognized how he had set up the barriers. They would wait until the marriage vows to be intimate again. His honor demanded as much. "I love you more than life, James Kerrington."

He kissed the tip of her nose. "You are a temptation, my Love." A deep sigh signaled his withdrawal as he slid from the bed. "If I do not leave now, you will have no reputation of merit left, and Fowler will become my enemy."

"Yes, my Lord." Ella brought the blanket around her shoulders and closed her eyes tightly. "I will just dream."

James stood, picked up his jacket, and walked to the door.

"Naughty dreams," she called out without looking at him.

James snorted with amusement as he reached for the door handle. "You do not play fair, Lady Eleanor."

"I have never had such fun *playing* before, Lord Worthing." She raised her head from the pillow and pursed her lips in a kiss.

James groaned—her disheveled appearance making her look adorably sexy. Striding to her, he shoved her back on the bed. "I warned you, Ella, when it comes to you I have no self-control—none whatsoever."

"Control is highly overrated," she teased, stretching out her arms to him.

"I have created a monster." His kisses trailed down her neck and across her chest. "A monster, indeed."

CHAPTER 13

~ ~ ~

"I TOLD YOU I EXPECTED FULL PAYMENT when I arrived in London! Then you forced me to track you to Kent!" Aidan Kimbolt lifted Louis Levering from the floor and slammed him against the nearest wall. "I am not a man who likes to be kept waiting!"

Levering staggered to his feet, rubbing his chin where Kimbolt's fist had made contact. "I do not have the money, but I should have it soon."

"I am tired of hearing you say *soon*. Nothing you promise ever comes about, whether it is the money or the ladies." Kimbolt threw the decanter of port against the wall, watching it soak the tapestry. They were at Huntingborne Abbey, and the place had seen better days. Portraits no longer adorned the walls, tattered and worn rugs "graced" the floors, and candle wax filled in the woodcarvings of the mantelpiece. Evidently, the baronet had sold everything of any value to cover his debts and feed his addictions. "By the way, what has happened to Lady Eleanor? Was she there when you arrived in London?" Kerrington had instructed Kimbolt to find out if Levering suspected Eleanor Fowler's whereabouts.

"The bitch still has not shown. I called at Briar House yesterday; Miss Aldridge put me off, saying Lady Eleanor was touring the Lake District with her friend Miss Nelson. The chit has no friend by that name; I know—we made it up, but her cousin was there with a newsy letter, and it was posted from the Lakes. That is why I came to Kent—I thought she might be hiding at Thorn Hall. I have a man there—a guy who owes me—so he will tell me when the Fowlers come and go. He says they have been in London since they left the estate eight weeks ago." Levering edged away from the wall. "I need to find her soon; she is my money purse."

Kimbolt made a mental note to warn Fowler of a traitor on his estate. "Is that your master plan? Marrying Lady Eleanor?" The viscount snarled in disbelief. "That is how you plan to pay me back? Obviously, Fowler's sister has no desire to marry you, Levering. She can hide out for a long time, and your debts will keep mounting."

"I have something she wants; the lady will not stay away."

Kimbolt walked around the room to assess the possibility of a hiding place. "You are a pompous ass if you think your charms strong enough to induce Lady Eleanor's return."

"Lady Eleanor is too cold for my taste, but she will return. I guarantee it." Levering moved to the nearest chair, keeping it between him and Kimbolt.

"Guarantee? What kind of guarantee?" The viscount fingered a vase on the nearest table, pretending to assess its value. "If you expect an extension, I want to see this guarantee—see where my money is going. Otherwise, you may be looking at debtor's prison. I do not see anything in this house of value—nothing to pay back the debts I hold on you."

"You have only two thousand," Levering insisted.

Kimbolt smiled deviously. "That is where you are wrong, Levering. I hold your scrip from several of your biggest creditors. I bought your blunt for pennies on the quid. You owe me close to twelve thousand."

Levering staggered backwards in disbelief. "Why would you do that?"

"I play my hunches, and my instincts tell me you are on to something big. It took balls or pure stupidity to bring a lady of Eleanor Fowler's stature to that hunting box. I prefer to think it is the former, and you have some sort of plan. I want a cut of what you make in addition to the debts you owe me."

"That is blackmail," Sir Louis protested.

"Precisely! Something with which I suspect you are very familiar. How else could you control Lady Eleanor? I observed the woman with Viscount Worthing on more than one occasion this Season; she affects him, and it would be a good match for them both. I doubt if either family would object. Then, all at once, you announce that the woman will marry you. So, I ask myself, what does Levering have that would make Lady Eleanor turn from a future earl to you. The only answer I have is blackmail. It must be something good. Tell me I am right, Levering." The viscount now stood menacingly over Sir Louis.

Levering tried to smile—a self-deprecating move. "And if what you say is true, what will it cost me?"

"The balance of your debt and another eight thousand." The Realm planned to back the baronet into a corner to force him to agree to their proposal.

"That is twenty thousand. Highway robbery! I will not do it!" Louis stormed away toward the window.

Kimbolt watched their contrived manipulation masterly fall in place. "Fine. We will do it the hard way—debtor's prison for you and a twelve thousand pound lien on this property for me. I am sure someone will give me the twenty thousand I want for it. Even in the shape it is in, property is still the safest commodity."

"Wait a minute!" Levering put out a hand to stop Kimbolt's departure. "We can deal together."

Lexford turned slowly, milking the moment. "I am listening."

"Five thousand plus the debts," Levering countered. "And you help me pull this off. Lady Eleanor liked you; she will respond to you positively." He mopped his sweaty brow with his handkerchief.

"Let me see what you have on the lady first—see if it is worth my wait. If it is as good as I believe, I will take an even fifteen thousand and leave you to the rest."

Levering's breathing became easier, and he tried to smile again. "Follow me." He stepped around the viscount, picking up a candlestick as he went.

With a satisfying smile, Lord Lexford followed, taking note of the direction so he might share it with Crowden. Finally, they came to a narrow staircase leading to an attic, probably a room to dry clothing, as they were in the steepled part of the house and a room for any other purpose was unlikely. Levering demanded that Lexford wait at the bottom of the stairs. The viscount thought to follow, but heavy dust on the steps told him Levering would see the footprints. So, instead he listened, counted the number of steps, heard the scrape of metal on wood, the sound of something heavy being moved, and steps returning.

"Ah, here we are." Levering returned from the hiding place.

Kimbolt lounged against the wall, trying to look casual. "Was it worth all this dirt?" He brushed at his sleeve.

"You tell me," Levering smirked. He handed Kimbolt the diary; for a moment, the viscount wanted to knock out the baronet and make off with the journal, but he had to be patient—to wait—to play out the hand: to make sure there were no copies, make sure no one else knew, and make sure Levering never told another soul. It was the Realm's way to be thorough, never impulsive.

"It resembles a lady's journal." Lexford turned the book over in his hands. "How can this bring down Thorn Hall?"

"Take a look at the December 5 entry, and you will understand." Levering folded his arms over his chest and waited for the expected reaction. "What do you think, Collins?" he snorted with self-confidence.

The viscount read the suggested entry and then thumbed through the book, examining the other entries. He needed to tell Worthing and Fowler what the book held. Lexford whistled under his breath. On more than one occasion, Fowler had shared the horror stories of his father's sexual appetite, but here was proof of not only the duke's unusual tastes, but that of Levering's parents. Instead of being appalled by what he read, Levering planned to exploit his own family's reputation to feed his need for cards and women and drink. Kimbolt did not know who was the more debased—somehow William Fowler moved up the rungs of the ladder. The diary went a long way toward explaining why Levering acted the way he did. The viscount realized the baronet waited for an answer. "I have to hand it to you. It is quite lascivious; is it true?"

"Who cares?" Levering took the book from Kimbolt's hands. "What is important is that Thornhill will be willing to pay to keep it quiet."

"Is it just the one book?" Kimbolt needed to know, to tell Crowden.

Levering tucked the volume under his arm and headed down the stairs to the sleeping quarters with Lexford following close on the man's heels. "There are two books. I keep them both under lock and key; they are my bread and butter." Reaching the main passageway, he turned to face Kimbolt. "Well, Collins, do we have a deal?"

The viscount paused, adding the needed suspense. "We have a deal, Levering. I will have my man of business draw up the papers. He will call on you later today." The Realm planned to send Lowery to act as Lexford's solicitor. "The debt will come due one week from the day you marry Lady Fowler. I will even help fund your courtship. Roslyn really enjoyed the gowns I gave her. They earned me three straight days in the lady's bed."

"I am happy one of us benefited from Lady Eleanor's departure. Fanny is still angry." Kimbolt truly found that fact amusing. Departing the house, he laughed freely at the image of the neutered Sir Louis Levering kneeling at Worthing's feet and begging for mercy.

~ ~ ~

"I will go tomorrow night," Gabriel Crowden told Fowler. They had sent word to Worthing of Kimbolt's success, and now planned to execute the next step, Crowden's removing the diary from Levering's possession.

"Why not tonight?"

Crowden leaned back in the chair, a mischievous smile turning up the corners of his mouth. "Too easy." He propped the heels of his Hessians on the corner of Fowler's desk. "No one there tonight but the servants. Lexford says Levering plans a little card party tomorrow evening with his friends. I prefer a challenge."

"I just want the diary; I do not personally care about the *thrill* you receive when you invade the place."

"You will take possession of the diary, Your Grace; I will warrant it. I just hate that no one will know until much later."

Fowler handed Crowden a package. "The Viscount made a guess on the appearance of the second book. The black one is what he believes Lady Levering used for the one he saw in Sir Louis's possession. We have written *creative* passages in place of the ones Kimbolt observed. It should be amusing anyway."

"I shall place these inside the box Levering used." The marquis took the package from Fowler's outstretched hands. "As soon as we have the original diary, are we still off to Derbyshire?"

"Eleanor and Worthing will marry on Friday. I want to give her the diaries before then."

Crowden thumbed through the counterfeit books, needing something to do with his hands. "How do you feel about their marriage?"

"I am having some difficulty in picturing my baby sister as old enough to be the mistress of her own house, although I know she is more than capable." Fowler traced his finger around the glass's rim.

"I thought you were going to say something about picturing her with child, knowing how she got that way."

Fowler frowned, pursing his lips. "I could have gone all day without the image of the Captain in bed with my sister. That is certainly not fair, Godown."

The Marquis laughed when his friend blushed. "Worthing is the first of us. Who do you suppose is next?"

The Duke paused, debating on whether to answer. "I suspected you and my cousin might be considering a joining."

Crowden lowered his heels and prepared to stand. "I was thinking, Your Grace, about retiring to Gossling Hill."

Fowler swallowed hard. "Alone?"

"Alone, Your Grace." Crowden stood and adjusted his clothing. "I thought I might leave from Derbyshire."

"You must wait until after Prinny's party. It would be a shame to miss what happens with Levering."

"Then after the Prince Regent's little soiree. I need the wildness of Staffordshire. London is too constraining."

Dressed completely in black, Gabriel "The Ghost" Crowden climbed through an open window on Huntingborne Abbey's second floor, having traversed a vine-covered trellis. The window, used to cross-ventilate the upper level, opened onto a long hallway, which led to the main staircase. Crowden stood in the shadows and listened for whether anyone had sounded the alarm with his presence. According to Kimbolt, Levering kept a bare-bones staff of only five in the house. Near midnight, Crowden did not expect to find any servants, although it was possible, as Levering and his friends played cards in one of the downstairs drawing rooms.

Crowden watched the game in progress from a patio window for some time, assuring himself of the condition of each of the house's occupants. Kimbolt had joined the group to help him if something were to go wrong with the heist. The party shared three women—local village whores who allowed themselves to be touched intimately by each and all. Aidan Kimbolt chose not to partake, although none of the other carders noticed, as the viscount occasionally slipped his arm around one of the women, purely for show. But he did not participate in the profligacy, nor did he drink beyond the occasional sip. Both Crowden and the viscount needed a clear head to stay alert to danger.

Crowden stayed in the shadows and worked his way along the wall. Kimbolt had drawn very detailed diagrams, which the Marquis had committed to memory. Now, he moved cautiously. It was a quiet night—no wind, and even the crickets were silent. Luckily, the moon made an appearance, providing a shaft of light the length of the hallway. He had earned the nickname of *The Ghost* after convincing one not-so-magnanimous French comte that he had imagined the dark stranger when the man awoke to find Gabriel Crowden going through the safe in the comte's bedroom. With his French better than that of many Frenchmen, Crowden assured the man that he had dreamed the theft and then waltzed from the room—a ghost—without anyone else in the household even waking.

Reaching the described stairway, the Marquis lit a stub of a candle. Being far enough away from the card room, the players would not see the light. No one had cleaned the stairway, and Crowden needed to step into Levering's footprints. The idea was for the baronet not to realize the exchange of books until it was too late. Crowden found he had to tiptoe at times because Levering wore so small a boot. "A boy's feet," he thought sarcastically.

He eased the room's door open. Kimbolt had guessed correctly: Someone had designed the room for drying clothes. Rope lines ran between metal hooks on the wall. Although the windows remained closed, they polluted two walls, providing light enough to see the room's layout.

Lord Lexford had counted the steps Levering had taken and had noted the sound of metal on wood, but the room was totally empty except for the drying lines. There was not one piece of furniture.

"All right—no chest or safe," he told himself. Immediately, he squatted to see if there were dusty tracks he could follow, but nothing showed in the subdued candlelight. "Eight steps," he silently mouthed.

Keeping Levering's height in mind, Crowden adjusted his stride, shortening it. He marked off eight steps toward the room's center, which proved fruitless—not even a loose floorboard. Dutifully, he returned to the doorway and went off at an angle to his right. Still nothing. He tried the same thing on the left with the same results. Feeling the frustration of retracing his steps over and over again, Crowden nearly missed the obvious. A second turn, at a different angle, offered no possibilities, but the same angle on the left revealed a shadow in the wall, which the marquis cursed himself for not seeing immediately. He began at the room's closed door again and went toward the darkened aberration. Eight steps exactly.

Raising the candle, he examined the area. A three-foot square cut into the wooden panels displayed a hinged door—the metal on wood that Kimbolt had heard. Crowden used a knife to get a finger hold and began to edge the hinged door open. After the first squeak, he lifted the door enough to ease the weight of it and managed to swing it wide open without any other sound.

A gaping black hole appeared before Crowden raised the candle to look inside. *Of all the absurd places!* Inside the opening stood the house's locked dumbwaiter, a knotted rope keeping it from moving. Crowden peered in, and lying on the flat plane of the small bucket was a book.

"Bloody hell!" he cursed silently, as he realized that only one book lay in the compartment. Quickly, he opened the package he carried under his shirt and placed the replica they had created as a replacement for the original. *The dummy in the dumbwaiter*, he kept repeating in his head as he closed the hinged opening. He would share the irony of the phrase with Kerrington and Fowler.

Now, he had to find the other book. Hurrying back the way he had come, Gabriel retraced the baronet's steps once more. The man's bedchamber seemed the most likely place, so he rushed toward the family quarters. He peered into several empty rooms before finding one strewn with remnants of leftover food and rumpled clothing. Evidently, Levering's small staff let the work lapse around the house.

"Pig." Crowden commented as he closed the door behind him. The chamber pot's stench filled the room with a strong urine odor. Unable to tolerate the smell, Crowden cracked one of the windows. "The arse will thank me later," he mumbled.

Lighting a single candle, he did a complete search of the room. He found dirty clothes and bed linens, but nothing even resembling a book. He searched the dresser, the mattresses, the wardrobe, and even managed to open a locked safe box. "Now where?" He began to reason. He could not search the whole house in one night. He had to think like a madman. "His study," Crowden decided.

This was more challenging than he had expected. He needed to traverse the stairs without being seen. Leaving the baronet's bedroom, Crowden turned toward the service stairway he had passed on the right hallway. Crossing the landing on the main stairway for the third time, he paused to hear a woman's squeal emanating from the open doorway before he slipped into the service passage.

Although he did not know the house, all English country estates followed certain principles in their constructions, and he made only two wrong turns before he stood in the hallway that held the baronet's study. Unfortunately, he needed to cross the drawing room's open doorway, as well as a footman snoozing in a chair beside the house's entrance door. This was a real problem. He needed a distraction: He needed Aidan Kimbolt's help. In the past, he and Kimbolt had staged similar forays. Easing along the wall and using a crossover step to keep in the shadows, Crowden reached the open doorway. Unfortunately, the marquis could not see Kimbolt to know whether his friend might respond. *I hope this works.* He reached up to the wall sconce and lit the candle he carried. Crowden brought it before him where Kimbolt might see it in the door's crack, and then blew it out, letting a whiff of smoke sneak through the opening. Then he held his breath and prayed his partner would see the brief change in the hallway.

"Is there another chamber pot?" Crowden heard the viscount ask a bit louder than necessary.

"What is wrong with the one in the corner?" One of Kimbolt's fellow players, who sounded a bit irritated, inquired.

Through the crack, Crowden saw Kimbolt shove his chair back. "I need some privacy."

"Use the one in my study," Levering mumbled without looking up.

Kimbolt stood and swayed in place, giving the impression of being inebriated to anyone who might have looked up. Crowden thought that Kimbolt deserved his reputation for dramatics. "Deal me out this hand." Then he stumbled toward the open doorway. When he reached it, he caught the doorframe and pretended to steady himself before calling over his shoulder. "To the right or the left?" As he made an exaggerated gesture, he pulled the door to him, closing it part of the way, allowing Crowden to slip past.

"Left." Levering and Montford called out in unison, without raising their heads, engrossed in the game.

"Right." The viscount took two steps. "I mean left. Right—it is left. That is funny." Kimbolt cackled with his own attempt at humor—a drunken cackle, which one of the women mimicked. The viscount stumbled out and turned to the room where the door stood ajar.

Entering the study, he locked the door before lighting a candle. When Crowden stepped from the wall's darkness, he asked, "What is wrong?"

"There was only one book in the drying room. Its mate is not in the baronet's bedchamber. I thought it might be here."

With no further discussion, both men began to silently search. Kimbolt took the desk and Crowden the stacks of paper piled in every corner. Slowly, the viscount eased a bottom drawer open. "Here," he whispered with urgency. He pulled the tome from the sliding receptacle in the desk.

Crowden moved quickly to make the exchange. "You have to make sure the baronet locks up the copy before he reads it again. He will know something is wrong, and Fowler says he cannot know until Prinny's party."

"I will take care of it," Kimbolt hissed. "Now, get out of here."

Crowden simply nodded and strode to the window. "I will be at Briar House tomorrow."

Kimbolt did not get a chance to answer: The door rattled from the outside. "Hey, Collins, what is going on?"

Kimbolt hurriedly loosened the top buttons of his front placket. "Nothing is going on," he barked as he jerked the door open. "Sometimes I like to take a piss in private." He rebuttoned his breeches.

"I think we have all had it for tonight." Montford walked toward the staircase. "We are staying here. Take any of the empty rooms you want." Heath Montford climbed the stairs slowly; one of the village women supported his weight. Danver Clayton followed with another of the women. Gavin Bradley had passed out on the chaise some time ago.

Returning to the card room, the viscount told the third woman, "You should find your way to Sir Louis's room." She looked at him with disappointment, after having vied for his attention all evening.

"The third room on the left from the second landing." Levering stacked the cards in the table's middle.

When the woman trailed the others, Kimbolt began to straighten the chairs. "Did you speak to Fowler?" He asked rather casually.

"Saw him yesterday." Levering downed the last of his drink before setting the glass a little too hard on the table. "The bastard received me himself."

"Any news of his sister?" The viscount propped his feet on a nearby hammock as he sat again at the card table.

Levering joined him so they might speak in private. "Fowler says Lady Eleanor plans to return for Prinny's party. That is less than a fortnight. When I asked where the lady might be, the duke claimed she had taken a holiday—supposedly traveling through the Lake District with that non-existent friend of hers, Miss Nelson."

"So, she is still in hiding?"

"The chit has to come home sometime—to either London or here. I even sent a man to Cornwall to see if she was at Fowler's house there, but that place is shut up. The servants from there are the ones the Duke has in London."

Kimbolt flipped the cards, using one hand to divide and shuffle them. "So what do you do next?"

"The Duke invited me to join them at the Prince Regent's party. I will reclaim Lady Eleanor then if not before."

"Prinny's party? You were invited to the Prince's party?" He pretended surprise.

"Well, not directly, but as part of Thornhill's party, I will be accepted."

"Only the cream of the *ton* is invited." Kimbolt set the trap. "It will be the perfect time to make connections—to feather your bed, so to speak."

"Being seen with Lady Eleanor on my arm before the *beau monde* will serve me well."

"Looks perfect." Lexford gave Levering a mocking smirk. "You have the books to keep the lady in line."

Levering stared off as if imagining the scene. "Yes."

"The books are in a safe place, are they not?" The viscount laid out the cards in a game of solitaire. He did not even look at Levering, but he knew what expression the man wore.

Levering stood suddenly. "I should not keep Lizzie upstairs waiting."

"I believe I will finish this game and then call it a night. I have business in Surrey day after tomorrow. I shall be out of town for a week. You will take care of the Fowlers while I am away?"

"Everything will be well. You have nothing of which to worry. I shall have your money before long."

Kimbolt continued to concentrate on the cards. "I trust that you will."

Levering slunk from the room. Out of the corner of his eye, Kimbolt observed the baronet scurry to his study. A drawer's slam indicated that he had located the phony diary. The viscount breathed easier when Levering immediately headed for the stairs. The Captain's expectations were sound: Levering proved predictable. Kimbolt put down the cards, blew out the candles, and sauntered in the direction of the main stairs. He climbed leisurely, listening closely for the baronet's footsteps. Sir Louis did not go directly to his chambers; instead, he climbed another level.

Kimbolt could not follow, but he could time Levering's absence and observe his composure when he returned. Within five minutes, the viscount heard the baronet's tread on the upper level. He dropped into an open door where he might see Levering's reappearance. The man, literally, spun around and strutted with confidence to his room. Evidently, he had not noticed the switch. Smiling, Kimbolt closed the door and began to undress. *It was all coming together.*

~ ~ ~

Crowden placed the two volumes on Fowler's desk and smiled. "Send word to Worthing that Levering's hold on your sister has disappeared like a ghost in the night."

"Any trouble?" The duke fingered the books' gold edgings, letting his curiosity caress the binding. Bran would read them before he turned them over to Ella. He knew Eleanor would never tell him the whole truth of their father's depravation. Reading the diaries would be a way to punish his soul for leaving Ella behind.

Crowden dropped into his favorite chair. "Nothing Kimbolt and I could not handle. The viscount knows how to stage a diversion. He should be around later to apprise you of the details. You will inform Worthing?"

Fowler turned immediately to lock Lady Levering's books in his safe. "I will write Worthing without delay." He and his future brother had sent multiple messages between London and Derby over the past week. Sometimes the riders had actually passed each other on the North Road. "The last impediment to his and Eleanor's marriage is resolved; I will wait for Worthing's response, but he had planned for next Thursday or Friday for the ceremony. I will not tell Aunt Agatha until right before we leave. I refuse to involve her in this mess until it is too late for Levering to make a countermove. I invited the baronet to join my party at Prinny's gathering. That is the Wednesday after Eleanor's wedding. She will return to London as Lady Worthing."

"Then we will leave on Monday?"

Fowler smiled deviously. "Monday seems appropriate. I will spread the word that we travel to visit the Duchess's family. Her son's estate is actually close to Worthing's, so no one will notice the difference."

"Will the Duchess accept the smaller wedding? I imagine she planned something more elaborate."

The Duke noted the possibility. "Worthing's mother is an old friend; plus, the idea that Kerrington and Eleanor chose to marry where the Earl might attend will be plausible for everyone involved."

"Worthing seemed happy." Both men stared off, each trying to envision such contentment in store for himself.

"He and Ella connected instantly; she stumbled and had fallen into his arms. From that moment, anyone with eyes could see where it would lead. I am pleased for them; they will find happiness with marriage, an unusual occurrence among those of our station."

"I have business to which to attend." Godown stood to leave.

"Will we see you at the Drake's garden party?" Fowler followed the Marquis to his feet.

"I think not." Godown straightened his waistcoat. "You should spend time with your cousin, Fowler. Quit playing games and simply declare your love."

The Duke said nothing, but the news of the near disaster involving Eleanor's marriage changed how he thought about his relationship with Velvet Aldridge. He would not leave it to chance any longer; it was time to convince her to marry him. He shook Crowden's hand when they reached the door. "I will let you know if anything changes."

Chapter 14

"WAIT HERE," JAMES CAUTIONED. He had taken Ella and Daniel riding across the estate, making each of them familiar with the land and the responsibility of his future as the Earl of Linworth. The household expected Lord Amsteadt's arrival tomorrow evening; the man had sent word of a one-day delay. Georgina had declined the need to inform him of Baby Eleanor's untimely appearance; James's sister planned an elaborate surprise for her husband. Therefore, this was likely the last quiet day he and Eleanor would have for the next week. As the three traveled the estate's perimeter, they came upon a broken-down carriage along a side road leading to the village. It was probably nothing, but James decided to take no chances. Levering had friends in nearby Nottingham, and he wanted no more troubles to haunt Ella's dreams. "Let me see who this might be first." He motioned for Ella and Daniel to remain hidden among the trees.

"Greetings, in the carriage!" he called as he rode his stallion down the low-sloping hill.

Hearing his voice, a middle-aged gentleman eased his way from the coach, mopping his perspiring brow with a handkerchief. A quick glance showed the coach to have a broken crank neck, as well as several broken spokes causing the wheel to come apart. "Ah, bless you for stopping." The man pulled himself up to speak to the mounted Kerrington. "We could use your assistance, Sir."

James did not dismount, still surveying the scene. "Hopefully, I will not disappoint. What are you doing out here? It is not a main road."

The man continued to pat his brow dry. "We travel from the Lakes to Kent. Where we stayed last evening, the innkeeper told our coachman of a shortcut to eliminate at least twenty miles from our journey. Unfortunately, the road was not well-kept, and we ended up here."

"Who are *we*?" James searched the coach's interior darkness, trying to see who might be hidden inside.

"My wife, Sir, and our niece." The man finally realized that James did not trust him. "I assure you, Sir, I am a viscount. We live near Edinburgh."

A matronly-looking woman's face appeared at the open carriage door. "Is there a problem, Samuel?"

"No, my Dear." The man now eyed James with equal suspicion.

Seeing the woman, James cautiously dismounted. "This road abuts my estate," he offered. "I am Viscount Worthing, and this is Linton Park." He gestured toward the land behind him before making an abbreviated bow.

The man first helped his wife to the ground and then a dark-haired girl. Turning to James, he began his own introductions. "Sir, I am…"

Before he could finish, Ella's voice rang out from the edge of the hill leading to the road. "Cashé!"

Everyone's heads snapped around in unison. Ella was off her horse and running down the slope toward the strangers. She opened her arms, and the girl ran straight to her. Squeals of laughter and happiness drowned out the greetings. Seeing the girl turn to the running woman, the genteel couple did the same. Soon, the four of them—Ella and the three travelers—stood in the road's middle in one gigantic embrace. James watched, mouth agape, as Daniel joined him, having caught the reins of Ella's horse and brought it alongside his father's before dismounting.

When the squeals died down and the initial joy subsided, Ella, her arm around the girl's waist, turned to where James stood patiently awaiting an explanation. "Oh, James," she actually laughed as she spoke, "this is one of Velvet's sisters."

Now that Ella had said it, the likeness became completely evident. However, he simply smiled and inclined his head to the woman he loved and waited for the introductions.

Belatedly remembering her manners, Eleanor turned to the couple and began the proper welcome. "My Lord, may I present the Viscount and Viscountess Averette and Miss Cashémere Aldridge. This is Velvet's aunt and uncle from near Edinburgh and one of her younger sisters."

Ella shifted to stand between James and Daniel. "Lord and Lady Averette, may I present James Kerrington, the future Earl of Linworth and my betrothed. And this will be my new son Master Daniel." Ella purposely placed her hands on Daniel's shoulders as she spoke.

"You are to be married, Lady Eleanor?" Lady Averette came forward to claim Ella's hands again even as her husband and Velvet's sister offered the obligatory bow.

Ella bubbled with excitement. "I am, Viscountess. Next week, in fact."

Lord Averette stammered, "We…we were holidaying in the western Highlands and the Lakes when word reached us of your father's passing, Lady Eleanor. We immediately set a course for Kent."

"Then you do not know; Brantley has returned home to claim the title."

A look of relief flooded the faces of the three Averettes; Lord Averette spoke their concern. "We prayed that the late duke's Cousin Leighton's claim to the estate might be thwarted." Sounding quite pompous, he continued, "The devil cannot remain at Thorn Hall. It has seen enough facinorousness." James noted that Ella's posture had changed.

"Shall you not be to Kent for the wedding, Lady Eleanor?" Miss Aldridge's sister spoke in a righteous tone.

Ella blushed, realizing how all this must look. "No, His Lordship and I will marry at the Linton Park chapel. The Earl is very ill and would not withstand the trip to Kent or London for the nuptials. Bran, Aunt Agatha, and Velvet will join us in three days. My betrothed and Brantley served together on the Continent and in the East. My brother's connection brought His Lordship and me together."

"Let us see everyone safely to Linton Park, shall we, Ella? Then you may continue renewing your acquaintance." James wanted to put an end to the censure he had heard in Aldridges's tones. He turned to the couple. "Lord and Lady Averette, I insist you become our guests for the wedding. There is certainly no reason for your traveling to London if those you seek there are coming to Linton Park."

"Thank you, Lord Worthing. That is most kind of you. We gladly accept." The gentleman said the proper words, but his attitude spoke of disapprobation—something which bothered James. He would not wish for Ella to face undue criticism.

"Ella, Daniel and I will return to the estate and bring my carriage for the Averettes' comfort. I will send someone to make the necessary repairs." He caught her hand and brought it to his lips, forcing her to look at him. With a tilt of his head, he indicated for her to walk with him to his horse.

She tightened her hold on his hand and allowed him to take her a few steps away from the others. "Be careful," he warned. "We are not completely clear of Levering—not until I hear from your brother." He glanced to where the Averettes waited. "When was the last time you saw your cousin's family?"

Ella's eyes followed his, but she shook off his objections with a turn of her head. "It has been since before my father took ill. The Averettes never approved of my father; they rarely visited, and Velvet never traveled to see them." She purposely smiled at him. "I understand your concern, but, really, no one will bother me; I shall seek the carriage's cover until you return." She glanced over her shoulder at her distant relatives. "Samuel Aldridge was Velvet's father's younger brother. He was but seventeen when he inherited. His mother could not see her way clear to raising all three of her grandchildren. That is how Velvet came to us, but he has done well by Cashémere since he reached his majority, and he would protect me if necessary. I am yours, James." She lowered her voice for only his ears. "You have left your seed in my body and your smell on my skin. Nothing will keep us apart."

James palmed her cheek. "You are a threat to my sanity, my Love." Expelling a deep sigh, he swung into the saddle. "We shall not be long." He winked at her before circling his horse in place. "Let us ride like the wind, Son. Our Lady needs our help." James kicked the horse's flanks and took off, Daniel's smaller gelding following closely behind.

Ella watched them ride away before returning to the Averettes. "It shall not be long now. Let us become comfortable while we wait." She gestured to the carriage, and they all climbed in.

"We have a smaller coach we expected to follow, but so far we have seen nothing of it. I suppose it had similar problems. We sent the coachman to look for a village." Lord Averette declared. "That was but a quarter hour ago."

"His Lordship's carriage will surely see your man. He will have to come by way of the main road. Lord Worthing will make everything right. You may depend on him, Lord Averette."

"If the man has your loyalty, Lady Eleanor, I will not question his worth." Lord Averette settled into the squabs. Again, his tone spoke a different story, and Ella fought the urge to contract into the coach's soft cushions.

"Tell us what happened to bring your brother home, Ella," Cashé implored, "and of what you and Velvet have been doing."

Ella took a deep breath and began her recitation. For nearly an hour, she spoke of finding Bran in Cornwall, of their surprise with Sonali, of the London Season, especially of Queen Charlotte's acceptance, and a perverted tale of how she and her maid had traveled to Derbyshire in order for Ella to meet James's family, specifically for his father, who wished to see his son settled before the elder Kerrington's illness took him to an untimely death. Throughout, Lord Averette made comments regarding Bran's poor judgment in deserting Thorn Hall, the unsuitability of Ella's going to Cornwall, Bran's impertinence in marrying a "heathen," and her impolite trek to Derby with only a maid as her chaperone. Ella spoke freely in the beginning, but she soon learned to guard her words. Viscount Averette's censure stung.

"You and Velvet enjoyed your first Season?" Cashé asked. "Was it as decadent as I have heard?" The middle Aldridge sister seemed a bit annoyed by the news of her sibling's new life, as well as more than curious about the unknown. "Is London truly a den of iniquity?"

Ella caught the girl's hand. "I would say it is more *glorious* than decadent, but it is also very stressful. There are so many rules and strictures. A woman is on display at all times. Personally, I found it quite restraining, even though I was fortunate enough to enjoy His Lordship's company on a regular basis, at least, until his family summoned him home to tend his father. I cannot imagine being subjected to not knowing if someone might judge me worthy of being his bride. Can you conceive of what it must be for those who spend several Seasons before either being chosen or accepting one's fate as being unmarriageable? The parties and soirees are exciting, but I believe your sister would agree with me when I say they are not worth it—not worth the underlying tension of being in a display case, waiting to be chosen by sometimes less than savory mates. It is a *game*—a game in which women often lose." Ella thought of how she could now have been looking at a future with Louis Levering instead of James Kerrington. How bleak that would have been!

"Well spoken, Lady Eleanor." Lady Averette straightened the seams of her dress. "I always thought English Society's perverted sense of propriety lopsided in its expectations for women. The Bible teaches us how God conceived a woman's place in the world. God created Eve from Adam's rib. I was fortunate to find an Englishman who presented me with the type of marriage a

Scotsman might allow me. If your Lord Worthing is the exception to the rule, you are fortunate indeed, Lady Eleanor." She slipped her ungloved hand into her husband's. "A woman's life is to serve her husband."

Ella watched the Averettes' interactions. She thought that she would never be Lord Worthing's servant: She preferred being His Lordship's partner. "My Lord has seen more of the world than the English countryside. Although he follows many of the most convenient modes of British Society, I do not expect to be placed on the shelf as a hunting trophy. Our relationship is based on a true affection."

"Ah…a love match. Excellent. I would be happy if each of my brother's children are so lucky," Lord Averette declared aloud; yet, he half-snarled in disgust, and Ella felt a sudden pang of guilt—guilt for what, she was unsure, however.

"Perhaps, your aunt and uncle will allow you to spend a few weeks in London with Velvet. I am sure Bran would extend an invitation to Briar House, and then you could judge for yourself whether a London Season is all you believe it to be. Only a few weeks are left before the *ton* disappears for the summer to their country estates."

"Would that be appropriate, Uncle?" Ella watched in distress as Cashé half-cowered. "Would it be sinful to wish to see the place, at least, once? I will not go against your precepts, but I admit to my curiosity."

Lord Averette's smile appeared strained. "We shall see. Let me speak to Thornhill first before we make our plans beyond a possibility. For now, we will celebrate Lady Eleanor's love match to her Viscount." Averette opened the Bible he had left lying on the coach's seat. "While we wait, let us continue our study."

A short time later, the sound of carriage wheels approaching from opposing directions brought Lord Averette to attention. He climbed from his coach's stuffy interior. Looking one way and then the other, he began to chuckle. "Notice the irony of life. My second coach carrying our luggage approaches from my left while Lord Worthing's rescue comes from my right."

Averette flagged down the smaller coach as James and his men helped the rest of the party from the damaged vehicle. "Let us see how Miss Nelson and our Gwendolyn are surviving." Averette opened the coach's door, hearing his child's excited giggles.

"Papa." A fair-skinned six-year-old reached for him. "We found you."

"You did, my Child." He helped a mid-twenty-something lady from the coach before lifting the girl to the ground.

"Ah, Worthing, I am pleased to see you." Averette motioned James forward. "This is our daughter, Gwendolyn Aldridge, and her governess Miss Grace Nelson."

James bowed to the two travelers. "It is good thing that I brought the larger carriage then." He led the governess to his coach and helped her in. They would transfer the broken carriage's baggage to the smaller coach. Averette and the child followed him. "I instructed your smaller coach to follow mine. My men are waiting at the turnaround with a flat wagon to bring your other carriage to my stable for repairs. Everything is arranged. Ella and I will ride together across the estate. My mother and sister are anxious to meet part of Lady Eleanor's family."

"You are most generous, Lord Worthing." Again, James experienced a twinge of unexplained caution.

James closed the carriage and motioned to his man to move out. He strode to where Ella waited by her horse. "Did you have a nice visit, my Love?" He lifted her to the saddle and handed up the reins before adjusting the straps for the stirrups.

"I did, Lord Worthing. I told the Averettes of their sister and niece." She smiled down at him. "And I spoke of a generous man who invites people he does not know to his home."

"In another week it will be your home, Ella; it is only natural to welcome your relatives. Soon, you and I will replace my parents." He swung up into the saddle and settled himself into the seat.

Ella's smile faded, and she leveled a serious look on him. "I am content to be your Viscountess for a long time. I prefer having a family—a mother *and* a father—to your succeeding to the title. You are the Earl in every other way, and the world knows it. I would hope your father might greet our children as he did Georgina's, and mentor them as he does with Daniel."

"God, I love you...sometimes you speak my most secret thoughts aloud. How is it you know me so well?" They sat staring into each other's eyes.

"Maybe it is because you speak to my soul, James Kerrington. I prefer the image of Eleanor Fowler I see reflected in your eyes. She is a woman worthy of being loved by a man such as you. She is no longer that lonely girl."

"And I am no longer a man lost to what fate had given me. Let us return home, my Love. The Averettes will be waiting for us."

"Shall we race?" Ella's complexion sparkled.

James chuckled at her constant need to prove herself commendable. "I will give you to the count of three as always, but if I win, I mean to claim a kiss as a reward."

Ella circled her mount. "And if I win, I mean to claim more than a kiss as a reward."

She kicked the horse's side, leaving him watching her retreating form. "You do not play fair," he called after her. For a second he debated letting her win; after all, losing to Ella would be exquisite torture; but James knew she would see through his ruse. Either way, she would end up in his arms. Thinking such, he nudged the stallion forward, picking up speed continually. He would lie with her again tonight. Soon, Fowler would be at Linton Park, and James would not chance taking Ella then, but he still had three days and three nights of Ella before he did the proper thing by her.

"You sent for me, my Lord." Mr. Lucas had summoned Ella to James's study.

"Yes, Lady Eleanor. Please come in. I have a letter from your brother. I thought we might share it together." James met her at the door, motioned Hannah away, and closed the door behind her.

"My Lord?" Ella's eyebrow rose in amusement when he purposely turned the lock.

James pulled her into his embrace, brushing his lips against hers. "If Bran's letter holds what I anticipate it does, I thought we might want to celebrate."

Ella laced her arms about his neck. "And in what type of celebration do you hope to participate, my Lord?" She kissed along his chin line.

"You did win our race, Ella. Shall you not claim your reward?"

"This reward, Lord Worthing?" She brushed an open palm against his manhood, making him hardened immediately before tilting her head to receive his open mouthed kiss. He ground his erection against the flat of her stomach. "We made love but eight hours ago," she protested.

"And we will make love again in less than five minutes." James backed her toward the chaise, lifting Ella's skirt as they moved. When the back of her legs touched the cushions, he edged her down onto the furniture. His hands shoved her skirt to her waist while his mouth kissed his way to her mons. He untied her drawers and drew them away. Ella's breathing told him she wanted him as much as he did her. "Open for me, Ella," he rasped out as he lowered his mouth to her sex. Ella spread her legs, and James began to lick and suck her, using his tongue and his teeth and his lips to stimulate her. Within moments, she arched to meet his mouth and began to tremble with desire.

Excited as she, James loosened his breeches, releasing his manhood. He lowered himself to her, filling Ella with one smooth thrust. "I shall not last long," he growled. "I cannot get enough of you, Ella. I want to bury myself inside you—feel your womanhood contract around me." He talked himself into the climax. His mind imagined the tightening before it came. His hips pumped hard and quick, drowning in his need for her. "I love you, Ella."

"And I love you," she whispered to his contorted face. Lifting her hips, she held herself still, where he might reach her more easily, allowing him to use her as a vessel for his desire. When she knew he was ready, Ella began to meet his thrusts with her own. Triumphantly, she watched as he succumbed to his desire—watched as his jaw locked in need—feeling his seed fill her.

He braced his weight on his forearm and hand. Finally, he smiled at her and opened his steel-grey eyes, the ones that had mesmerized her from the beginning. "You were magnificent; I may never win another horse race," he teased.

"Oh, I am not finished with you, Lord Worthing." Seductively husky, her voice made him hard again. "You will be in my bed tonight, and I will have my way with you. You will not touch me, but I will touch you, my Lord. That will be my reward."

James's groin responded to her suggestion. He wanted her again, immediately, although he knew they could not remain locked in any longer without someone coming to look for one of them. "You are such a tease, Eleanor Fowler. I will be hard the rest of the evening, and you will torment me with images of your bed." For good measure, he ground his hips against her before pulling out and standing to restore his clothing.

Purposely, Ella left her body exposed to his gaze. "I want you to remember me as I am now," she whispered before lowering her skirt. She loved this power she held over him; it validated her as an independent woman even as she gave herself to him.

"Damn!" James forced his gaze from her body, hearing Ella laugh in the background. He turned his back on her and adjusted his manhood behind his closed breeches. Then he helped Ella to stand and to straighten her clothing and hair, although he purposely averted his eyes from her face. Irritated that he took away her control over him, Ella went on her tiptoes to nibble on his ear. James groaned, "Please stop tormenting me, Ella."

"I do not mean to torment you, James. I just wish to love you." For a split second, James heard the voice of the sleepwalking Ella begging for her father's love. Part of her would always be that girl looking for someone to love her. He would need to prove his devotion over and over—not a bad sentence for a man who desired her night and day.

He kissed the tip of her nose. "You may touch me any time—any place—I welcome your interest—your desire. If you hear me complain, it is only that I fear someone will interrupt, and I will not be able to stop when I take you in less than private places. I would never dishonor you."

"I will behave myself for now." She moved away to sit in a nearby chair. "May we share Bran's letter?" James took a deep breath and returned to his desk. He took the letter from the tray and handed it to Ella. Surprised, she said, "You want me to read it first?"

"You may read the letter to yourself and never tell me what it says, or read it to me, or we can read it separately. It is your life, Ella, and I give it back to you. I know the gist of what happened years ago, but I never need to know the specifics unless you wish it. If it helps you to deal with your past by telling me, I will listen. If you prefer to keep some things private, I will respect your silence because I know it has nothing to do with whether you love me. I have made choices in my past—some I will share because I need to voice my thoughts before I can give myself absolution. Some others—I may take those to my grave. But none of those choices change how much I love you. You gave me the freedom to realize that some choices do not make me all bad—evil even. If I were evil, you could not look at me with that innocent wonder. I pray you see the same acceptance in my eyes."

With a silent agreement to all he offered, Ella broke the seal on the letter and began to read aloud.

Worthing and Eleanor,

It is with a happy heart that I tell you that our plan progressed as we designed it. Our men have performed admirably in this endeavor, as we knew they would. Crowden presented me the two volumes of Lady Levering's diary today. I will bring them to Linton Park as a wedding present.

Ella looked up, tears misting her eyes. "Can it be?" she whispered, and James nodded his affirmation. Letting the beginnings of a smile kiss her lips, Ella returned to the letter.

As planned, Kimbolt presses Levering for his debts; Sir Louis is most anxious to make Eleanor his wife, to claim her dowry. The baronet is making bold promises and foolish assumptions. As you instructed, Captain, I have invited the baronet to join my party at Carlton House. Everything is in place.

"Must I truly face the baronet again?" Ella looked up, distress rising again.

Worthing's voice took on a soothing tone. "It is the only way to silence the man completely. You must trust me, Ella. I will not allow Sir Louis to hurt you again."

Although not totally convinced, Ella took a deep breath and continued to read.

I will tell Aunt Agatha of the marriage on Sunday. We will be on the road by Monday morning and see you on Tuesday. We will travel under the guise of visiting Agatha's son and his new wife for a few days, claiming she has family business. I let it slip to Levering that Ella will return from the Lakes in time to attend Prinny's bash.

Kimbolt leaves for Derbyshire tomorrow; Swenton will follow on Saturday. Crowden will travel with us. Even Shepherd plans to make an appearance. Your wedding will be a joyous event.

Ella, I love you with every breath I take. I would give my life to change what has happened to you. You are an amazing woman, and I am humbled by your strength of character. I once thought myself the strong one in the family, but next to you, I pale by comparison.

Captain, I would follow you into hell. You are the best of us. Make my little sister happy, and you will earn my undying devotion. Both of you deserve to know love.

Your brother,
B

"Then it is nearly finished," James thought aloud.

Ella bit her bottom lip. "Seriously, James, I do not know whether I can face Sir Louis again."

"This comes from the woman who delivered an undeliverable baby while facing down the Earl of Linworth within his own home."

"That was easy compared to this."

"Ella, you have nothing to fear; you will have the full force of the Realm behind you. I will protect you. You will be my wife, and Sir Louis will never be heard from again. I make you that promise, but we must silence him forever. For that, you must be in the baronet's presence once more to end this."

Ella's voice held her vulnerability. "You will not let me out of your sight?"

"One of the Realm will be with you in every move you make. It will work, Ella. Trust me. In this, I am the expert."

"I trust you, James." She paused before taking a steadying breath. "If we must do this, may I make a suggestion?"

"Certainly."

"The Averettes' governess is *Miss Nelson*."

James studied what she suggested but half of a heartbeat before he made the connection. "And the lady was traveling in the Lake District. You are brilliant, Eleanor Fowler. Absolutely brilliant!"

Kimbolt reappeared that very afternoon at Linton Park. Lady Linworth rallied her energies and became the perfect hostess. All of James's unit planned to attend the ceremony, and close relatives and neighbors received invitations. Linton Park hosted a houseful of well-wishers. James watched with delight as family and friends came to his home to celebrate his love for Ella.

"Lexford," he called as the viscount entered the room. "I am so pleased to see you." James extended his hand.

Ella stood by his side. She grasped their visitor's hand in hers—an unusual act, but James ignored it. "How may I thank you, my Lord?"

Kimbolt smiled; he had thought Ella quite remarkable when he had met her, and his opinion had not lessened. "Keep this one home." He indicated James Kerrington. "Fill his life with children and love, and anything I did for you will be paid in full."

"That is an easy penance, Viscount Lexford."

He kissed the back of Ella's hand. "Part of my master plan, Lady Eleanor." Then Lexford raised his eyes from Ella's face to find a pair of emerald green ones staring at him, watching him with an intensity he had rarely felt. Lady Eleanor said something else, but Kimbolt heard none of it. Coal-black hair framed a cheek, which begged to be caressed, and a pouty mouth he immediately imagined kissing.

James read his friend's mind perfectly. He suspected his face had held the same silly expression when he first laid eyes upon Eleanor. Kimbolt's brows furrowed in confusion, while a profound smile of satisfaction graced the viscount's lips.

James touched Kimbolt's arm. "Allow me to introduce you," he said with some amusement. He led Kimbolt to where his sister kept company with the Averettes. "You remember my sister Georgina, Lexford."

The viscount bowed over Georgina's hand. "Lady Amsteadt, I am pleased to see you."

James waited and then redirected his friend to the waiting trio. "Viscount Lexford, may I present Viscount and Viscountess Averette. The Averettes are Miss Aldridge's aunt and uncle, and this is her sister Miss Cashémere Aldridge. Miraculously, we came across the Viscount's party on their way to Kent. Naturally, with Fowler bringing everyone here, Lady Eleanor and I extended the invitation to join our gathering."

His friend continued to watch the girl, although he followed the formalities of the new acquaintance. Kimbolt bowed to the Averettes, but he remained in tune only to Cashé. "Miss Cashémere, may I comment on the uncanny resemblance to your sister."

"As it has been several years since I last saw Velvet, I must accept your opinion, Your Lordship."

"Then Miss Cashémere, I will anticipate your reunion."

At that very moment, Thomas Whittington, Lord Amsteadt, strode into the room. "It appears I have arrived just in time for a party," he announced good-naturedly to the room.

"Thomas," Georgina squealed, breaking away from the group.

James followed his sister and mother to greet the arrival of their family. Georgina wrapped her arms about her husband's waist, and he kissed the tip of her nose.

"Your timing is perfect, Amsteadt." James clapped him on the back.

"What is the special occasion?" Amsteadt looked from one face to another—none of whom he recognized.

James guided Thomas's gaze to Ella. "I am to marry, Brother." He reached out to catch Ella's hand. "Thomas, may I present my betrothed, Lady Eleanor Fowler. As I suspect you have surmised, Ella, this is Georgina's husband, Thomas Whittington, Lord Amsteadt."

Whittington bowed over Ella's hand. "Welcome to the family, Lady Fowler."

"Thank you, my Lord, for your attention and your well-wishes." Ella laughed lightly. "However, I believe you might wish to take a closer look at Lady Amsteadt."

"Pardon me?" Amsteadt stared at Ella for a split second before his head snapped around to really see his wife. "Georgina?" he stammered, registering the difference in her size.

"Your daughter rests in the nursery, my Lord." Georgina's eyes danced with happiness.

"My…our daughter?"

Georgina giggled, grabbed his hand, and pulled her husband toward the open door. "We will return later," she called over her shoulder.

Total silence lasted the length of a deep sigh before everyone talked over one another. "Did you see the look on Thomas's face?" Lady Linworth wiped at the tears of joy she could not control.

James kissed the back of Ella's hand. "We certainly overloaded Lord Amsteadt with news, did we not?"

"His Lordship shall think twice about walking into a private party again." Lady Linworth returned to her other guests, a cheerful smile filling the room with happiness.

Chapter 15

~ ~ ~

ELLA KEPT HER PROMISE; she took her reward from James over a two-hour period before falling asleep in his arms. With a house full of company and Bran's appearance at Linton Park, they agreed to spend the last few evenings leading up to their marriage in their respective rooms. Their commitment to each other complete, the reading of the vows was all they needed. In their eyes, they were already married. They spent time daily with Daniel, and James began to introduce her to the Linworth tenants, establishing her as the estate's future mistress. Ella won over everyone she met with her knowledge of agriculture and her natural sincerity and good humor.

Swenton followed the day after Kimbolt. Carter Lowery and Marcus Wellston arrived on Monday. James spent many hours in their company—perfecting his plan for Levering, but also reminiscing over time together in the service. Linton Park filled with those sharing a common bond. Even the Earl managed a few hours out of bed each day, bringing a renewed flush to his cheeks and a brightness long gone from his eyes.

Midafternoon on Tuesday brought the Thornhill crest into the drive, and Ella was out the door and in Bran's arms before he could help either the Duchess or Velvet from the carriage. Ella had missed him more than she would admit to anyone, even herself. Surprisingly, after years of hating him for leaving her behind, she wanted to be nowhere else but safely in her brother's arms and feeling her family around her.

"It is well, Ella." He stroked her head as she clung to him.

She sobbed into his chest. "I am sorry, Bran. I did everything wrong."

He bent his head to speak to her alone. "We both made mistakes. You did what was necessary to survive in our father's world; I do not blame you. If anything, I blame myself for not being there to protect you. Now, that will be Worthing's province. Yet, it shall be my true pleasure to exact revenge on Levering. I will rid you of the evil at last. Now, enough of regrets. This is a happy time—a time for you to begin a new life."

"I do love His Lordship," she confessed.

"Then let us celebrate that love." He turned her toward the rest of her waiting family.

Worthing handed down the Duchess and Miss Aldridge, bowing over each lady's hand. An elongated hug from Aunt Agatha nearly brought a return of Ella's tears. "Ah, my Child," the Duchess caressed Ella's cheek. "It has long been my wish to see you so happy."

Next, Velvet hugged Ella and jokingly warned, "You have much explaining to do, Eleanor Fowler." However, Ella easily distracted her cousin by pointing out the Averettes patiently waiting for her on the outside steps. Predictably, Velvet's eyes misted over in happiness as she scurried up the steps to throw her arms around an obviously emotional Samuel Aldridge and his niece. "I cannot believe you are here," she gasped.

Meanwhile, Aunt Agatha latched onto Camelia Kerrington, and the two began to chatter their way into the house. Ella took some comfort in their reunion. Her new mother needed friends with whom she could commiserate. "And Linworth is feeling better?" Agatha inquired as they climbed the steps to the main house arm in arm.

"Martin has had a positive turnaround," Camelia explained with some caution. "He will adore talking to you. He regaled Eleanor with tales of your Harold. The three of us have a different perspective from the young folks. After you refresh your things, I want you to meet my newest grandchild. Baby Eleanor favors her father Lord Amsteadt, I fear, but Georgina is in there somehow."

"Baby Eleanor?" Agatha looked about in surprise. She shot an ambiguous-looking reprimand over her shoulder at Ella, and Eleanor knew her aunt would not rest until she knew everything.

Camelia stopped in midstride. "You do not know. Of course, you do not. Your niece and I delivered Georgina's daughter less than a week ago."

"My niece?...Eleanor?...Delivered Georgina's baby?" Agatha's voice held more pride than contempt, and Ella let out a breath of relief.

"God sent Eleanor to this house just in time to save James's heart and Georgina's life." James's mother spoke with pride also.

Agatha started moving forward again. "Well...well, it seems I have been left out of the inner circle. I was not aware that Eleanor had been at Linton Park for more than a few days. You and I, Camelia, must place our heads together later. I need to know everything you know." Ella laughed lightly as she watched them go.

Fowler and Crowden judiciously joined Kimbolt and Lowery by the main door. Together, they went through it, enjoying each other's company and speaking of the ills of traveling in the summer and the need for something refreshing to drink.

They all drifted into the brightly decorated hall, leaving James and Eleanor alone in the driveway except for a few footmen unloading the carriages. He looked amusedly to where the others entered the main door. "Well, my Love, are you sure I cannot convince you to take a quick trip to Scotland and the anvil?"

Ella's eyes followed his to the retreating party. "It becomes more tempting by the moment."

"Do you suppose they would realize we were missing?"

"Maybe when they reached the church on Thursday, and we were nowhere to be found." Ella slipped her hand into his outstretched one, feeling the warmth of his fingers as they encircled hers.

James coaxed her to his side. "Two nights," he whispered as she smiled up at him.

"Too long," she teased.

"Amen."

Ella glanced around to make sure no one else could hear. "Would you retrieve the books from Bran? I want to burn them before the wedding."

"I was thinking a casual supper on the patio tonight…alfresco… maybe a bonfire…a picnic without the blankets…a little cricket… some croquet and quoits and pétanque while it is still light out. What do you think? A purely spontaneous idea, mind you."

"An excellent cover for burning a book. You are brilliant."

"It is too warm for lighting fireplaces," he noted.

"A perfect solution to our problem, and no one will know."

James caressed her cheek. "I plan to taste your lips in the moonlight, my Love."

"I shall be counting the moments."

Two days later, everyone gathered in the Linton Park chapel. Shepherd, as James expected, was the last to arrive. The man who had formed James's unit of the Realm looked on as one of his finest returned to a normal life. James paced the front of the chapel like a caged animal. Judiciously, earlier, he had asked Daniel to stand with him, reinforcing the family unit. Bran would escort Ella down the aisle. As James waited for her appearance in the vestibule, he reflected how much his life had changed in a mere three months. From their first moment together, he had desired Eleanor Fowler, but it was much more than that base lust. Ella filled a gaping hole in his soul. Recently, he had told her that if he met Elizabeth Morris now, he would not choose the woman as his wife, and he meant what he had said. Of late, he had realized that his first "perfect" marriage had lacked the depth he once thought it possessed. He pursued and won Elizabeth Morris because she was the prettiest girl of that Season—a purely male thing—all competition. She fascinated him and played to his ego, but, in reality, Elizabeth knew nothing of the hardships of life. She was a beautiful trophy for an immature aristocrat.

With Ella, something different existed. She possessed physical beauty—although maybe not as stunning as Elizabeth's, but with much more character. More importantly, Eleanor made a difference in people's lives—Daniel's, Georgina's, Bran's. She owned layers—like an onion to be peeled away, exposing a poignant personality covered by a thin façade. And he loved her with a passion he had never felt possible.

A rustle from the back of the church told him that Ella had arrived, and pure anticipation shot through his veins. Finally, he saw her, holding tightly to her brother's arm, and James's world righted. "Exquisite," he murmured to himself. James had used the word before about Ella, but never so appropriately.

Lovely in his grandmother's gown, Eleanor's eyes danced with happiness as she prepared to make the short walk into a new sensibility, full of the warmest gratitude for a new family. She wore a round dress of pale yellow crape with a demi-train and a fuller skirt. Satin flounces trimmed the bottom, bound with ivory satin ribbon. Laced from behind and pulled tight to accent Ella's soft curves, the V-shaped back and square front neck were shaded by a double frill of ivory lace. Full three-quarter length sleeves tapered into a band of crape and ivory ribbon. Ivory satin slippers matched the satin hat ornamented by a plume of white feathers and the white kid gloves. "Exquisite," Ella heard James say as she approached. It was the word he had used many months ago to describe her, and today she finally felt it. With James, Ella knew family at last. He and Daniel waited to claim her as wife and mother; she could not be happier.

The guests stood as she and Bran made their way to James—Ella's eyes locked on his. His father sat beside his mother on the front pew, having insisted on being carried downstairs in his rarely used wheelchair. James heard him tell his countess, "Eleanor is nearly as beautiful as you were wearing that dress, my Dear."

Finally, she reached him; Fowler placed Ella's hand in his, and they turned as Doctor Perry began the service. James thought that Ella looked perfectly composed, but even through her gloves he could feel her pulse racing, and somehow that gave him comfort. He squeezed her fingertips to let her know he understood, and Ella flushed with the most becoming color.

When Doctor Perry said his last "in the name of the Father, the Son, and the Holy Ghost," James's heart made a somersault. Ella was his for all time. Happily, he led her up the aisle to sign the registry. She was his most precious asset. "I love you," he whispered close to her ear.

"And I love you, my Husband." Ella laced her arm through his.

James leaned in closer. "Might I convince you to skip the wedding breakfast, Countess?"

Ella laughed lightly, but she shook her head in the negative. "You possess a one-thought mind, James Kerrington."

"I waited until we married," he protested.

"You must wait a bit longer, my Love." Ella caressed his cheek. "I believe everyone is outside, anticipating our appearance."

James brought her knuckles to his lips. "Oh, the joy of being pelted by rose petals."

"Do not take all the tradition of the marriage ceremony away from your wife, my Lord. I know you prefer a more manly challenge, but your wife is of a more delicate nature."

"A more *delicious* nature," he teased.

Ella struck his chest with the back of her hand in a playful gesture. "You are a wretched man!"

"I am simply a man in love."

"You are so beautiful, my Child," Aunt Agatha caught Ella up in her arms. "Your mother is surely the happiest of God's angels today."

"Thank you, Aunt. I feared you might be disappointed because His Lordship and I did not choose to marry in London." Ella continued to hold the woman's hand, needing to restore the connection lost while Ella dealt with Levering's demands.

The Duchess reached to caress Ella's face. "Oh, no, Child. Your happiness was always more important than the *ton*'s idea of performance. You must know, Eleanor, how happy Amelia was the day you were born—how very much my sister wanted you. She would send me letters drowning in details of your every move—to the point where I felt I spent the day holding my niece in my arms. If I have a disappointment today, it is Amelia's not surviving to see this. She would want this for you. My sister would also want her daughter to reach out to family and to allow that family to care for her. Amelia taught both you and Bran about responsibility. Share the responsibility for Thornhill's future with your brother. Together, you are an unmovable force."

"I did so many wearish things." Ella blushed with a flash of color and looked away quickly.

"The adults in your life, including me, let you down, Child; and despite our shortcomings, you became an incredible woman. Lady Linworth related what you did for Georgina. An unmarried woman of our station should not even have been in the same room with Lady Amsteadt in her condition. Yet, you set that aside. You fought to save His Lordship's sister because you knew how it would affect his family, a family you planned to join and claim as your own. I spent several hours with the Earl and Lady Linworth yesterday. They cannot be happier with Worthing's choice of you as his wife. They are aware of the changes in their son since his return from Thorn Hall, and they attribute those changes to you. After being together for many years, they are also aware of what it takes to keep the land strong. The aristocracy is in flux, and only with an exceptional match will the earldom survive. The Kerringtons believe their son has made such a match with you. They understand that your life has held its own imperfections, but those flaws give you the strength to be the kind of wife Kerrington needs. They assured me his first wife was incapable of what they see in you. The

Earl even says you will be a better mother to Daniel than his real mother. He has already noted that the child refers to you as *Mama* in private."

Ella smiled with the news. "Does he?"

"The boy does because you are here in this time—a time he needs you. Do not live in the past. Brantley and your husband have everything well in hand. Trust them to protect you."

"As long as I have kept your affections, Aunt."

"It would take more than the ruffling of William Fowler's ghostly wings to destroy the love Amelia Fowler shared with me until her own death. Even with your poor childhood choices, you are a better woman than many who knew no hardships. You and James Kerrington will become the stalwarts of change for the nobles in the Peak District. I predict it, and I am never wrong." Aunt Agatha puffed up with pride, indicating they should join the others.

Ella took no more than a half-dozen steps, however, before Velvet caught her arm. "Ella, may I speak to you privately?" she implored.

Eleanor nodded her assent, and they stepped into the main hallway, away from the rest of the wedding party. "What is it? His Lordship wants to make our departure soon."

"Ella, you must help me. The Averettes plan to return to London with us."

"I am afraid I do not understand how that is a bad thing. It seems to me you would want to spend time with Cashé." Ella searched Velvet's face for the source of her cousin's anguish.

"I will enjoy Cashé's company, especially with your *fortunate defection*, although you understand I deem you more of a sister than either Cashé or Satiné. However, that is not the problem. My aunt and uncle insist on my returning to Edinburgh when they leave. With your marriage, they consider it inappropriate for me to remain at Thorn Hall. I am not Bran's wife and cannot act as the mistress of his properties. We cannot live in the same house together once the Duchess returns home. What am I to do? I have no desire to live in Scotland; it is so far away from Kent. If I leave, Bran will choose Mrs. Warren."

Ella nearly laughed in Velvet's face. Her cousin's crises always concerned Bran. Velvet knew nothing of real adversity. "I will inform my brother of Lord Averette's declaration, but that shall be the extent of my interference. If you want my brother, earn his devotion. Bran has you on a pedestal. You need to climb down from that perch and show him you are a flesh and blood woman. Do not accept your fate. Take initiative and complete your own happy ending." Impulsively, Ella gave Velvet a quick kiss on her cheek and then hurried away to find her new husband.

"There are you, my Love." James caught her to him when she returned to the room. "Shall we make our farewells?"

Ella touched her fingers lovingly to his lips. "Absolutely."

He brought the back of her hand to his mouth. "I need you in my arms," he murmured into her hair.

"Lying with you as my husband," she whispered. "How heavenly!"

James smiled mischievously. "You know just what to say to taunt my need for you."

Ella protested, "I speak the truth."

Without taking note of the others in the room who watched their every move, James lifted her chin and bent to kiss her lips briefly. "Heavenly it is then."

"Let me make my farewells to Bran, and then we may leave." Ella squeezed his hand and made a quick curtsy. James watched her walk away, totally enthralled by the sway of her hips.

"The new Lady Worthing is quite exceptional." A familiar voice behind him caused James to turn quickly. The man they all knew only as *Shepherd* stood imposingly at Kerrington's right elbow. "When I partnered you with Fowler, I never expected such an outcome, although I should have thought of it as a possibility. Fowler's sister has always been of a nature you would consider admirable."

James quickly made the connection and stood accusatorily. "You knew of Eleanor's troubled youth and did nothing about it?"

Shepherd did not even blink when he answered. "Of course, I knew. It is my job to know everything about each of the men I recruit. And what would you have me do? We live in a society in which a man owns his wife and family. How could I legally change what happened in the Fowler household? Even if I had tried to remove the girl, she would have never left the other one behind, and if I had told Fowler, he would have rushed home to kill his father. The British government would have lost one of its best agents. Lady Eleanor handled it, and, in reality, the Duke protected her in the end."

"She should not have been left to suffer," James hissed, his rage rising quickly.

"Your lady," Shepherd lowered his voice, "has become a woman of compassion and empathy because of her life choices. We all give part of ourselves away to earn the right to finally know love. Lady Eleanor does not concede to the role Society expects her to play. Remember—one of the reasons you, of the stoical nature, found the lady so intriguing was her inscrutable spirit—without it, your wife would be stripped of her appeal."

James looked frustrated by what the Realm's leader said. "How is it you reduce all actions to a minimalistic motivation? Shepherd, you need to get out of the office and find that real life is not all black and white—shades of grey exist in nature too."

"Is that not what I did today, Kerrington?" Shepherd offered James a proper bow. "I plan to return to London immediately. I simply wished to offer you my congratulations."

James returned the bow but made no open acceptance of the man's well-wishes.

"I might remind Your Lordship," Shepherd's voice was now hard and enigmatic, "that destroying Levering does not eliminate the danger to which the Realm is susceptible. Sir Louis took credit for the Hyde Park attack, but what of the two attacks at Thorn Hall? And, for your information, there were two shooters in the park that day. That is why you fought two men and noted two coaches.

I believe the baronet's plan to worm his way into Lady Eleanor's life foiled those of Shaheed Mir to find the emerald. Danger is not a thing of the past, Kerrington." With that, their secretive leader strode away, leaving James to wonder who might be next and what he should do about it.

~~~

James and Eleanor spent three glorious days locked in the estate's manor house. It would be the Dowager house when his father finally passed, and his mother relinquished her title. For them, it was a period of exploration and investigation. They shunned formal clothing and simply learned about each other's likes and differences.

"You despise cooked carrots?" she teased as she filled him a plate from the serving table the servants set out for them before astutely disappearing.

"And you love them?" he retorted. "Will our marriage survive such diverse tastes?"

Ella placed a kiss at his temple before setting the plate on the table. "Of course, it will. You, my Lord, will finish my sentences for me. At supper, I will eat your carrots, and you will devour my peas. When grey shades your temples, I will tell you that it makes you look distinguished; and when I predictably gain weight after bearing your children, you will tell me that you prefer a woman with fuller curves."

"Will I now?" James laughed at her reasoning. "I am quite fond of the soft curve of your hip as it is." He slid his hand between Ella's back and the chair.

"Oh, poor Lord Worthing. As my mother passed long before we met, you have no idea how I will look when I age. For all you know I may turn out to be quite pleasingly plump." She stuffed a bite of potato in her mouth and puffed out her cheeks before chewing the food. "Whereas, I know exactly how you will look, my Love. I have seen the Earl."
~~~

"Amazons do not become plump," he countered.

Ella reached to where his plate rested and speared a carrot with her fork. "Yum." She rudely smacked her lips to emphasize her taunt.

James mimicked her but instead chose the peas. "Delicious." He licked the butter from his lips.

"See…our marriage is perfect."

"I never doubted it…from that first kiss, I knew you were the Amazon for me." A brief kiss led to another and then another. Soon they forgot all about food and greying hair and thicker waistlines. Those things were part of a bright future; for now, it was just about the love. As James carried Ella to their bedroom, all he knew was how it felt to touch her. To feel her soft skin under his fingertips. To know how Ella responded to his entreaties. To smell the lavender oil she used in her bath as it lingered on her skin. To recognize his need for her. To be consumed by the look on her face as he made love to her. "My life's blood." James nuzzled her neck as he placed her on the bed.

"Make love to me," she growled into his ear.

James's hands pushed up her breasts to where he could taste them. "Anything, Amazon. Any time. Any place."

~ ~ ~

They returned to reality after their too-brief respite. "We will be at Worthing Hall through this coming weekend," he informed his mother as footmen loaded his carriage. "Ella and I should return the first part of the following week."

"Why do you not spend a few extra days in London as man and wife?" His mother straightened his cravat. "Your father is doing better, and I am sure there are several households who would want to offer their own congratulations."

"We will discuss it. If we choose to stay longer, I will send word." James kissed her forehead before turning to his son. "I expect you to tend to your grandfather and your lessons, but I have also given the groomsmen orders to take you riding and to allow you time in the stables."

Daniel placed his arms around James's waist. "Thank you, Papa. You and Ella enjoy your trip."

"Being invited to the Prince's party is part of what a future earl must endure. I am more of the persuasion of spending time with my son and my wife." James held the boy at arm's length so he might see his face. "However, when one's prince issues an invitation, a gentleman responds appropriately. Do you understand, Daniel?"

"Yes, Papa."

"Go help Ella into the carriage and say your farewells. I want a last look at my niece. Lord Amsteadt plans to depart for Devon before we return from London."

James cornered his sister's husband in the main hallway. Motioning him to a private alcove, he warned, "Thomas, add an extra guard or two about the estate."

"Can you not tell me why, James?"

"It is probably for nothing, but I must be sure. An old enemy of the Realm has been unpredictable of late. I would not wish for that enemy to try to get to me through Georgina. I expect no such attempts; yet, I must be cautious."

"I will see to it. No one will touch my family."

James implored, "Keep it from Georgina."

"Do you keep it from Eleanor?"

"Although Ella knows more than most outsiders—mainly because she was in the midst of two attacks—I will not confide everything I know to her. Like you, I protect my family."

Thomas looked around to be sure of privacy. "Should I contact Shepherd?"

"Shepherd is aware of our situation. He will communicate with you directly if things change dramatically."

"You will let me know if you need help. I have been away from the Realm longer than you, but I have not forgotten my skills."

James shook his brother's hand. "If things shift toward Devon, you will be the first to know."

~~~

Fowler's carriages and those of the Averettes traveled together to London. The rest of the Realm returned individually, spreading out their arrivals to avoid suspicion. James timed his return to arrive shortly after dark on Wednesday. He did not wish anyone to see Ella enter the house so they debarked behind the town house in the mews and entered through the servants' doorway. Ella fidgeted the whole day, anticipating her encounter with Sir Louis on Thursday evening. Nothing James said or did made a difference. Anxiety ruled her mood and her appetite.

"Do you wish to go to Briar House this evening?" James wanted to take her into his arms to offer comfort, but he knew Ella would find it too confining.

She shook her head in the negative. "It is likely Sir Louis will call there to check on my return. He may have someone watching the house."

"I have someone watching his quarters," he said flatly. "I will know if the baronet makes any unpredictable moves."

"Even with our burning Lady Levering's diaries, I still fear Sir Louis's retaliations," she confessed.

"I will protect you, Ella. I know Louis Levering as well as he does. Between your brother and me, we know what the baronet had for breakfast and how many times he looked out his window today. The man makes no move of which we are not aware. This is what we do, and we were trained to do it well."

She did not argue with him, but Ella could not shake the feeling of dread spreading through every pore. "I believe I will retire early," she said softly as she stood.

"Do you wish to sleep alone?" James did not want to be in his own bed, but he recognized her anguish.

"I am not sure I can sleep alone," she murmured. "Yet, I am not of the mind to deprive you of your sleep."

James heard the meaning behind the words. "I will see then when I come to our chamber."
~~~

Ella stopped by his chair and leaned down for a kiss. "I apologize for my irritability."

He made circles with his fingertips on the inside of her wrist. "I understand." He kissed her palm. "Shall I have Hannah bring you some warm milk, or a brandy, even?"

"No, just ask her to come help with my dress and hair."

"May I escort you to your chamber?" James stood, extending his arm to her.

Ella looked a bit indecisive, but she wrapped her arm through his. As they entered the main hall, he sent a footman scrambling for Hannah to report to her mistress's room. Outside her dressing room, James paused to open the door for her. "Eleanor, you will be free of all this by the end of tomorrow evening. I know that is hard for you to conceive at this point, but the Realm has a reputation for protecting British citizens, especially women and children. We remove impediments. Leave it all to me." He kissed the back of her hand.

"Thank you, James." She slipped into the dressing room. Closing the door behind her, she leaned against the cool wood of the doorframe and let out a deep sigh. Her husband meant well, but he did not know the evil found in Louis Levering. She did—she had experienced it firsthand. The past few weeks at Linton Park, Ella had known contentment; she deceived herself into believing Levering had never existed. Now, her brother and her husband expected her to face the man who knew her most damaging secrets. Tears found the corners of her eyes and rolled down her cheeks. When she heard Hannah enter from the other room's door, she quickly dashed away the tears with her knuckles. She would get through this; even if James learned how depraved she had once acted, he would not turn from her. At least, she did not think he would.

It was near two in the morning when James heard her stir in her chamber. Although he did not lie with Ella, he remained close.

Knowing what fretfulness did to her, he made a pallet inside her dressing room so he could offer protection if necessary. The clicking sound of the door closing behind her set him on alert. Immediately, James fled through the other door, shadowing Ella in the hallway. Today was only her second time in his house; she might fall on the stairs or hurt herself somehow. Therefore, he moved in unison with her. Surprisingly, she turned into his bedchamber and stopped. Even though her eyes were open, she saw Thorn Hall in her mind.

"Is Mama going to die, Bran?" She glanced at the bed, seeing her mother's figure there. James stepped up beside her, taking on the role of her brother. He knew this scene by heart, having heard Brantley Fowler describe it in many a drunken stupor. "Not much longer, Ella."

"Why is Papa not here?" she pleaded, clutching at his hand.

James swallowed hard, feeling the grief of the thirteen-year-old Ella in her voice. "I could not find him." James knew the lie he told. Fowler had found his father making love to a housemaid on the floor of his study while his wife lay dying of the pox he had given her. The Duke and Fowler had fought about it later that evening after Lady Fowler's passing. It was the reason Bran had stormed from the house, never to return while his father lived.

"She is asking for you, Bran." Ella shoved James toward the empty bed. He sat on the edge, seeing what she saw. "We are here, Mama. Bran is here, and I have sent for Velvet." Ella dropped to her knees beside the bed and began to say the rosary, her fingers working at the beads that only she saw.

James watched her carefully, stroking her golden hair. He let Ella finish her prayers and have her cry before he bent to help her to her feet. "It is over, Ella," he whispered as he steadied her shoulders. "Your Mama is one of God's angels. Come, Sweetheart." James lifted her to his chest, clutching her tightly to him. He carried Ella to her bed and gently laid her against the pillows, arranging her hair across the cushions.

She stirred and opened her eyes for real. "Is something the matter?" She looked about the unfamiliar room.

"I was just checking on you." He caressed Ella's cheek with the back of his hand.

She smiled lovingly. "You are too good to me." Ella lightly kissed his fingertips. "Come lie beside me."

"Are you sure?" James placed a knee on the bed's edge.

"I want to lie in the safety of my husband's strong arms."

James slid in beside Ella and pulled her into his body, cradling her head on his shoulder. "I love you, Eleanor," he whispered into her hair.

"I am blessed by your love, and some day I will be worthy of it." Ella kissed his chest and wrapped her arm across him. He felt her warmth along the length of his body. She inhaled deeply before closing her eyes to the outside world. He took a steadying breath, filling his lungs with the scent of her. James's fingers mindlessly traced lines up and down her bare arm. He wanted so desperately to make things right for Ella. Tonight his prayer would be for his elaborate plan to work. Maybe if it did, their marriage might bring her the happiness that she had brought to him.

~ ~ ~

Carlton House glowed with a thousand lights as Thornhill's party entered. Fowler purposely told Sir Louis that his party would leave Briar House at nine when, in reality, they left shortly after eight. That way, frustration would follow Levering to the Prince's private quarters, and the pompous baronet would react impulsively. The duke had instructed his staff to "play dumb" when the baronet fussed about being left behind. Mr. Horace and Murray knew the drill; that is why he had brought them from Cornwall; Thornhill could trust them.

The Averettes, Cashémere Aldridge, and Miss Grace Nelson joined Fowler, the Duchess, Velvet Aldridge, and Gabriel Crowden. The duke ushered them to their assigned seating after they were announced very royally. To ready them to play their parts in the farce he had concocted, James Kerrington positioned Aidan Kimbolt, Carter Lowery, Marcus Wellston, and John Swenton about the room.

"Are you prepared?" James whispered as he handed his card to the waiting footman.

Ella's voice shook. "Not at all."

"Let us think of this as our first public acknowledgment of our nuptials. I placed a notice today in the *Times*. You are my wife and countess, and I want the world to know of our love."

"It is more than a public celebration," she insisted.

"It is what we wish it to be, Ella, and I wish it to be a declaration of our joining. I shall introduce you to our future king as my wife. As a countess, you hold great sway in this country." James placed her hand on his arm.

Ella looked chagrined when she said, "I apologize, James. Of course, our first appearance as a married couple should be my focus. You have given me the protection of your name and have done everything possible to wipe away my sins. I can never thank you enough."

"I have no use for your gratitude, Ella. We are partners in life, and we will see this through together."

Before she could answer, the captain of the guard announced, "Viscount and Viscountess Worthing," Almost immediately, well-wishers surrounded them, allowing them to relate the story of his father's illness leading to their rushed marriage. "Yes, Lord Linworth attended the ceremony," she told one group of acquaintances, as James assured three elderly gentlemen, "We had planned to wait until the end of the Season, but the Earl insisted that we lay the groundwork for my eventual assumption of the title." Most of the *ton* felt very smug, having recognized Lord Worthing's interest in Eleanor Fowler and her preference for him over the lowly Sir Louis Levering. Ella heard Lady Lucas tell the Dowager Lady Martindale as they returned to their table, "I told you repeatedly Fowler would never tolerate his sister's alliance with a baronet when a future earl waited in the wings."

Finally, they made it to Fowler's table. "Phase one is complete," Crowden muttered as Worthing seated Ella next to his friend.

"Now, we just must wait for the baronet to fall into the trap," James whispered to his friend, but he shot a worried look at his new wife.

"What do you mean the Duke is not here?" A red-faced Louis Levering looked up into the wrinkled chin of Fowler's butler, Mr. Rogard Horace—the man's upper-servant face made of pure granite. The Realm had scripted the baronet's reaction.

"His Grace waited until a quarter past the hour, but he felt he could not keep the Prince waiting longer."

"But His Grace specifically sent word that we were to leave at nine."

Mr. Horace kept the smirk from his lips. "I cannot say, Sir. Let me ask Murray." With a flick of his wrist, Mr. Horace summoned the footman forward. "What message did you leave at Sir Louis's residence today?"

"Sir Louis was not available so I told his landlady what His Grace had instructed me to say. I told her to inform the baronet that His Grace would leave Briar House at eight so his party might be seated at Carlton House *before* nine."

Levering cursed under his breath. "Now what am I to do?"

"Shall I hail a hack, Sir?" Mr. Horace followed Fowler's orders exactly.

"A man cannot arrive at the Prince's residence in a hired hack!" Levering's face turned a deeper shade of red.

"I suppose not, Sir, but if you do not mind my saying so, it would seem a larger offense, if invited, not to appear at Prince George's gathering. One could always dismiss the hack a few blocks away and arrive on foot."

Levering jammed his beaver on his head. "Then order the hack immediately, Man."

Mr. Horace kept a hired carriage already waiting just down the street, having paid the driver well to refuse other fares. Within a minute, the coach pulled up before the residence; Mr. Horace held the door for the baronet, and Levering was on his way to what he thought would be a renewal of his scheme.

Right before Mr. Horace closed the coach's door, Levering asked, "Was Lady Eleanor part of His Grace's party?"

"I did not personally see His Grace's sister, as I was in another part of the house when the Duke departed, but I am of the understanding Lady Eleanor will attend." As the carriage rolled away, Levering touched the diary he brought as insurance to Ella's behavior. A smile played across his face as the nighttime shadows swallowed him in their grasp.

Chapter 16

LEVERING DISMISSED THE HACK two blocks from his destination, but a very damp misty rain greeted his steps for those two streets. When he entered the hall, the first person he saw was Aidan Kimbolt, whom Worthing had posted by the door as part of his plan.

"What are you doing here?" Sir Louis barked as he wiped his face with a cloth provided by one of the servants. "Checking on me?"

"Of course not." Kimbolt smiled deceivingly, taking in Levering's disheveled appearance. He wondered if the Captain had ordered the rain as well. "I am escorting the daughter of a viscount who is new in town—just arrived from Scotland. By the way, Thornhill appeared some time ago; I thought you had backed out."

"A mixup on times," Levering grumbled. "Is Lady Eleanor here?"

"She is."

"Good! I am tired of her games!"

The viscount leaned casually against a doorframe. "Prinny is making his way about the room, greeting his guests. If you hurry, you can be at Thornhill's table when the Prince speaks to them. It would go a long way toward solidifying your claim on the lady if the Prince believes her to be yours."

Levering straightened his waistcoat and jacket. "The chit will have no choice." He tapped his inside jacket pocket to feel the security of the diary under the lining.

"By the way, Worthing is here also."

"He had better stay away from Eleanor." Levering strode to the door and handed his card to the captain of the guard to announce.

From his vantage point at the top of the stairs, he could see the Thornhill party bowing to the Prince. "Just in time," he muttered as the servant called out, "Sir Louis Levering of Huntingborne Abbey."

"Levering is approaching the building," Worthing whispered to Bran and Crowden. "I am stepping away from the table. Support Ella as best you can."

James kissed Ella's hand and whispered, "Keep your chin up. You are a Viscountess—a Duke's daughter and the wife of a future Earl. That means something in England. You are above this." Ella nodded, but she did not look at him. "Crowden is beside you, and I will be less than ten feet away." He paused before adding, "I love you."

Her head turned to him. In a plaintive voice she added, "I love you, James Kerrington."

Indulgently, he smiled at her, recognizing her anxiety before he walked away to talk to Marcus Wellston. He knew that what he planned would not sit well with his new wife, but it was for the best—the way to be rid of Levering forever.

Prinny's entourage appeared before the table, and Thornhill's party rose to their feet to bow low to their country's future king. A rippling murmur of "Your Highness" filled the area.

"Your Grace," Prince George acknowledged Bran. "I am pleased to see Thornhill now attending our simple gatherings." Prinny gestured with a heavily ringed hand to the settings for nearly two hundred attendees.

"We are honored by your continued acknowledgment, Your Majesty."

"I am told you served us well in the East." Prinny looked carefully at the others about the table, lingering over the females in the group.

"Thank you, Your Highness."

"Might you make the introductions, Fowler?"

"With pleasure, Your Majesty." The duke turned to the others in his group. "I am sure you are familiar with my aunt the Dowager Duchess of Norfield."

"Your Grace." Prinny kissed the back of Agatha's hand.

"Gabriel Crowden, the Marquis of Godown."

"Ah, another of Shepherd's sheep."

Crowden bowed again. "Yes, Your Highness."

"My cousins, Viscount and Lady Averette, and their niece Miss Velvet Aldridge, as well as Miss Grace Nelson."

Prinny inclined his head toward all of them and took a full canvass of each of the young ladies.

"And my sister, Your Majesty, Lady…"

Before Bran could finish, the Prince interrupted, "Lady Fowler." He bowed over her hand. "Queen Charlotte was quite taken with you."

Ella curtsied. "Thank you, Your Highness, for remembering, but it is now Lady Worthing."

"Lady Worthing?" An amused eyebrow rose. "And when did you become Lady Worthing?"

"Just last week, Your Highness."

Bran picked up the conversation. "My sister and Viscount Worthing had expressed their affections for some time, but I stubbornly refused because I felt Lady Worthing had been denied Society during my father's long illness. I asked them to wait until she had experienced a Season, but the Earl of Linworth took a turn for the worse. He was anxious to see his son well settled, and as we had no real objections to the connection, I reluctantly agreed to a private ceremony at Linton Park, where the Earl might witness the marriage himself."

"Very compassionate of you, Thornhill." Prinny leaned in to speak privately to Ella. "I had considered asking you to walk with me about the room, Lady Worthing, but you are too new a Viscountess to be interested in the attentions of even a prince."

Ella blushed to think the Prince Regent found her attractive. "I am honored, Your Highness, but you understand the early affections of marriage."

Prinny opened his mouth to respond, but Louis Levering appeared from nowhere and caught Ella's arm sharply in his grasp.

"Your Highness," he bowed to Prinny, "I am Sir Louis Levering of Huntingborne Abbey, Lady Eleanor's betrothed." Everyone in the vicinity of Fowler's table gasped, aware of Levering's audacity in speaking to the Prince without being spoken to first, and in his manhandling of Eleanor Fowler Kerrington.

Prinny rarely stuttered in surprise, but today was the exception. "Lady…Lady Eleanor's betrothed?"

"Yes, Your Majesty." Levering, not understanding the break in propriety he offered, puffed up with confidence at being recognized by the Prince.

Instantaneously, Worthing materialized. He caught Levering's hand, the one he used to hold Ella, and bent it backwards, causing Sir Louis obvious pain. James knew that Levering had abused Ella in a similar manner, and he could not help but return the favor. "You will never touch my wife, Sir!" James menacingly declared. "No one, including our most Royal Highness, would dare deny me satisfaction, Sir Louis."

Fowler pushed forward, as did Crowden. "I will be your second, Worthing."

"Your husband?" Levering ignored the clear invitation to a duel issued by Worthing. "How can that be, Eleanor? You are betrothed to me."

James purposely shoved Levering into Crowden so the marquis could deliver a perfectly disguised punch to the baronet's kidneys.

Worthing's arm came around Ella's waist, pulling her out of Levering's reach and giving her the confidence to confront the baronet. "I never gave you permission, Sir Louis, to use my familiar name," Ella retorted as she sought her husband's protection.

Totally out of his element and too angry to think straight, Levering blurted out, "I need no permission to use your familiar name, Eleanor. I have been more familiar than that with you." Another gasp reverberated throughout the room. Ella buried her face in James's shoulder, ashamed of what everyone had heard.

"Sir Louis," Prinny's amused voice caught everyone's attention. "I do not believe this is the time to make such charges."

"But, Your Highness, you do not understand—they…" He pointed to the members of Fowler's party. "They have thought themselves above a baronet. Ask them if you do not believe me. I escorted Lady Eleanor about town on more than one occasion with the understanding that she would be mine at the Season's end."

Thornhill placed himself beside Levering, while Crowden remained behind the baronet. Bran answered Levering's accusation. "Sir Louis, Your Highness, is our nearest neighbor to Thorn Hall in Kent, and while I was away in the East, my family held an acquaintance with him before our trip to London, although it is my understanding it had been several years since they last saw him. When we first arrived in our nation's capital, my sister had a riding accident in Hyde Park, and Sir Louis happened to be there and came to her aid. Those two factors allowed me to give permission to Eleanor to ride out with the baronet, but there was never anything beyond neighborly gratitude on my sister's part. Lord Worthing engaged her heart long before we took residence in London."

"Then why did you allow Lady Eleanor to travel to Nottingham with me?"

Ella sobbed into James's shirt, and Velvet moved to shield her cousin from the prying eyes of the *ton.*

"My sister, Sir Louis, never traveled anywhere with you," the duke's voice boomed out. "What craziness is this? You are a madman!"

"A madman?" Levering sputtered. "We will see about that. Ask him!" Sir Louis pointed to Kimbolt, who lurked along the perimeter of the gathering crowd. Cashé held his arm, and Carter Lowery made part of their trio. Prinny motioned the viscount forward. "Tell him, Collins."

Kimbolt bowed respectfully to the group. "Your Highness."

"It seems Sir Louis believes you might corroborate his story. Is there a reason Levering calls you *Collins*?" Prinny evidently thought this the best party he had thrown in a long time, for he gestured several of his party forward so they might hear better.

"That is his name," Levering declared. "Allister Collins. He was in Nottingham with Lady Eleanor and me. In fact, I gave her to him for the evening."

By now, the dining room rang with silence. Except for Ella's sobs and Levering's labored breathing, everyone else waited for what the baronet might say next.

The viscount did his best thespian imitation, looking concerned for Levering's sanity and empathetic for Lady Eleanor. "Your Majesty, as I am not Allister Collins, I have no idea of what this gentleman means by his rantings. I am sure you are aware, Your Highness, that I am an associate of Thornhill, Crowden, and Worthing. In fact, this evening I entertained Fowler's other cousin, another Miss Aldridge." He motioned for Cashé to join him. "Your Highness, may I present Viscount Averette's niece, Miss Cashémere Aldridge of Edinburgh."

"Miss Aldridge." Prinny's acknowledged the newcomer with an eye for her beauty.

Levering could have simply left in embarrassment at this point, but he heard the *ton* tittering behind him, and in a panic, he plowed ahead, trying to save his tattered credibility. The question of flight played through his mind. Within his bosom the thoughts rang true, but he did not flee. A quick glance at Velvet Aldridge confirmed the identity of her sister, and an echo of what the man he had known as Collins had said, *I am escorting the daughter of a viscount...just arrived from Scotland*, echoed through his mind. "Then if you are not Allister Collins, what is your name, Sir?" Sir Louis demanded.

"I am Aidan Kimbolt, Viscount Lexford of Cheshire, as if it is any of your concern, Sir."

"And I guess," Levering now pointed to Carter Lowery, "he is not your man of business!"

Lowery joined the group. "Your Highness, I am Carter Lowery, Baron Blakehell's son. I work in the Home Office, but I am no solicitor by profession."

Levering turned on Fowler again. "Are you going to claim your sister never removed herself from London, Thornhill? She ran off from me in Nottingham and has been hiding ever since."

The Duke used his best condescending tone when he responded. "Each time you called at Briar House, I explained that my sister took a holiday to the Lake District. I simply did not tell you that she traveled to Derbyshire to meet Lord Worthing's family when the Earl's health demanded it. It was none of your concern, Sir."

"You allowed a duke's sister to travel alone?" Levering charged.

"Besides her maid, Eleanor spent time with Miss Nelson."

"There is no Miss Nelson!" Levering's voice resonated in the room.

Ella flinched, but James wanted her to stand up to the man. While her brother argued with Sir Louis, he surreptitiously bent his head to speak to her ear. "Listen, Ella, to what is happening. No one believes him. You are my Countess. Be the aristocrat. Do not give Levering domain over you the way you did your father. Take back your life."

For a few brief seconds, she did not respond, then Ella's shoulders stiffened, and she raised her head at last. "I believe, Your Highness, that my brother has introduced you to Miss Nelson." Her voice trembled, but Ella raised her chin in defiance.

"I believe he did, Lady Worthing." Prinny turned his attention to the school teacher-looking woman standing quietly among the Thornhill party. In a silent request, James prayed the Prince would ask the right questions.

"Miss Nelson."

"Yes, Your Highness." The woman refused to raise her eyes to Prince George.

"You will tell me the truth."

"Yes, Your Highness."

"Have you recently traveled in what is known as the Lake District of England?"

"Yes, Your Highness."

"And have you spent time at Viscount Worthing's estate in Derbyshire?"

"I have, Your Highness. It was an honor to be among Lord Worthing's guests at his wedding to Lady Fowler."

"Are you related to either the Fowlers or the Kerringtons?"

"No, Your Highness. My parents were Baron and Lady Nelson of Lancashire."

"It is impossible!" Levering seethed with anger. "I made her up. There is no Miss Nelson."

The snickering became more prevalent, and Levering whirled around to silence his critics. "So, you do not believe me. Well, you will believe this." He pulled one of the black diaries from underneath his coat. "Read it, Your Majesty. It is my mother's diary. In it, she describes her relationship with the late Duke of Thornhill and a very young Lady Eleanor." The crowd pressed forward to hear better what Levering said.

"Easy," James cautioned in Ella's ear. "Stare him down. We burned the real books."

With James by her side, Ella looked down her aristocratic nose at the baronet. "My father was a duke, Sir. He would have had nothing to do with a man who only achieved his title because three cousins died in a freak drowning accident. My family has controlled the dukedom for nearly two hundred years. As for your mother, she threw herself at my father, but he loved only the Duchess Amelia Braton Fowler."

"May she rest in peace," Aunt Agatha made the sign of the cross. "My sister was of the finest cut."

"Here, here." Lord Witherspoon confirmed. "Have we not heard enough of this whippersnapper's lies, Your Highness?"

"Read it, Your Majesty," Levering insisted, his expression sobering his critics. "Read it aloud for all I care. It is not very flattering to my parents, but I am willing to shoulder their shame to prove why Thornhill and Worthing despise me and why they have set about to smear my good name."

Prinny took the book and handed it to one of his footmen. "Ask the captain of the guard to come to us."

"Yes, Your Majesty." The man cleared a way through the crowded room.

"Do you have a favorite entry, Sir Louis?" Prinny motioned for the servant to take up the book.

"December 5, Your Highness."

"Please read to us the entry dated December 5." Prinny leaned on his walking stick, looking casually amused by this scene.

"At once, Your Highness." The guardsman turned to the required page, cleared his throat, and read in a voice that reverberated off the gold inlay of the walls.

December 5

Robert took too much to drink again tonight. Between the port and his love of the black powder, he is often incapacitated, although from the beginning, he was never much good that way. This evening, I found him passed out in his bed, dressed in my favorite nightgown. Sometimes I believe he looks better in it than do I.

"Stop it!" Levering ordered, before charging forward to grab the book from the man's hands. "That is not what it says. It must not be the right diary."

"It is *your* proof," the Duke's hatred became more evident. He turned to the Prince. "Your Highness, I believe we have tolerated Sir Louis's tirades long enough. He has slandered my father, my sister, my friends, and me. Everything he said was false. I am a loyal Englishman and do not wish to break English law, but I demand satisfaction. I will not let Worthing do this; he has a family—an ailing father, a mother, a son, a sister and brother, a new niece, and a new wife, my sister. I have only my daughter, and I am willing to give up my title and return to the Continent for the gratification of running Sir Louis through with a sword."

Levering began to edge to the side, but Crowden and Swenton blocked his retreat.

"If you do not mind, Your Grace, I find this all so amusing, and I would like to hear more of Lady Levering's words." Prinny placed a good-natured pat on Bran's shoulders before motioning the guardsman to again take possession of the book and to continue his oration. James and Bran exchanged a worried look. They had planned to issue a challenge to the baronet. Now, they would have to play the hand the Prince dealt them.

Louis recently lost more money at the tables. I wish he spent as much time in his university studies as he does in the gaming hells and houses of ill repute. Of course, what should I expect? The boy is exactly like his father, and I do not mean Robert. If he were Robert's son, I would need to dress him as my daughter.

Again, people began to laugh, including the Prince's cortege, and everywhere Levering looked smiling faces and pointing fingers greeted him. "Cease!" he demanded, rushing at one group and then another. "Stop it this moment!"

"Sir Louis would look fine as a female; he has attractive eyes," Lord Witherspoon taunted. "Maybe he is Levering's son, after all."

"If he is not Levering's son, then he is not the baronet." Marcus Wellston's voice silenced the growing turmoil. He maintained his distance from the Fowler group, appearing to be part of the interested throng.

Prinny laughed, and all his cronies laughed, and then the rest of the guests and servants followed suit. "You are correct, Lord Yardley, and if Sir Louis is not the baronet, Huntingborne Abbey is not his."

"Your Highness, you cannot mean to take away my home." Levering now stood alone. A semicircle of the cream of the *ton* surrounded him.

"By your mother's own words," the Prince began, "you are not Robert Levering's son. If so, you are not a baronet, and by your mother's own words, you were born on the wrong side of the blanket."

"I am not a bastard!" Levering bellowed. "I am a baronet!"

Prinny bristled at Levering's tone, his amusement with the scene dwindling. No one spoke to him that way. "You are a baronet, Sir, only if I say you are." Prince George's tone warned of an atmospheric change. "And I, Sir, say you are no longer a baronet. England owns Huntingborne Abbey. In fact, I have a better idea. Mr. Lowery?"

"Yes, Your Majesty." Carter bowed properly.

"You, Sir, are a second son, are you not?"

"That is correct, Your Highness. My elder brother Lawrence is my father's heir."

"Would you care to be a baronet, Sir? You may take possession of Huntingborne Abbey tomorrow if you accept. At least, I know that you have served England faithfully."

"It is a great honor, Your Highness. I am speechless."

"I hope you have the ability to agree to my offer."

"Yes…" Carter stammered. "Yes, I gratefully accept your offer, Your Highness."

"No!" Levering threw himself at the Prince, half in anger and half in disbelief. "It is my home!" He took the Prince by the shoulders and shook him violently. Guards immediately grabbed him and bent Levering over a nearby chair, but he fought until they subdued him completely.

"He attacked the Prince!" someone from the rear of the room exclaimed. "Sir Louis attacked Prince George. No one attacks England and lives!"

"Throw him in Old Bailey and throw away the key." An elderly man supporting a grey-haired matronly woman declared.

Worthing spoke at last. "I suggest transportation. Australia's penal colony for life would satisfy me. What of you, Thornhill?" James had orchestrated this whole charade, but he had never expected Levering to grab the Prince. He had only hoped for a turn of the royal head while either he or Fowler faced Levering on a dueling field.

"I would accept transport," Bran bowed to the Prince, "if you deem it appropriate punishment, Your Majesty."

"In the olden days they would have cut out his tongue for speaking such invectives against the good name of the English aristocracy," Witherspoon added.

The elderly lord observed, "In King Henry VIII's time, the man would have had no head."

"Immediate transportation seems reasonable." Prinny motioned the guards to remove his attacker. They carried a screaming and combative Louis Levering from the room. When the fracas died away, the Prince acknowledged Fowler again. "You shall have to attend my parties more often, Thornhill. I cannot remember the last time I was so entertained. Lord Worthing, I offer you and your viscountess my apologies for allowing Sir Louis's mad ramblings to smudge your reputation, but then how else might we have proven him insane? Imagine a woman of your quality even looking at a man such as Louis Levering out of more than pity. You are too benevolent, Lady Worthing."

"I am, Your Majesty. It is a character flaw upon which I will seek improvement, although my heart sometimes controls my head." Ella tried to smile, but she wondered how many people would believe Levering.

"Your wife will suit you well, Worthing, but I insist she walk with me about the room."

James eased Eleanor from his hold. "Lady Worthing would consider it an honor, Your Highness." He bowed as the Prince extended an arm to Ella.

Dutifully, she accepted the prince's proffered arm and strolled by his side. Each time they stopped, Prinny introduced her as one of Queen Charlotte's favorites, relating the Queen's tale of Ella's strong sense of propriety and her upholding of the traditions of Society. He rejoiced in making her known to those in attendance, but Ella still smarted from the previous scene.

As they moved to another group, the Prince leaned in to whisper, "I knew your father's tastes permeated your household, but I am pleased to see that you and your brother have risen above the late Duke's reputation. Now, Viscountess Worthing, for the rest of the room, I wish for you to converse and smile as if Levering was nothing more than the fly you have just killed on the wall. Viscount Worthing was correct. Whatever he told you about not letting the likes of Louis Levering defeat you has served you well. Dare these people to question your worth by showing them a woman who faces life as it is. They will believe what you want them to believe. Cower, and they will promote the accuracy of Levering's rants. Hold your head high, and they will see him as a madman."

"Thank you, Your Majesty, for doing this."

"For thwarting an attack on the English nobility? Think nothing of it; it is my destiny." Prinny took her free hand and brought it to his lips. "Are you sure you would not prefer a prince to a future earl, my Lady?" he teased.

"Maybe some day I will tire of the Earl." Ella smiled at him and caught his arm a bit tighter.

Prinny barked out a laugh. "You are delightful, Viscountess."

After an hour, Prince George returned Ella to James's side. "You are a lucky man, Worthing."

"I am, Your Highness. I have found something few men of our stations can claim." He extended an outstretched hand to Ella, and she curtsied before leaving the Prince's side.

"Thank you, Your Highness, for your kindness and your attention."

"Good evening, Lady Worthing." With those words, Prinny returned to those who waited attendance on his every wish, and Ella walked into a life of which she had never allowed herself to dream.

Thirty minutes later, the Fowlers and the Worthings offered their excuses before making their way to their carriages. Of course, various "friends" stopped them to lend their support and to capture the moment, adding their own slants to Levering's bizarre display. However, finally they achieved their goal of the privacy of their coaches.

"The rest of the Realm will be to supper tomorrow," Bran declared as he assisted the Dowager Duchess into his largest coach. "You will join us, Worthing?"

"Ella wishes to take tea with the ladies. We will come early."

"That would be entertaining." Fowler laughed audibly before touching his hat in a salute to his sister. "Rest well, Eleanor." He bowed before following Velvet and Cashé into the carriage.

Silence blanketed the newlyweds. In their coach, Eleanor and James said nothing for several minutes. He simply took her in his arms and held Ella close, offering comfort and protection. "It is over, Sweetheart." His voice caressed the hair by her ear, although he realized the explanation sounded too simplistic, even to him.

"Yet, so many know of my downfall." Sobs shook her shoulders as the truth came crashing in.

James's fingers stroked her temple. "They needed to hear it—the *ton*. Now, you will never fear the past again. It is out in the open, and any truth behind it will be buried in Sir Louis's insanity. Yes, there will be the occasional gossip who prefers Levering's version, but with the Prince's attention and Queen Charlotte's support, you, my Dear, shall rule Society. When that lone gossip beshrews your name, he will be shouted down by a dozen who will swear they were here tonight when our future King proved Louis Levering a madman and a liar."

"This was your plan, my Husband?" Ella drew back to where she might see him in the dull light of the carriage lantern.

He smiled at her, the image of a squirming Levering being carried from the room turning up the line of his mouth. "I did not plan for Levering to self-destruct and to grab the Prince," he chuckled. "But I do admit to planning to make Levering appear a fool."

"At my expense?" she whispered, her voice shaking.

"It was for your liberation, Ella. Your brother and I discussed it, and we decided you should never fear being exposed to public shame again. Who is to say Levering did not tell one of his cronies, and someone might threaten you or Thornhill or Linton Park? We had to crush Levering's hold on you, and the only way was to face it without blinking an eye. Levering knew your brother's penchant for staring down the *ton*, but he ignored that well-known character flaw because greed and revenge were all he considered when he saw you."

"Did you read Lady Levering's diary?" Ella demanded.

"I told you I would not, Ella. If you want me to know specifics, you will tell me."

"Did Bran read it?"

James paused briefly, trying to find the right words. "We never shared that information; however, knowing your brother, I would assume he did. Yet, does it matter, Ella? Brantley Fowler believes in his sister—in his words, he would move mountains for her. And your husband, Eleanor Kerrington, loves you beyond reason. He would be the one clearing the way to make those mountains fit into your world. Two men love you unfailingly—know your faults, but find them miniscule in comparison to the magnitude of the woman you are. How is that an unfavorable situation?"

Tears rolled freely down her cheeks. "How can I argue against such reasoning?" Ella bit her bottom lip tentatively, considering what he said. "Did you not trust me enough to tell me all of what you had planned?"

"I do not wish you to believe it was a matter of trust for it was most certainly not. I thought it best to protect you. If you had known, Ella, what Levering would say tonight, there is no way you would have agreed to make an appearance." Eleanor acknowledged the truth found in his words. "You must know, Sweetheart, how much I wanted to rip out Sir Louis's heart and serve it to my hounds for his laying his filthy hands on you; but, to free you, I swallowed that hatred and allowed the man to hang himself. I simply wanted the pleasure of running him through with a sword. The fact that the Prince now sends Levering to a penal colony was never part of my thoughts."

"What if Sir Louis talks while in prison?"

"Who would listen to the man?"

"It is not your reputation, James," she objected.

Worthing's arms clasped behind her waist, nudging her to him. "I must take exception, my Dear. You are my wife, and what happens to you concerns me. However, I care not for what Levering says. I know an Eleanor Fowler he will never know—a woman of tenderness and empathy and passion. My son respects you. My parents and my sister adore you, and I cannot breathe unless you are in my life. Without wishing to minimize your feelings, we could analyze this all evening, but nothing would change. I wanted to give you freedom to choose and beg for you to choose me, Eleanor."

She hesitated, picking at the invisible lint on his coat. "It was quite delightful to witness Sir Louis's coup." She kissed his lips briefly. "And the Prince was most kind to favor me."

James grumbled, "Much to my chagrin."

"Were you jealous, my Husband?" She accepted another brief kiss from him.

"Is it mutinous to consider calling out one's King for the attentions he gave my new wife?" James settled her in his arms.

Ella snuggled into his chest. "I could become the future King's mistress if I tire of you," she teased.

"That shall never happen."

"Your words smack of conceit, my Lord."

"I promised to please you." James turned her chin so he might kiss her properly. "And if I ever fail to do so, you may freely choose his Royal Highness or any other man with my blessing."

"I choose James Kerrington, Viscount Worthing." Ella nibbled on his ear as he lifted her to his lap. "I choose to be your Viscountess—your wife—the mother of your children." She met his lips in an open-mouthed kiss.

"Such a life with such a wife," he mumbled as desire overtook his reason. "Even Shakespeare could not complain."

"What do we do about Fowler and Kerrington?" The two men clung to the shadows of the misty street corner outside of Carlton House.

A dark line crossed one man's face as he pulled up the long coat he wore. A cold shiver ran down his spine. Although it was midsummer in England, the dampness of the country sank deep into his bones. It was certainly nothing like his homeland—a place where a man might sleep without his clothes and still never feel the chill. "I have an idea," he snarled. "We find what pleases them most and take that away."

"We trade for the emerald?" his friend looked hopefully at a passing hack, thinking that they might seek the comfort of a dry room now that the Duke and the Viscount had withdrawn from the Prince's party.

"First, we must deal with those incompetent nobodies with whom you formed an alliance. Mir will not be happy if we leave any witnesses." The man strode forward into the muted lamplight to hail the cab. "You would not wish to make Mir unhappy."

"No...no, I would not wish that on any man."

Epilogue

TWO MONTHS LATER…

They would see the port of Calcutta by morning. Louis Levering had remained on deck even though it was well after dark. He hated the hole with a passion. Raised as a gentleman, he could not tolerate the absolute crudeness of his fellow inmates. It was strange that he had managed his own vulgarity before, but now he found crudeness beneath him. The others smelled of filth and decay, and the stench in the hole nauseated him beyond belief. Of late, he had bribed his jailers to allow him to stay on deck. Sleeping in the open, even chained to one of the masts, was a hundred times better than what awaited him below decks. Tonight, the wind, unseasonably cool, blew steadily, and a blanket was not to be used. He needed a bath—needed a change of clothes—needed to find a way out of this mess. Without a trial, the Prince had ordered his transportation to Australia, and now he found himself aboard ship with a penal colony as his destination.

Only once during his short incarceration in London did any of his former friends come to see him in prison—all of them afraid to associate with the man who had attacked the Prince Regent. The thoughts of his "so-called attack" brought a sneer to his lips. He had foolishly allowed Fowler and Worthing to manipulate him. Viscount Lexford, the man he had known as Allister Collins, practiced a sham for which he fell, costing him everything. Belatedly,

Sir Louis had discovered that Gabriel Crowden held a reputation for being a "ghost" of a thief. He had played into their hands, and now he would pay the ultimate price. His only chance lay in Calcutta. Once before, he had aligned himself with a man known to hate both Fowler and Worthing. He had convinced his friends Heath Montford and Gavin Bradley to contact their former associate about what the Realm had done to him. Finally, a week later word came—a note on his meal tray—all it said was that help awaited him in Calcutta. Levering knew not what form that help might take, but he would gladly accept release. He would even serve the dark-skinned emissary he had met but twice before. Anything but Australia!

Restless, unable to sleep, he made his way to the railing. His chain barely allowed him the movement, but if he angled toward one of the three wooden traverse bulkheads, he could stand along the railing and feel the wind and mist in his face. "A few more hours," he told himself as he looked out into the darkness. A star-filled sky had given him the hope that things would soon change.

Engrossed in his thoughts, Levering did not hear the sailor behind him. In a split second, the man held a knife to his throat, and Levering abandoned his thoughts of struggling. "I paid to be up here," he croaked—the pressure of the man's forearm across his Adam's apple choking him.

"No one cares." The sailor's warm breath stung Levering's cheek, a sharp contrast to the chilly air.

He tussled, desperately trying to see his attacker. "I do not understand."

The man tightened his hold. "You caused my employer many headaches with your petty plans." The menacing voice hissed near Sir Louis's ear, and for once, Levering knew real fear.

"I can fix this." He began to bargain. "I have friends meeting me in Calcutta. Tell me what you want, and I will make it right… amends can be made."

The assailant chuckled lightly. "I am the one you were to meet in Calcutta." Levering went still; the expanse of his problem spread wide to his imagination. "I want the emerald one of the Realm holds, but your bungling greed alerted them to my search. Now, I must find another way. Everything was progressing in my favor until you stepped in with your pathetic plan to blackmail Fowler." Each word slithered from the man's mouth, biting away Sir Louis's confidence. "I resent such interference; a man who cannot control his own business is a pitiful excuse for a man."

"What do you require of me?" Sweat rolled down Levering's face despite the windy conditions.

"I require your death, Mr. Levering. Your ineptitude will haunt this earth no longer." With a jerk of his wrist, the knife sliced Levering's neck, cutting his carotid artery. Immediately, the man released Levering's body, allowing it to drape like a drunken sailor over the railing. The chain held Louis Levering in place; his body dangled from the waist over the wooden banister, the blood draining from his blype and into the dark water of the Indian Ocean. Sir Louis, unable to fall into the water and incapable of climbing back on board to seek safety, his life dripping away, fought no more.

As the light broke on the horizon, the sailing master summoned the captain to the scene. "Who is he?" Levering's body was laid out on the upper deck, the sailors who discovered him retrieving the lifeless form onto the wooden flooring.

"The one who attacked the Prince." An old sailor jabbed at Levering's body with the toe of his shoe, making sure the corpse no longer moved. "What shall we be doin' with him, Captain?"

"Have the quartermaster fill out the proper paperwork—inform his family—let the Home Office know. Then dump him overboard. I do not want him littering the deck when we hit Calcutta. We would have too many questions to answer."

"Yes, Sir." The boatswain motioned for the two sailors who had found the body to come forward. "Should we find out who did this, Sir?"

"Why?" The Captain leveled a steady gaze on his junior officer. "Would anyone care? The man bribed someone to be up here. He took a chance by leaving the safety of the hole. If anyone asks, we let him out for exercise. A swift wind sent the mast turning, and the sail accidentally knocked him overboard. We tried to save him, but as it was night, we lost the man in the dark waters. For the record, tell everyone it is likely he was unconscious when he hit the water. We will hear enough from the port authorities for allowing him a moment of freedom, but it is nothing we have not heard before."

"Yes, Captain. I will see to it, Sir."

"Are you sure, Lucifer?" A little over a month later, Worthing and Kimbolt sat in the study at Linton Park.

The bulky-looking man turned his hat over in his hand. "I spoke to the sailor who found Sir Louis's body the morning the *Star of the East* docked in Calcutta. He be swearing someone slit Levering's throat during the night and left him to bleed to death. The captain ordered the men to throw Levering's body overboard. Otherwise the Indian port authorities would be holding them to investigate the crime."

Kimbolt added without thinking, "Shaheed Mir?"

"Probably," Worthing contemplated this new information. "Levering's attack in Hyde Park overlapped the Baloch's one."

Viscount Lexford and Lucifer had gone to Calcutta when the Realm discovered the note sent to Levering, but they were unable to prevent the attack on Sir Louis. Lucifer's common-man appearance allowed him to move freely among the unwashed throngs found on Calcutta's docks. He pretended to seek employment on the *Star of the East*, buying drinks for several sailors on day leave. "Most of the sailors, Sir, blended in easily with the natives," Lucifer reported. "I followed as many as I could, but nothing proved worth the time I be spending."

"Thank you, Lucifer, for your dedication. A bonus should come your way." Worthing shook the man's hand. "Why do you not find something to eat in the kitchen? I will have a room made up for you."

"Yes, Sir." Lucifer headed for the door, but he paused before leaving. "Excuse me, Viscount Worthing." The man actually blushed with embarrassment. "I be wondering, Sir, if Hannah might be still serving your wife."

Worthing laughed lightly at the probability of a love affair springing up between the two servants. "Hannah should be in the garden with Her Ladyship. I am sure she will be happy to acknowledge your return to Derbyshire."

"Thank you, Sir." A broad smile broke the lines of the giant's face before he disappeared into the bowels of the house.

"One of us is going to lose a servant."

Lexford ignored both the sarcasm and the truth in his friend's words. "It appears likely."

James took the seat behind the desk. "It will be with twisted pleasure that I tell Eleanor about Sir Louis's 'accident.' Maybe that will give her the peace she has yet to find." Kimbolt nodded his agreement. "Any other news, Kimbolt?"

"The Averettes and Miss Cashé have returned to Edinburgh. They insisted Miss Aldridge accompany them. Fowler grumbles about everything—nothing at Thorn Hall pleases him, but I expect you knew this already."

"Surprisingly, I did not." Worthing pretended to straighten a pile of letters. "And your relationship with Miss Cashémere?"

"The trip to Calcutta cut that short. It is all for the best, though; nothing could have come of it. I was just bored with London and the like."

"I said the same thing when I visited Fowler at Thorn Hall." Worthing said no more; he let Kimbolt draw his own conclusions. "How long will you stay with us?"

The viscount looked away, lost in his own thoughts. "Only for a few days; I need to return to my estate. My steward sends word that my presence is needed to deal with some of the cottagers."

"Stay as long as you like."

"I will give Lucifer a few days with Lady Worthing's maid." Kimbolt stood suddenly. "I think I will see if that boy of yours would enjoy a long ride."

"I guarantee it. I told Daniel I would take him to Tattersalls soon. Ella and I want a few days in London before the weather changes. Derbyshire winters can be very confining."

Obviously preoccupied with his own thoughts, Lexford did not comment. "I will have our horses saddled if you will send for Daniel." Without looking back, Kimbolt strode from the room.

Watching him go, Worthing laughed to himself. "He has it bad."

"Who has it bad?" Ella stood in the doorway.

James looked up and smiled, always happy to see her. "Kimbolt." He rose to ring for a servant. "The Viscount is declaring a lack of interest in your Scottish cousin." He caught Ella's hand and brought her to a nearby chair. The servant appeared, and he asked for tea to be sent to them and for someone to fetch Daniel. "The Viscount swears that London bores him and now his estate needs him."

"Sounds very familiar." Ella mumbled as he bent to kiss her lips before taking a seat across from her.

"I said the same thing before I came to Thorn Hall to visit your brother, and look what it brought me."

Ella arched an eyebrow. "An Amazon?"

"Exactly."

"Lord Lexford has brought us news, which I hope you will find satisfying," James began.

Ella looked up in anticipation. "Yes?"

"His Lordship and Lucifer have recently returned from Calcutta. Shepherd received word of someone wishing to aid the former baronet, and he sent the Viscount to stop the attempt to free Louis Levering."

"And?" Ella held her breath.

James leaned forward for emphasis. "Sir Louis Levering has

breathed his last breath. Those he sought as his friends have seen to his death. The former baronet aligned himself with Shaheed Mir, but Sir Louis did not understand how treacherous a Baloch warrior can be."

"Then, it is over." Ella expelled the words in a gush of air.

For long minutes, neither of them spoke, absorbing the news and how it might impact their lives. "It is," James murmured softly. It was over for Ella, but he knew Mir still remained a danger to them all.

A light tap at the door announced his son. "Did you need me, Papa?"

James swallowed his thoughts and motioned the boy forward. "I wondered if you would do me favor?"

"Of course, Papa."

"Viscount Lexford is staying with us for a few days, and he would enjoy a riding partner; but, unfortunately, I have other obligations. I thought you might keep Kimbolt company."

Daniel's eyes lit up with excitement. "I would like that, Papa."

"Good. The Viscount is having your horse saddled. I suspect you should hurry along then."

"Did you hear, Ella? I am to ride with the Viscount."

Ella touched his hand, family suddenly taking center stage. "You will be careful." James recognized how she tried not to smother his son with her attentions. Daniel wanted to be treated more as an adult; however, of late, she could not help herself, and James found that quite agreeable. "I worry when you take unnecessary chances."

"I will ride with care," their son assured her before bowing out of the room.

Tea arrived, and she poured them each a cup. "Daniel enjoys your mothering him," James noted as he sipped the tea. He still was unsure how Ella took the news of Levering's passing.

"Do you believe so? Sometimes I wonder if I do the right thing by Daniel. I want to protect him, but I know he needs his freedom."

James smiled cautiously, as she completely ignored the repercussions of the baronet's murder. "Trust me, if I told Daniel to be careful, he would think I treated him as a child. Yet, he thrives when you say such things. He never knew a mother's love until you arrived at Linton Park."

"Do you believe I could be a good mother? I mean, with my history, could I make a child a competent parent?" Ella bit her bottom lip, never a good sign as far as James was concerned. That action indicated something major troubled her, and he suspected that he understood.

"Ella, you are already a good mother. If you could hear Daniel go on and on to his friends about his mother, you would never doubt your worth. It is not of Elizabeth he speaks; it is of you." It was a conversation they had had before. James placed his cup on a table and moved to kneel before her. He was waiting for the reality of life to hit her. "What troubles you, my Love?"

"Nothing." She looked away, biting down harder on her lip.

James touched her mouth with his index finger. "This lip tells me otherwise. Talk to me, Ella; we are in this together." He felt her shiver, but not with anticipation—with worry. James prepared to offer his comfort.

For several moments, she fought the tears misting her eyes. Finally, gulping for air, she blurted out, "I am with child." She paused briefly before continuing. "This is not the way I had planned to tell you; something more romantic was hidden away in the back of my mind." She paused longer, mustering her courage. "I have no time to learn to be a good mother," she nearly whined. "I must know how now."

James froze, her words impaling him to the spot. He had expected tears—expected self-recriminations—even expected some hysterics. He had not expected this. "Are…are you sure?" he stammered.

"I missed my courses twice, and now I can barely look at food without running to the chamber pot. I am as sure as a woman may be."

She was not the least concerned with her former troubles. James had read her completely wrong. Yet, even now understanding her qualms, he still did not move. James's mind calculated how far along she might be with child. He too had forgotten about their former difficulties. "Three months, maybe a bit more," he thought aloud.

"I had my courses right before Nottingham. It is likely from before our vows or those early days in the manor house. Probably three and a half—closer to four." Ella now noticed how frightened he looked. "You are happy, are you not, my Lord?"

Her words shook him out of his thoughts. He now considered how he would protect Ella. He had lost Elizabeth to childbirth, and nearly Georgina; James could not imagine what life might be without Ella. He almost wanted her never to bear him a child, to keep her safe. "Of course I am happy, my Love. You simply took me unawares." Instinctively, he cupped her chin to kiss her tenderly. "We are…we are to have a child," he continued to stutter. Meanwhile, his thoughts were on finding the best medical help possible. The village midwife would not do.

"I thought we might tell your parents together." Ella spoke, but she remained unsure of his true feelings.

Allowing the news finally to speak to his heart, he was on his feet in one movement, lifting her from the chair. "I will carry you," he insisted. "Anywhere you want to go." He turned in circles, swinging her through the air. "We are to have a child." He started toward the main staircase with her clutched to him. "First, we will tell the Earl." Servants scurried to open doors.

"And then?" she giggled, noticing the dark desire now found in his eyes.

James stopped on the landing to nuzzle her neck with his lips. He whispered in her ear, "Then I plan to show you how much I adore you, Eleanor Kerrington. To prove you are the most precious thing in my life."

"I love you." She kissed him although several servants looked on. "Your father," she reminded him when he responded to her.

"My father." James smiled mischievously as he took the steps two at a time. Outside the Earl's chambers, he motioned for Ella to open the door. When she did, James swept in, carrying his wife close to him.

"James?" his mother squealed, observing the odd display from her favorite chair.

Without ceremony, he announced, "Ella and I came to inform you that we are to have a child." He turned immediately to leave with her still held close to his chest. "We will tell you more at supper. You will eat with us tonight, Sir," he called over his shoulder as he left the room and turned toward his own bedchamber.

The Earl sputtered and then started laughing as soon as they were gone.

"He is certainly your son, Martin," Camelia Kerrington noted with amusement, before tucking in her husband's blanket, moving to sit next to him on the bed.

"I carried you everywhere for a week, if I recall correctly, my Dear." The Earl caught her hand and brought it to rest over his heart.

"You did." Camelia touched her husband's cheek. "James did no such thing for Elizabeth."

"Our boy loves this one, Camelia. It is not just youthful fascination."

"James will be a good earl, as good as you, Martin." A gentle caress spoke of a lifetime of devotion. "He and Ella will surpass us, as it should be."

The Earl kissed the palm of her hand. "Close and lock the door, Camelia," he whispered huskily.

"Martin? Are you sure?"

"I am ill, Camelia; I am not dead. I want to lay in this bed with my wife, the woman I have loved for over thirty years."

"I love you as well, Martin Kerrington."

"Then lock the door, Love, and come and show me."

Camelia smiled as she stood to do as he had said. "With pure pleasure, my Lord."

Preview of Book II in The Realm Series

~ ~ ~

WHEN THE MESSAGE CAME, he could not believe his eyes; now Brantley Fowler raced across the English countryside. He had ridden throughout the day and much of the night, having stopped only long enough to change horses. He had taken a room at a posting inn for several hours, although he had slept very little. An overnight thunderstorm had driven him from the road. Riding an unfamiliar horse in a driving rain was nearly impossible. Now, he kicked his latest horse's flanks. It was a miserable-looking nag, but it was all he could secure at the last inn. As the animal clopped into the gravel drive at Linton Park, he threw the reins to a waiting footman as he slid from the saddle. At a run, he took the steps to the main door two at a time. Mr. Lucas, Kerrington's butler, pulled the door open just as Bran reached it. "Your Grace." The offering of a quick bow came as Bran flung his hat and gloves at Mr. Lucas.

"Where is Viscount Worthing?" Fowler demanded.

"I believe the Viscount and Viscountess are in their chambers, Your Grace. Shall I let them know you have arrived?"

Bran glanced toward the main staircase before he started to move. "No, I will announce myself."

"But, Your Grace..." the man called as Fowler bolted up the stairs.

Rounding the post and turning to the left, Bran knew where Kerrington slept. Within seconds, he pounded on Kerrington's door. "Worthing!" he hit the door again. "Worthing, I need you!"

The door opened ever so slightly. "Fowler?" Kerrington looked disheveled and a bit angry.

"I need your help." Bran ignored what he had probably interrupted.

Kerrington nodded and eased the door closed. Bran paced the short distance of this private quarter debating whether to hit the door again when it suddenly opened. Bran plowed into the middle of the room before he realized Kerrington wore only his breeches, and worse, Ella wore a nightgown and robe in the middle of the day. Seeing his sister in what was obviously an intimate moment took his breath away, and he froze, just staring at her.

"Ella?" he rasped.

"Yes, Bran." She looked amused by his reaction, but still she flushed with color.

Bran stammered, "I…I did not think."

"Sit down, Fowler," Kerrington ordered from somewhere behind him as the viscount slipped a shirt over his head.

The familiarity of his friend's voice brought him to his mission. A shake of his head cleared his thinking. "Velvet is in trouble." He turned his back on his sister, not wishing to picture her in Kerrington's bed.

"How so?" Worthing took Bran by the arm and led him to a nearby chaise.

"I received a note from Shepherd yesterday morning. The Home Office intercepted information regarding a plan by Murhad Jamot to take Velvet as a bargain for the emerald. Shepherd sent Wellston to Scotland because the Earl was in Northumberland and the closest to Edinburgh." He ran his hands through his hair as he gathered his thoughts. "Yet, Berwick did not reach the Averettes' home in time. By the time of his arrival, Velvet was missing. Viscount Averette thinks that his niece ran off to meet me somewhere, and he gives pursuit, working his way toward Thornhill; but Miss Cashé thinks otherwise. She claims that she and Velvet saw a man—a dark-skinned man—lurking around the estate on and off for the past week. Plus, because I have never answered one of Velvet's letters, she assumes I have chosen Lucinda Warren instead. Velvet told Cashé I forgot her quickly."

"How long ago?" Kerrington asked as he dressed.

"The original information was dated nearly a week ago. Shepherd sent word that Jamot expects a ship at Liverpool next weekend. I have five days to find her."

"Will the man hurt Velvet?" Ella now stood beside her husband.

"I do not know. I have no idea where to look—who to ask for help." Bran dropped his head in defeat. "But I have to do something."

Kerrington touched his shoulder. "Get out of here, and let Ella and me dress. We will meet you downstairs in a few minutes. Lexford is here—just arrived today; he and Daniel are out riding. Lexford is from Cheshire; he can help us with Liverpool."

Bran's head snapped up. "Thank God." Ready to take action, he stood immediately. "May I send someone out to find the Viscount and your son?"

"Certainly." Kerrington edged Bran to the door. "We will meet you in the library in a few minutes." As they reached the open portal, Kerrington took Bran by both shoulders. "We will find Miss Aldridge, Fowler. You will know what I know with Eleanor. You will have the same kind of happiness."

Bran glanced at his sister standing quietly behind James Kerrington. "Ella, you look quite beautiful," he stated.

"Most women with child do," Worthing whispered close to Bran's ear.

Bran looked at his friend in disbelief. "I am to be an uncle?"

"Yes, Bran," Ella uttered the words. "We have just told the Earl and Lady Linworth. When Daniel returns, we plan to tell him."

"Oh, Ella," he rushed past Kerrington to catch his sister in his embrace. "Even in all this madness, you have given me hope. I do so love you." He clasped her to him.

She held Bran tightly, needing to know his love. "Now, go!" she finally ordered, tears streaming down her face. "We need to find the woman you love."

Bran walked to the doorway as Eleanor rushed into her husband's arms. "Take care of him." Bran heard her plead as Kerrington closed the door.

"I always have," came the reply.

She did not know how long they had traveled; she guessed six days, but as he had kept her drugged, she could have easily lost count. Not sure where he took her, Velvet fought for some sense of what had happened. She remembered confronting the man for being on her uncle's property; she remembered the struggle when he grabbed her—but little else since then.

Rocking back and forth on the seat of the carriage, she kept her eyes closed, not wishing him to know the drug no longer coursed through her veins. For the past two nights, she had slept in the carriage—locked in, gagged, and bound, unable to even move and with no way to signal for help. Her captor had slept in an inn. She knew it to be an inn because she had recognized the sounds of the comings and goings of the other carriages and of the stable hands as they handled the horses. Other than the driver, she did not think anyone else accompanied them on this journey.

At the moment, she regretted that confrontation in her uncle's orchard, but in reality, Velvet knew he would have taken her eventually. He, obviously, targeted her for his own reasons, reasons she suspected had something to do with Bran and with the earlier attacks on her and Ella. Although if her captor thought Bran would come for her, he was sadly mistaken. Three months ago, she had left London for Scotland. Her Uncle Samuel had demanded that she leave Briar House and Bran behind, and she had foolishly acquiesced. Velvet thought she did it for Ella and for Bran, but she now realized that she had done it for herself. She had wanted Bran to prove his love, literally, to come for her—to be her prince—her knight in shining armor. Yet, he had not come—had not even answered her letters. Instead, Brantley Fowler had abandoned her to the attentions of some Scottish border lairds, too crude for her sensibilities—men who openly spoke of bedding her. Now, all for which she could hope was that her uncle might seek her release. However, Velvet expected she would have to design her own rescue. She would have to be Joan of Arc, Elizabeth I, and Scheherazade all rolled into one—a fighter, a strategist, and a conspirator combined.

"Open your eyes, Miss Aldridge."

Acknowledgments

MY DEEPEST GRATITUDE goes to the many people at Ulysses Press who took a chance on a public classroom teacher and gave her one of the best experiences of her life. Thank you for taking another risk with me by moving into the Historical Romance genre.

About the Author

~ ~ ~

REGINA JEFFERS, an English teacher for thirty-nine years, considers herself a Jane Austen enthusiast. She is the author of several novels, including *The Phantom of Pemberley*, *Darcy's Passions*, *Darcy's Temptation*, *Captain Wentworth's Persuasion,* and *Vampire Darcy's Desire*. A Time Warner Star Teacher and Martha Holden Jennings Scholar, Jeffers often serves as a consultant in language arts and media literacy. Currently living outside Charlotte, North Carolina, she spends her time with her writing.